A TABLE BY THE WINDOW

Suellen Grealy

For Joel, compagnon de route

PROLOGUE

AMERICAN SOCIALITE FOUND DEAD

Nice, June 20

American heiress Mrs Natascha Barron was found dead last night in a shop in Nice, France, according to the local newspaper Nice-Matin. *Police have not yet issued a statement concerning the cause of death, but witnesses reported that Mrs Barron, 29, had been seen at 9pm slumped in the shop window.*

Mrs Barron, the daughter of Russian-American millionaire Uri Raskilovich, who died in New York last year, had been visiting the Côte d'Azur with her husband, yachtsman Michael Barron, Jr. Previous editions of Nice-Matin *have reported on the planned refurbishment of the shop, which was to have opened later this summer.*

Michel Norriet, a spokesman for the emergency team that attended the scene, was quoted as saying: 'We can confirm that an ambulance was called at 9.13pm by a woman known to the deceased, but that the young woman in question was not revived.' A person of interest, reportedly with Mrs Barron at the time of her death, is being held for questioning.

American lawyer Michael Barron, Sr, Mrs Barron's father-in-law, is expected in Nice from New York today. He asked that the family be shown compassion at this time but has not yet issued a statement.

Part One

CHAPTER ONE

'Alexandra, darling, listen. All you need to do is lock and unlock the door, and answer the phone. It's all I ask.' Alex Coates could hear Chantelle Charpentier, on the other end of the line, inhale her cigarette. A siren droned nearby. Was she leaning out of the window of the apartment in Manhattan? Alex pictured Chantelle's manicured, freckled hand waving as she spoke, rings glittering in the morning sun.

'Of course,' Alex said. 'But four Americans called this morning. They're all interested in properties in Bellet, and we don't have any in the files. I thought you should know.'

'Bellet? Where the vineyards are? But darling Alexandra, listen; here's what you must do.' Alex smiled. She no longer felt intimidated by her new French boss's theatrical exasperation. Chantelle reacted the same way to everyone. 'Take their numbers, tell them all our pretty houses have been, how do you say in English, snazzled up, and I'll take care of it when I get back to Nice.'

'Snapped up?' Alex said. Chantelle insisted on speaking English with her.

'Snapped up, yes! That's why I asked you to work for me, you understand what the foreigners are saying. Don't worry. I'll call you tomorrow afternoon French time, to see what has happened.' Another siren droned in and out. '*Au revoir*, Alexandra.'

'Take care, Chantelle. Have fun with your cousin.'

Alex hung up and turned to look at the map on the wall behind her.

Chantelle Charpentier's real estate business stretched more or less wherever she discovered a property to sell or to rent. The map showed Nice at the centre of a series of half-circles that extended from Marseilles in the west to the Italian border to the east. Alex traced her finger along the coast, then further inland, until she found Bellet. She'd tasted the wines grown there in the hills behind Nice, but she hadn't had a chance to visit the area yet. She looked at the familiar names – Antibes, Cap Ferrat, Monaco, Cannes. They reminded her of the map spread, coffee-stained, over the kitchen table in London as she and Rod planned where they would live when his redundancy came through. Nice wasn't on the list – they'd spent too many idyllic holidays in the French countryside to ever consider a town. All they wanted was birdsong in the background, a patch of garden to grow vegetables – and space for their two grown daughters and their grandchildren to stay, of course.

A sudden thud against the shopfront startled Alex. She peered between the property ads that lined the glass to see a town worker in his yellow overalls tugging a hose across the pavement outside. A sheet of water, aimed accidentally onto the window, slid down the glass. The daily *Libération* food market in the street outside was finished for the morning, and the clean-up operation had begun.

As she tidied up the desk, Alex noticed a familiar customer from the restaurant nearby. He'd double-parked his BMW in front of the office. An energetic-looking man in his sixties, he wore a camel-coloured raincoat, despite the early spring warmth, and waved angrily at the careless street cleaner. It was lunchtime, and lunch was just one of the pleasures Alex had decided she would enjoy *à la Française*.

She took her linen jacket from the back of the office chair, and ran her fingers through her short hair. She applied a slick of dusky-pink lipstick. She knew she looked good for a woman her age – she was as slim now as she'd been in her twenties, thanks to long, energetic walks. But now that she was working at a French estate agency, she made an extra effort. She angled her small mirror so she could see the way her new haircut waved at the nape of her neck. She'd let her hair go a bit after Rod's death, but it was over a year now. She was waking up again. She took a satisfied look at her new reflection and turned over the sign on the door so it could be read from outside: '*Fermé pour le déjeuner*'. Closed for lunch.

Chez Maxie was next door to Chantelle's agency, Immobilier Charpentier. The restaurant's *terrasse* was popular with office workers, local people and occasional tourists sipping rosé, but Alex preferred to sit inside. Even diffused under the red and white parasols, the lunchtime sun was too bright for reading.

'*Bonjour*, Madame Alex!' Maxie's mother Françoise surveyed the restaurant from the bar. Behind her, bottles were reflected in mirrors lining the glass shelves. Wine glasses hung from racks above her head. Coffee cups were stacked atop the enormous silver coffee machine at one end of the bar. At the other, curling photographs of birthdays and festive dinners papered the old cash register. Alex took a moment to locate Françoise amid the jumble. She couldn't have been more than four foot 10, and only her head – neat grey bob, red-framed glasses and red lipstick – was visible. Once Françoise had called out her greeting, more of her body came into view as she climbed onto the little stepladder that Alex knew she kept behind the bar. She reached up for a champagne glass.

Maxie, a darker, faster version of her mother, had a plate of grilled John Dory in each hand, but she jutted her chin in the direction of a table for two in the corner. '*Là, Madame*, there,' she said. 'Push Honda off the chair.' It wouldn't be the first time Alex had shared her table with the Jack Russell, so she let the dog be and chose the empty seat. His tail wagged lazily when he saw her – a long way from the panting welcome he gave Chantelle.

The man in the camel raincoat sat facing the bar. His eyes followed Françoise as she made her way towards Alex, holding a glass of champagne in one hand and a copy of *Nice-Matin*, the local newspaper, in the other.

'*Voilà*,' Françoise said, placing the glass in front of Alex. She wasn't a young woman, but her size gave her an ageless air. It was Chantelle's habit to have a glass of champagne as a lunchtime aperitif, and everyone at Chez Maxie assumed that

Alex would join her. Alex no longer tried to differ. Françoise put the newspaper on the table.

'You must be busy today. *Regardez*. Look.' She tapped on one of the articles. 'This says that a big American newspaper has mentioned our own Immobilier Charpentier by name. Chantelle hasn't lost a moment!' Françoise spoke slower, more formal French than her daughter. She still referred to Alex as '*vous*' in the polite way, while Maxie had almost immediately started using the more familiar '*tu*'.

'But I just spoke to Chantelle, and she didn't say a thing, 'Alex said.

'According to the Americans, Bellet is the hidden secret of the Côte d'Azur. Time to buy!' Françoise laughed. 'Do they really think they haven't found everything yet?'

Alex started to read the article. Her French was good, but despite the evening classes she and Rod had taken together, reading took time. After a couple of sentences, Françoise whipped the paper away. It was a familiar sensation. Whenever Alex began to feel included in the *quartier*, something would remind her she was a stranger.

'The *daube* is excellent, by the way,' Françoise said, tucking the paper under her arm. Much as Alex loved this regional speciality, the rich beef stew was too heavy for lunchtime. She watched Françoise zigzag back among the tables, nodding at the man in the camel coat. '*Ça va*, Alain? Do you like our *daube*?' The man smiled at Françoise over half-moon glasses. He had thick grey hair, which he kept under control by absently pushing it back with the flat of his hand.

'I recommend everything from Maxie's kitchen,' he replied. His French was clear, though quick, and Alex easily understood. Maxie squeezed between their tables with two carafes of water in one hand and a basket of bread in the other. She leaned down to give the man a noisy kiss on the cheek. 'Aha! Monsieur Alain Hubert, former commandant of the *police judiciaire* of Nice, recommends my restaurant. Now, Madame Alex, will you try the *salade de chèvre chaud* as a starter?

Everyone wants my goat cheese *salade*.'

The little neighbourhood restaurant hadn't disappointed Alex so far, either for the food or the atmosphere. It was somewhere she'd miss if she decided to return home to London, yet every day she felt a bit more deeply ensconced in this new life.

The interior of the restaurant was filling up. Monsieur Hubert was joined by a younger man wearing, in the Niçois style, too much gold. Even though he usually sat on his own, Monsieur Hubert often received a stream of visitors throughout his lunch. From what Alex could overhear, he and his companion were discussing *les Américains* and *les Russes*, the Russians. Maxie joined in as she passed. She could carry on conversations with three or four tables at once.

'Oh, you two,' Maxie said, swooping past, laden with empty glasses. 'You'll give me a bad name talking like that. Americans and Russians are the biggest spenders on the Riviera, why do you think they're all criminals?'

'Here comes one now,' Françoise called from the bar. She stared pointedly out toward the *terrasse* and Monsieur Hubert, the young man, Maxie – and Alex – all turned to look.

A man in a grey leather jacket was looking at Chez Maxie's menu. Alex's first impression was that his black hair was dyed.

'It's him!' Monsieur Hubert's companion said excitedly. 'The guy I've been telling you about. He bought that 1967 Mercedes 250 SL from my brother-in-law, for 35,000 euros, cash!'

Monsieur Hubert shifted so he could see outside. Alex too leaned forward. 'It's true – 35,000 euros!' the young man continued. 'My brother-in-law couldn't believe his luck. He'd only taken delivery of that beauty at his garage the week before – in perfect condition, except for two little holes the size of bullets. You think someone shot up a treasure like that? But you know what he said, that guy out there? He said, don't fix the holes.'

Maxie grabbed the young man's arm. 'Felix, he's paid more than he could afford. Look, he's off; even my 14-euro menu is too much for him.'

'You should start doing borscht, Maxie, or caviar,' Monsieur Hubert said. Alex joined in their laughter, and was momentarily embarrassed to be caught eavesdropping.

She watched the Russian disappear down the street. Alex turned to see Monsieur Hubert studying her. His face was deeply lined, but his inquisitive eyes were startlingly blue.

'*Excusez-moi*, Madame, but does Chantelle have many Russian clients?' He addressed her across an empty table.

'One or two, I think,' Alex said. 'But we are only managing their properties. I don't know of any Russian buyers at the moment.' She tried to sound brisk and professional, but she knew that her English accent, however much she tried to disguise it, was strong. Chantelle had already told her some people in the neighbourhood weren't happy to see an Englishwoman working at Immobilier Charpentier. Alex didn't want to believe that the genial Monsieur Hubert might be one of them.

'Of course,' Hubert said. 'Chantelle has been managing properties, I'd forgotten. Anything new lately?'

Alex inhaled. Should she divulge information to Monsieur Hubert, and Felix in the process? The former policeman was probably just making conversation; perhaps it was an old habit, gathering information in every exchange. It was best to be vague until she could speak to Chantelle. After all, the agency was Chantelle's business. She'd been building it up for years on the power of contacts and leads picked up in even the most casual conversations.

'Possibly. I haven't been working with Chantelle long. Barely three months.'

'And you were one of her clients before that, weren't you? But we haven't been officially introduced,' he said. Alex tugged her skirt down half an inch over her knees. 'I am Alain Hubert, and this is my nephew, Felix. Are you settled yet? It's a beautiful apartment building, Les Jolies Roses.'

It didn't surprise Alex that he knew where she lived.

Hadn't she herself just learned about the car-buying habits of a complete stranger? There was something to be gleaned at every one of Maxie's tables.

'I'm happy, thank you. I couldn't have been luckier to find it – I mean to find Chantelle, who found it for me.'

'If there's anything you need while she's in America, let us know,' Monsieur Hubert said. 'It's not easy being on your own in a new country.' Alex glanced at Felix, who smiled in a bored way. She often had the impression that she was being observed and even teased by the locals. But perhaps it was just that her French wasn't quite good enough – yet.

Françoise stepped between them, with a sheaf of paper tablecloths under her arm. Monsieur Hubert straightened his shoulders. 'Isn't that right, Françoise? Madame Alex is among friends here.'

'Oh, as long as she pays her bill – like everyone else.'

The *daube*, as predicted, was delicious. Alex had tried to reproduce the classic southern French beef and red wine stew herself, but never managed the same depth of flavour. Maxie, always delighted to discuss her dishes at length, explained that the secret to the velvety texture of the sauce was in the reduction.

The kitchen at Chez Maxie, at least what Alex could glimpse of it on her way to the *toilettes*, was tiny. She wondered how the asthmatic-looking chef and his boyish assistant could produce such consistently delicious dishes. The little restaurant was one of several around the Place du Général de Gaulle in the northern part of Nice, but Chantelle had told her confidently, it was the best.

Maxie, Françoise and the pretty *serveuse* who helped out at lunchtimes welcomed each customer with a singsong *Bonjour!* and often a kiss on both cheeks. Alex was beginning to remember their names. She was even now included in the amiable greetings as the customers trooped in. Beatrice, whom Alex recognised as one of the tellers in the local bank, nodded at her. The man everyone called Monsieur le Professeur, in the same baggy brown jacket every day, smiled as he nudged aside the books piled on his table. One lunchtime the mayor of Nice had arrived, which prompted even Françoise herself to climb down from behind the bar to offer up her cheek. He and his colleagues had precipitated a commotion in the restaurant. Maxie moved faster than ever. Only Alain Hubert was unruffled, calmly finishing his mouthful of roast duck as the mayor waited to shake his hand.

When Alex returned to the office, she could hear the phone ringing as she put the key in the lock. She picked up just before the answering machine clicked in. It already showed five messages.

'Alex, where have you been?' It was Chantelle, breathless. Alex looked at her watch guiltily, but it was only 2.30pm, an acceptable time to be returning from lunch in the south of France.

'I've been at Maxie's. Everyone sends their regards.'

'Oh, yes, lunch! I'm mingled up about the time difference.'

Surely Chantelle meant mixed up, but Alex didn't interrupt.

'I've been calling and calling. Something exciting has happened! We have been mentioned in the American press! And someone important saw it. She got her people to get in touch with me. Natascha Barron, Alex! What a *coup!*' Alex heard what sounded like Chantelle's heels clicking on a wooden floor.

'I'm sorry, Chantelle, I don't know that name. Should I?'

There was a silence on the other end of the line, followed by a long sigh. Alex immediately realised her *faux pas*. It hadn't taken her long to learn that Chantelle had an encyclopaedic knowledge of who was who in the society pages of glossy magazines. 'But how is it possible you don't know this family?' Chantelle had asked more than once, incredulously, as Alex tried to recognise one socialite or another among the issues that littered the office.

'Natascha Barron! But you remember her as Natascha Raskilovich, the daughter of Uri, the multimillionaire. Her wedding last summer was the biggest event in New York. She married into one of the best families in the United States.'

Alex thought she might have heard the name, perhaps from the English papers – Rod had read the business pages voraciously. She knew it wasn't worth trying to resist. 'Of course! Natascha Barron! What does she want?'

'She's not interested in Bellet, needless to say, she'll need Cap Ferrat, or Cannes, somewhere important. Her people tell me she and her husband want to establish themselves on the Côte d'Azur. She'll need something special. Somewhere big.' The heels clicked furiously as Chantelle recited the names of the most beautiful properties on the Riviera.

Alex didn't share Chantelle's gossipy interest in her clients, but she couldn't resist her excitement.

'The Barrons are one of the oldest families in North America, all lawyers. So well-respected. If only the Menier villa were available… How perfect! But of course, you don't know that one.' Chantelle sighed again. 'Now listen Alex, *chérie*, you must do the floorwork before I get home.'

'You mean groundwork? But Chantelle that reminds me. That ex-policeman was asking me about our clients today. I wasn't sure what to say.'

Another silence. 'Which clients?'

'Just generally. If we have Russians on the books.'

'Hmm. When Alain takes an interest in something, it's best to take an interest, too. Except in Françoise, of course!' She laughed throatily. 'Now, *oui*, the groundwork. I expected it to be quiet in Nice for the moment – who could have predicted this surprise? We must find out what's happening with all the best villas – when will they be available, who is interested, who is for sale, and so on.'

Alex frowned. So far, she had visited just a few properties in Chantelle's company. The extent of her own local contacts ended at Chez Maxie. When Chantelle had suggested Alex come to work at Immobilier Charpentier, it was only because she was English, and could communicate with the clientele Chantelle wanted to attract. Alex had accepted to keep herself busy.

'Chantelle, I wouldn't know where to start.'

Chantelle's laugh made Alex hold the phone away. '*Chérie*, I don't expect you to do my job! Natascha Barron will arrive in a few weeks. I'll be back in a week or so. But I want you to go through all the records and prepare a dossier for me – a big file. Look in the bottom drawer of the cabinet, you'll see plenty of information to start.'

Alex could reach the drawer from her chair, and she tugged it open. It was stuffed with yellowed newspaper cuttings, filed in among estate agents' details and pages torn from notebooks. She pulled out a coffee-stained envelope on which was written, possibly in lipstick, an address and phone number. The postmark on the other side was 10 years old.

'You've been keeping notes,' Alex said.

'If anything has changed hands in the past 20 years, it's in there. As you can see, my housekeeping is imperfect. But you, Alex, you are so organised. I saw it the moment you walked into my office with that handsome husband. If anyone can make my dossier work, it's you.'

CHAPTER TWO

Sorting out Chantelle's dossier was going to be equal amounts pleasure and pain. First Alex would need to record the scores of properties it contained alphabetically, along with whatever details she could find. It would be time-consuming, and it would challenge her French, but she could do what she loved – cross-referencing, cataloguing, indexing and mapping.

She'd started working as an indexer when her daughters Meghan and Beth were tiny; it was an easy if poorly paid way of staying at home with them. Publishers sent the final proofs of biographies and histories, which she pored over, pencils and highlighters poised. As the years went by, her stacks of index cards on the kitchen table were replaced by a computer on a roll-top desk, but the essence of the work was the same. Her contacts in Britain still kept in touch, pleading with her to take on one more job, but no, this was her new life.

Now, as she unfolded the cuttings, her fingertips lingered on the crackling newsprint. It had been a while since she'd opened a fat galley proof, sharpened pencil in hand, and entered another world with each new job.

Many of the cuttings were agents' advertisements from back copies of *Nice-Matin*. Others were a testament to Chantelle's powers of observation. An article about a car crash showed the widow of the deceased, a wealthy entrepreneur, photographed leaving her house in Monaco to attend the funeral. '*Demande à Boubil*' Chantelle had scribbled on it; 'Ask Boubil'. Alex recognised the name of the biggest estate agent in the area. The sale of that house, Alex knew, would have earned someone a handsome commission.

Before long, she found an article snipped from a magazine about the new owners of a house she'd noticed earlier. She flicked backwards. There, a country house, the kind locals called a '*mas*', for sale near Menton, in need of work. No date.

But she could see it was the same house as the one in the magazine photo, beautifully refurbished. She paper-clipped the two pieces together, and laid them to one side. She selected a new notepad from the shelf of stationery Chantelle kept near the kitchenette at the back of the office. On the first page she wrote 'Mas' and 'Menton'.

When she heard someone tapping on the door, she looked at her watch and saw a couple of hours had gone by.

'It's open,' she said, waving for Chantelle's handyman to come in.

'Madame! Still here?' Guillaume Chapel's southern accent was strong. He craned his tanned neck to look at the spread of papers on the desk.

'Chantelle asked me to look through her file,' Alex said quickly. Would he think she was nosing through Chantelle's business? Could Guillaume be one of those people who didn't care for the new Englishwoman?

Guillaume's rough hands scratched over the yellowed *Nice-Matin* articles. 'Ah, look at this. The Menier villa just outside Villefranche, that terrible fire.' He read the story, shaking his head slowly. Menier, Alex thought. It was the name Chantelle had mentioned on the phone. The coastal village of Villefranche was just a couple of miles from Nice.

Guillaume made rare, unannounced appearances in the office, overpowering even Chantelle's signature Eau d'Issey scent with the odour of diesel or woodsmoke that clung to his blue overalls. Sometimes he stayed to chat with Chantelle; other times he slipped in silently to collect keys or look over invoices. Chantelle depended on him completely. He roamed among the apartments and villas that Immobilier Charpentier managed in a pick-up truck so laden with tools it reminded Alex of a hut on wheels. 'We need him, *chérie*,' Chantelle had said, 'so we will put up with whatever mood he's in today.'

This afternoon his overalls smelled of rosemary.

'Three people dead, including a child,' he said. 'That was a beautiful place, an artist's house.' He put the article back on the desk.

Alex wrote 'Menier', 'Villefranche,' 'Artist' and 'Fire' in her notebook. When she had finished, she saw that Guillaume had been watching. He quickly looked away. 'Was it destroyed?' she asked.

'Not completely. But after the tragedy, only Chantelle would take it on. The owner was old, and his family were hard to find. But Chantelle worked hard, and eventually she convinced the cousins who had inherited to let her sell what was left. The cousins couldn't resist her, of course. Who can?' Guillaume smiled, as if unable to resist her himself. 'It went for a good price.'

'Who bought it?'

'A Parisian who rebuilt it as a luxury rental, but he has an agent in Paris manage it for him. You can imagine how angry Chantelle was about that lost opportunity! I noticed the owner this morning in the market, Patrice LeBlanc. He's not usually in the area, so perhaps he's looking for a tenant again.'

Alex wrote 'To let?' in her notebook. Guillaume pulled binders from the shelves and flicked through the files. Eventually he dug into his hip pocket and pulled out a keyring with a noisy collection of keys. He unlocked the cabinet behind Chantelle's desk and stood scratching his scruffy grey hair.

'There it is,' he said at last. 'I couldn't get in today when I went to check on the gardeners in the Avenue Jean Cocteau on Cap Ferrat. There's been a complaint from the next-door neighbours – feral cats, they say. The noise wakes them up.'

'Oh!' It wasn't the kind of problem she'd expected to face. 'Can we get rid of them?'

She saw distaste in his brief glance. 'First I need to see if they're a genuine problem, or just a problem for people who don't like cats.'

Alex felt scolded. Her daughters, Meghan and Beth, had a rescue animal as children – a scarred ginger tom with half a tail. They were devoted to ensuring his long ninth life made up for the previous eight.

'Do you know the house I'm talking about, Madame? We manage the maintenance while no one is there. It's just beyond Villefranche, 15 minutes' drive? I might need some help. Can you come?'

Oh yes. Of course she could.

The wrought-iron gates at the villa on Avenue Jean Cocteau opened onto a curved drive edged with mimosa and cypress, and Alex couldn't contain her sharp intake of breath. It was beautiful. The gates closed automatically behind Guillaume's pick-up, and when he turned off the engine there was nothing to hear but the tick of the cooling engine and the trees brushing in the late-afternoon breeze. The house, cream stucco with orange tiles on its undulating roof, faced the sea. Splashes of Mediterranean turquoise flickered through the branches of a rhododendron hedge, which lined the perimeter of the garden. The drive divided into two, with one side veering off towards a small building in similar style – a three-car garage. Guillaume crunched over the gravel towards it.

As Alex began to follow, a hedge, which divided the property from the one next door, began to rustle. She tensed, remembering the feral cats. But a young couple appeared through a sizeable gap, brushing leaves off their clothes.

'Excuse us,' the man said. 'We've been meaning to have this fence fixed, I hope you don't mind us slipping through. We heard the truck. You must be Madame Charpentier.' The man came forward, his hand outstretched. There were discreetly expensive logos on his sunglasses that he politely took off.

'No, you're mistaken,' Alex said. 'Madame Charpentier is away. I'm Alex Coates, her...' She hesitated. There had never been any discussion of a title. 'I'm her assistant.'

'*Une Anglaise!*' the woman said, switching to perfect English. She pushed her sunglasses up into her stylishly cut blonde hair. 'One can never speak enough English, don't you agree? There never seems to be the opportunity to converse.'

'Oh Lili, *si'l te plait!*' said her husband. 'Madame Coates speaks French well. I'm sure she doesn't need to speak English with us.'

Alex looked from one beautiful young person to the other.

'I've had more opportunities to speak English than I can count,' She said in French, 'so I welcome every chance to improve my French.' She hoped it was sufficiently diplomatic.

The man laughed. 'I am Henri Valentin, and this is my wife, Liliane. My great-uncle Auguste owns the house on the other side of the fence.' He waved towards the bushes. 'I mean, owned. Sadly my uncle died recently.'

Guillaume, hovering near Alex, now moved forward. 'My sympathies,' he said. 'I knew Monsieur Valentin wasn't well, but I didn't realise...'

'We've been coming down from Paris every few weeks to get the feel of the place again,' Liliane interrupted, addressing Alex. 'But it's just too big for us. Six bedrooms!' She put her sunglasses back on as she spoke, and Alex watched her own reflection nodding in the convex blackness.

'My uncle stayed in the house until it was no longer possible,' Henri said. 'He insisted, of course. He'd been here since the late 1930s. I've always loved it. So many wonderful times here!' Henri looked towards the glinting sea. 'I learned to swim in the bay, and to sail. My first girlfriends...'

'Henri,' Liliane said firmly. 'We're concentrating on the future now.' Alex smiled at her husband. She imagined those slim, tanned girls on the beach below.

'Of course. Please excuse me, Mrs Coates. He too put his sunglasses back on. 'But first there is the problem of these cats.'

'*Affreux*,' said Liliane, flaring her delicate nostrils and, repeating herself in English, 'Frightful.'

'Guillaume came to see about that,' Alex said. 'He thinks they might be living in the garage.'

Guillaume, who had been standing on the edge of their conversation, turned towards the garage. As they followed him, Liliane's tan suede loafer crunched on something. There were some well-stripped chicken bones scattered over the gravel.

'Their food!' she screeched. 'Horrible creatures, like vermin. Henri, let's go home. But Madame Coates, we'd like to discuss what we can do with the house. We certainly don't want it for ourselves. Will you join us for an *aperitif* while your man does what he needs to do?'

Alex thought immediately of Chantelle's new client Natascha Barron. She turned to Guillaume, but he was already walking behind the garage. He was clearly not the type for cocktail chitchat.

The Valentin house was breathtaking. Although the furniture and décor were dated – his great-uncle, Henri explained, had been 96 years old when he died – every room was flooded with light reflected off the sea. It had been built in the 1930s, with living areas interconnected through wide, arched doorways round a paved courtyard. Each bedroom had its own bathroom, with walls tiled in marble the colour of poached salmon, and black and white chequerboard floors. Alex stood with her hand on one of the worn Bakelite door handles, pretending for a delicious few seconds that this was her home.

'We don't know what to do,' Henri said over a pastis in the living room. Liliane had insisted that she and Alex have gin and tonics, even running outside to pick a lemon from the garden. 'Everything is so dated. To rent, we'd need to do so much work. To sell, we wouldn't get the best price in this condition.'

The house was tired, without a doubt. Paintings had been removed, and the ghostly frames showed up how yellowed the walls had become. The kitchen, refitted to what must have been the chicest standards in the 1970s, also had a nicotine tint. The wooden cabinets were chipped and the Formica worktops worn and singed. But the pine table, with its eight Provençal ladder-back chairs, was positioned perfectly to see all the way across the sea from Villefranche to Cap d'Antibes. The vanilla scent of late-flowering mimosa permeated the courtyard.

'Chantelle is an expert in this sort of thing,' Alex said. 'She could tell in an instant if you should market this as a house full of history to the English, or if you should modernise it for an American rental. She can even tell you what to sell for reclamation. The bathrooms, for instance... so beautiful.'

'It has character, as they say in English,' said Liliane. She looked disdainfully around the living room.

'And such possibility,' said Henri. 'My uncle was quite a bohemian, and he used to throw incredible parties even in his nineties.'

Alex sipped her drink and settled into the sofa, eager to hear more, but Liliane put her hand on Henri's arm.

'Darling, that's over. Madame Coates doesn't want to hear about the past. You'll let Madame Charpentier know about this, won't you?' She stood up to show Alex to the double-width front door, with its ornate ironwork hinges, slightly rusting.

Twilight had fallen while Alex was with the Valentins. She gulped in the scent of pine and eucalyptus in the silent darkness before launching herself back through the gap in the hedge. She crept forward, hands in front of her, pushing branches away and aiming towards the dull light that filtered through the side windows of the garage. Guillaume had evidently managed to get in.

A branch snapped back in her face, and she laughed out loud at the sight she'd be if anyone were there to see. Her linen jacket and white cotton shirt were speckled with dust, and there were leaves in her hair. She stepped out onto the grass and vigorously brushed herself off.

Guillaume's head was just visible in the garage window and he seemed to be talking to someone. She strained to hear.

'*Petit minou*,' he said. 'Pretty puss. Don't be scared. You'll be safe here.' There was a scuffling noise, and Alex stiffened. Guillaume's murmur continued. 'Fresh fish every day soon, eh, sweethearts?'

Guillaume was far from luring the animals into a trap. He was chatting to them.

She stamped in the dried leaves and coughed. 'Guillaume, are you in there?' she called.

He appeared at the rear of the garage. 'Come,' he said. The garage was piled with wooden packing crates and he pointed inside one of them. 'Here.' A skinny white cat with a black tail was nursing a litter of kittens.

'And here,' he said, pointing under a workbench on the back wall. He pulled back a packing blanket to reveal another cat and her kittens, all identical, white with black tails.

'They're not feral,' Guillaume said. He tickled the top of the mother's head. 'Not yet, anyway. They're fine here, until the litters are old enough to be moved.'

'But what about the Valentins?'

Guillaume puffed out his cheeks – a French expression Alex had learned to translate as, 'Who knows?'

'There won't be much noise until the mothers are ready to mate again. I'll drop some food off now and again.'

They watched the little families in silence, then Guillaume gently lifted up each kitten for a closer look.

'I wouldn't have taken you for a cat-lover,' Alex said.

'I'm not.' He looked at her but his gaze faltered, and he looked quickly away. 'But I married a woman who loved anything with four legs. My daughter, too. I got used to cats quickly.'

'I had to do the same thing,' Alex laughed. 'My two girls couldn't be more different from one another, but they always loved their cats and dogs. They're both grown now. One's here in France, in fact. She's a painter. She got a grant to work in Paris...'

Her voice suddenly seemed loud. He didn't appear to be listening. He put the kitten back with its mother.

Alex asked, 'How old is your daughter now?'

He crossed his arms and stared at the floor. 'She would have been 33,' he said. 'A scientist. An accident, in Marseilles. She did industrial research….'

'How awful. I'm so sorry, Guillaume. I…'

'It killed her mother, too,' he said. His eyes seemed to harden. 'She couldn't…she couldn't manage.'

Alex thought immediately of Rod, of the exhausting, lonely blankness he left behind. She couldn't have faced it without Meghan and Beth.

'It must have been unbearable,' she said.

Guillaume cleared his throat. His eyes flickered towards hers before he turned back to the cats. 'How was the Valentins' place? Chantelle has been waiting for that villa to become available.'

'I must speak with her about it as soon as possible. It's a beautiful house. But someone will have to spend a lot of money to bring it into the 21st century.'

Guillaume jangled the keys and switched off the light.

'There might be someone soon,' Alex continued, following him outside. 'Chantelle's expecting an American couple, looking for something spectacular.'

Alex and Guillaume crunched back towards the pick-up. 'Then the Americans will have come to the right place.'

Back at Les Jolies Roses, Alex flung open her living room windows and leaned on the railing to watch the scene below. Her third-floor apartment was not far from Immobilier Charpentier. As well as the parquet-floored living room, there was a small kitchen, a bedroom that faced the overgrown garden of a villa behind, and a second bedroom, for which she'd bought flat-pack spare beds, still lying unassembled on the floor. It would be tight, but Meghan and the children wouldn't mind.

It had been Chantelle's idea for Alex to move to Nice. They'd bumped into each other in the square in Fayence several months after Rod's death. Alex recognised Chantelle straight away as one of the estate agents they'd met when they first arrived. They'd rattled around the countryside in

Chantelle's car a couple of times. She'd obviously formed the wrong impression when Rod explained that he'd taken early retirement from his firm of lawyers. The redundancy settlement had been generous, but nowhere near the amount they'd need to buy the expensive properties she was convinced they'd love.

'But you absolutely cannot stay in Fayence on your own,' Chantelle had said over an aperitif in a village café. 'A widow must lead a new life, *comme un chat!*' Like a cat. It made Alex think. She had started to notice, once the girls no longer came out from England so often to keep her company, that the little house she and Rod had rented now felt isolated rather than rural. The vegetable patch, Rod's vegetable patch, was already going to seed. Chantelle rang the following week. 'I've found the perfect place for you,' she said. 'But you must make up your mind today.'

Alex didn't need to consider it for long. She knew what Rod's advice would be, if she could've asked. Let's go. Life is short. It was what he'd said to convince her that moving to France while they were still young enough was the right decision in the first place.

Within two months, Chantelle had taken care of breaking the lease on the house, and Alex was surrounded by boxes at Les Jolies Roses. Barely a week after that, she'd started working at Immobilier Charpentier.

She sipped a glass of rosé from the Bellet vineyards in the hills behind Nice, which Maxie had recommended, and listened to the conversations that floated up into the flat from the street.

When Alex's phone rang and she saw that it was her daughter Meghan calling from London, she momentarily considered not answering. Conversations with Meghan required all her energy.

'Hello darling. How are you?'

'Exhausted, of course. I've just packed the kids off to bed. It was piano night for Robert and gymnastics for Olivia.'

Alex knew from the tone of her elder daughter's voice that a good 20 minutes of detail would follow. She topped up her glass.

'Poor you, sweetheart.'

Meghan had a cleaner, an au pair girl, a personal trainer, and a contract with a garden maintenance firm. Once a month a flamboyant Argentinean hairdresser, much in demand in her exclusive part of London, came to the house to retouch her roots. There was scarce free time in the children's schedules, and then only by accident.

Alex couldn't recall how all this had happened. Was this fierce high-heeled organiser really the biddable child who once lay on her stomach under Alex's desk, whispering to a menagerie of plastic animals? Rod put the change down to all the wrong boyfriends, ones who wanted to be something in the City instead of writers or social workers. Alex was more compassionate. Being a good wife and mother was much harder than it was 30-odd years ago, she'd reminded him. It had become a competitive sport. She would wait out Meghan's full-on parenting years patiently, until her grandchildren were older and the pressure had eased.

Unfortunately, in the meantime, Alex had migrated to the top of Meghan's 'To Do' list.

'I saw a wonderful flat for you today, Mum. Close to the tube station. You'll love it.'

'Hmmm.' Alex had caught a glimpse of a familiar raincoat on what she could see of the Place du Général de Gaulle. 'Don't forget I've got my job now, darling. Don't worry so much about me.' She leaned a little further over the railing. 'And besides, Chantelle is away. I have to take care of things for her.' Monsieur Hubert was standing on the pavement, hands in his pockets, intently watching something on the other side of the Place.

'What did you say? She's away?' Meghan's voice squeaked. 'Mum! You're on your own?'

Alex followed Monsieur Hubert's line of vision. Only a tiny

part of the Avenue Malaussena was visible from her window, obscured by the spring leaves of a tree. But she saw the black-haired Russian sauntering out of sight, just as he had earlier in the day.

'Yes, she is, actually,' Alex answered. 'In New York, visiting a cousin.'

'No! Are you alright? Shall I come over and keep you company? Oh, I'm sorry, Mum, I forgot, I can't, Tim's off to Hong Kong for a conference... Maybe Beth could come down. Is she still in Paris? Not that my sister would tell me if she were. God, she can be grouchy.'

Monsieur Hubert continued to watch what Alex couldn't see. Then he took his mobile phone from a breast pocket and made a call. He paced up and down as he spoke.

'Don't worry, sweetheart, I'm fine.'

'Don't let anyone take advantage of you,' Meghan said. 'You're far too nice. You don't owe that Chantelle anything, you know. Is she paying you extra while she's not there? Are you sure you're safe? We don't know why you took this job, Mum, we really don't. I wish you'd come home. You know you'll be better off here.'

A tram whirred past on its way towards the sea. Just as the last car passed, Monsieur Hubert was walking towards the police station next to Maxie's. Alex leaned even further over the railing as he disappeared through the door. Across the road, the waiters at the Café des Soldats were beginning to bring in the tables for the night.

'I'm sorry, sweetie, what were you saying?'

CHAPTER THREE

The *Libération* food market was already lively by 8am the next morning, as Alex wound her way past trestle tables piled with fruit and vegetables on the short walk to the office. A stallholder with a wind-burned face looked up from slicing the leaves off a cauliflower and waved at her, knife in hand. His neighbour winked from behind a mountain of fruit. So far, however, no one had offered her their sweetest produce as they did, unasked, to Chantelle.

When she shut the door of Immobilier Charpentier behind her, the hubbub of the market suddenly dulled, as if she'd put in earplugs. The light on the answering machine was already blinking. There were two more messages from Americans who'd read the newspaper article, one in lumbering French, which Alex listened to several times before she understood the mangled phone number.

The third message made Alex feel queasy. An efficient-sounding Dianne Steer, personal assistant to Mr Michael Barron, was calling to inform Madame Charpentier that Mr and Mrs Michael Barron had changed their plans and would be arriving in Nice considerably earlier than had been discussed with Mrs Charpentier. They were expecting to see the potential properties Mrs Charpentier had said were available. Ms Steer would be in touch again next week to confirm the arrangements.

Next week! Alex would call Chantelle the moment the time difference allowed – she'd probably want to catch the first flight home. Meanwhile, Alex distracted herself answering emails and opening the post, rearranging a schedule for one of the cleaners, and calling Guillaume to let him know a tenant had complained about the stiffness of a cold-water tap in the shower.

She turned her attention to the dossier. She had begun to pile the cuttings according to the location of the property, in alphabetical order, divided for now by sheets of paper on which she'd written large initials. In her notebook, she kept a half-page for each property, jotting down details. Some houses appeared again and again. The villa of an ageing Italian pop star, of whom Alex had never heard, showed up in five reports of scandalous parties. One covered the pop star's death by drowning in his own kidney-shaped pool in a town called Villeneuve Loubet. She wrote 'V' in the notebook. Underneath, she wrote 'Villeneuve Loubet'. Then she added 'Valentin'.

As she scanned the stories, she turned over the cuttings to look at the other side. *Nice-Matin* was a relentlessly local paper, full on the one hand of innocent stories about school swimming competitions, and on the other about knifings and shootings, reported with enthusiastic forensic attention. Chantelle's scissor snips and rough tears often prevented Alex from reaching the end of a story. There were plenty of cuttings from glossy magazines and gossipy weeklies, too. Alex couldn't have been happier sifting through the years' worth of local news.

Chantelle's mobile still went straight to voicemail. Alex left her message about the Barrons' imminent arrival, expecting an excited return call, but none came. She thought an espresso at Chez Maxie might ease her impatience.

She was returning papers to the file when a woman's face pressed against the glass of the door. Alex jumped. She rushed to open it, but the woman was hurrying away.

'*Excusez-moi!*' Alex called after her. 'We're open. Come in!'

The woman turned slowly and looked Alex up and down. Alex tried not to do the same, but the short, round woman was quite a sight. Her jawline was fleshy and her straight hairline seemed drawn in charcoal across her broad forehead. Gold bracelets tinkled on her wrists, and gold chains cascaded over a leopard print scarf onto her solid bosom. The remarkable paste diamonds on her fingers matched those in her ears. Her lips and her fingernails were fuchsia. Alex was momentarily dumbfounded.

'Madame Charpentier is away,' the woman said haughtily.

'Yes, that's right.'

'My name is Paulette Bitoun. We are old friends.'

Alex racked her memory. Could she have possibly forgotten meeting a woman like this?

'I am the interior decorator. Madame Charpentier and I have worked together over many years. Liliane Valentin called me, and I want to discuss it.'

'Of course. I met Mrs Valentin yesterday,' Alex said. 'The house needs work, lovely as it is. It would be a wonderful job.'

Paulette took a gold pen and a notebook from her bag and held them poised. 'And you are?' She opened her mouth in what Alex took to be a smile, showing tiny yellow teeth.

'I'm working with Madame Charpentier now. My name is Alex Coates.' She held out her hand.

'English,' Paulette said. She put away her pen without writing anything down and offered Alex the cold tips of her fingers. 'Well, I'll wait for Madame Charpentier to get in touch. Goodbye.'

Alex watched her go, noting with satisfaction her thick, shapeless calves.

Chez Maxie's tables were set for lunch. The pretty waitress was talking on the phone as she leaned on the wall near the kitchen, an unlit cigarette in her hand. There were two customers at the bar, and Françoise was absorbed in her newspaper.

'So,' she said, when she looked up to see Alex. 'I see the Valentins want to sell on Cap Ferrat.' She tapped the *Nice-Matin*. 'The family are in financial trouble. Hardly a painting left.' She read on for a moment before closing the paper. 'I remember those parties. I went to one or two myself. The family's losing money hand over fist now. Obviously that nephew doesn't have a head for business. 'Will you have an espresso, Madame Alex?'

Before she could answer, Alex saw Françoise's face light

up. She followed her gaze to Guillaume, followed closely by Monsieur Hubert, coming through the door. The asthmatic chef appeared from the kitchen, wiping his hands on his apron, to shake Guillaume's hand.

Alex tried to follow the group's banter as they drank small glasses of red wine. Françoise leaned over the countertop, touching Guillaume's arm and laughing like a girl. He seemed to glance as furtively at her as he did at Alex herself, and he said little. His companions didn't seem to mind. Today a well-pressed blue shirt was stretching taut over his stomach. He pulled repeatedly at the open collar.

Eventually the little group turned their attention turned to Alex. She straightened her shoulders. There was warmth in Hubert's intelligent gaze and in Françoise's expectant smile. Had they said something she hadn't understood?

'Bad timing for Chantelle to be away,' said Alain Hubert. 'Every agent on the Côte d'Azur will want the Valentin villa now.' Who but Guillaume could have told them about meeting the Parisian couple?

'Even worse timing than she could have predicted,' Alex replied. 'I've had a call from an important American contact of Chantelle's, who is coming next week and expecting to be shown the best properties.'

'Ha, isn't that what they all want?' said Françoise.

'But Chantelle will be back by next week,' Guillaume said.

'That's the problem,' Alex said. 'Viewings will need to be arranged in advance. This is a new client Chantelle is anxious to please.'

Françoise folded her newspaper and put it under the bar. 'Madame Alex, I think Chantelle will sort everything out, even from New York. Who is this client?'

Alex hesitated. The restaurant was always full of eager listeners. 'An American couple, newlyweds, wealthy and well connected,' she said. 'They want something close to Nice.'

'Cap Ferrat,' said Alain Hubert confidently. Guillaume, Françoise and the chef nodded.

Françoise put an espresso on the bar, with a paper-wrapped biscuit on the saucer. 'The Valentin villa might be right,' she said. 'But it must be an old wreck now.'

'You'd be amazed how easily things can be fixed,' Hubert continued. 'Isn't that so, Guillaume? Money can take care of everything.'

Guillaume and Françoise laughed.

'In any case, Madame Coates, there is a house that could soon be available near St Jean on Cap Ferrat,' said Hubert. 'On the Avenue du Phare. It could be ideal for Chantelle's new client – your new client. An ex-colleague just told me the owner might want to sell. I haven't seen it for years, but I'd like to. Perhaps I can arrange for us to see it?'

'That's kind of you,' Alex said. 'But I must speak to Chantelle before I take any steps.'

Hubert's sparkling eyes were hard to resist. 'Chantelle wouldn't want two potential properties to slip through her fingers while she's away,' he said. He turned to the others. 'Would she?'

Alex looked at Guillaume for reassurance, but he refused to meet her eyes. Were they teasing her? She could feel her cheeks beginning to flush. She said, 'I'll let you know as soon as I can.'

She left the money on the bar for the coffee, and said goodbye.

There was still no message from Chantelle. Impatiently, Alex flicked through the filing cabinet that contained the list of properties. She wanted to get started, but how could she get going without Chantelle's advice? Nothing struck her as exactly right. There were two elegant villas for sale near Cannes, but neither was particularly private. There was a small villa in Antibes, although it did have a tennis court and two swimming pools in its extensive grounds. There was also a penthouse apartment near the Negresco Hotel, the landmark building on the seafront Promenade des Anglais with its candy-pink dome, visible for miles around. The apartment took up the entire top floor of a Belle Époque building, but the elderly owner was insisting on a price that even Chantelle considered greedy.

Chantelle knew the owners of all these places. She charmed them, remembering the names of their children and cooing over their pets. Alex couldn't disappoint her new boss. She checked the key cabinet, feeling the satisfying weight of each set of keys as she found them, and replaced them on their hooks. Where on earth was Chantelle? Why hadn't she called right back? If the Americans were arriving earlier than planned, she'd need to get down to work the moment she arrived home in Nice.

Alex looked again through the notes she'd made for her dossier. Was Natascha and Michael Barron's dream property in there? She scrabbled among the papers until she found the yellowed article on the fire in the Menier villa. Chantelle's favourite property, Guillaume had said. A seven-bedroom residence, the cutting reported, with a guesthouse by the pool. Hadn't Guillaume mentioned something about the owner looking for a new tenant? She put the cutting on top of the pile of details, and read it again.

She tried calling New York once more, but all she got was Chantelle's imperious command to *laissez un mot* – leave a message. Alex knew every breath of it by heart now.

After a few more silent minutes turning over the pages of the dossier and making notes in her notebook, she could no longer keep her curiosity in check. She scanned the map for the quickest route to Cap Ferrat, and grabbed the keys to Chantelle's car.

The scent of L'Eau d'Issey still lingered in Chantelle's Citroen Xsara. Alex gripped the wheel nervously. She'd always been a confident driver, but in Nice, she wasn't used to the speed everyone else seemed comfortable with. When, beyond Nice, the coast road opened in front of her, she relaxed. A few minutes later, as she turned in towards the bay of Villefranche, she glanced repeatedly at the view. The sky and the water lit the bay so brightly that even at a distance, each leaf of the bougainvillea spreading across the towering wall between the beach and rail track seemed minutely defined. This is the light the artists came for, she thought.

She continued on round the bay, past the village and towards Cap Ferrat, the green spit of land that reached out into the sea towards a white lighthouse, the *phare*. Through tall hedges and over solid gates, there were tantalising flashes of orange or green rooftiles.

She checked her map several times before she found what must be the Menier villa. She had already parked when she noticed the security cameras above the gates. Alex could see nothing but blue sky above the white front wall, but she noticed an alley between the Menier grounds and the house next door. She hardly looked like a cat-burglar in her slim skirt, she thought, and marched confidently towards the house, hoping to get a better view from the alley. The camera turned in her direction.

There was a car in the alley. It was an old one, a small, dark-green two-seater, perhaps a Mercedes. She could have used the polished chrome bumpers as mirrors. Nearby two men were talking. She recognised immediately the shorter one as the Russian who'd been looking at Maxie's menu; he was becoming familiar. The other one, a similar age, was wearing a sweater in the sort of pastel yellow she and Rod used to laugh at. She stopped beside some mimosa hanging lushly into the alley over the wall. Suddenly the men's voices rose. She realised that between the parked car and the branches, she was hidden from sight, and stood motionless. The taller man punched his fist into the opposite palm. A moment later, he banged aggressively on the bonnet of the car, shouting what sounded like '*Nyet, Nyet, Nyet*'. The other grabbed his arm, swinging him round with enough force that he stumbled.

Alex gasped. The two men turned towards her. There was an unpleasant menace in the coolness with which they looked at her. Before she could think of anything to say, the Russian got into the car, started the engine and pulled rapidly out of the alley, forcing Alex to flatten herself against the wall.

The man in the pastel sweater smoothed his grey-flecked dark hair and smiled. Deep dimples appeared in his cheeks, and an amused gleam replaced any trace of hardness in his eyes. 'Excuse me,' he said in French. 'We've surprised you.'

'Yes,' Alex said. 'But I suppose that's not surprising.'

The man laughed. There was extra weight on his tall frame, but he looked comfortable with it. 'I haven't seen you in the neighbourhood before,' he said, changing effortlessly to English when he heard Alex speak. She was unsure of his accent. 'Could you be trespassing?'

'This is only an alley,' she said defensively. She realised he might be the owner of one of the houses nearby. 'I'm not sure if it's private property. So the answer is…maybe.' They both instinctively looked up at the Menier villa's security camera. 'To be honest, I just wanted to have a look at this house. It's got some history, and it's supposed to be very pretty.'

'Everything's pretty here,' the man said, and waved his hand dismissively towards the greenery. 'That's the point of here.' He was wearing a gold ring on his right hand, one that, had Rod been around to listen, Alex would describe as vulgar. For now, it seemed exotic. His black slip-on shoes were shiny – a bit Euro, her daughter Meghan might say. 'And most villas have a history, too,' he continued. 'People kept their mistresses in the houses; artists used to paint these views.'

'I'm interested in more recent history,' Alex said.

He took a step towards her. Alex stiffened. 'I can cover the past few decades for you,' he said. He lingered a fraction of a second too long on vowels, and over-stressed his Rs. 'Where would you like to hear about it? There are some pretty restaurants, since you like pretty, down on the waterfront.'

The man, close now, smelled of leather. He cocked his head as he looked at her, waiting for an answer. Alex frowned and put her hand to her throat. He seemed aware of her confusion, and stepped back. She was both relieved and disappointed.

'Thank you,' she said. 'I have another appointment.'

She walked back to Chantelle's car and drove off as calmly as she could, not thinking about where she was going. In the rearview mirror, she saw the man walking in the direction of the Menier villa.

CHAPTER FOUR

Alex had immediately clicked through the few messages she found blinking on the office phone, anxious to hear Chantelle's voice. Still nothing. She went back to Les Jolies Roses and changed into trainers. Walking had always helped calm her down.

The Promenade des Anglais hugged the beach for two miles along the curve of the city, and Alex slipped in amongst the usual crowd of joggers, dogwalkers, rollerbladers, strolling tourists and cyclists. She moved fast. As a child, she'd won all the school prizes for running and jumping, and even now Beth or Meghan told her to slow down as they trotted after her.

The open sea and sky of the bay permeated the air with intense, calm blue. At dusk, when the streets of Nice had already passed into night, this strange colour retained a peculiar light that didn't belong to the coastline at all, but rather to another world along the horizon. There was something uplifting and hopeful about the clarity of the evening, though when the last light had gone, the matt blackness that began beyond the breaking waves unnerved her.

She reached a quiet stretch of beach where once or twice Rod had tried his luck along with the early-evening fishermen.

Alex stopped to watch them now when she felt her phone vibrate. She reached into the warmth of her fleece jacket to answer it.

'Beth, darling!' Her younger daughter couldn't have called at a better time. 'You'll never guess where I am. Do you remember when Dad and I were fishing on his birthday and you phoned? I'm here again!'

Beth laughed. 'Fishing? What's come over you?'

There were voices in the background, the occasional toot of a car horn. Beth must be at a café near her studio in Paris.

'No, not fishing, silly. I've been walking.' A fisherman

glanced round as Alex's voice carried over the stones.

'Were you thinking about Dad?'

She'd barely thought about Rod this afternoon, with so much going on. That was beginning to happen. His grip on her would relax, moment by moment, day by day. It was healthy, she knew it. She couldn't be lonely forever. Beth, however, unlike her sister, wouldn't be happy to hear it.

'Not really, darling,' Alex said. 'Not today. I've been at work, and just wanted a walk. Things are getting interesting.'

Alex made no mention of her growing sense of frustration at Chantelle's silence, nor her experience in the alley. Instead, she turned the impending arrival of the Barrons into an entertaining anecdote for her daughter. Beth was in good spirits. Each time she laughed, Alex felt a surge of pleasure. It was rare enough.

Beth had been a fretful child who'd turned into a resentful teenager, quick to take offence, and even the way Beth closed a door could still make Alex tense her jaw, ready to watch every word. It was exhausting. Now, sometimes weeks went by when their only contact was a brief email. Alex, guiltily, appreciated the peace. To have Beth in this easy, talkative mood was heaven.

'I've been thinking of coming down, Mum. I've been stuck in the studio for ages and Paris is so grey. I could use some light.'

'I'd love it, Beth. I can't wait for you to see the flat, and there's plenty of room.' She knew Beth would love the market, and Chez Maxie. She imagined them wandering through the market, choosing ingredients for dinner at Les Jolies Roses. 'I can set up a workspace so you can paint.'

'Don't worry, Mum. In fact, I have a friend down there, someone who was at art school with me. I'm not expecting to work too hard. Besides, I've been doing good stuff here in Paris. I'll be able to head home with a load of work to justify my grant.'

Alex knew better than to ask about either Beth's work or her friend. Meghan would have provided every last detail, but Beth would consider any questions prying. Her oversensitive, wary self could reappear in a breath.

'Whatever you want, sweetheart. You know I'll be happy whenever you get here.'

'Not if you're busy with that job, though.'

Beth's sudden sharpness unsteadied Alex. 'Chantelle should be back soon,' she reassured her daughter. 'Things will be back to normal.'

'I hope so,' Beth said. 'I wouldn't want to get in the way of your new life.'

Alex ignored the sudden new layer in their conversation, but as they said goodbye, it left her with a dull sense of regret. Beth could twist things so adeptly that Alex had often provided her with ammunition before she knew it. She watched the fisherman pack up their gear and had set to walking rapidly back home when the phone rang again.

'I hope I'm not disturbing you,' a familiar voice said, in French. It took Alex a second to place it. Alain Hubert. Did he get her number from Guillaume? He had called to say he could arrange a visit to the house he had mentioned.

'Please, say if it isn't convenient.'

Alex apologised for what sounded like her lack of enthusiasm.

'Still no news from Chantelle,' she explained. 'It's worrying.'

The line went silent. She thought Hubert had hung up, but when he spoke again, she imagined him smiling.

'This isn't the first time our friend Chantelle has visited New York,' he said.

'So she said,' Alex replied. 'All that shopping!'

'Yes, the shopping. It's very... rejuvenating.'

The fairy lights that wrapped around trunks of the palm trees along the Promenade came on all at once. Alex checked her watch. It was later than she'd thought. 'Unfortunately I've never had enough money for shopping like that,' she said.

'Chantelle comes home without bags,' Hubert said.

'No? I thought that's why she went.'

'I mean without bags under her eyes.'

She stopped walking the second she realised what Hubert meant. She disguised a laugh by clearing her throat.

'Ah,' she said. 'I see what you mean.'

'I'm telling you so that you know that for a short while Chantelle might not be able to get in touch,' he continued. 'Do you understand?

CHAPTER FIVE

Two days later, still with no word from Chantelle, Alex went to Chez Maxie to meet Alain Hubert as they had agreed. Maxie was sitting next to her mother behind the bar, peering at paperwork through wire-framed glasses and stabbing at a calculator. She didn't look up as Alex entered. The restaurant wasn't officially open yet, and Alex didn't sit down. In the kitchen, a radio was playing an old French song, and the chef was singing along. The young sous-chef was telling him a story in insistent, guttural French.

'Bonjour Madame,' Françoise said. 'He's just parking outside. He took his granddaughter to school. Café au lait? Thé? Nescafe? I'm never sure what the English prefer in the morning.'

Alex wondered why Hubert hadn't suggested meeting at the office. She was going to refuse the offer to save Françoise the trouble, when Maxie put her pencil down.

'*Voilà!*' she said. She dropped her glasses on the table, smiled, and seemed familiar once more. 'Alex will have a café au lait, Maman. Everyone thinks money flows like water in a restaurant, but you have to be so careful. Today, for instance, the skate wing in black butter...*Mon dieu*, I had to work hard with my supplier on that! I have a reputation for driving a hard bargain.' She looked smug. 'Only the freshest fish will do. And I even know where the butter was churned. Shall I set one aside for you?' Maxie waited less than a heartbeat for an answer, then continued: 'It's always popular. I'll see what I can do for you, but I can't promise anything.'

Françoise put Alex's coffee on the bar, along with the morning's *Nice-Matin*, in the spot Maxie had vacated. 'Look,' she said, pushing the newspaper towards Alex. 'Here are your American newlyweds.'

Alex tried to read the short report. There was a headline about the forthcoming arrival of the American socialites.

'Mr and Mrs Michael Barron expected on the Riviera from New York,' Françoise read out. 'Recently married…blah blah blah… Old family, wife a beauty, daughter of an art collector… *oui, oui*…Natascha…' She looked up. 'A Russian name, *non*?'

'Perhaps,' Alex said. She would buy her own copy of the paper as soon as she could.

When Alain arrived, Françoise put the *Nice-Matin* under the bar. She served him an espresso and busied herself wiping down the coffee machine. 'Do you remember the house on the Avenue du Phare, Françoise? Those parties?' But she seemed not to have heard. Something that Hubert was tapping on the bar caught Alex's attention. She was looking at it when he turned to her and said, 'I've met the owner once or twice, though that's going back a long time now. Something in the art world, people say. His wife disappeared. He's in no hurry to sell, but my contact says he'd consider a good offer.' What he was tapping seemed to be a small piece of wood or stone, painted gold.

Hubert drained his espresso and watched Françoise, so that Alex was unsure to whom he was speaking when he said, 'It's a beautiful house. Romantic.'

Hubert's scratched and dented BMW was double-parked outside. He took a different, quicker route out of Nice than the one Alex knew. The baby-seat in the back was unexpected.

'Grandchildren,' he explained. 'My main duty these days is to drive the children around. I understand you have two yourself.'

Alex laughed. 'How do you know that? I don't remember mentioning them.'

Hubert expertly overtook a bus, sliding the BMW back into lane with barely a hair's breadth between the wing mirror and an oncoming van.

'You told my cousin. He delivered your bunk beds,' he said. Then he winked. 'Nice is a small town. We don't ignore our neighbours the way they do in Paris and London.'

As they arrived in the Avenue du Phare the villa's iron gates were open, and a police car was nosing in. Hubert pulled closely behind it, flashing his lights. The policeman in the passenger seat peered angrily at them through the rear window, but when he saw Hubert he waved, motioning them to come through.

'It's Cuscolini,' Hubert explained. 'This is out of his way. He's based just up the coast.'

Alex gripped the side of her seat. She was already feeling a bit out of her own way, accompanying a man she didn't really know to see a house that may or may not be for sale. Now that she saw in front of her a woman shouting and running towards the police car, the feeling turned to queasiness. She sunk down low. She wouldn't be telling her overly concerned daughter Meghan about this. Hubert, on the other hand, leaned forward brightly, like a cat ready to pounce.

'*Enfin!*' the woman said. Finally! She threw her arms around the beefy Cuscolini as he climbed out of the police car. With her mousy hair and shapeless floral dress, she could have been in either her 50s or her 70s. Whatever she was shrieking about was at first muffled by Cuscolini's belly. He patted her arm. 'He told me never to call the police without telling him, but what could I do?' Alex heard her say. 'The front door was wide open.' She let go of Cuscolini momentarily to point towards it.

'You're safe, don't worry,' Cuscolini said. 'No one is hurt.'

The woman bit her knuckles. 'I went into St Jean and I came back to discover the alarms were off. I was only gone for 20 minutes. If Monsieur Bronz finds out, he'll be furious! I've never seen such a temper in my life!'

As Cuscolini led the woman back to the house, Hubert got out of the car. He slapped the other policeman on the back, shook his hand and for a few minutes they stood talking quietly. Soon the policeman followed his partner into the house.

'That's Suzanne, the housekeeper,' Hubert said to Alex through the rolled-down car window. 'Cuscolini is her nephew.

He thinks she probably just forgot to set the alarms herself.'

'But aren't we supposed to be meeting the owner here?'

'Suzanne expects him back in half an hour, that's why she's so eager to have her nephew look the place over before he gets home.'

Alex shifted in the seat, which was beginning to feel too warm through her jersey skirt. 'So if nothing seems to be missing, the owner will be none the wiser?'

Hubert nodded.

'Except that we all know.' She frowned. 'That doesn't seem right.'

Hubert stood up straight, so that Alex could see only the stomach of his buttoned jacket as he spoke. 'Maybe in London they do things by the book, but here we take care of each other,' he said. 'I'll have a look around while we wait for him.'

She watched him walk over the perfect lawn towards the far wall and look it up and down.

Hubert was right: the house was romantic. It was a tall, square, Belle Époque villa, painted chalky yellow, with ornate lintels above the windows. The white shutters were mostly closed, but on the third storey, two circular windows were visible, framed by plaster curls. Alex counted six windows on each floor, all topped by lintels decorated with a tangle of plasterwork flowers. She assumed that the hedges on either side of the house hid later additions, or perhaps a pool house or garage. She would soon find out.

The BMW was warming up rapidly in the morning sun. Alex got out and went to stand beneath one of the two eucalyptus trees beside the entrance gates. The shade there was deep and cool, and she breathed in the minty tang.

As Alex was examining the front door, Cuscolini, his partner and the housekeeper came out. The aunt pointed and gestured, wringing her hands. Eventually they walked back to the police car, and after some animated kissing of cheeks and hugging, the two policemen backed the car up and turned around. The aunt disappeared into the house. The gates opened as the policemen approached, and they waved cheerfully at her as they passed.

The sound of the engine soon faded. There was no sign of Hubert and the front door remained closed. It occurred to Alex that he wasn't doing her a favour at all: he wanted to see this property, and she was the perfect excuse. Alex waited. If this were her house, she decided, she'd put in lavender bushes along the driveway so the scent would drift through the windows.

After 10 minutes, Hubert returned.

'The grounds must be big,' she called out. She was relieved to see him. What if the owner had returned to find her lurking in the shade of his trees?

'It's a fine property,' Hubert replied. 'There's enough room to hide another building at the back. Come, let's remind auntie we're here.'

The housekeeper took some time to answer the door, and when Hubert explained why they were there, she looked momentarily shocked.

'Oh! I'd forgotten. Monsieur Bronz must be expecting you, he said he would be back. Please come in, Alain, how are you?' They followed her into a hall with a white marble floor so highly polished Alex thought of ice. The hall was dominated by a curved stairway with an ironwork balustrade, topped with a gold handrail. Too fussy, Alex decided, though she liked the worn edges of the stone steps.

'You won't tell him, will you, Alain?' The aunt began wringing her hands again. 'He has a terrible temper, that Monsieur Bronz. He's a fanatic about security. He'd be so angry if he knew I'd forgotten the alarm...' She turned to Alex, as if seeing her for the first time. 'Madame! You mustn't let him know I made such a silly mistake.'

'Don't worry,' Alex said kindly. 'What he doesn't know won't hurt him.'

She led them into the kitchen, where she must have been putting away the purchases she'd made in St Jean. The table was almost big enough to play pool on, spread for the moment with bulging brown paper bags and a baguette. The wood was scrubbed to the colour of whalebone. Alex ached to start kneading dough on it, shucking green beans, mixing cakes. But the rest of the kitchen, she thought, was made cold by stainless steel and black granite.

They waited for Suzanne to bring them glasses of water in a reading room that faced the back lawn. The Art Deco armchair Alex had chosen to sit in was just the right inclination, and there was a glass side table that was just the right size for her bag. In contrast with the kitchen, someone had spent a lot of time thinking about how to make this room comfortable. Hubert wandered around, hands clasped behind his back, looking at the framed photographs and paintings that lined the walls. There was a burnished walnut desk in a corner near the French windows. One wall was entirely lined with bookshelves. Alex could only read the larger titles – art books, mostly.

Hubert leaned in to look closely at one particular picture.

'Christ,' he said. He fumbled inside his jacket for his glasses and put them on. 'Could it really be?'

'What?' Alex said. She jumped up and went to look, but the front door slammed, and there was a confident tap of heels on the marble floor.

'He's here!' Suzanne hissed at them as she put their water tray on a lacquered coffee table. 'Don't forget, you don't know anything!'

'Have they arrived, Suzanne?' a deep voice called.

Alex was about to sit down again, but there was no time to compose herself. Monsieur Bronz hesitated for barely a second when he saw her.

'A pleasure for the second time,' he said, approaching her, his hand outstretched.

Adrenaline rose in a rush through Alex's chest. It was the taller man in the pastel yellow jumper from the alley by the Menier villa.

'But I thought you were Russian,' she said, realising immediately how foolish it sounded. She hoped the flush she felt at her neck was hidden by her scarf.

'You're very astute, in that case,' Bronz said in English. His hand held hers a moment too long. 'My soul could be Russian.'

He turned to Hubert, who was watching them with a bemused smile. Alex didn't know whether or not he understood English.

'*Comment allez-vous?*' Bronz said, continuing in French. 'Suzanne, bring us champagne! This is superb! Hubert, please, introduce me to your friend.'

It was far too early for alcohol, even champagne, but Alex said nothing. Bronz and Hubert seemed to know each other, though she noticed Hubert was cool. Suzanne mouthed a shy 'shhh' at Alex as she whisked the water glasses away, and again as she put a champagne bucket on the coffee table.

'The sale of this house is entirely conditional,' Ed Bronz explained when he had settled himself in the desk chair, swinging languidly to face Alex and Hubert, and then the garden. 'The reasons I stay here may change.' Alex now noticed that he rolled some of his Rs, but not others. 'If I leave I must sell, or rent. That, Madame Coates, is why I'm happy to speak with an estate agent I can trust.'

Alex cringed. When on earth was Chantelle going to get in touch? She shouldn't have agreed to come with Hubert – she felt she was on the edge of making a fool of herself.

'The rental market in the South of France has almost no boundaries,' she said, 'but it's seasonal, as I'm sure you know. And a house for sale, as with anything you have to sell, is only worth what someone will pay for it. We'd have to find that someone.'

Ed Bronz was listening to her intently. His brown eyes never moved from hers. Did she sound credible, or did he have what Rod had called 'bullshit radar'?

'But surely it's you who have to find that someone? In any case, I haven't decided yet,' Bronz said. 'But you'll need to see the house.' He looked from Alex to Hubert, but Hubert raised his hands and laughed.

'I'm not the professional here,' he said. 'I've simply made the introduction. I'll let you get on with business while I sit with my *amie* Suzanne and catch up on her news.'

Alex felt a pang of alarm. Her own bullshit radar was overheating. She wasn't sure if she could keep it up over the entire house. She grabbed her glass of champagne from the coffee table. 'We could have a quick look,' she said, reverting to English now that Hubert was gone. 'Just an idea for now, while you consider your options.'

CHAPTER SIX

'Mum! Oh my God! What do you mean, this man wants to have a drink with you?' Meghan's voice squeaked with the strain of stressing the last word. Alex moved the phone away from her ear, and put it on loudspeaker. She knew her daughter was rolling her eyes, personally affronted by this latest turn in her mother's life.

'Yes, he asked me out. Isn't that how you say it these days?' She blotted her lipstick with tissue, the final part of her morning makeup routine. Meghan often called early, to share the first coffee of her day.

'You're not going, are you? I mean, what if he's married.' Her voice lowered on the word 'married' as if a nosy neighbour were within earshot.

'Hubert said his wife had gone to South America, but Ed didn't mention any wife,' Alex said. 'He only wants to show me around Monte Carlo. Anyway, I haven't said yes or no yet.'

Meghan snorted. It was a familiar noise; one Alex had been hearing since Meghan was a child. It worked as exasperation, embarrassment, irritation and, as Alex knew in this case, inarticulate worry.

'He's charming,' she assured Meghan. 'He hardly strikes me as a murderer.' She took her cup and wandered to the living room. As she spoke, she straightened the Turkish rugs with her toe.

'It just doesn't seem … seemly. You're a woman on your own, Mum, and you don't know anything about him. You don't even like his house!'

Alex agreed. It was a shame about the villa on the Avenue du Phare. The house had seemed cool and impersonal, and Ed Bronz had shown her round it as if he himself were the estate agent, opening each door as if unfamiliar with what he might find. The perfect proportions of the rooms had been overwhelmed by colour and pattern. To his credit,

Bronz had explained that every room, except the reading room where he spent most of his time, and the understated, masculine bedroom, had been conceived by an insistent interior decorator called Paulette Bitoun. Alex remembered the overdressed woman she'd met outside the office, and wasn't surprised.

'I'm not planning to buy the house,' Alex pointed out to Meghan. 'But it might suit Natascha and Michael Barron. It's big enough. Apparently there used to be amazing parties there. Hubert said...'

Meghan snorted again. 'That's another thing, why would that old policeman want to look around? It sounds strange to me, Mum. I'm glad Beth is coming down soon from Paris, I'll get the full story from her.'

The image of her two girls deep in discussion about her welfare made her smile. So far, she had indulged them, but now, on her own, she was just beginning to imagine that one day she might be grateful for it.

It was Sunday, and Immobilier Charpentier was closed. Perhaps that's why Chantelle still hadn't phoned, Alex thought; she wanted to give Alex her weekend off. But she was beginning to worry. Faced with the Barrons' imminent arrival, she planned to spend some time in the office working on the dossier. But first she wanted to drive out to Bellet to see for herself what the American newspaper was referring to.

In Chantelle's fragrant Citroen, she rolled down the windows, turned up the morning news on the radio, and negotiated her way onto the highway that would speed her through Nice and out of town. The temperature was beginning to climb. Alex had felt it that morning as soon as she opened the shutters to look out over the market. Her leather handbag on the car seat beside her became supple in the sunshine. She rested her hand on it as she drove, feeling the warmth.

As soon as she turned off the highway, the narrow road started to twist and turn. Within minutes, she was among vineyards. Rows of bare, stumpy vines stretched over the line of the hills. Here and there a muddy track led towards a house surrounded by scruffy outbuildings. It was unlike the graceful vineyards she'd seen in Bordeaux, but she knew there was no comparison. Bellet was the tiniest of the French wine regions, run by just a few families. She noticed a hand-painted sign that said '*Dégustation*' – tastings. She slowed down to look, and glimpsed a squat building with empty tables and chairs scattered on the grass. She'd remember the way for another time.

Alex parked in the tiny village and ordered an espresso at the only café. It was dead quiet. Perhaps this was one of the things that had so appealed to the American journalist who'd written about the area. A waiter leaned on the bar, spinning his tray and watching the few passers-by. After a while he returned to Alex's side.

'Another espresso, Madame?'

Alex said no; she would have a glass of Perrier, no ice.

'*Vous êtes Américaine*? We've just been written about in an American newspaper. Are you on holiday?'

'I live in Nice, but I've come for a look. Do you get many Americans?'

'They could be English. What do I know?'

'Americans leave tips.'

The waiter laughed loudly, exposing several gaps in his back teeth.

'I think I know who wrote that article, and he must have been American, because he left five euros every time.' The waiter held up his right hand and spread his fingers wide. 'One beer for him, five euros for me. He was here for a week. Someone told me he wanted to buy the château.'

Alex had been about to remind the waiter of her Perrier, but she stopped.

'The château?'

'It's not really a château. That's what we've always called it. It's a ruin. We all used to play in it as kids. People say some crazy foreigner owns it.'

Alex took her notebook out of her bag and put it on the table. She noted Bellet; Ruin; Foreigner. The waiter's eyes followed her pen.

'I hope it's not for sale,' he said. 'Messing around in the château is part of growing up here. Your first cigarette, your first kiss…' His tray spun round and round. 'It's about a kilometre beyond the village, if you want to see.'

Chantelle probably knew all about the château; perhaps everyone did. It wouldn't be any good for the Barrons, and Alex would be wasting her time. But she couldn't resist a good wreck. She and Rod had gone through a period of believing they could take one on. A single trip out from London spent inspecting dilapidated walls and caved-in ceilings had brought them to their senses. At least that phase had expanded their French vocabulary; Alex could still remember words for septic tank, joist and termite.

She glanced at the crude map the waiter had drawn in her notebook. If she had followed it correctly, the château was just the other side of the overgrown hedge where she had parked the Citroen. On the other side of the road, an elderly woman was working in a vineyard beside a farmhouse.

The size of the two-storey building surprised her. The grey stone façade was intact, but the side walls had collapsed in sections, leaving gaping holes. The roof had partly caved in, and what was left sagged perilously like a worn-out mattress. No doors or windows remained. Alex circled it, stepping carefully to avoid catching the toes of her shoes in vines that twisted into the fallen stonework. Insects flew out of the undergrowth as she passed. At the back of the house, the vines had engulfed the rusted skeleton of what must once have been a fine veranda. There were steps leading up to it, overgrown but for a central path trampled clear, probably by local children. She took off her sunglasses. It was irresistibly inviting.

Once she was inside, however, Alex felt the chill of the stone. She was in a large room with a wall full of glassless windows covered almost completely by knotted vines. Dim light came from where part of the ceiling had crashed through the floor, exposing the room above as if it were a doll's house. The parquet floor was fissured and dry, and slivers of varnish clung to the loose tiles. They clicked and clacked under her feet as she crossed them. A sour animal smell hit her when she looked down a narrow corridor that ran the length of the building. A shaft of sunlight lit the opposite end. Halfway along, she could see some kind of console table.

It amazed her that there was any furniture left in a house that had been abandoned for decades. Except for the acrid odour, the château was dreamlike – just the sort of place children would play out their fantasies. Beth would have loved it here, a perfect stage for the princesses and dragons she drew endlessly when she was small.

As Alex approached the table, there was a screech from behind. She whirled round, dropping her canvas shoulder bag. There wasn't enough light to see clearly. She stood as still as possible, her hand on her stomach, where her heart seemed to be pumping. But of course, she told herself, it was only a cat outside on the veranda, or a bird.

She dusted off her bag. Alex had never been prone to imagining burglars and rapists at every turn, but she knew it was imprudent to be here. The structure was dangerous, no one knew where she was, and it was isolated enough for anything to happen, not to mention the fact that she was trespassing. Still, she'd risk just a quick look at that table.

Close up, it was an ugly, squat piece of furniture. It was also rotten, infested with woodworm and split along its hefty barley-twist legs. Dragging it along the hall would have been a problem for anyone. Only one of the three drawers remained. Alex pulled at it. At first it wouldn't give, so she bent down to look underneath. When she poked it, a cloud of acrid dust puffed out. She pulled again, and it opened with a jerk. Her stomach leapt once more, and she tried to slam the drawer shut, taking a step backwards. The tendon in her heel ground as she hit the wall too hard. Whatever she'd glimpsed had moved.

Her heart was beating rapidly now, and there was a film of perspiration on her upper lip, but the drawer wasn't closed, and when she looked again, she could see that inside was the maggot-infected body of a mouse. It lay on a piece of paper torn from a school exercise book, on which someone had written 'Boo!'

'For god's sake,' Alex said out loud. Whatever teenage boy – it couldn't be a girl – had thought up this prank would have been pleased with his handiwork. Her pulse was beating uncomfortably in her throat, and her heel felt bruised. She headed towards the sunlight at the end of the corridor, thinking she'd prefer to climb out of the frameless window than face what had been screeching on the veranda. The uneven floorboards required all her attention. When, suddenly, a shadow fell across her feet, she gasped so deeply her ribs seemed to cramp. Someone grabbed her wrist firmly, and Alex, who had never fainted before in her life, felt her knees give way.

CHAPTER SEVEN

When Alex opened her eyes, she saw motes of dust floating in the fading sunlight. Every beat of her heart seemed to press her back into the wall where she was sitting upright, her feet in front of her. She patted the floor for her bag, and pulled it to her chest. There was no noise beyond the birds outside and the diminishing whine of a motorbike.

'Who are you?' she called out. There was a pen in her bag, and a wooden cuticle stick. Would she be able to do any harm with them if she had to?

'Who are you?' Her voice cracked. 'People know where I am.'

She thought of the waiter, who would surely have forgotten her by now.

She listened until she couldn't hold her breath any more. Her wrist was braceleted with mottled pink, and it tingled as she rubbed it. Could she have imagined that hot, firm grip of a hand on her wrist? She fumbled for her wallet, keys and phone, her hands shaking. Her throat tightened as she felt a sob rising. She wouldn't let herself cry, however. She almost never let herself cry. She stood up slowly and smoothed her shirt.

By the time she had clambered out of the window and walked back to the Citroen, Alex had just about convinced herself that her imagination had got the better of her. It was probably just a cloud passing over the sun, and she'd already been feeling jittery because of that dead mouse. Who did she think she was, traipsing around private property? And why was she trying to take care of everything in advance for Chantelle? Perhaps she should just shut the office and wait for her new boss to come home.

When her hands no longer trembled, she pulled the car into the lane. Tears continued to prick her eyes. If only she could tell Rod about all this, he'd soon make her laugh, as usual. Surely tripping over your own toes while doing something as patently silly was no reason to feel as anxious as this.

All the way back to Nice, Alex's resentment with Chantelle's silence grew. The moment she got back to the office, she marched in, leaving the door wide open. She knew Chantelle's number by heart now, and punched it angrily into the keypad. Her message was brief, but even someone as thick-skinned as Chantelle would understand that Alex was losing patience with her.

Making the call calmed her down. She rubbed her wrist. She must have scratched it as she tripped, that would explain it. She'd never fainted before; perhaps the fact that she couldn't remember exactly what had happened was perfectly normal. She'd try not to think about it.

The phone rang again just as she was about to leave the office. Not again, she thought, not someone else calling about Bellet. She would have ignored it if she hadn't heard an American man's voice on the answering machine address her by name.

'Hello, Mrs Coates, this is Harry Bormann, a friend of Chantelle Charpentier's.' Alex stood still, listening, the *Closed* sign in her hand. 'I know you've been trying to get in touch with Chantelle.' He had a breathy, girlish way of speaking, and Alex imagined him as slight and fair-haired, pursing his lips as he cleared his throat to continue. 'There's a little problem. Chantelle was undergoing a...a minor procedure, I don't know if she told you about it?' He paused. Alex knew she didn't have the energy for this phone call, not the way she was feeling. She sat down, and listened to Harry Bormann go on: 'We're not exactly sure what's happened, but I guess I better let you know: so far she hasn't regained consciousness.' The sentence ended with what might have been a tiny sob. Alex returned to the desk and her hand hovered over the phone. Harry sniffed. 'That's literally all I can tell you right now. So, if you want to call me back at your convenience...' He left a number, which Alex jotted down. She'd barely finished when the phone rang again. This time she snatched it up immediately.

'Ah, Mrs Coates, I'm glad you're there.' A familiar, efficient voice. 'I'm glad to catch you on a Sunday. This is Dianne Steer, Mr Michael Barron's personal assistant. I'd like you to send me all the details of the properties the Barrons will be seeing.'

'Ah…'

'Mrs Charpentier advised us there were several suitable possibilities.'

'Yes, she's…'

'I need to know, Mrs Coates, which is why I have to call you over the weekend. The Barrons are planning their departure. Mrs Barron in particular likes to have things well organised.'

'I'm sorry, but…'

Dianne Steer interrupted her with a loud sigh and said, 'Is Mrs Charpentier back in Nice yet?'

Alex was reminded of her first Saturday job at Harrods, where an ogress-manager in the ladies glove department expected her to know the location of every item of stock. Here she was again, waiting impatiently for a reply.

'Mrs Charpentier is unavailable for now, but don't worry,' Alex said, putting one hand on the wall to steady herself. 'I'll send you details tomorrow. Now, may I confirm your email address?'

When Alex had hung up, she ran both hands through her hair. She could barely remember writing down the two phone numbers she saw on the blotting paper on her desk. There was so much to do, but what? She should probably lie down after the morning's unsettling experience, but what she really wanted was a *coupe de champagne*.

CHAPTER EIGHT

The Sunday lunchtime crowd at Chez Maxie was beginning to dwindle, and the professor had piled his papers on the now-empty table beside him. He stood up to shake Alex's hand as she passed, and his baggy jacket knocked one of his books to the floor. She handed it back to him – *An Architectural History of the Mediterranean.*

Maxie, coming out of the kitchen with a crème caramel, made straight for her. '*Oh malheur,*' she said, what a situation. She frowned. 'We've heard. Maman! Champagne for Madame Alex!' With her free hand she steered Alex around the professor to the corner table. Alex sat. Was the unexplained event at the château already making the rounds of the Place du Général de Gaulle?

Françoise scuttled towards her through the tables. 'Chantelle shouldn't have gone; we have plenty of good surgeons in Nice. I don't know why she insists on New York.'

So, Alex thought with irritation, everyone except her must have known exactly why Chantelle was in the United States. Alex swallowed the first sip of champagne gratefully, soothed by the icy tickle on the roof of her mouth.

'I've just heard about it myself,' Alex said. 'When did you find out?'

'Before lunch. But didn't Guillaume tell you, too?' She cocked her head. 'His motorbike was outside, so I thought he was next door with you. Poor Chantelle! I can't bear to think of her alone in New York in a coma!' She crossed her arms and bit her red lips. 'I hope she has her insurance in order.' She gazed out the window for a few seconds, probably imagining the worst, until she patted Alex on the shoulder. 'She'll be alright. Chantelle is tough.'

Alex was exhausted. She felt she ought to be making plans of some kind, but couldn't focus on what they might be. When her glass was almost empty, Maxie appeared and poured another. The little dog Honda hopped up on the chair opposite Alex and lay down with a satisfied grunt.

'We're all praying for Chantelle,' Maxie said. 'What a shock! But she'll be fine. My ex-husband went to the Clinique St Georges for his gallstones. It was supposed to last 15 minutes. He woke up three days later!'

'Was he ok?' Alex asked.

'He married one of the nurses, so yes.' She laughed, carefully holding the champagne bottle. '*Tant pis*. Too bad. I'd be receiving his pension now if he weren't.'

It wasn't reassuring. Even if Chantelle regained consciousness this afternoon, she wouldn't be back home in Nice soon enough to take care of Natascha and Michael Barron.

'Maybe Chantelle will marry one of her doctors,' Alex said as cheerfully as she could. 'But meanwhile there's her business to take care of. The American newlyweds are coming soon and I don't want to let Chantelle down.'

'You won't,' Maxie said. 'Whatever you do, it will be your best.'

Alex nodded. It was exactly the kind of advice Rod used to offer Meghan and Beth.

'Now, I've asked Chef to prepare a little *steak au poivre* for you. It will give you strength. And some *frites*, of course. The beef is from Charentes, the best in France. And Maman will bring you a nice glass of Pauillac, from my cousin's vineyard. You need it, Madame Alex. There's a lot to do.'

The steak was cooked perfectly, tender and bloody pink in the centre, crisping at the edges. Drinking a wine as fine as the Pauillac with chips was just the sort of indulgence she needed. As Honda snoozed, Alex began to relax.

But when Alain Hubert arrived, she was reminded of her predicament with a start.

'Worrying news about Chantelle,' he said, after chatting with Françoise. 'And of course it puts you in a difficult position.'

'You're right, Monsieur Hubert. Who will run her business?

I can't! I spent my life in books, not property.'

'You can only do your best. Chantelle will appreciate it. And of course you have Guillaume.' Alex would have preferred it if he'd advised her to put a closed sign on the door. 'And, please, call me Alain.'

As he fumbled in his pocket, she was suddenly reminded of him in the villa on the Avenue du Phare. 'I meant to ask; what was it that caught your attention on the wall at Ed Bronz's house? You seemed surprised.'

'Ah, not good. A policeman has to have a poker face. Do you play poker?'

Alex wouldn't be put off. 'Was it that photograph?'

Alain looked out at the Place du Général de Gaulle as if he were mulling over his answer. From his pocket he pulled out the little gold object and rolled it between his fingers.

'A picture of Bronz,' he said. 'It made me think about an old case, going back a long way. I'm not even sure I can remember the details now.' He closed his fist over the object. 'But I must be going – my granddaughter needs picking up from a party. *Courage*, Alex.'

On his way out, he said '*bon appétit!*' to Maxie and her team, who were sitting by the kitchen eating together now that the lunchtime service was over.

'Madame Alex, we have another house for the Americans,' Françoise called over. It was by now quiet enough to talk across the tables. 'Go ahead, Sammy, tell your story.'

The young sous-chef looked down at his plate shyly and shook his head.

'Oh, for goodness' sake,' Françoise said. 'Sammy's mother is a maid for a couple in Eze, a few kilometres from here. They just told her they'll be moving to Los Angeles.'

'But maybe Maman can work for the new guys,' Sammy blurted out. Françoise, Maxie, and the *serveuse* turned to him expectantly, but he stuffed a forkful of *ratatouille* into his mouth.

'Sammy's mother says they're going to rent out their house,'

Françoise said. 'It's a palace, right Sammy?'

He nodded, swallowing. 'I've never been inside, you know.'

Françoise rolled her eyes. 'But your mother has. Don't make us squeeze it out, Sammy, tell us.'

'Get on with it,' the *serveuse* said. 'I want to know, too.'

Once he was no longer expected to address Alex directly, Sammy took off, but she had trouble following his rapid delivery. 'Maman says they have silver like in a museum – bowls and pots, y'know? She has to polish it all. The owner he's, like, a movie director. They have lots of people to stay, y'know? Maman has to change the sheets every day, like a hotel. Lots of bedrooms, y'know? They have a cook, too, y'know, and gardeners. And an infinity pool, y'know? You can see all the way to Corsica.'

'You said you'd never been inside,' said the *serveuse*.

Sammy smirked. 'Well, just once, when the owners were away.'

When Alex asked him if he could give her their phone number, he seemed to deflate all at once. He mumbled to his plate about asking his mother, and went to the kitchen to phone her. When he returned, he offered Alex a piece of kitchen roll on which he'd written 'Madame Eze' and a number.

There was a sudden scrape of chair legs on the floor tiles, and everyone turned to the professor.

'I couldn't help but overhear. Are you looking to rent a house, Madame?' he asked. He placed a hand on his books, and took off his rimless glasses. Colour crept up his pale neck, and Alex realised that his receding hair and baggy jacket added years. He couldn't be more than 35.

'For a client,' she explained. 'For Immobilier Charpentier, next door.'

'I happen to know of a place that might be of interest. In the course of my research, I have recently visited a house above the village of Villefranche, towards Cap Ferrat. The housekeeper was kind enough to let me into the garden.' The professor giggled nervously. 'She saw me as a potential tenant, I think.

She was mistaken. I believe the previous tenants have just vacated.'

'A big house?' Alex asked.

'Enormous. I was most interested in the architecture, because of a particular detail – the windows. As she walked me past the house, and I remember thinking that even if my book – I'm writing about the architectural details of the Riviera – sold thousands of copies, I'd never be able to afford such a home.' He looked from one face to another, and Maxie, obligingly, said she'd buy two copies. The professor continued, 'I understand there was a tragic fire there some time ago.'

Alex's stomach lurched.

'Fortunately the exterior was rebuilt to look as it did at the turn of the century, which is what I wanted to examine,' he continued. 'We're privileged to be surrounded by architectural delights here, but most commonly it is the small detail…'

'The house, Prof, what's it like?' Maxie interrupted, like a heckler.

'Oh, yes, of course. I'm sure you don't want to hear all about the unusual shutters on the Menier villa, do you? But it does give the house…'

'The Menier villa!' Alex repeated.

'Some people still refer to it by that name,' the professor said.

'And it's to let?'

'I believe so.'

Alex could have hugged him.

'That would be perfect,' Françoise said. She patted Alex's hand. 'See? We'll soon be ready for the arrival of Monsieur and Madame Barron, won't we?'

As Maxie had predicted, Alex was fortified by her good lunch, and she returned to the office ready to call Harry Bormann in New York. He was hardly reassuring.

'She was so excited about the Barrons, and now…' he gulped. 'I called Guillaume because Chantelle had mentioned him, and

I found the name in her phone. My French is hopeless, so I didn't think he understood. I just don't know what to do.'

So that's how Guillaume had heard. Why on earth hadn't he called to tell her right away?

'But what about Chantelle's cousin?'

Harry sniffed. 'Cousin? Here in New York?'

Alain Hubert had been right. Chantelle wasn't going to visit a cousin at all.

'We'll have to locate some family,' she said authoritatively. She'd never heard Chantelle mention anyone, but Alex hoped there was a brother somewhere, someone calmer and more manly than Harry appeared to be.

There was nothing to do but plough on. She opened her notebook to 'M', flipped through Chantelle's ancient Rolodex, and found a number for Patrice LeBlanc, the owner of the Menier villa.

Perhaps it was the champagne that had given her confidence, but after an hour or so, she was able to lean back in her chair with a satisfied sigh. There on the desk in front of her were the notes she'd made during several calls. Patrice LeBlanc had said he had a long-standing relationship with an agent in Paris, but if when the Americans arrived the villa were still available, perhaps he and Chantelle could come to an arrangement. He would send some details. He had pointedly asked Alex not to mention the name Menier – that tragedy was long ago.

Sammy's piece of kitchen roll was stapled under 'E'. Alex's call caught the film director's wife in Eze by surprise. She addressed her as Madame Eze, as Sammy had noted, and the woman burst into a croaky smoker's laugh. Alex realised her mistake in a second. Her name, she said, was Julie Eichenbaum.

'I haven't had a second to think about the move yet.' There was a dog barking in the background, and a man shouting. 'But yeah,' the woman said. 'We should do something about it. Sure, come later this week. Why not?'

There was also the note of a strained conversation with Guillaume, surrounded by Alex's anxious doodles.

'You've heard about Chantelle, haven't you?' Alex had asked him.

There was silence for a moment, before Guillaume had said suspiciously, 'Is that all you want to talk to me about?'

Alex was taken aback. 'We have so much to talk about, considering the circumstances, don't you agree?'

'There's an explanation,' he'd said quickly, before ringing off.

Clearly Chantelle had more patience for his moods than Alex.

The mark around her wrist had faded, but she kept touching the faint ring. When she tried again to think through exactly what had happened, she ended up shaking her head. The best thing to do now would be to go home and rest.

CHAPTER NINE

Two days later, when Alex opened the shutters to see who was ringing her bell so early in the morning, she saw her daughter Beth on the street below. 'Sweetheart!' she shouted down, waving. Beth looked up, but she didn't wave back. Alex inhaled deeply. As soon as the lift sighed to a stop and the cage opened, she knew from the shadows in the corners of Beth's eyes that something was wrong. Her skin looked dry, its usual porcelain luminosity – from Rod's mother – had turned flat as paper. She was dressed in a shapeless black sweatshirt. Alex hugged her gently; a faint, familiar odour of linseed oil rose from Beth's lank hair. She was shorter than Alex, much finer-boned; she always felt fragile, so different from her sturdy, energetic older sister. Beth clung to her mother briefly before letting go.

'Why didn't you let me know you were on your way, darling?' Alex asked.

'I was driving, wasn't I?'

Beth dropped her canvas knapsack on the hall floor and looked around. Alex had stacked pictures against the wall, still undecided as to where they should hang. Beth ran her fingers along the tops of the frames. Alex's books were piled on the floor beside them, and she quickly moved some aside to make room.

'Did you drive down from Paris overnight? You must be exhausted.'

'I had to get away. I hired a car. I told you I was coming, didn't I?'

Beth's teenage petulance had never entirely disappeared, despite the fact that she was now in her early thirties. Alex, however, had outgrown her patience for it. Rod would have stepped in here, teasing in a way Alex never knew how to manage, gently cajoling Beth out of a mood before it had a chance to settle. But for Alex, a feeling of inadequacy accompanied Beth like that scent of artist's linseed oil. She could already tell that whatever she said would be wrong, and felt tired even before she opened her mouth. She smiled anyway.

'Are you hungry? Look, sweetheart, I'll open the window and you can sit in the sun while I make breakfast.' Alex took Beth's hand and led her into the living room. Beth followed like a child.

Alex could see her lift at the sight. She had brought some of the old furniture to Nice with her, including a round table with four bentwood chairs. She'd thrown a cream cloth over the table, which was now almost dazzling in the morning light. She cleared away papers and envelopes, as well as some yellow blossoms that had fallen from a jug of mimosa branches.

'Oh Mum, it's gorgeous! It looks like home.' Beth touched the books on the shelves lovingly and looked at some of the silver-framed photographs. 'This is just what I need.'

'Has it been hard work in Paris?'

'That dreadful studio is freezing, and I can't stand the other grant students. I'm supposed to spend so many hours a week there. It's part of the arrangement with the Foundation's tutors. And then that hostel! I can't get up in the morning without throwing books on the floor to scare the mice away.' Beth hunched her narrow shoulders.

'Oh dear,' Alex said.

'It started getting to me.' Beth looked accusingly at her mother. With Meghan, there was never a subtext. She was candid and honest, and never understood, or cared, why she ruffled feathers. She would have made an uproarious drama out of living with mice. But with Beth, every sentence was loaded. What did she want now – sympathy, or pity?

Since Rod had died, Alex's relationship with her two girls had been redrawn, the weight redistributed. Meghan had become the grown-up. Right from the first midnight phone call at the hospital, Meg had launched into providing every support. Her husband Tom was detailed to busying himself with practical duties, like installing new double locks on the house in Fayence. The children were uncharacteristically quiet and attentive, almost shy. Meghan relished her dutiful daughter role; it helped her cope with her own grief. Alex accepted it, grateful and bemused.

But without Rod, Alex no longer had an interpreter or referee, no guide to navigate the submerged obstacles that blighted her relationship with Beth. Where had they come from? Even when Beth was a baby, she seemed to smile for Rod, and to whimper when he wasn't there. Alex had always felt second best. When, after Rod's death, she was first alone with her daughter in Fayence, Alex had felt something near panic.

'You're here now, sweetie. And I don't have mice. Shall I scramble some eggs? Buy some croissants? There's a bakery right downstairs.'

'Actually I bought some pain-au-chocolat just as I got into Nice. I stopped to ask directions and the bakery was the only place open.' Beth pulled a squashed bag from her knapsack, and held it out with a timid expectation that made Alex's heart open.

'Perfect! Come, I'll show you the kitchen and put on the coffee.'

Beth lingered behind, looking at Alex's pictures and books. When she came into the kitchen, she opened each of the cupboards, standing on tiptoe to pick out cups and bowls.

'You've got everything from Fayence,' she said.

'Of course. You know I gave up the lease on that house.'

Beth put together a cup and saucer, white porcelain with a gold handle. 'But this is your good stuff. Shouldn't it go home?'

'It is home, darling.'

Beth seemed to consider this for a moment before putting the china back in the cupboard.

Once Beth had showered and was napping on one of the still-unassembled bunk bed mattresses on the floor, Alex planned to work on the document she would send Dianne Steer. She left Beth a note and went, as Beth had asked, to buy a parking ticket for her rental car. She looked for it in the public car park behind the derelict 19th-century train station. Its surreal hulk was all provincial solidity on one side, and on the other an unsightly mess of breeze blocks, graffiti and pigeon droppings. Cars now packed into the tarmac-covered space where once steam trains had disgorged winter visitors laden with trunks for a glittering sojourn on the Riviera.

In the car park, she noticed Guillaume chaining up a motorbike. She headed towards him, relieved. He could have put in more of an appearance at the office, she thought. She'd barely seen him at all since they'd heard about Chantelle. He must know she needed his help. As she approached him, Alex couldn't catch his eye. He repeatedly repositioned the bike and double-checked the lock, then took off his jacket and folded it carefully on the seat. Perhaps he didn't want to work with the *Anglaise* at all. But if she wanted to keep Immobilier Charpentier going, she'd have to work with him somehow. She planted herself in front of him.

'Guillaume, there you are!' she said. 'Will you be coming into the office this morning? Please?'

He rooted in the motorcycle's saddlebags until he found his sunglasses. He said, 'Perhaps later. Around noon.' He moved to leave but Alex put her hand on his arm.

'I want to keep things going for Chantelle,' she said. 'It will be impossible without you. I hope you won't mind giving me your advice.' She hoped flattery would help, but he brushed her hand away. He walked off with a dismissive wave.

Alex watched him go. Whatever connection they'd formed over the kittens had gone. Was he angry with her attempts to keep Chantelle's business running? Jealous? Did he regret telling her about his wife and daughter? She had obviously misunderstood something, but what? She walked back to the office slowly, oblivious to the noisy swing of the *marché* around her. The fuzziness frustrated her, as if the solution to a crossword clue was staying resolutely on the tip of her tongue. She would understand if only she could put her mind to it.

Unfortunately, now wasn't the moment. There was Dianne Steer to think about instead.

Alex spent the rest of the morning working on the proposal, and when she finished, she read and re-read her handiwork with satisfaction. It was crucial she sent something out today. If she didn't, it would be perfectly reasonable for Dianne Steer to get in touch with other agents. Alex wanted to make sure the Barrons felt Immobilier Charpentier was their best option. ('But *chérie*, it *is* their best option,' she imagined Chantelle saying.)

There was an element of uncertainty in the six-page proposal, but Alex hoped she'd disguised it as exclusivity. She assumed money was no object, so left prices 'to be confirmed'. In describing the villa in Eze, which she wouldn't be able to see for a few days, she made much of its suitability for entertaining, highlighting the guest bathrooms and secluded pool Sammy the sous-chef had described. She turned the Menier villa's location into an irresistible selling point. Anyone reading it would overlook missing details, which were to be divulged once an interest had been declared. She emphasised the fact that the Valentin villa and the house on the Avenue du Phare had been specially selected to offer the Barrons a range of styles, from faded Mediterranean glamour to the height of contemporary chic. She added the overpriced apartment near the Negresco for good measure.

At last, when she'd toned down a couple of flowery phrases, she attached photographs from the Menier details, which arrived in her inbox just in time, as well as some views over the beach at Eze. They were probably at least partially visible from the infinity pool, she decided. Then she attached an English version of Chantelle's terms of business, signed it on behalf of Chantelle Charpentier, *directrice d'entreprise*, and sent it on its way. It was 50 per cent rubbish, but would buy her time.

The completion of her task raised Alex's spirits, and she was genuinely pleased to see Beth walk through the door. Her nap had restored her humour as well as the colour to her cheeks.

'Bonjour Madame, I'm looking for a small house,' Beth said in a falsetto voice. 'It must have orchards and stables and a garage for my Ferraris and views of Monte Carlo and a berth for my yacht and, oh, don't forget the heli-pad.'

Alex laughed.

'This is great, Mum. It's so close to the flat. It must be the shortest commute to work ever.' Beth examined the wall of photographs of Chantelle. 'You're right about the boss. As French as they come. When did you say she'd be back?'

'I didn't,' Alex said. The truth would have altered the mood between them, and Alex wanted this companionable moment to last.

Beth sat at Chantelle's desk, her slight body enveloped by the chair, peeping into drawers. Every now and then someone Alex recognised passed, and she pointed them out. 'Thug,' Beth commented when Alain's nephew Felix swaggered past; 'Nerd,' when the professor shuffled by. They giggled. Why couldn't it always be so easy?

Soon Beth started to fidget. She wanted to see Chez Maxie, but Alex was anxious not to miss Guillaume if he did come in before lunch, as she'd asked.

'He'll know where to look,' Beth said, and though Alex knew she was right, Alex didn't want to give him any chance to miss their rendez-vous. There was no point in trying to explain Guillaume's behaviour to Beth; she was still trying to understand it herself. She particularly didn't want to say anything that would intrude on the rare intimacy with her daughter. But Beth unfortunately could take care of that herself. She stood up abruptly and said, 'Quite the indispensable Madame Coates in your new single life, aren't you?'

Alex ignored the old bitterness in Beth's voice.

'He won't be long now, sweetheart. Are you starving?'

Beth opened her mouth to answer as Guillaume appeared at the door. He glanced from side to side furtively as Alex introduced her daughter. Beth was suddenly charming. Her

French had been good even as a child, inspired by a gifted teacher who'd read the class *Babar* in both English and French. Guillaume couldn't possibly have noticed the sarcasm with which Beth wished them a productive time together when she decided to go out for a walk. She would see Alex later.

In silence, Guillaume flicked through a ring binder full of neatly compiled records of services due, guarantees, schedules. He made pencil ticks and copied details into a dog-eared diary.

'I had another call from the rich Americans' secretary, Guillaume,' Alex said, when she could stand his silence no longer. 'The ones Chantelle was so excited about. I hope I'm doing the right thing. I've sent some information about houses they might like.'

'Good,' Guillaume said. He continued flicking and ticking, never meeting her eyes.

'Guillaume, is something the matter? I mean, of course there is, but… something I've done?'

fidgeted, but said nothing.

Alex threw her pen on the desk in irritation and started to clear up. She could catch Beth in time for lunch. But after a couple of minutes Guillaume, without her noticing, had slid up behind her.

'You're right to want to help Chantelle,' he said. She jumped. There was still a file in his hands, and he opened and closed its silver ring as he considered what to say next. Alex thought that if his skin weren't so weathered, she might be able to tell if he were blushing. 'But things are always more complicated than you think. People aren't always what they seem here.'

Alex laughed, but if Guillaume wanted to unnerve her, it had worked. 'That's why I need your help. We must work together, for Chantelle.'

Guillaume cleared his throat. He looked directly at her for the first time with sad, tired eyes. 'Have I done anything to make you mistrust me?' he asked.

Yes, Alex thought. You've let me down. But she needed him

now, so she shook her head and smiled as if the suggestion were absurd. She said, 'Chantelle trusts you, so I do, too.'

He kept her gaze for a few seconds, and Alex felt as if she were being sized up: the *Anglaise* getting her feet under the table a little too quickly. 'I am only the maintenance man,' he said. 'I don't know much, but I think that the owner of the house on the Avenue du Phare might not be worth knowing.'

'Ed Bronz?' Alex thought of the angry altercation in the alley. What on earth could Guillaume have heard?

'There have always been rumours.'

Was this why Guillaume had been so shifty recently? Surely Alain wouldn't put Chantelle's business in jeopardy.

'Why didn't you tell me before I went to the house with Alain?'

'Alain's curiosity is insatiable,' Guillaume said. He had raised his voice, but lowered it again, as if embarrassed. 'He spent his life working with men who thought nothing of danger. Being a *grandpère* isn't enough for him. He needs something to entertain him between the nursery and the school gates. Sometimes I think he's still working on old cases.'

'Ed Bronz seemed nice to me,' Alex said weakly. 'The house was impressive. Anyway, I've already let the Americans know about it. It would make a nice commission for Chantelle.'

She handed Guillaume a copy of the proposal she'd sent to Dianne Steer. 'Look, I've been working on this.'

He looked at it for several minutes, putting each page down neatly on the desk as he finished, then said, 'But I don't understand English.'

Alex tapped her foot under the desk. 'I know,' she said. 'I just wanted you to see it. Chantelle will be home by the time there are contracts to sign, but at least we can keep things moving. I haven't even seen the Menier villa or the place in Eze yet!' She pointed to the photos.

'You've made it all up?' For the first time, Alex heard Guillaume's quiet laugh. 'Chantelle is a good teacher. This is just the kind of thing she'd do herself.' His face quickly became serious again. 'But what a sad twist,' he said. 'Chantelle is such a beautiful woman, why does she do these absurd things?'

They looked silently at the wall full of photographs.

'Chantelle may have a brother,' Guillaume announced, scanning the pictures.

'Oh?' Alex was buoyed by the thought of someone wading in to take charge.

'Yes, here.' Guillaume pulled at the tack that held up a fading photograph of Chantelle dressed in a puff-shouldered gown, the only woman in the centre of a group of greying men in evening dress. On closer inspection, one could perhaps have resembled Chantelle. 'But they haven't spoken for years.'

Alex sighed.

'And there's definitely no cousin in New York?'

'Not that I know of,' Guillaume said.

'What about Chantelle's friends? A close friend?' She remembered Paulette Bitoun. 'The interior decorator?'

'No,' he said firmly.

In Guillaume's presence, Alex felt less overwhelmed at what she had taken on. Despite insisting that he knew nothing but plumbing and gardening, Guillaume was aware of exactly how Chantelle ran her business. He answered Alex's questions by first meekly protesting his ignorance, and when pressed by producing an avalanche of practical information. He rattled off figures for rents he thought the properties might attract as if he'd been considering it for some time. 'But that's just my opinion,' he said apologetically, rubbing his chin.

When Beth returned, looking less irritable, Alex was feeling almost optimistic.

'He's an odd one,' Beth said, as they watched Guillaume head back towards the car park behind the station. 'Has he got something to hide?'

'I think he's just shy,' Alex said.

She knew she was going to have to tell Beth about Chantelle. 'Come on, I'm sorry you missed your lunch. Let's go and have an aperitif in the Old Town instead.'

70

CHAPTER TEN

They chose a café on the Cours Saleya, the wide pedestrian street in Nice's medieval Old Town. It was quiet now with no sign left of the busy morning flower market that made it famous. The late-afternoon sun didn't reach the ground between the 17th-century buildings, but the suggestion of heat radiated from where the sun still fell across the upper storeys of their mango- and lemon-curd-coloured façades. Beth's feet were surrounded by shopping bags. There were plenty of galleries on the narrow streets of the Old Town, beside open-fronted butcher's shops where skinned rabbits hung upside down above the counters, and dark, fragrant stores that displayed small mountains of spices.

Beth examined some lavender soaps she'd bought for her tutor in Paris. She inhaled their fragrance and laid them in a row on the table.

'I'm glad you live here, Mum,' she said. 'It's selfish of me, but the thought of being able to come here whenever I need warmth is reassuring.'

'I'm glad, darling. I want you to come whenever you can.'

'Meghan's always on at me to talk to you about going home.' Beth poured a scant drop of water into her anise-flavoured pastis. 'She thinks you'd be happier being hands-on gran to the kids. She thinks you just won't admit that you're lonely.'

'She likes to have everything in order, she was always like that. And besides, I'm hoping to see more of Robert and Olivia on holiday over here than I would at home. I've been thinking I might buy a car, you know. There are so many things nearby the children would enjoy.'

'Well, well, a job and a car, too,' Beth said. She started putting the soaps back in their paper bag. 'That's quite a commitment. You're adjusting quickly to life without Dad, aren't you?'

Alex felt the barb, but didn't respond, distracted by the arrival of a group of Italian tourists. They discussed loudly which table to sit at before the three men in the group sat down beside Alex and Beth. The women, tightly trussed in short leather jackets, wandered indecisively before choosing a table on the other side of the café. The men, resigned, got up to join them.

'Thank god for that,' Beth said, watching them move.

'Has it been helpful, being in Paris?' Alex asked. The grant Beth had received allowed her to paint without worrying about money for a year. Six months of the year were to be spent in Paris, studying under several more established contemporary artists. Alex had been proud but surprised when the grant had been awarded, shortly before Rod's death. She didn't understand the repetitive, geometric abstracts Beth painted on her huge canvases. She'd never felt Beth was as passionate as an artist should be, nor as disciplined as success would require. But they rarely talked about it. Each discussion ended in sulks and pouts.

'I suppose so. I've been doing lots of sketches and colourwashes. I have to get down to the real work now.'

'That's always the hard bit, isn't it?' Alex said.

Beth's nostrils flared. 'What do you know about it? You've never painted anything.'

Alex shut her eyes briefly. Beth was always vigilantly on the look-out for the wrong word, the misplaced emphasis.

'It's what people say, sweetheart. I only meant that I understand how difficult it is to put it all together.'

'No, you don't, Mum. You don't know what you're talking about.' Beth swirled the ice cubes in her glass angrily until drops of pastis slopped onto the tabletop. 'I've been working on this for ages, and can't even be sure it'll turn into anything. I can't just splash paint on a canvas. You might think that's what I do, but it's a lot more than that. I didn't study fine art to do any old thing, however you see it. My tutor in England is on my case every week, too, asking me how I'm doing. And Dad went and died in the middle of it all. Why don't you give me some platitude about that?'

Alex imagined slapping her, but just now the easier option was to say nothing. She watched the Italians, one of whom seemed to be the joker, telling a story that required him to waddle up and down like a penguin. The others shrieked with laughter.

Beth blew her nose.

'What's *he* been drinking?' she said after a few minutes, nodding towards the Italian.

Perhaps Alex ought to have lost her temper with Beth more often. She'd always given in to Beth's neediness, to her tears and foot-stamping tantrums, and later to her moodiness, and this walking-on-eggshells approach had become habit. She imagined turning to her daughter and slamming the table so their two glasses jumped, shouting, 'And what about me? *Me*?' But she was as likely to do that now as she was to join the penguin charade in front of them. Instead she waited a moment, then said, 'It seems that Chantelle Charpentier won't be coming back home for a while. She's become quite ill.'

'Uh-oh.'

'Perhaps that's why I've been a bit tetchy. I'm worried. Not just about Chantelle, of course, but about her business.'

'Can't Guillaume take care of it?'

Beth leaned forward to catch every word as Alex told her about the American newlyweds. Chantelle would be so disappointed if she missed the opportunity. Beth nodded enthusiastically. Then Alex added, lying, 'Perhaps I'll rethink coming home if I can just keep things on the go for her until she's back.'

Beth was intrigued. She was just about to say something when suddenly Alex sat up straight and crossed her legs. Beth followed the direction of her smile.

Ed Bronz had appeared through the archway that led to the sea on the opposite side of the Cours Saleya. He and Alex had caught sight of each other at almost the same instant. He headed towards them.

'Madame Coates, what a pleasure yet again.' Bronz's leather

jacket looked soft and expensive. 'I've been thinking a lot about our meeting.'

Beth looked at her mother, and Alex could sense her excited curiosity. Bronz continued, 'I'm afraid I still haven't come to a decision.' He turned to Beth. 'But excuse me for interrupting. We won't talk business now, of course.'

Alex introduced Beth, who, while explaining her reasons for being in France, made her progress in Paris seem further along than it actually was. Bronz listened with interest, but he didn't sit down. The Italian women at the nearby table watched him over their wineglasses.

'I'd love to hear more about your work,' he said, 'but I have an appointment here in the Old Town.' He looked at his watch. 'Perhaps I could hear about it over dinner tomorrow evening? It would be a treat to have two such interesting women at my table.'

Beth gave her mother a frantic 'how do we get out of this?' look, which turned to open-mouthed surprise when Alex said that they'd love to.

CHAPTER ELEVEN

Alex could barely stop looking at Beth once she was ready for their evening out. She'd bought two inexpensive pink scarves in the Old Town and tied them around the waist of a white sleeveless silk T-shirt borrowed from Alex, which she wore with tight black jeans. She'd arranged her long hair in a low chignon, carefully pulling strands out with a pencil so they fell over the nape of her neck. With such perfect skin, all she needed was lipstick. Mostly, however, it was playfulness that illuminated her face. When she was happy, Beth was beautiful.

'We should go to Monaco every evening,' she said to Beth. 'It makes you look gorgeous.'

Alex chose a black gabardine shift with a wide patent belt, and a silvery-grey embroidered shawl.

'Understated,' Beth announced, lying on the bed and watching her mother twitch the shawl first over one shoulder, then the other.

Alex examined her reflection in the mirror. She particularly liked that shawl; it always made her look more sophisticated than she felt.

'No more than understated?'

'Do you want to look anything else? For that man?'

Alex turned away. 'I'd make more of an effort if I were trying to attract *that man*, but believe me, I'm not.'

Beth laughed. 'You're hardly his type. I'm sure he prefers women who wear big diamonds. Did you see the size of that watch?' She puffed out her cheeks.

Monaco had become a familiar excursion for friends visiting from home ('the request stop,' Rod had called it), but she and Beth had never been together. She noticed now that Ed negotiated parts of the tiny city she'd never seen before, then headed for a steep street behind the elegant Hôtel de Paris. His metallic-blue Audi slotted effortlessly into a parking spot beneath the orange trees as if it were waiting for him. When he opened the door of the car for Alex, she pressed her ankles together as gracefully as she could. He had a well-mannered way of keeping the conversation going, but so far there was no click between the three of them. It was enjoyable, but vacant, like Monaco itself. Perhaps he was tired. Alex couldn't imagine, tonight, what had interested her when she first saw Ed arguing in the alley.

The evening was warm for the time of year, and they walked towards the main square. If anything gave the principality of Monaco its fairytale atmosphere, Alex observed, it was spotlessness. Barely a leaf had fallen onto the pavement; the roads could have been swept moments before.

Beth's mood had become almost buoyant since her early-morning arrival. She and Ed chatted amiably about Paris, which he appeared to know well, but Alex noted that still he gave little away. Whatever she knew about his life she had gleaned from his comfortable reading room, his polished shoes, and the quality of his well-tailored jacket. Its cashmere softness had surprised her when she spontaneously touched his arm in response to a joke.

They detoured through lush, sloping gardens and stood at the top of a flight of steps to appreciate the full effect of the coloured lights that played over the fountain and the grand façade of the famous Casino. The building turned from green and blue to purple and pink, matching the fountain beneath it. Jets of blue water shot up high, bubbled in yellow and turned pink as they shrank back down into a green shimmering pool. In front of the Casino, crowds milled around the cars watched over by parking valets, as if Bond-like figures would saunter past accompanied by women in diamond tiaras. In fact, most people in the Place du Casino were tourists. Even so, it was a beautiful place, enlivened by the *frisson* of romance and wealth. Somehow it made visitors collude with its own image. Tonight, Alex allowed herself to be bewitched, too.

Inside the Hôtel de Paris, it was a different story. Walking around the Place du Casino outside might be free of charge, but it cost a good deal of money to have dinner at the hotel's Michelin-starred restaurant. Beth's eyes widened when she saw the prices on the menu.

'Are you sure Mr Charm is paying?' she whispered, nodding towards Ed after he'd excused himself to say hello to an acquaintance. Alex nudged her, reminding her it was Ed who'd insisted on taking them there.

Alex's bouillabaisse was heavenly, but she wondered if it were any better than one she'd had recently at Chez Maxie, which was, she calculated roughly, one-third the price. Beth raved about her tournedos, but Alex watched in mute horror as she set its layer of pâté de foie gras aside distastefully. Alex scooped it up with her sauce spoon and ate it in two mouthfuls. The Château Pontet-Cantet Beth was sharing with Ed made her giggly, her eyes shining. Alex couldn't stop looking at her, liberated for the evening by her daughter's good temper.

When Beth's phone rang and she walked quickly away to answer it, Alex watched her go longingly. Ed had been scanning the room constantly throughout dinner, but the moment Beth was gone, his focus rested on Alex. She realised that what had been missing until now was his complete attention.

'Favourite daughter?' he asked.

'You're not allowed to have a favourite child,' Alex said. 'To be honest, Beth is much more difficult than her sister, but tonight she's in such a good mood, it's wonderful. She's also much more interesting than her sister. Am I allowed to admit that?'

'You have to be honest about relationships.'

'So you favour one child over another?'

'I wouldn't know. My wife took our son with her when she left me 30 years ago. God knows what she told him about me. He won't even take my money now.' He said it without rancour.

'I'm sorry to hear that.'

'Don't be.' Ed shrugged his shoulders. 'It's my own fault.'

It struck Alex as harsh. She took a sip of water, suddenly aware of how much wine she'd been drinking, and looked around for Beth.

A man like Ed Bronz wouldn't have fitted easily into Alex's former life. Most of the men she knew were her friends' partners, editors she'd worked with, Rod's tennis crowd, friends from school. None had the aura of restlessness and expectation she sensed in Ed, as if he were waiting for something to happen. When she spoke, he placed his hands on the crisp white tablecloth and turned his face to hers, listening intently. His skin was lined, but looked soft. The whites of his dark brown eyes were as clear as a child's. He smiled at her, and Alex wondered if she'd been naïve accepting his invitation so quickly.

'Have you lived in the Avenue du Phare all that time?'

'I've owned the house for a long time,' Ed said. 'But I don't need it. Which is, fortunately, why we've met.' His smile was easy and open, but Alex felt, once again, out of her depth. She wondered where Beth could have got to. 'Letting that interior decorator get hold of it was a mistake,' Ed continued. 'I barely recognise it now, except for my reading room. I wouldn't let her touch that. Paulette something. I wouldn't want to get on the wrong side of her, and I've been on the wrong side of many people in my life.'

The wine Ed had chosen was probably helping, but his story of fighting off the attentions of the gold-encrusted Paulette Bitoun made Alex laugh out loud. She hardly noticed when Beth slipped back into her chair.

'Getting on like a house on fire, I see,' Beth said. Alex hoped she had only imagined the reproach in her voice. 'Listen, Mum, that was the friend I told you about, who's down here. He's nearby, in Menton. He's on his way here to pick me up.'

All Alex had been told about this friend was that one existed. 'Aren't you coming to the casino with us?' She suddenly felt chilly, and pulled her shawl around her shoulders. But she said, 'I'm feeling lucky.'

'I'm not,' Beth said sulkily. She thanked Ed, resisting his offers of more wine, dessert, coffee, a digestif. When he innocently asked the questions Alex wouldn't have dared to, she discovered that Beth's friend – Raymond – was an American artist whom she'd met in Paris a couple of months before, and that he was now in Menton where he was teaching English. Hardly a friend from art school, Alex thought, but once again said nothing.

'Thank you,' Alex said, when Beth had gone.

'For?'

'Beth and I don't always get on well. It's been special this evening.'

'But Alex, you sound as if it's over.' Ed rubbed his palms together and widened his eyes. 'I thought you said you were feeling lucky.'

The constant rattle of tokens pouring from slot machines raised Alex's pulse, even though she wasn't a gambler. The noise was as vivid a feature of the casino as the low, golden lighting and the thick carpet, as integral to its character as the sparkling chandeliers. Ed guided her through the crowd, gently touching the inside of her elbow. Around the edges of the enormous room were cashiers behind small windows, and a long, high bar where customers drank in celebration or consolation, leaning towards each other to be heard above the background din. People fed the slot machines seated on velvet stools; others, at the roulette tables, called out in eager anticipation as the tiny ball clacked into its niche. Groups of friends gathered round winners at the baccarat tables; tourists watched a high-roller whose blackjack table had been roped off, hoping to witness a fortune being won or lost. Everywhere there were bursts of laughter, shouts of joy, or a communal groan at a loss. The expressionless croupiers rolled the dice and doled out chips and dealt out cards, observing everything.

Alex viewed whatever money she lost at the casinos in Monte Carlo as the price of admission. They watched the crowd at one of the roulette tables before squeezing in between a hefty, cheerful, American man who whistled softly during every throw, and a young French woman in a black, strapless cocktail dress. Her husband hung over her shoulder telling her what to do. At first Alex and Ed bet prudently on red or black to win. As the ball landed on their colour, Alex clapped excitedly. It didn't matter that she was winning almost nothing; she was winning. With each turn of the wheel, she waited almost until the last moment, just as the croupier said 'Rien ne va plus,' no more bets, to place her chips on the table. Ed began choosing individual numbers, without much luck. Then he started to pile chips so that they covered four squares at once, hedging his bets so there was more chance a number would come up, but no chance of winning big. Soon afterwards, he opened both hands and shook his head, to show he had nothing left. He took two glasses of champagne from one of the waitresses who wandered the casino with cocktail-laden trays.

'I'm about 150 euros ahead, I think,' Alex said above the din, leaning towards him so he could hear. The fringe of her silver-grey shawl slipped over his hand. 'What would you do?'

'That would buy lunch in a bistro somewhere, but it's hardly anything to lose, either,' Ed said.

Alex laughed. 'That's not an answer,' she shouted.

'What if it were a thousand euros?'

'I'd walk. There, now you know how much I'm worth.'

'Put it all on eight.'

Alex looked at the table. The square was empty. Her chips were piled in two neat towers in front of her. The croupier had spun the little ball onto the track of the roulette wheel, and it clattered around the edge.

'No time to think,' Ed said. 'Quick! Quick!'

Suddenly exhilarated, she pushed all her chips on the number eight square. The American whistled loudly and said, 'Good luck, lady.'

The croupier called 'Rien ne va plus.' Alex held her breath. Her shoulders tensed as the ball jumped into the eight pocket, but bounced out again and came to rest in number 10. Ed put his hand on her shoulder. 'Sorry,' he said, close to her ear. 'Be sure never to trust me.'

The croupier gathered up her chips with his long rake and dragged them towards him.

As they walked back towards the car, Alex shivered in the cool air. She regretted losing the money she'd won. It wasn't much, but she was unused to throwing money away. She was just about to mention it when she realised how silly it might sound to a man like Ed. He hardly seemed like someone who would be concerned about a few hundred euros. She still had no idea what he did for a living, or if he did anything at all. There'd been no further mention of his wife, or wives. Whenever she asked a question, his answers seemed candid, but somehow they would soon be discussing something else altogether. Even when she asked if Russian were his mother tongue, she felt she was prying. She was always aware of that throaty 'R'.

'So many people of my generation had to learn Russian,' he replied. 'Every schoolchild from the Baltic states, all the Iron Curtain countries. It was the obvious choice, the way English was for western Europeans – and is now, for everyone. Russian is a beautiful language. Sometimes it sounds harsh to unfamiliar ears. I don't use it often. There's no need. And you, Alex, what other languages do you speak?'

As she told him about her schoolgirl experience with Spanish, she realised she was none the wiser. Another question evaded.

The quickest way back to Nice was on the highway which cut inland high above the Mediterranean, but Ed chose the road skirting the coast, twisting through seaside villages lit with fairy lights. She calculated what Ed might have had to drink. She and Beth had had most of the Bordeaux, but she remembered a second gin and tonic in the Hôtel de Paris, and a 20-year-old cognac as a digestif, before the champagne at the casino. The cushioned door handle gave lightly in her hand as she gripped it when an oncoming car illuminated his face. He didn't slow down, but hugged the jagged rock on the side of the road, guiding the car with one hand resting low on the steering wheel.

'You drive like you gamble, as if you're not concerned with the outcome,' Alex said nervously.

'It was hardly a risk to lose a few euros tonight for fun. And this car is always in control. It's built for that. I don't gamble with anything important to me. Not now in any case,' he said.

'So you did once?'

'The biggest gamble is to trust people. Isn't your whole life based on trust, Alex? You trusted your husband, yourself, your work, your family?'

Alex nodded. She had been luckier than most.

'I backed the wrong horse early on,' Ed said. 'By the time I realised it, it was too late.'

Alex imagined his wife, an elegant foreign beauty.

'Someone you loved?'

'Someone I hated. It's my fault, of course. You can't blame anyone other than yourself for your mistakes. But some people are evil. They haven't a shred of compassion for other human beings. I stupidly, perhaps greedily, put my trust in someone like that.'

The headlights fell on a rough wall of rock as the road swerved to the left. Ed accelerated and Alex put her hand on the seat to support herself as the car turned.

'Hey,' she said. 'Slow down.'

'Sorry. We can make irreparable mistakes when we're angry, don't you agree? When I remember all of that...well, I scare myself.'

Alex glanced at him in shifting light. He looked angry, and she was momentarily alarmed; she remembered Suzanne the housekeeper saying she'd never known such a temper. But for all Ed's sophisticated confidence, he looked lonely too.

'All of what?' she asked

'Long ago and far away, Alex. I don't like myself when I think about it. You wouldn't like me either.' They drove through the next village in silence, and at a stoplight, Ed touched the back of her hand as it rested in her lap. He was smiling. 'Too serious,' he said. 'Now, tell me what you would do to my house if Paulette Bitoun hadn't got her claws into me.'

CHAPTER TWELVE

'Beth is a grown woman' Alex said to Meghan the next morning. 'She met up with her friend last night. She said she was coming down to see him too. I'm just glad she didn't try to get back to Nice in the dark.'

Meghan's voice burbled angrily through the earpiece as the coffee grinder whined.

'Listen, Meghan, I'm not calling Beth at 7.30am. And don't you call her either.'

Alex squeezed the phone between her ear and shoulder as she flicked through the clothes hanging in her cupboard. She could tell even this early that something in the atmosphere had changed overnight. There was heat in the air, fanning the scent of ripe fruit from the market up into the flat. She slipped the dry-cleaner's plastic off an olive-green cotton skirt.

She'd worried momentarily when she saw that Beth hadn't slept in the guest room, but had shrugged it off. Beth sometimes spent weeks out of touch, during which time Alex didn't fret about what she was doing. Why should it be different because she was nearby? She had little influence over her daughter. She just hoped that this Raymond was kind.

'No, she hadn't mentioned him to me before either, Meghan.' After the toast popped up, Alex sat at the table by the open window, the phone still squeezed on her shoulder. As she sat down, she realised with a jolt that with everything that had happened over the past couple of days, she had neglected to tell Meghan the news about Chantelle. She steeled herself for the predictable response.

Meghan listened, then shrieked. 'For Christ's sake that's it, Mum. Honestly. That's really, really it. I'm coming over as soon as I can.'

'Don't be silly, Meg. How would you help?'

She snorted. 'I would bring you to your senses. What have you let us in for? Working for some mad Frenchwoman who disappears off to America, gambling with a Russian gigolo, and now you're rooting about in strange houses all over the Riviera for some spoiled rich couple. What would Dad think?'

There was silence on the line while they both contemplated it. Alex had woken up that morning thinking not of Rod, but of Ed Bronz.

'Actually, I think your dad would have loved it. It's better than sitting around watching movies on TV.'

'I wouldn't worry if all you were doing was watching movies.'

'I think you'd worry about anything, sweetie.'

Fortunately it never took long to put Meghan's fears to rest. Alex was soon on her way to the office, lingering briefly at one of the stalls as she selected a dewy bunch of white asparagus. Beth loved it; when she came back from Menton, Alex would steam it for her and make a hollandaise sauce.

As she unlocked the office door, she was aware of a woman's voice calling her over the chatter of the market. Liliane Valentin's white knee-length shorts showed off the early spring colour on her long legs. Gold glinted at the neckline of her sailor-stripe T-shirt. Her wicker basket brimmed with fruit and vegetables from the *marché*. Heads turned as she strode towards Alex.

'Mrs Coates, I was just on my way to see you,' Liliane said. 'May I come in?'

Liliane waited, posing glamorously, while Alex opened the door.

'*Mon dieu*, those cats,' she said, once they were inside, reverting to French. 'We heard them again in the night. This cannot go on. I thought your *gardien* was going to put them down.' She smiled helplessly at Alex, as if expecting her sympathy.

'I'm sorry you're still being disturbed. I'll ask Guillaume to check again, but there were only two cats, each with a litter. I think perhaps he found it difficult to... Well, I'll ask him to move them somewhere else as soon as possible.'

'Ah, yes, Guillaume, that was his name. We happened to see him the other day in Bellet.' Liliane looked at the pictures of Chantelle on the wall as she spoke, uncurling the older ones with her manicured fingers 'I was there with Paulette Bitoun, my interior designer. Do you know her? We went to visit someone who imports chintz. I love chintz, don't you? But what an out-of-the-way spot for a supplier to set up.'

Alex took in what Liliane was telling her slowly. She gripped the edge of the desk. Guillaume in Bellet?

'Madame Coates?' Liliane frowned at her. 'Are you unwell?'

She shook her head, but sat down. 'Yes, sorry. I'm fine. Of course, chintz...so versatile.' Actually she hated the fussy traditions chintz represented, the stiff scrape of it against her legs. It was no surprise that the dragon Paulette loved it.

'I know we're waiting for Madame Charpentier's ideas on how we should progress, but I couldn't resist talking to a decorator. I need some cheering up. The press are on our doorstep, it's awful.' Liliane's pretty face looked momentarily glum, but Alex got the impression she found it entertaining.

'Oh dear,' Alex said. 'What do the press want?' She said it distractedly. What she was really thinking about was Guillaume.

'I won't speak to them, of course. They keep asking about Uncle Auguste's paintings. Myself, I can't stand looking at all those empty spaces. We removed anything of value after Auguste died – the Matisse was the first thing. Of course we had to tell the police, just in case. The insurance...'

Liliane waved her hand, jingling her slim gold bracelet. She sat down by Alex's desk. 'We're not staying at the villa any more, you know,' she continued. 'I convinced Henri to take a room at the hotel in Beaulieu for now. Frankly, Mrs Coates, I find that house depressing. I would love to do it up with Paulette.'

The moment seemed right to let Liliane know the situation – not the full story, but the fact that Chantelle could be away for a while. Liliane's eyes widened as she listened, looking increasingly horrified.

'But I have marvellous new clients,' Alex added quickly. She didn't, for Chantelle's sake, want to let the Valentin villa slip through her fingers. 'They're a society couple from the United States. They'll adore your villa.'

Curiosity calmed and brightened Liliane's face like a balm. She looked almost smug when Alex told her how much rent a villa like that might fetch.

'That should encourage the Valentin family,' Liliane said. 'Too many artists and not enough heads for business in that crowd.' She looked towards the door, then leaned slightly over the desk. 'Publishing is the family business,' she said, 'but they've been selling off the old man's pictures for years to keep it afloat.'

Alex loved indiscretion. She remembered Françoise's comments about the Valentin family's financial trouble. 'No!' she said. She felt suddenly better.

'Yes,' Liliane continued, 'But there's hardly anything left. They hung on to the *pièce de résistance* hoping it would save them, but now its authenticity is in question. That's why the press are here, you know.'

'The *pièce de résistance*?'

Liliane shrank back, as if Alex's ignorance offended her.

'The Matisse, Mrs Coates. The one the artist himself gave to Uncle Auguste. So everyone thought, anyway. Drouot the auctioneers in Paris have been valuing and authenticating it. They're the most reputable auctioneers in the country, and they can't sell something if they're not 100 per cent sure about it. The family aren't happy, needless to say. It's embarrassing for them, don't you think?' She picked at invisible specks of lint on her T-shirt. 'It was stolen once, you know, years ago. Old Auguste should have had it valued then, but he was so eager to have it back he paid the ransom. That's what they do, these art thieves. They ransom the paintings they steal, like kidnapped children. Now we'll see if the family paid up for the real thing. Fortunately my own family has been much more successful in business than my in-laws.' She stood up to go. 'I'll be at the villa this afternoon,' she said 'I don't mind it during the day. It's only at night the place is too, too depressing. Let me know about the Americans – and the cats!'

CHAPTER THIRTEEN

Alex sat motionless, processing the flood of information Liliane Valentin had provided during her short visit. Then she went to the kitchenette to make herself a cup of tea. She'd brought in her own kettle, which Chantelle, who only drank her coffee and *infusions* in cafés – found eccentric.

When she had settled back at the desk, she turned on the computer and typed in the name 'Auguste Valentin'. She was surprised that she herself recognised some of the artist's own work, particularly the scenes of Nice's Promenade des Anglais and its pebbly beach, flecked with parasols. But there was little about the artist himself, save a few biographical facts. Most sources hadn't even been updated to include the date of his recent death.

There was, however, a short, recent story in *Le Monde*. Auguste Valentin was listed as the owner of a minor Matisse that had appeared not long ago in a collection of paintings discovered in a New York vault after the death of the art dealer and collector Uri Raskilovich.

Alex sipped her tea. She'd heard that name.

She had to look up one or two words in her French-English dictionary. The mystery, said *Le Monde*, was that the Matisse painting found in New York had been reported stolen, then later found and returned to the owner. Yes, thought Alex. That's what Liliane had said. Didn't she say it was in Paris, at the auction house?

Alex read on. Sources reported that following the death of Auguste Valentin, the family intended to sell the Matisse he owned. It had been sent for valuation and sale to Drouot in Paris. In the course of authentication, the remarkable similarity with the newly discovered painting from the New York vault came to light.

Well, Alex thought, that's possible. Sometimes, she had to admit, she had difficulty telling one of Beth's canvases from another.

The discovery, *Le Monde* reported, had convulsed the art world: there was now one painting in New York, and its double – or one almost impossible to differentiate – in Paris. Initially the Raskilovich estate had suggested they would consider a sale of the new-found paintings, but they had now issued a statement that this was not the case. The art world had had a brief glimpse of the hidden Raskilovich pictures, and now with the revelation that there were two versions of at least one of the paintings – the Valentin Matisse – the hunt was on to find other instances of doubles. The provenance of scores of paintings around the world would have to be re-examined.

Now Alex understood what Liliane had been referring to. If there was any doubt about the authenticity of the painting, the Valentins would never be able to sell it.

She glanced up at the collection of photographs on the wall and was reminded of Chantelle with a shiver. She was so vivacious in the pictures, taller than all the women, smiling more brightly, more glamorously dressed. It was hard to imagine her any other way. But when Alex's gaze returned to the desk and to the dossier in the filing tray, she felt a wave of irritation. Meghan might be right. Perhaps she should walk away from all this. It was too much responsibility. She hadn't heard from Dianne Steer yet: why shouldn't she tell her that for now Immobilier Charpentier couldn't help? She closed her notebook.

The morning's post had brought some cheques, as well as bills. Chantelle kept her records by hand in a hardbound ledger of a type Alex hadn't seen since her very first job. She heaved it down now from the shelf by Chantelle's desk. The smell of musty paper and L'Eau d'Issey rose from its pages, which were minutely filled with pencilled notes. For Alex, who banked online and kept track of her accounts on a laptop, the ledger seemed impossibly old-fashioned. In the 'Debit' column, Alex could see her most recent salary cheque, noted as 'A Coates, March'. Under the 'Credit' column she noticed a payment from the owner of the villa where the cats had taken up: 'Ave. Jean Cocteau, six months.' She felt sneaky looking over the list of regular rentals, a few commissions, even a monthly payment to Chez Maxie, and she felt even worse noticing that the totals in the two columns weighed alarmingly on the 'Debit' side. She couldn't leave Chantelle in a mess. Chantelle had thrown her a lifeline, and she would throw her one in return.

After replying to some emails and ordering on account from the *quincaillerie*, as requested by Guillaume, a set of shower mixer taps for one of the managed flats, Alex filled in the amount of the morning's cheques in the ledger. She knew that Chantelle kept the business chequebook in the top drawer of her filing cabinet, but forging her signature to pay the bills seemed unnecessary for the moment. She took it with her, however, when she closed the office and crossed the Place du Général de Gaulle in the direction of Chantelle's bank.

When Alex reached the counter, the teller took one look at her and slapped her hand to her tanned and leathery décolletage, shaking her bottle-blonde head slowly. Her equally leathery hand was covering her name tag, but as soon as she removed it Alex remembered that she was Beatrice, a lunchtime regular at Chez Maxie.

'*Quelle histoire*, Madame Coates,' the teller said. 'What a story! The whole *quartier* is praying for Chantelle. Praying to God!' She squeezed her hands together piously, then flipped open the drawer in the counter beneath the glass that divided her from Alex. 'Any news?'

'Nothing so far,' Alex said. She dropped the chequebook and the cheques into the drawer. Beatrice examined them with interest before she looked up again.

'Such a hard worker, our Chantelle, how unfair it all is!' Beatrice said. She passed a form through the till. 'We've known her for years, all of us at the bank; we just can't believe it. You have to fill in one of these, you know, if you want to make a deposit.'

Alex had to ask for the chequebook back, so she had the

correct information for the form. Beatrice pushed through a pen at the same time. 'Are you a signatory?'

'Do I need to be a signatory to make a deposit?' Alex asked.

'Of course not, Madame, but if the situation should continue...' Beatrice lowered her eyes.

'Oh dear,' Alex said. 'Let's not think about that yet.' She wondered how Chantelle would feel knowing that everyone in the *quartier* was discussing her misfortune over their banking transactions and glasses of *rosé*.

The tips of Beatrice's thin fingers reached into the drawer and tapped the metal divide. Alex didn't know if it was an attempt at consolation or eagerness to have the form returned. 'Don't worry, though. We're all friends of Chantelle's here. Is Guillaume a signatory?'

'I don't know. No, I don't think so. He would have mentioned something.'

Beatrice pursed her lips. 'Chantelle might have had some doubts about making him a signatory, considering his history,' she said. She took the completed form and stamped it enthusiastically. Alex noticed the tell-tale orange of fake tan on her nails.

'His history?'

'Well, you know, that time...after the death of his daughter...' Beatrice licked her lips to say something more, then apparently thought better of it. 'But no matter. Chantelle is so kind to him. Poor Chantelle.' She put her hand on her breast again. 'But Madame Coates, we are at your service. Please just let us know what we can do.'

Outside, the *marché* was packing up, and Alex zigzagged to avoid stallholders hefting what remained of the morning's produce back into vans and trucks. Now and then an orange or tomato rolled past into the gutter. She crossed to the sunny side of the street, where the cafés were full of people still lingering over coffee or just arriving for lunch.

When Alex's phone rang and she saw that it was Beth, she turned down a side street, away from the noise.

'Darling! How are you? Did you have a nice evening? Wasn't Ed fun?'

Their evening in Monaco already seemed long ago.

She strained to hear Beth's description of her night out with Raymond. They'd gone out dancing, she said. She'd stayed up until almost sunrise; she sounded tired and happy. She should have phoned sooner, sorry. Raymond would probably drive her back to Nice, she wasn't sure when. Perhaps they might stay in Nice for dinner, if Alex didn't mind.

Alex thought immediately of the white asparagus, just enough for three. 'I'd love that, sweetheart. I could make something for us, something simple.' She walked back to Immobilier Charpentier feeling almost lightheaded with relief and anticipation.

CHAPTER FOURTEEN

Alex tried to imagine Chantelle sitting beside her when, later that week, she rounded the hill beneath Julie Eichenbaum's villa at Eze. Chantelle's little car handled well, and Alex felt confident enough, despite the steep incline, to flip into third. The medieval hill-top village with its narrow, cobbled streets and far-reaching views along the coast was firmly established on the tourist trail, but Alex today barely noticed it as she passed. She was intent on following the directions Julie Eichenbaum had given her over the phone. 'You'll see it above you just before the turn,' Julie had said. 'Looks like it'll fall over on top of your head.'

Julie was right. The ultra-modern house seemed to defy the rules of physics, jutting out over the cliff it was built on like a fat gull's breast and threatening to roll down onto the scrub. Alex pulled the car in at the turning and got out for a better look. The bleached-wood entrance gate was in front of her, but there was still a considerable climb to the house. She imagined the driveway rising up to it in a series of alarming hairpin bends. The house appeared to have several tiers, each with balconies facing the sea. Its glass walls glinted fiercely in the sun. Every level seemed to hang slightly over the one next to it, like a pile of wooden blocks balanced by a mischievous child who hoped to see them tumble. It made Alex dizzy.

'Come on up,' Julie said, through the entry phone.

Alex waited. After three or four minutes there was a hydraulic whoosh from behind the bleached wood. A moment later, the door divided down the middle and each half slid into the wall on either side. It looked like an ordinary garage. Alex began to nose the car in. A voice, which Alex realised was a recording, instructed her to drive in: '*Avancez s'il vous plait*! Move forward please! *Avancez s'il vous plait*! Move forward please!' When she could go no further and had already turned the car off the voice said 'Stop your engine! *Coupez le moteur*!

Stop your engine!' It continued insistently as the hydraulic whoosh restarted, and the entire garage began to shudder. Alex gripped the steering wheel, but quickly recognised the noise and the sensation: she was inside a lift.

The voice was still telling her to stop her engine when, after less than a minute, the doors opened and Alex was blinded by a burst of light. Almost at the same time, on her left, something was scraping the side of the car. Moist heat blew through the open window. She instinctively put her hands over her face.

'Dammit,' someone shouted. 'Is that thing broken again? Down, Lolly! Help, where's that button? Get down, Lolly, leave her alone! Where's the damn button?'

The recording stopped. Alex opened her eyes. Lolly, a gargantuan dog, had its paws on the car door. It looked excitedly from Alex to the woman she assumed was Julie Eichenbaum, spraying drool through the window with each movement of its massive brown head.

'That recording thing is still screwed,' Julie said. 'Drives me crazy.' She dragged the dog away by the collar. 'It's supposed to shut up as soon as you're inside.'

Julie Eichenbaum was about the same age as Alex, and was smoking a yellow Gauloise. Her short, tousled hair had probably been carroty red at one time. She was barefoot, wearing faded denim overalls with a black sleeveless T-shirt that exposed her wiry arms. Lolly pulled away from her grip, but she didn't release him. She must be strong, Alex thought, to hang on to that monster.

'Like dogs? He's big but he's harmless. A Great Dane mixed with an Irish wolfhound.' She had a smoker's cracked laugh and a lean, creased face. 'Pull the car into the carport.' She let go of the dog, who lolloped off. Alex pulled across 20 feet of tarmac and parked next to a vintage open-top Jeep. In her rear-view mirror, she could see the doors of the lift closing, set in a vehicle-sized sugar cube of white-painted stucco. Julie was waiting for her on a wide stone stairway that wound up towards the house.

'I don't think I've ever been in a lift like that,' Alex said.

'Weird, huh? There's a drive up to the back of the house, but we only use it for deliveries. The elevator was my husband Sal's idea. Look how it works.' She leaned over the railing at the back of the carport, and Alex joined her. The little lift had travelled sideways from the road up a funicular. 'He got the idea from a house we had in Cape Town.' Julie started padding up the stairs. 'He thinks big.'

Sammy the sous-chef hadn't done the house justice. Alex followed Julie through a patio door, across a cool, white room scattered with Indian rugs, through a hall with a green mosaic floor, past a dining room where a coloured glass sculpture twisted above a table set for 12, and into a sitting room where one wall was painted luminous turquoise-blue. Alex realised she was already lost. As she sat on the cream, L-shaped sofa, waiting for Julie to come back with iced coffee, she realised that the blue wall at the end of the room was actually the sky. From this angle on the cliff top, surrounded by light and air, the house felt as if it were flying.

As she waited, a man wandered in. He was on the phone, and stopped to look at her, though she could tell his mind was on his conversation. 'So how long will it take? The bastard said I'd have it by Friday. Tell him to quit fucking around!' He breathed heavily into the phone through a fleshy, open mouth as he listened to the other speaker. He plucked absently at the buttons of his white shirt, which billowed over khaki shorts. His hairy calves were the size of rugby balls. Alex avoided looking at them. This, disappointingly, was likely to be Sal Eichenbaum. 'Tell him to do the fucking job. Don't ask me how to fucking do it!' He wandered out the way he had come in, his expletives fading away into other rooms.

At the far end of the room was a dividing wall created out of niches of varying sizes. Alex could see through them into the other half of the sitting room. Each niche contained one piece of silver; bowls, plates displayed on Perspex stands, vases, boxes... Sammy's mother's hard work with the silver polish was evident. Each object reflected the turquoise sky.

When Julie returned, she carried a silver tray, and the delicate silver handle and feet on the glass jug of iced coffee matched the two glasses. The ashtray she had also brought, however, was yellow plastic singed with brown. When she filled the glasses, she offered Alex a cigarette.

'No thanks,' Alex said. 'I quit years ago, under duress. My two daughters wouldn't leave me alone. I'm tempted though, once in a while.'

'Children are the worst,' Julie said. 'My grandchildren look at me as if I'm clubbing baby seals every time I light up – got two. My son works for *The New York Times*. But France is as bad now. We might as well be back in LA.' She took a silver lighter from the chest pocket of her overalls and lit up. 'So, you think we should rent, huh?'

Alex was taken aback. 'That's up to you, of course. But I might have a tenant, if you decided that's what you want to do.' If anyone had bullshit radar, it would be Julie, Alex thought. She liked her.

'We've been here five years, but with my husband's new project, he's going to be in LA, 18 months minimum.' Julie had unusual tawny eyes, an animal colour. 'I don't want to go. The studio there is nowhere near as good as here.'

'The studio?'

Julie waved her cigarette towards the wall of silver. 'Silverwork,' she said. 'Jewellery mostly, but this stuff, too. Want to see? Bring your glass.'

She followed Julie across a small atrium open to the sky, where shiny-leaved plants climbed up the walls, and up a narrow staircase to a room lined with windows. A radio chattered quietly in English. There were battered wooden trestle tables against three walls, and against the fourth there was a small furnace on a stone plinth, beside a squat steel safe with a combination lock. The words 'City Bank of Hollywood' were engraved on a plaque above the lock. There was a singed, metallic taste in the air. Julie picked up a tiny piece of metal from one of the tables, polished it with her thumb, and handed it to Alex. It was a minuscule palm tree, each frond clearly defined.

'For a necklace,' Julie said. 'Each tree will be a loop in a chain.'

'It's beautiful,' Alex said. Julie took it back and examined it closely. She sat down on a stool by one of the tables, and said, 'Not yet.' Alex immediately wanted to sit too, but she couldn't see any other chairs. She noticed a large, hairy dog bed under the table.

'I imagine you'll miss this studio,' she said.

'You're right. In LA the light's not the same,' Julie said. 'We only spend a couple of months every year back home, so I never get around to fixing up the studio there.' She picked up a stick of some kind and started scraping at a ball of wax. For a few minutes, neither of them said anything.

'I think I must have come a bit too early in your decision-making process,' Alex said at last.

Julie looked up, surprised. 'No, no. We have to make up our minds about this. He's not going to, that's a fact.' She nodded towards the door. 'He doesn't want to rent. He thinks we can keep it here ready and waiting. But he doesn't see the bills.' She shrugged. 'Men. Are you married?'

'My husband died of a heart attack over a year ago,' Alex said. She always tried to say it matter of factly. People rarely knew how to respond, and Alex felt vaguely responsible for their discomfort. Julie's tawny eyes fixed on Alex.

'Huh,' Julie said. 'I hope it was quick. Kids?'

Alex could have hugged her. She quickly sketched a picture of Meghan, the happy, uncomplicated daughter, and Beth, the thoughtful painter. This wasn't the moment to mention that Beth hadn't yet returned to Nice, having texted simply that Raymond's studio had a good view. Alex had eaten the white asparagus on her own.

'Arty ones,' she said. 'Always trouble. Tell me more about this American couple.'

Alex liked Julie's brassiness. Before long, she was telling her all about the Barrons and Immobilier Charpentier, though she left Chantelle's dignity intact by saying simply that she had fallen ill in New York. Julie listened, rapt.

'This is the house for a couple of kids who want to set up on the Riviera. We've got a bar in the pool and a movie theatre. I'll show you. Sal loves that stuff.'

As they moved towards the door, however, Sal Eichenbaum's voice boomed up the stairs. 'Fuck 'em,' he shouted. 'It doesn't matter what the fuck he says! He arrived in the doorway, panting from the short climb. 'Yeah, yeah, yeah, tell me another time.' He clicked the phone shut angrily and stood staring at Alex. 'Asshole.' Alex prickled, old enough to be shocked by casual swearing.

'Not you,' he said to Alex. He turned to Julie. 'Who's this?'

As Julie explained about Immobilier Charpentier and renting the house, Eichenbaum appraised Alex with his mouth open, scratching his chest through his shirt. Alex tried not to look. Perhaps he was enormously talented, she thought. Perhaps he had been handsome long ago. There must be some explanation for this apparently stupendous mismatch.

'Yeah, I remember your office. Down by the market? Next to a great little restaurant, Waxy something?' he asked.

Alex didn't bother to correct him.

'I tried to get hold of one of your guys once.' Alex waited for further explanation, but Eichenbaum roamed around, sifting through bits of his wife's silver.

'What's the rent again?' he asked, directing the question to Julie. She told him.

'And their take?'

Alex assumed he meant Immobilier Charpentier's fee. She told him, though Julie repeated it, as if translating.

'We leave our shit?' He was looking out of the window now, his mind elsewhere.

'They may want it furnished initially, if you're prepared for that,' Alex said.

'Yeah, I know, it was something to do with the daughter.'

He turned to face Alex, and his chest-scratching became more excited. 'There was some guy working for you, been in prison. Tried to torch a car somewhere in Nice?'

Alex told him he must be mistaken.

'Nah,' he said. 'We were doing a documentary about revenge, I remember him, little quiet guy. It's usually that kind.' He laughed loudly. 'Wouldn't talk to us.'

Could he possibly be talking about Guillaume? Alex hoped not. Even the thought of Sal Eichenbaum in her office, in her neighbourhood, near her little restaurant, gave her a sickly feeling.

'I'd love to continue with the tour,' she said to Julie. She turned towards the door, not caring if it seemed rude.

'I don't give a shit if we rent the place, Julie,' Eichenbaum said as they were at the top of the stairs. 'It's up to you. But that contract better be fucking watertight.'

'Sal's big on contracts,' Julie said, as they crossed the atrium. 'Anything like that would have to go through his lawyers.'

'That wouldn't be a problem,' Alex said.

Alex made some sketches in her notebook under 'E' as she followed Julie around the villa. She needed to note the way that one room led into another, the unexpected steps and stairwells, the way that every space faced the glinting sea.

As they stood beside the infinity pool, Sal Eichenbaum reappeared with a towel wrapped around his huge waist. He padded up behind her and she could feel the heat from his body.

'Shame we didn't get that guy. It was the kind of story me and my people do best. A revenge tale. I'm sure it was him, daughter did research somewhere, got killed.'

Alex backed away just as he flung off his towel and heaved himself into the pool. He was naked.

'Oh, Sal,' Julie sighed. She grabbed Alex's arm and steered her towards the carport. 'Sorry you had to see that. Pity me, though. I have to see it every day.'

As Alex sat in the shuddering car on the way back down to

the road, she wished that Sal Eichenbaum would hurry up and leave, and that Julie would stay behind.

CHAPTER FIFTEEN

On her way back to Les Jolies Roses, Alex looked through the window of the office to see if the answering machine was winking. She didn't want to miss any word from Harry Bormann. Alex played the first message several times, standing in the dark as she tried to understand.

When the door opened, she swung round, hoping to see Beth. But it was Françoise. 'You're here!' she said. 'I saw the door open but no lights on, and I thought...' She stopped as she looked the office over, as if sizing it up.

'I'm glad it's you,' Alex said. She rewound the machine. 'Will you listen to this? The accent is too strong for me.'

Françoise frowned, looking absently at the wall of photographs as she concentrated on the message.

'Well, well,' Françoise said. 'That old witch! I haven't thought about her for years! Odile Perrin, from Bellet. Play it again.'

Alex replayed the message, but could still barely catch more than the first few words.

'She's not happy with Immobilier Charpentier.' Françoise was clearly amused. 'She obviously doesn't know about Chantelle, but she must have heard that Bellet is suddenly the *destination du jour* for Americans. She's blaming it on Chantelle.' She giggled. 'Oh, I must tell Alain! We've known Odile for decades.'

'She called to berate Chantelle?'

'That wouldn't surprise anyone, Madame. Odile hates tourists, she hates foreigners, she hates rich people, she hates people who sell their houses, she hates the people who buy them...' Françoise counted Odile's complaints enthusiastically on her fingers. 'She puts up with Chantelle, but the only person in the world she really likes is Guillaume. She has a farm up near that ruin. She still tends her vines, too. She's produced a few good wines in her time, I'll give her that.'

She turned to the wall again, her face changing subtly from a squint to a flicker of a smile to a frown and back again as she scanned the photographs. She even pointed at one, tutted and shrugged her shoulders.

'I went to see the house where Sammy's mother works this afternoon,' Alex said.

Françoise put down the Galeries Lafayette bag she had been carrying and sat down beside the desk.

'And?'

It was useful for Alex to follow her route back through the villa at Eze as she tried to recall each detail for Françoise. Françoise interrupted now and then, asking for clarifications that focused Alex's memory. No, she told Françoise, she couldn't remember seeing a walk-in fridge, but yes, all the bedrooms did have mirrored closets. Alex pencilled in a few additions to the notes and sketches she'd made while following Julie through the house. She would type them out tomorrow, before she lost track of what her scribbles meant. She could get them into good enough shape for Dianne Steer.

'Françoise, Mr Eichenbaum seemed to remember Chez Maxie and Immobilier Charpentier. He said that once he wanted to interview someone here about a car fire. Could that be right?'

It was getting dark now, and Alex turned on the desk lamp between them. It felt cosy.

'Interview? For a movie?' Françoise seemed puzzled.

'A documentary. About revenge I think he said.'

Françoise considered it silently before a look of disappointment crossed her face.

'Oh, why don't they let him be,' she said. 'So much time has passed since then.'

'Who?'

'Guillaume, of course. I'll tell you something, I would trust Guillaume with my life, with Maxie's life. Anyone might have done what he did. Anyone can be provoked beyond the limit.'

'But what did he do?'

Françoise shifted in her seat and her face moved out of the comfortable halo of lamplight they shared. She waved her hand as if the light were too bright.

'I must be going. I only came in because I saw the door was open. The *quartier* isn't like it used to be, with all these strangers.'

The office felt still after Françoise's abrupt departure. Alex made a note of Odile Perrin's phone number in the dossier, under 'B' for Bellet, and deleted the message. Did Françoise mean strangers like her?

The only other message was from Guillaume.

'The cats won't be bothering Liliane Valentin any more,' he said, and hung up. Alex imagined him rattling angrily down the Avenue Jean Cocteau with a basket of mewling cats on the pick-up's front seat. He would no more have harmed them than she would herself.

The dossier sat next to the phone, and she leafed through it. She'd moved it into an alphabetically tabbed accordion file she'd found in Chantelle's stash of stationery. There were still swathes of unallocated cuttings stuffed into the 'Z' pocket, but they were all yellowed – far too dated, she'd thought, to offer up any useful nuggets.

She took her notebook from her bag, and picked a red pen from the desk drawer. She would mark with a series of stars the villas she thought just right for Natascha and Michael Barron. She had no idea how she would follow it up, but surely this is what Chantelle wanted. As she worked in the lamplight, she felt as if she were indexing again. Something, at least, that she knew how to control.

CHAPTER SIXTEEN

The days passed, but Alex still woke each morning feeling anxious, her thoughts never quite settling on one thing or another. Sometimes her nervous energy got her up so early that with the time difference she could even catch Harry in New York before he went to bed.

'How long can it go on?' he asked plaintively. He was a reluctant visitor to Chantelle's bedside, but he seemed a dutiful friend, sitting beside her and reading to her from gossip magazines. He was becoming familiar with the comings and goings of her doctors and nurses, and even more reluctantly being entrusted with information about her prognosis.

'I hope they don't ask me to make any decisions,' he said. 'I mean, I have a life, and this isn't supposed to be part of it.'

Alex felt sorry for him. He, too, had been accidentally co-opted into responsibility for Chantelle.

'Something will happen soon,' she said at the end of each conversation. But her heart was beginning to sink, especially when Harry told her that the doctors had mentioned moving Chantelle to a long-term facility. A woman from the registrar's office had called him to discuss insurance. 'What could I say?' he said, his voice rising. 'What do I know about all that stuff? You've got to help me, Alex.'

'We can't keep on waiting,' she said whenever Guillaume came in to collect keys or check paperwork. 'Someone has to make decisions on Chantelle's behalf.'

At the restaurant, everyone relentlessly asked after Chantelle. Alex began to wonder out loud if there was someone she should call.

'Not that layabout brother, *certainement*,' Françoise said confidently from behind the bar. 'Even if we knew where he was.'

'Her ex-husband died years ago,' Maxie offered, 'so he won't be much help. And what a loser he was, eh, Maman?'

'Handsome, though,' Françoise admitted.

'Isn't there a relative in the north?' Beatrice from the bank asked. 'I can't say anything, of course, you know we have to respect client confidentiality, but until not so many years ago, Chantelle used to make a regular payment to someone in Brussels.'

Alex looked at her hopefully. 'Could you find out?'

Beatrice threw up her orange hands. 'Not me, of course. Oh no. I'll have to ask my directors.'

Alain shook his head. '*Non*,' he said decisively. 'It's time to get in touch with Chantelle's lawyers.'

Thank god, Alex thought with a flood of relief. How could they not have thought of contacting her lawyers before? They'd know exactly what steps to take. There would be a procedure to follow. 'Who are they?' she asked.

But when she telephoned the firm of *notaires* that handled Immobilier Charpentier's legal work, she found they had nothing to do with Chantelle's personal affairs.

Even the return of Beth, slinking back into Les Jolies Roses on her own with no notice at all, had barely shifted Alex's attention.

'Someone will have to get into her apartment,' her daughter suggested. 'That Guillaume bloke must know how to break down a door.'

Alex's first mistake on Beth's return had been to look over her shoulder into the hall as she came into the flat.

'No,' Beth said, with a tired sigh. 'Raymond hasn't come. It's just me. Isn't that enough for you?'

Alex overlooked it. 'Then you can help me put your room together,' she said. 'I don't want you sleeping on a mattress on the floor.'

Beth, despite her slight build, was much more capable of assembling the beds than Alex. She, not Meghan, had patiently watched Rod put up shelves and curtain rails, and chattered to him while he changed washers or valves, handing him spanners and wrenches. Thanks to him, she could use a drill more confidently than Alex could ever hope to.

Beth laid out everything she needed for the job, counted up screws and dowels, and meticulously went through the instructions. It was exactly what Rod would have done. As Beth concentrated, she clenched her jaw in the same way. When something slipped, a screwdriver or a hammer, she didn't whine or curse, as Meghan would have done, but calmly started over, her lips pursed even harder. Alex could have watched her all day, but Beth eventually looked up at her in irritation, and said, 'What?'

Alex brought her cups of tea, and helped hold bulky pieces of the frames in position.

'You know, I've looked up a few things on that Ed Bronz,' Beth said. She was kneeling on the floor, tightening bolts while Alex stood above her, steadying a piece of baseboard.

'Don't tell me. An ex-con who cheats estate agents out of their business?' Alex laughed, but Beth didn't.

'He used to have his own art gallery. I think he had one in Paris, and definitely one in Monaco.'

There was wood dust in Beth's hair, and Alex leaned down to brush it off. Beth ducked away.

'Hold that piece straight, Mum. All the bolts need to be even. I can't find much about the one in Paris. He must have represented a few contemporary artists because there are references to shows. Small stuff. Can you pass me those other bolts?'

In silence they laid the wooden base down and turned it back up on to the opposite side, so that Beth could fix the other corners. It was heavy, and they were both sweating.

'I found a couple of mentions of the one in Monaco,' Beth said. There was an ominous creaking sound as she turned the wrench, but she continued what she was doing. 'He had some expensive things, Kandinsky, Malevich. Plus a bunch of Eastern Europeans I've never heard of.'

Alex relaxed. Why had she been expecting something unpleasant?

'I'm sure he'd be happy to talk about it,' she said.

'Maybe not. Apparently in the 1980s everything was sold off all at once.'

'He must have wanted to do something else.'

Beth stood up and rocked the base gently. 'Tell Robert and Olivia not to jump on these beds when they come over,' she said. She and Alex tightened the fixings. Beth inspected Alex's work, tapping and adjusting just as Rod would have done.

'The thing is, the name of the gallery came up a couple of times in the art press. There were questions of provenance about stuff that came through his gallery.'

'What does that mean?' Alex recognised a certain smugness in Beth's voice. Whatever she had discovered, she was pleased with it.

'It's possible that some of the things he dealt in weren't what they seemed.' She started pulling the bed slats from their plastic wrappings.

'Poor Ed. I expect that wasn't good for business.'

Beth gave her an exasperated look.

'What if he knew?'

'What if he didn't? Besides, Beth, just because you've found information on the internet doesn't mean you can trust it.'

'I know. I'm going to keep looking. I'll probably go back to Menton tomorrow.' She turned back to the bed, and Alex could see in the set of her narrow shoulders that she was pleased with having irritated her mother.

CHAPTER SEVENTEEN

No one wanted to force their way into Chantelle's flat, but everyone agreed it had to be done. When Alex suggested it to Guillaume, he said nothing, contemplating the list Alex had made of everything she needed: brother's contact details, solicitor's phone number, insurers. Alain had even offered to send along someone he knew to take care of the lock. There was no risk, he assured her; if worst came to worst, they would send the police in sooner or later anyway.

'I don't understand why it has to be you,' Beth said. Alex had gone home to Les Jolies Roses for lunch, unsure, as usual, whether she would find Beth there or not. This time, Beth had made a salade niçoise. The market was packing up beneath the window as they sat at the round table.

Alex had suggested it should be Alain, but he said he had 'rifled through enough women's drawers'.

Françoise also refused. 'It's not quite like that,' she explained. 'In the end, we are only acquaintances. It wouldn't be right.'

'Oh, for Christ's sake,' Beth said. 'They're being so French. They don't want to take any responsibility themselves but they want someone in there to get hold of the goods. I'd say they're all looking for a scapegoat in case it goes pear-shaped.'

Alex had wondered the same thing herself. Would it be convenient to blame whatever went wrong on the *Anglaise*?

After a few days, Guillaume reluctantly agreed to help.

'I believe Chantelle left some spare keys in the cabinet,' he said, and to Alex's relief, there they were. The ring was marked 6b/25.

Alex had expected that Chantelle's flat would be in a building similar to her own, but 25 Boulevard Las Planas was an unprepossessing, square, 1970s building, However, it was painted rose pink, and was in a beautiful location up a winding road, just far enough away from town to be peaceful. Chantelle had bought it off-plan for next to nothing, Guillaume recalled, along with one or two others in the building, since sold.

It was stuffy and dark inside, but the odour of stale scent and cigarette smoke was oddly comforting. Guillaume opened the shutters, then hung back by the open front door. He said, 'I can't stay. I have to pick up some paint.' He stared at the floor, as if afraid that he might see something he shouldn't. It seemed to Alex that they hadn't looked at each other directly for days. She signed in relief when he left.

Alex could understand exactly why Chantelle might have chosen a flat like this. It was on the top floor, with a deep balcony that offered a view stretching from the hills across a small built-up valley and over the rooftops of Nice to the sea.

Chantelle was neat. Apart from a coffee cup on the polished oak dining table, with a lipstick stain on the rim, the flat was spotless. There was a large oak armoire against the living room wall, a matching chest of drawers on the opposite wall, an old-fashioned sofa upholstered in tweedy dark green, and two matching bergère armchairs. The flowery tapestry cushions on each one were plumped up. Alex examined the few paintings on the walls: dark Northern landscapes, and a couple of views of Venice, framed in gilt. Only one painting interested her: a bright pink and blue Cubist-style portrait, which she stared at for a moment before deciding the subject was a much younger Chantelle.

She inspected the knick-knacks that were arranged around the room. Most were glass; colourful Murano vases, glass Daum *pâte-de-verre* fruits, clear Orrers candlesticks from Sweden, swirling like streams of water gushing from a tap. Alex enjoyed the weight of them in her hand.

But she wasn't there to look at Chantelle's glass collection. Where would her important papers be? Alex kept her own things in an old steamer trunk, found years ago in a junk shop. Rod had made file hangers out of plywood, and stained them to match the paper-lined interior. They kept all the usual things there; deeds, certificates, diplomas. Meghan had even added a file marked 'Dad', for Rod's death certificate and *certificat d'incineration*. 'It's all in here, Mum,' Meghan had said, pointing. At that stage, Alex couldn't look. 'It's France, Mum. You've got to keep this stuff for ever. They'll never believe he's gone if you can't prove it.'

There was nothing like a desk anywhere. The bigger bedroom had a delicate Louis XIV-style painted dressing table under the window, but there was nothing in the drawers except half-used compacts and expensive-looking lipsticks worn to nubs. There was nothing much in the bedside tables, either, other than empty aspirin packets and piles of magazines, each one hedgehogged with strips of paper where Chantelle must have wanted to make a note.

Alex at last saw something promising in a hall cupboard. It was a walk-in cupboard, bigger than Chantelle's bathroom, lined with cheap wooden cabinets. A naked bulb hung from the ceiling. There were shelves for shoes, and hanging space for clothes zipped up in plastic bags. There was even a stepladder leaning folded against the wall to access the higher shelves, which were full of boxes helpfully marked, including *'Photographes'* and *'Cadeaux de Noël'*. One was tantalisingly marked *'Jeunesse'*. Alex considered it for a few seconds, but knew there was no argument at all for going through Chantelle's 'Youth', neatly labelled and filed away in one dusty cardboard box.

Most of the cabinets were packed with either clothes or china and wine glasses, but one was a proper office cabinet complete with file drawers. Chantelle clearly intended to be organised; the files were all marked, but the top, flat drawer was stuffed full of paper. Alex slid it open. As it gave way, a sheaf of papers exploded onto the floor. She left them where they fell. She felt the same mix of elation and hopelessness elicited by the dossier back at the office.

Alex separated the papers with the toe of her shoe, and bent over to see more clearly. There were some recently dated statements from her bank in Avenue Jean Medecin, and a few letters – one was confirming the extension of Chantelle's car insurance. Then Alex saw a letter that made her stomach flip: the letterhead was from Quelin & Company, Solicitors. 'Chère Madame Charpentier,' Alex read, 'We are pleased to enclose a copy of your *testament authentique* amended recently to your instruction...'

Chantelle's will. 'Bingo!' Alex said out loud. The letter was dated only four months before. Had Chantelle already imagined these tragic circumstances? Despite a paper clip at the top, there were no attachments, but it didn't matter. Alex had found the name of the solicitors in whom Chantelle must have already placed her trust. She felt an enormous rush of hope, as if this alone would make Chantelle sit bolt upright in her New York hospital bed, demanding her phone and cigarettes.

Alex knelt down and shuffled the papers on the floor into a pile. She pointedly tried to avoid reading, but her eyes fell on notepaper from the '*Maison d'arret de Grasse*' – the prison at Grasse. It was addressed to Chantelle at Immobilier Charpentier, and the subject, in bold type, was Guillaume Chapel.

She gasped. So Sal Eichenbaum had been right.

'What on earth are you doing here?' Alex heard the screeching voice just as she became aware of the bulk blocking the doorway. She scrambled to her feet so quickly she made herself giddy. The prison letter fluttered from her hand.

'This is outrageous, Madame Coates!'

Alex recognised Paulette Bitoun's voice before she could identify the interior decorator's generous silhouette.

'No, no,' Alex said. 'I came to help.'

'Help? Nosing through Chantelle's personal effects without her permission? Is that what they call help in England?'

'Let me explain...' Paulette Bitoun had entered the tiny cupboard, and Alex instinctively backed up flat against the cabinets. Today the decorator's lips and fingernails were frosty pink, and her hair was plastered into a ponytail tied with a pink bow. Her white jeans had lurid pink stitching on the pockets and seams.

'I'm shocked to find you here, Madame Coates. What right have you to enter? Madame Charpentier will not be happy to hear about this.' Her little eyes darted from shelf to cabinet to clothes rail as she spoke. 'And what's this? All of her private papers strewn about like leaves?' She bent down and picked up a handful of the papers Alex had left on the floor, scanning them greedily.

Alex stepped forward. 'Actually,' she said, snatching the papers from Paulette's hand, 'I'm here with the agreement of Chantelle's friends, including the ex-chief of police Alain Hubert.' She gathered up the correspondence and held it close to her chest as she glared at the decorator. Her heart was beating madly and she could feel the colour rising in her cheeks. Paulette looked at her coldly.

'So you have all agreed to go through her belongings, have you? Poor Chantelle. People she considered her friends.' Paulette fingered the clothes bags hanging nearest her. 'Not that you can be counted a friend, of course. Where did you say you were from?'

Alex was unnerved by Paulette's unpleasantness. 'The situation in New York is serious,' she said. 'We're hoping to make Chantelle's family aware of it.'

'Serious?'

There was curiosity without sympathy in Paulette's tone. Alex realised that now she had the upper hand.

'As a friend of Chantelle's, you must know how we can get in touch with her family,' Alex said.

Paulette sniffed. 'I'll think about it,' she said.

'Her siblings, or aunts, uncles, nephews, and of course her true friends,' Alex emphasised the word 'true' – *ses* vrais *amis*.

'Yes, yes,' Paulette said. She looked voraciously around the cupboard before turning back to the hall. As she tottered out, she halted suddenly.

Alex heard Guillaume's voice. 'You!' he said. 'Where is

Madame Coates? How did you get in?'

Guillaume's face appeared at the cupboard door. He seemed relieved to see Alex.

'I have a client in the building,' Paulette said haughtily. 'I was on my way out when I noticed Chantelle's door was wide open. Naturally I thought she was home.'

'No, she's not home,' Guillaume said. 'Let me show you out.' Alex was surprised by his confidence. Guillaume virtually manhandled Paulette Bitoun towards the front door. The clatter of her pink heels on the marble floor sounded like a startled horse. He closed the door firmly behind her and watched through the peephole.

'Now, Guillaume, why do I get the impression you don't care for that woman?'

Guillaume rubbed his hands together as if he were wiping away crumbs. He looked at her, his eyes filled with anger, before his expression returned to its usual downcast frown. '*Salope*,' he said. 'Bitch. She's nothing but trouble. She follows Chantelle around like a hyena. She tells everyone they're friends and colleagues, but Chantelle wouldn't trust her for a moment.'

Alex suddenly remembered the sheaf of papers she was holding. She scrambled for the rest of them on the floor in the cupboard, shoving to the back the letter from the prison, on which she picked up only the words 'probation' and 'reference'. She'd be unlikely to find out what it said now, but then it was clearly none of her business. She hated the idea that Sal Eichenbaum had tried to make it his.

'I've got something,' she announced. She turned off the cupboard lights, shut the door and walked into the living room, forcing Guillaume to follow. 'See? It's recent. What do you think?'

Guillaume refused to look. 'It's not my place to know,' he said. He went to the balcony, and leaned over the railing, scanning the cars in the parking area below. Alex folded the letter and put it in her bag. Then she went into the kitchen with the coffee cup and washed off the lipstick. 'Yes it *is* your place to know,' she whispered angrily to herself, but then remembered how ugly resentment could look – she'd seen enough of it on Beth's face over the years. Alex had chosen to help Chantelle; she would do it with good grace. Still, the thought of phoning the lawyers Quelin and Company made her want to sing.

'There she goes, Bitoun's getting into her car, the silly cow,' Guillaume called from the balcony. Alex smiled. Perhaps she'd learn to feel comfortable with Guillaume after all. 'It's safe for us to go now. But you can count on Paulette Bitoun to be spreading nasty rumours even as we stand here.'

CHAPTER EIGHTEEN

When Alex called Quelin & Company, *Maître* Amedeo Quelin himself listened politely and promised assistance for his dear friend Chantelle. But after the third or fourth call nothing happened, Alex wondered if they were such dear friends after all. She knew she would have to be patient. First of all, said Quelin, the situation would have to be verified. Then, understandably, the company would have to verify Alex. Then they would have to undertake their research. And then, of course, there was no cast-iron guarantee that they would be able to help. If the situation continued for much longer, however, an *administrateur judiciaire* would have to be appointed to intervene in Chantelle's affairs.

'What did you expect?' Meghan asked scornfully during their morning phone call. One of the children was playing *Greensleeves* on a flute in the background. 'It's France. You have to produce your great-grandmother's birth certificate before they'll even admit you were born.'

Beth was still in Menton. The spare room, strewn with her clothes, diffused the faint odour of linseed oil mixed with new wood from the so-far unused beds. Alex could smell it now, lightly rising from her silk cardigan, even above the aroma of roasting beef coming from the kitchen of Chez Maxie.

'Things will take their own course,' Maxie said, serving her a piece of camembert ripe to the point of melting. She waited for Alex to taste the cheese from the edge of her knife. '*Bon*, eh?' she said. 'From my ex-sister-in-law's farm near Bayeux. She sends me a wheel once in a while.'

As Alex searched for a red wine on the board where Francoise chalked up her daily choices, she noticed the professor on the *terrasse* outside. He was shuffling faster than usual.

'Madame Coates,' he called, making straight for her, 'Did you visit the Menier villa? I've been eager to hear!'

There were beads of sweat on his forehead.

'Not yet,' Alex said.

The professor's face was childlike with disappointment. He put his books on the chair opposite Alex, balanced his briefcase on top, and pulled out a plastic folder of papers.

'Please,' he said. He handed her a photocopied photograph of an elderly man standing in front of a wall of paintings. Alex looked at it closely. Nothing was familiar.

'Hmm,' she said. 'Who is it?'

'I'm not entirely sure, but look at this.' There was a window behind the old man, and the professor tapped it with his finger. 'The subject of my investigations. If only you had seen the Menier villa, you might have recognised the background.'

Alex looked again.

'The shutters, Madame Coates. They're so unusual for this part of the world. They're more like carved Indian screens, are they not?'

'Hmm,' Alex said again. The shutters seemed to be covered with elephants, but she couldn't be sure.

Maxie appeared beside them and put two glasses on the table. 'Madame Alex, I can't bear to see that camembert without this Cabernet beside it,' she said, pouring. 'And you, Monsieur le Professeur? Have your buildings driven you to drink?'

The professor looked at the floor shyly and took the glass.

'The house was owned by an artist. Do you think this could be him?'

Alex and the professor lowered their heads together over the photograph.

'The family – distant family, apparently – donated their papers to the Municipal Archives after the fire, but they didn't provide any notes. If I went through them all and it came to nothing, it would be such a waste of time.'

The professor wiped his forehead with the sleeve of his jacket.

'If I could only uncover something interesting about the

house or the owner, it would justify more research about the shutters. Sometimes the architectural detail on its own doesn't provide sufficient interest. Publishers want intrigue and secrets and...' The professor grimaced before continuing. '...romance'.

Alex pressed the melting camembert to the roof of her mouth with her tongue, and sipped the Cabernet.

'There's always the fire. Publishers love tragedy.'

The wine warmed her throat. She was already thinking of her after-lunch siesta. Unfortunately, the professor was rooting in his briefcase.

'I'm not good at tragedy,' he said. He laid more photocopies on the table and Alex was forced to move her plate to one side.

'I also found these at the Municipal Archives.' He fanned out the papers – a few handwritten letters, and some pencil sketches. Some of the drawings looked like childish sketches over crumpled bills or invoices, of a girl in a summer dress.

'And they're definitely from the Menier villa?' They didn't look hopeful to Alex.

The professor blew out his cheeks.

'It's hard to tell, but one would assume there's a connection, if there's a photograph taken inside the house.' He looked hopefully at Alex. 'Wouldn't you agree? If any of these documents mention the shutters, I'll be able to make something of it.'

The phrase needle in haystack came to Alex's mind.

'I wish I could have seen the shutters up close. The housekeeper who let me into the garden wasn't so accommodating once she understood that I wasn't a prospective tenant.'

'Don't give up hope. This might hold what you're looking for.'

The professor shuffled the papers back into the folder. He petted it as if it were an animal, with slow, loving strokes. 'I'll have to read them all first, though. And we'll need to get into the villa.'

CHAPTER NINETEEN

When Alex walked outside onto Maxie's *terrasse*, the crystal brightness of the spring air tempted her away from Les Jolies Roses and a siesta. She strolled instead through the side streets towards Boulevard Gambetta, stopping to look in the windows of shops in which she couldn't imagine spending her money. She stared for several minutes at a display of dog and cat beds; miniature gold-painted four-posters with satin cushions and, for the cats, matching litter trays. Further along was a minuscule shop with nothing but plaques for house numbers behind its plate-glass window, along with a desiccated copy of *Nice-Matin*.

It was rare for Alex to walk far in Nice without coming across a lingerie shop, and now she noticed one she hadn't seen before. She crossed the road to look, always in awe of the silk and satin confections. She imagined the itchy discomfort of the ruffled bras displayed on inflatable plastic busts suspended from the ceiling. It was moment before it occurred to her that this selection of underthings was saucier than the norm. She leaned in, and saw that what she'd taken for the usual French assortment of lacy knickers included leather and rubber. As she turned to go, the entrance door to the small block of flats next door opened and a man appeared.

She immediately spun in a half circle and headed in the opposite direction fast when she saw that it was Ed Bronz.

What would he make of her looking at this sort of tat? She'd only taken a few steps before she turned around again, telling herself not to be ridiculous.

She was about to call to Ed when a woman came out of the same building. She glanced at Alex. Mascara ran down her cheeks. She was neither young nor slim, and her short yellow-blonde hair was obviously dyed, but Alex was struck by the sensual way she gripped her black dress to her chest. She was barefoot, and looked frantically up and down the street. When she saw Ed, she shouted angrily, '*S'il te plait! S'il te plait!*' Please! Please!

Alex darted into the doorway of the lingerie shop. This was definitely not the time to bump into Ed. She heard the woman shout again, and then the door of the building clicked shut. Alex peeked out. Ed was standing on the opposite corner of the nearby intersection with his back towards her, and seemed to be on the phone. She waited, expecting the woman to come tearing back out, this time wearing shoes.

When nothing happened, Alex was disappointed. She stepped out of the doorway and walked as nonchalantly as she could towards Ed. At the intersection, she crossed the road, coming up behind him and aiming to pass within inches. But he moved off, without looking behind him. Alex called his name, but he didn't turn. The distance between them widened.

She reminded herself of a schoolgirl, trying to engineer a meeting with the object of a crush. It made her feel silly, and she was about to give up and turn down the next street when the Russian she'd seen before appeared at Ed's side.

Alex's pace quickened. Ed was still on the phone, and the Russian walked alongside him. Alex tried to keep up. They stopped briefly when Ed finished his call. He slapped the Russian on the back in a friendly way, but spoke to him urgently. It was easier once they turned onto the Boulevard Gambetta, where they kept to the shady side of the street. There were more people here, but it was quiet nonetheless. Among the grocery stores and carpet shops there were still small family businesses that closed for a stretch in the afternoon, giving the avenue a sleepy atmosphere.

Alex weaved between people on the street, and stayed for a while behind three teenage girls with identical rainbow tattoos on the smalls of their backs. She found Ed and the Russian again just as they were crossing the road half a block ahead. There was a lull in the traffic, and she darted across, reaching the other side just as they did. When they turned a corner, she broke into a gentle jog.

As she turned into a narrow street, she stopped short. At the far end, she recognised immediately the dark-green car she'd seen near the Menier villa. Ed was standing beside it as the Russian looked for something in the boot. Alex stepped into the doorway of a restaurant, and pretended to examine the menu as she watched. The Russian found what he was looking for: a reddish folder, or perhaps a slim case of some kind. Ed snatched it, unzipped it, and partially lifted something out. He stuffed it back in, slapped the Russian on the back again, and started walking towards Alex. Damn! Her stomach somersaulted. He'd be beside her within seconds. The restaurant's 'Closed' sign was level with her shoulder. It swung violently as she pushed the door and almost fell inside. A woman behind the bar looked up. '*On est fermé, Madame.* We're closed. Would you like to make a reservation?' Out of the corner of her eye, she saw Ed walking past. When she turned around fully, she saw the Russian getting into the car.

For the first time, it struck her that this must be the car Alain's nephew Felix had mentioned, the Mercedes with two small holes.

'Madame?'

'Oh, yes, later,' Alex said. 'I mean, another time. Sorry! *Merci!*' She felt ridiculous, but left the restaurant as calmly as she could.

The blue eyes that were looking directly at her when she closed the door behind her were familiar. Alain Hubert was sitting at the wheel of his BMW, parked directly across the street.

He was grinning, and he called out, 'Fish not fresh enough for you at Maxie's?'

'I had other business,' Alex replied quickly. She was pleased with herself. She hadn't missed a beat.

'So I see.' Alain leaned out of the open window to see the Mercedes pulling out, and started pulling out himself. There was no sign of Ed.

'I'd never have put you on surveillance duty,' Alain

continued. 'You should be more careful if you want to play these games.' He jerked his thumb in the direction of the sea as his car slowly accelerated, and said, 'He went thataway.' The slow, heavily accented English imitated American movies: *'e went zataway*. Alex blushed hotly. How much sillier could she possibly look?

As she began to calm down, she tried to make sense of what she'd seen, but each scenario she constructed seemed more absurd. Perhaps the barefoot woman was Ed's sister. Maybe he'd upset her by mistake. But she had looked desperate, and Ed had looked surprisingly, and attractively, determined. Alex had lived a sheltered life, really – it was something to be grateful for. That blonde had led a different life indeed.

And Alain – she put her hands over her eyes. How embarrassing! But why was he sitting on his own in the car? Could it be that he was waiting for the Russian?

Her legs were beginning to feel heavier as she walked. She thought about stopping at a café and sitting down to call Meghan, who would listen in thrilled horror to her story of tailing Ed. But it would only give her daughter renewed energy for her campaign to nag Alex to come home. She even thought momentarily of calling Beth, on the pretext of telling her about the professor's book. But Beth would be likely to take jealous offence at her mother's interest in someone else's work.

The person she really wanted to talk to, of course, was Rod.

She saw him sitting at the kitchen table in Fayence, wine glass in hand, laughing as if her stories were the funniest he'd ever heard. But all he could advise now would be just what she knew already: I'm sorry, Alex; you'll have to manage on your own.

When Ed suddenly blocked her path, her energy seemed almost completely run down. He had walked out of a building right in front of her.

'What a surprise!' he said, his dimples appearing. 'But if you'll excuse me for saying so, you look like the sky's fallen in.' He kissed her on both cheeks, and Alex couldn't decide if she could smell aftershave or perfume. 'Have you had bad news?' He rested one hand on her shoulder as he searched her face. There was no folder in the other hand. Alex glanced behind him to the building he'd just left. The brass sign listed architects and accountants, along with the usual Niçois smattering of physical therapists, the *kinésithérapeutes*.

Alex straightened up. 'No,' she said. 'I just wish things were… simpler.'

'Ah,' Ed said knowingly. 'There's a remedy for that. Look, over there.'

On the other side of the road there was a café with tables and parasols set up on the pavement.

'Their sorbets are the cure for all sorrows. And besides, I owe you your gambling losses.'

Alex laughed. How could she suspect him of anything other than being kind? They headed for an empty table. Ed ordered them both an agua limon, finely crushed ice flavoured with tangy lemon, which was the house speciality, then turned to her expectantly. 'I'd hoped I would see you again sooner,' he said.

'Our American clients haven't arrived yet,' she explained, pushing back her shoulders. 'Things will be on hold till I hear.'

'I didn't mean that, Alex.'

She wasn't sure what he meant. She thought of the barefoot woman. 'And of course there's no news about Chantelle Charpentier, so I'm keeping things ticking along. And Beth is still around, of course.'

Ed looked at her intently for just long enough to make her glance away.

'I saw Beth the other day, did she tell you?'

'Oh?' Alex drummed her fingernails lightly on the table. What on earth was Beth up to?

'Yes, her man and I have an acquaintance in common, a gallerist in Monaco. Raymond – it is Raymond, isn't it? – he does a bit of painting.'

Alex nodded, but she barely knew anything about

Raymond. The waiter delivered their orders.

'I've known the gallerist for some time, and he's honest with me. His opinion is that Raymond has more confidence than talent. But confidence has value in the art world.'

Alex stopped eating, waiting for Ed to say more. Perhaps Beth's smug appraisal of Ed Bronz and his past business dealings had some truth. Today, she didn't care.

'Poor Raymond,' she said.

'When I bumped into him and your daughter, he had just been told that the Greenwood gallery wouldn't accept his work, so perhaps I didn't meet him at the best time. That gallery might be a bit too established for him. But other dealers might like his style.'

Alex noted the name. 'Oh? You saw his work? What's it like?'

Ed pursed his lips and looked at the passing traffic.

'Ah,' Alex said.

'You have to be a genius to be truly original. Quite abstract. His use of colour is assured, but the technique needs refining. And the subject matter was cliché – chipped shutters on a Provençal farmhouse. Let's just say his best work is in front of him. I hope your daughter's not thinking of buying.'

'You sound as if you know what you're talking about.' She waited for him to add something, to mention the gallery Beth had read about, but he said simply, 'Anyone can be an art critic. It doesn't cost a penny.'

'I might have had enough of shutters for today,' Alex said. Ed swallowed large spoonfuls of agua limon as she described her conversation with the professor. She had expected him to laugh at her imitation of the professor stroking his pile of letters, but he remained silent, reflecting.

'I expect every old villa has a few secrets to hide,' she offered, to fill the silence.

Ed didn't appear to have heard.

'And he was actually walking around the garden of this villa? What's this professor's name?'

Ed's emphasis on the word professor seemed aggressive, and

Alex frowned. She had never heard anyone refer to the gauche academic by name. 'Well I don't know. I can find out. He's often at Maxie's. You think the professor might be on to something?'

'How long has he been working on this book?'

He also pronounced the word 'book' as if it were something unsavoury.

'Not long, from the sounds of it.'

Ed watched her as she ate, but she could tell he was thinking of something else.

He finished his ice and waved to the waiter.

'Your story has reminded me of something.'

'And you're not going to tell me what?'

'I don't want to bore you.' His full attention had returned to her now, and she took smaller, more delicate mouthfuls. 'But what I would like to do is have dinner with you again. Soon.'

Things were not getting simpler at all. This time, Ed Bronz was clearly asking her out, and without her daughter. And this time, accepting his invitation would clearly mean that she knew what he was doing. He pulled out a worn leather money-clip and put some notes on the table. 'There's something I must do,' he said. 'Can you forgive me for deserting you?'

'I think I won't be the first woman to do that, will I?'

Alex ordered a coffee when Ed left, and watched him as he walked, unhurried, back up Boulevard Gambetta. She imagined laughing with Meghan about the European swagger of his gait, but for once, it was something she couldn't imagine telling Rod.

Her phone rang as she swallowed the last of her coffee. The voice on the other end of the line could have belonged to a young girl.

'Hi, Mrs Coates? This is Natascha Barron.'

Part Two

CHAPTER TWENTY

When the sun is out, no matter what the season, there are sunbathers on the narrow strip of beach at Villefranche. The enormous bay is embraced on one side by the deep-green undulation of Cap Ferrat, and on the other by the medieval citadel above the village, overlooked by a bluff punctuated by houses burrowed into the rock. Together they protect the village and the beach, and the water is usually smooth, lapping onto the beach like the tiny waves of a transparent lake.

Alex floated on her stomach, watching flashes of silver fish darting among the leaves of seagrass beneath her through her dive mask. The only sound she could hear was the gentle pull and push of her own breath, and the mysterious scratchy roll of sand and salt – the noise of the Mediterranean. As she raised her head halfway above the water and looked at the beach, she could see Beth turn a page of her book. Alex swam gently for several minutes, parallel to the beach, glancing at her daughter now and again. Beth sat cross-legged on a rush beach mat, her head lowered to read. She looked up once, panning the water for her mother. They'd made themselves a huge *pan bagnat* this morning, the Niçois sandwich of tuna, olives, tomatoes and onion dripping with olive oil, which was packed in the basket at Beth's side. Alex was looking forward to it.

She pushed up her mask and rolled over to float on her back. The sky was a cloudless, piercing blue. For a few peaceful moments, Alex thought of nothing but the sway of her body in the water, but when she glanced up at the luxurious villas nestled in the rock above the beach, she thought again of Natascha Barron.

Nice-Matin had described the Barrons' arrival in detail, right down to the number of Louis Vuitton suitcases that were driven away from the airport. Natascha had been described as an exotic beauty, but when Alex was summoned to meet her over morning coffee at the Negresco hotel, she'd found a pale, tired girl with dark hair pulled into a loose ponytail.

True, Natascha was tall, with a model's long legs and natural elegance. Her skin had a flawless, airbrushed quality, emphasised by her high cheekbones and a broad forehead. Her knitted silk cardigan and tight leather jeans were simple, but Alex knew expensive clothes when she saw them. The diamond studs in Natascha's ears were small, but her left hand sparkled. She didn't look around the room, as if perhaps she would find too many people looking back. She hastily dismissed some of Alex's suggestions with a graceful flick of her hand, as if she were anxious to give the impression of being in control. Yet when Natascha accidentally upset a jug of hot milk over the table, she'd jumped up and dabbed frantically at the drops on Alex's skirt with a starched napkin. Her smooth cheeks instantly turned pink, and Alex saw nothing but childish vulnerability.

Alex couldn't tell if Michael Barron was a good match or not. He lolled with his legs apart in a chair beside Natascha, more interested in the other customers in the hotel's restaurant than in the conversation. He, too, was tall, and good-looking in an American sort of way, broad-shouldered and muscular beneath his light sweater. His teeth were alarmingly white, as if he'd never drunk coffee or red wine in his life. Not once, she noticed, did he return Natascha's touch as she rested her hand on his arm. His gaze swivelled towards Alex now and then, but each time she met his blue eyes, she saw boredom and impatience. She disliked him immensely. She was pleased when the upset milk splashed onto the crotch of his chinos, and he was forced to sit up properly and cross his legs.

'We found Mrs Charpentier so charming when we were introduced to her in New York,' Natascha said to Alex. 'Didn't we, Michael?'

Michael said, 'Mmm.'

'She seemed to understand right away what we want. Something simple but versatile, where we can be comfortable. She mentioned several places she thought would suit us.'

Natascha waited hopefully for Alex to confirm.

Alex hesitated before she said, 'Of course. Shall we start with the villa in Eze?'

Remembering Natascha's expectant smile, Alex shivered in the water. She swam for shore.

'Refreshing?' Beth asked. 'You were in for ages.'

Alex found her watch in the basket along with her towel, and checked the time.

'Only half an hour. It's given me an appetite.'

Beth put away her book and unwrapped their lunch as Alex dried herself off. She also uncorked a bottle of rosé wine and splashed a couple of inches into glass tumblers. They ate in companionable silence.

It was Meghan's birthday, and they had agreed to call her together.

'Time?' Beth asked.

Alex nodded. Beth wiped the oil off her hands and rang her sister. As Meghan answered, Beth waved her finger like a baton, counting them both into a chorus of Happy Birthday. It was raining in London, and Beth gleefully described the sky, the sunbathers, the shimmering water. She added a couple of degrees to the temperature. 'And we're toasting you with a nice little Côtes de Provence, too. Don't you wish you were here?' She held the phone out as she clinked her glass against Alex's.

'Don't overdo it,' Alex mouthed.

She listened as her daughters chattered. Meghan always had gossip about people they knew in common, and Beth's side of the conversation was punctuated by gasps of incredulity or derision, and bursts of laughter. Whatever mood Meghan found her sister in, she ploughed on regardless. Her attitude to Beth's changeable disposition had been to simply ignore it. Somehow that worked between them. But after a few minutes Beth frowned and looked at her mother over the top of her sunglasses. 'She didn't say anything to me about that,' she said to Meghan. 'Here she is anyway. Happy Birthday.' Beth shoved the phone towards Alex and whispered, 'Don't be long. This call's expensive.'

On the other end of the line, Alex could hear voices and laughter. Meghan was celebrating with Tom's family, and Alex felt a pang of longing. She'd sent Meg a present, a little silver palm tree she'd bought from Julie Eichenbaum – though Julie had so far refused to let Alex pay.

As soon as she took the phone, Alex heard Meghan hiss, 'Why didn't you tell Beth you'd agreed to go out with Ed Bronz again? You've dropped me in it now, Mum. She'll be furious because she didn't know.' It was true: Beth's expression had hardened. 'Don't blame me, will you?' Meghan continued. 'God, listen to me! I absolutely cannot believe that I have to avoid talking about my mother's *boyfriend*.' Alex could almost hear her slapping her hand to her forehead. 'Anyway, call me later, won't you? I want to hear the latest about Natascha Barron. Is the weather really lovely there? We must come as soon as Tom can get away.'

Alex poured more wine. 'Sounds like Meg's having a good birthday,' she said.

One look at Beth's face told her that Meghan's prediction was right. Beth was pouting like her grumpy eight-year-old self.

'Why didn't you tell me you'd seen Ed again?'

'Why didn't you tell *me*? 'Alex snapped back. She regretted it instantly.

'I forgot,' Beth said. 'It was so quick, he was just coming out of a gallery. You know, he's not your type, Mum.'

Alex laughed. 'What is my type?'

'Dad is, of course.'

 In the silence that followed, Beth picked up her book, and Alex lay back in the sunshine. The smooth stones cradled the small of her back through the mat. Just as she was beginning to doze, Beth cleared her throat.

'And anyway,' she said. 'Raymond's art dealer in Monaco says that Ed's still married.'

Alex didn't open her eyes. 'So what? We're not having an

affair. Why shouldn't I have dinner with him?'

'And that art collection? His wife sold most of it, all in one go.'

Alex sat up. 'Did she? How interesting.'

'It is not interesting, Mum! There's something sordid about it. It doesn't sound right at all.' She threw a stone petulantly into the water.

'What's not right? It must have been valuable. Anyway I'm not paying attention to your gossip.'

'Ha.' Beth began reading again, but before long she held her glass out for more wine. 'So does he have any children?'

Alex knew her daughter's curiosity would win out.

'A son, I think. Grown up. I don't think they're in touch.'

'That's sad. He must have done something awful to him.'

'Oh Beth, honestly. These things happen in families. Natascha and I will be seeing his house on the Avenue du Phare in the next few days, why don't you come too? You got on with Ed, so you can interrogate him yourself.'

'Very funny, Mum. I don't think I want to spend my time with Skinny Miss Moneybags, anyway. Just reading about all her Louis Vuitton travel trunks in *Nice-Matin* is enough to put me off.'

'You have better things to do with your time anyway,' Alex said. 'Have you been using Raymond's studio?'

The brim of Beth's sunhat hid her face as she slouched backwards. She sighed loudly. 'I've only been here a couple of weeks,' she said. 'What are you getting on my back for? This is supposed to be a break.'

'Of course it is, darling. I wondered, that's all. I love having you here. But you said yourself that your tutor was putting on pressure.'

Beth said nothing.

'The sooner you make progress, the sooner you'll be able to come back and really relax here. It'll be fun.'

'Nothing will be fun until that bloody Chantelle comes home. I don't know why you're making such a song and dance about taking care of her business.'

Alex could see Beth's pout beneath the brim of her hat.

'I can't abandon her, can I? It'll be sorted out soon. Anyway, you're changing the subject, sweetheart. I don't mind if you're not working, but you...'

'Then why are you asking?' Beth sat up and emptied what was left of her wine onto the stones. She started packing the basket.

Alex shook her head. Would she ever learn to see Beth's traps before they snapped shut?

'I'm really looking forward to when Meghan and the children come,' she said, but she could hear the strain in her own voice. 'By then you could've finished so much work. You won't have to worry about it. You can spend as long as you like here. It will be lovely when everyone's here, won't it?'

Beth stopped packing for a second, as if gathering strength, before turning to Alex.

'Well, everyone's never going to be here!' she shouted. A couple of terns that had been flitting along the beach flapped off in alarm. 'Don't you ever think about Dad any more?'

She got up, stumbling on the stones, and dropped Alex's jeans, cardigan and the keys to the Citroen on the beach mat.

'Don't be silly, Beth. Come on, stay with me.' But Beth was already stomping along the beach towards the steps that led to the train station. Alex lay back down and closed her eyes, rolling two pebbles in her fingers like worry beads.

CHAPTER TWENTY-ONE

Alex had started looking forward to her chats with Harry Bormann in New York. Chantelle's condition remained worryingly unchanged, but so far, the medical centre and the insurance company seemed to be managing the unusual circumstances between themselves. Relieved of that onerous responsibility, Harry had begun to relax.

'You know what, Alex, I feel weird admitting it, but I kind of *like* going to visit Chantelle, you know? I mean, she's so peaceful, and I just feel like I'm doing a good thing, you know what I mean? Like it's my good deed or something.'

He loved more than anything to discuss Natascha and Michael Barron.

'I swear Chantelle looks a little happier when I tell her about them,' he said. 'Like maybe she's trying to smile? Of course I tell her they love every property you show them. I don't want to upset her now.'

Alex had the impression that during their conversations, Harry made notes to relay to Chantelle. He interrupted her in mid-sentence to ask what Natascha had worn to see the villa in Eze. 'Prada,' he said confidently, after Alex had described all the way down to the elegantly comfortable suede lace-ups. Alex enjoyed this game.

It had been obvious from the start of the visit to the Eichenbaums' villa that it wasn't right for the Barrons. Natascha had looked almost stricken in the noisy lift, which had juddered to a brief, claustrophobic halt halfway up the hill before resuming its ascent.

When Alex got lost taking them through the maze of rooms, Natascha patted her shoulder comfortingly. She said, 'That's OK, Mrs Coates. Maybe this one is a little out of the way anyway.'

But she'd made a childish fuss of Julie Eichenbaum's monstrous dog, kneeling down to hug it, oblivious to the slobber he spattered all over her. She was delighted when she noticed that his paws were bigger than her own fists.

'I have to put up with this all the time,' Michael Barron said. There was no indulgence in his voice. 'She likes animals better than people.'

'They're nicer than people,' Natascha replied tartly.

Her attention had overexcited the dog, and soon his thick nails scratched the side of her thigh. Julie jerked him away by the collar so quickly he yelped.

'Don't do that, Mrs Eichenbaum! I can't stand to see an animal mistreated.'

Julie laughed. 'Is that what you call it? I'd call it saving your bacon.'

Natascha continued petting and cooing over the dog until at last Michael got back into the car, slamming the door hard.

'I'll leave the dog in the house with the furniture if you like, no extra charge,' Julie said.

'I wish,' Natascha replied. 'My dog Bruno died a few months ago, and this is the first time in my life I haven't had any pets.' She looked in Michael's direction and lowered her voice: 'We wouldn't be in Europe now if Bruno was still alive. I'd never have left him.'

After their frustratingly slow start, Chantelle's solicitors Quelin & Company had managed to get a few things moving. Quelin himself had come to the office to meet Alex. He was very much her idea of a capable expert, early 60s, tall and slim, with a patinated leather briefcase and shoes of a similar hue, but at first what he had had to say was disheartening. 'I can't divulge the contents of Madame Charpentier's *testament*, needless to say,' he'd explained slowly, as if he thought Alex's French wasn't up to it. 'My firm is to act as her executor. There are no direct relatives who would inherit, as is the case with French law, her estate, so the situation would be more complex without a will.'

'Oh dear,' Alex said. 'I don't think we're at that stage yet.'

'No,' agreed Monsieur Quelin, eyeing her over his reading glasses. 'But there is a will, and there are no named individuals with a potential to benefit from the estate. And of course we are looking for named individuals who may be able to make decisions on Chantelle's behalf.'

No named individuals. Certainly no brother. Had Chantelle left her estate to an animal charity? Alex couldn't imagine it.

She'd been glad he'd spoken slowly. What he said was becoming legalese.

'No cousins?' Alex asked.

'I can divulge absolutely nothing. *Absolument rien.*'

'But for the moment, Immobilier Charpentier has responsibilities. We need someone who has the authority to make decisions about the properties that Chantelle manages. Look, they incur costs.' Alex had put together a file for Monsieur Quelin. She waved it under his nose. He'd looked through the bills doubtfully.

'The suppliers will have to be patient until the *administrateur judiciaire* is satisfied.'

'Electricité de France won't.'

'I believe they have *résponsables* who occupy themselves with such situations.'

Alex had felt hopeful. 'When can you get in touch with them?'

Monsieur Quelin took off his glasses and put them back into a shagreen case. He snapped it shut. 'Considering the circumstances, we have applied for power of attorney, and we must wait for the power of attorney to be finalised before we can take an action of that sort. We must wait for the *administrateur.*'

It would probably take weeks. Nothing happened quickly when French bureaucrats were involved.

After her meeting with Monsieur Quelin, Alex had slumped over an espresso at Maxie's. Françoise leaned across the bar and patted her shoulder. 'Don't give up,' she advised. 'Quelin is good. His people are always in the newspaper. They're a big firm. They have clout.'

'Then why don't they use it? Why do things have to take so long in France?'

Alain was double-parking outside, and when he came through the door and saw Alex, he stood still and clasped his hands together.

Alex felt doubly hopeless as she remembered Alain sitting in his car, watching her hide from Ed in the restaurant doorway.

'Alex, you look defeated!'

'I feel defeated. The solicitors aren't in any hurry to help.'

'But they're doing things correctly,' Françoise said. 'The French way, *n'est-ce pas*?

She was already putting Alain's coffee on the bar, and wouldn't catch Alex's eye. How could Alex have forgotten she was the *Anglaise*?

'Of course they are. It wouldn't be for the best if they did it any other way. But Monsieur Quelin doesn't seem as eager to get things sorted out as I am.' She repeated her story to Alain.

'What do we know about Quelin, Françoise?' he asked. Françoise didn't answer, but Alex thought she saw her smile slyly.

Two days later, Monsieur Quelin rang Alex. He almost sounded apologetic. 'But Madame Coates, you didn't mention that you are a close friend of Alain Hubert's. He's told me how generous you are being with your time to Madame Charpentier, taking on so much on her behalf. I will after all make a few inquiries to see if we can expedite the situation.'

And quite soon the *administrateur judiciaire* had taken on the overdue bills that Alex dropped in to the firm's office.

Alex shared her progress with Harry Bormann. 'Wow, it's like Chantelle is charmed,' he said, as Alex was finishing her notes of Chantelle's insurance details. She'd pass them immediately to Quelin & Company. Harry backtracked quickly. 'Well, I mean… You know what I mean, charmed…in a certain kind of way. Don't you think?'

After her conversation with Harry, Alex sat in the late-afternoon sun on Chez Maxie's *terrasse*. Nearby, a young mother was doing a crossword while her toddler made a mess of a scoop of chocolate ice cream. Near the door, three businessmen had put their coffee cups aside and were crouched around a laptop on the table in front of them. Maxie came out now and again and stood with her hands on her hips, moving her head like a bird as she glanced from one side of the Place du Général de Gaulle to the other. Honda trotted about by himself, giving the toddler a wide berth. At the Café des Soldats opposite, the *terrasse* was empty.

Alex closed her eyes, but was roused within a minute by a warm, wet feeling on her arm. She jumped. Julie Eichenbaum was pulling her dog away.

'Sorry, sorry,' Julie said. 'Back, Lolly!' She sat down next to Alex, and the dog sat down beside her on the pavement. It was so tall that its head reached comfortably above the table, its snout resting within drooling range of Alex's cup. Julie didn't seem to notice. 'He gets over-excited in town. Only time I ever risk it is when I take him to the vet. He's had his teeth cleaned.'

The toddler had noticed the dog by now, and was hiding behind his mother's chair.

'He's trampled kids that size before, just trying to be friendly.' Julie laughed, then coughed, then lit a cigarette with the lighter she kept in the front of her overalls. 'So, no Mr and Mrs Barron for us, huh?'

Julie didn't seem in the least disappointed.

'I'm sorry nothing came of it,' Alex said, 'The location just wasn't right for them.'

'Aw, don't worry about it.' Three perfect smoke rings floated across the table. 'I didn't think they'd be so young, those Barrons. Too bad they married each other, they could've spread the money around.'

Alex would've agreed, but she still wanted to appear professional.

'Yes, I understand they're both from wealthy families.'

'You're not kidding. The girl alone could be in line for megabucks. My husband asked around, did a little research on them. There's some big fuss going on, about Daddy's art collection. Looks like Daddy might have made a few duff purchases – or else he was up to no good.' Julie settled back in her chair and stretched her legs out, resting them on Lolly's back. 'Maybe it's a good thing the groom has his own back-up fortune.'

Alex recalled what she had read in *Le Monde* about Uri Raskilovich's art collection. She was niggled by a worry that she had underestimated the sort of house the Barrons would expect. With that sort of wealth, perhaps they were interested in much grander places than she could possibly ever imagine – much grander than Julie's villa in the sky. She thought back over the dossier. Had she seen any châteaux?

While Alex had another coffee, Julie had a whisky on the rocks. Lolly slurped water out of Honda's water bowl, and passers-by were either drawn or repelled by the giant beast. 'Half dragon, half Chihuahua,' Julie said with a deadpan expression to one teenage boy who asked about the dog's breed. 'His mother was a gargoyle, his father was a greyhound,' she said to another. Her French was faultless, though her strong accent made Alex wince.

'So, that guy Sal was talking about, he still works here?' She flicked her cigarette ash towards Immobilier Charpentier's office.

Alex looked around for Guillaume's truck or his motorbike, and was relieved to see neither. She nodded.

'Sorry about Sal. He gets hell-bent on whatever he does and has no idea he comes over like a steam train.'

'My boss loves Guillaume. Everyone seems to.'

'Maybe Sal's got the wrong guy.' Julie's toes wriggled in the dog's fur. 'But he's usually right about things, damn him.'

When, after another cigarette, Julie said it was time to go, Alex found she was disappointed.

The sun dipped below the buildings on the west side of the Place, and the sudden shade felt chilly. Alex put on her sweater and went to pay. There were two men in workers' overalls drinking beer at a back table, but otherwise the restaurant was empty. Maxie sat behind the bar, surrounded by paperwork. '*Quelle bête!*' she said. 'What a beast! You could get a few chops out of that dog. Which reminds me, Alex, your friend Mr Bronz came in a few days ago. He had the *gigot* – that was my *plat du jour,* leg of lamb. We're beginning to see beautiful lamb from Sisteron, so don't worry, you haven't missed it altogether. He asked after you. That's how I knew who he was. No dessert, though, not even a coffee.'

'Oh? Alone?' Alex didn't bother trying to disguise her curiosity.

'*Non.* But he sat with the professor. I heard them mention the Menier villa, and I thought he'd be happy, our intellectual friend, but he looked quite pale. I must encourage him to eat more *gigot*. It'll be good for him.'

Ed Bronz talking to the professor? Her shoulders slumped as she went over the conversation she and Ed had had the day that Natascha had first phoned. The poor professor would crumple under Ed's aggressive interest in the shutters.

Alex had been over the properties in Chantelle's file so many times that she knew them almost word for word. Now, back in the office, she flicked through the dossier, hopeful she'd missed something grand. But there was nothing; Alex couldn't turn up more choices than she already had. Unlike Chantelle, she had no contacts that stretched back years, and certainly none of her employer's ruthless, if charming, guile.

She absently smoothed some of the papers from the back of the dossier, where she'd put what seemed like the oldest and least hopeful cuttings. The news stories seemed so dated now. A van transporting a delivery of electric typewriters had skidded off the road near the village of Peille, killing the driver. She turned this cutting over to find the date, and saw with a start what looked like Ed's house. There were the two circular windows in the upper storey that she'd admired.

Chantelle hadn't made any notes on this cutting, but it was snipped neatly. Yes, it was definitely Ed's house. The story reported that police had been investigating anonymous claims that the house was being used as a drop point for stolen goods. Alex took out her dictionary to look up the phrase. She wrote it in her notebook. There were suggestions, the story said, that stolen art was passing through the house. After keeping the property under surveillance for several weeks, the police entered. Nothing was found. However, a person in the grounds who was challenged to stop assaulted a policeman, breaking his jaw. He jumped over a garden wall and escaped in a car parked on the other side. Police fired two shots at the car, but it got away. The owners of the house were said to be Russians. They were unavailable for comment. Investigations were continuing.

The full date on the cutting had been obliterated, but Alex could tell from what remained that it was an edition from September 1980. She turned the pages of the notebook – she'd already instinctively cross-referenced some dates, and she'd made one for 1980. So far, there was only one entry, also from September: the catastrophic fire at the Menier villa.

CHAPTER TWENTY-TWO

Natascha and Michael Barron were staying in an apartment on the Promenade des Anglais owned by Michael's uncle. On the day of their appointment to view the Valentin villa, Alex pressed a buzzer set into brass beside the plate glass of the entrance door, and stepped back to look up at the modern building.

Before there was a reply, the glass door opened, and Michael Barron leaned against it as he waited for Alex to enter. His blond hair was either wet or slathered with something greasy, and he seemed to be on his way out.

'Oh,' said Alex. 'I haven't made a mistake, have I? Aren't you expecting me? To see the Valentin villa on Cap Ferrat?'

'Yeah,' Michael said. 'Come in. She's upstairs. Top floor.' As he left, and Alex entered, Natascha's girlish voice came through the entry phone outside.

'Mrs Coates?' She sounded anxious. 'Are you there? Can you see Michael?' Her voice was rising. 'Is he there? Mrs Coates?'

Alex waited for Michael to do something. She was seized with a curious mix of embarrassment and interest. He let the door click shut and put his face up to the glass from outside, raising a finger to his lips like a child playing a game. Then he headed towards the Negresco Hotel.

'Mrs Coates?' Alex could hear Natascha's voice on the Entryphone through the heavy glass. She heaved it back open and leaned out to speak into it.

'Yes, Natascha, it's me.'

Natascha answered the front door of the apartment wrapped in a short white towel, another white towel turbaned on her head. Alex thought her eyes looked puffy.

'I am so sorry,' she said. 'I should have called to let you know we were running behind schedule.' She beckoned Alex into a long, white hall. The only visible colour was on Natascha's manicured scarlet toes.

'Did you bump into Michael as you came in?' She led Alex through one of several doors along the hall. She glanced briefly over her smooth bare shoulders.

'I was too busy admiring the foyer,' Alex said. Liar, liar, pants on fire, the girls used to shout when they were children.

The living room in which Natascha, apologising again, left Alex while she went to get dressed, could have been a vintage furniture shop. There were 1960s-style white sofas with matching armchairs, square glass coffee tables with stainless-steel legs, and stainless-steel lamps with shades like beauty salon hair-dryers, which swung into awkward places on thin, arched stands.

The apartment was just about level with the tops of palm trees on the Promenade des Anglais below, and Alex watched them dance in the breeze through tall windows. She mentally redecorated the room, keeping only a mirrored-glass cocktail cabinet and one of the sofas, which she'd discovered to be soft and giving. But by then she was becoming impatient.

She peeped out into the hall. Somewhere, water was running. She walked in the opposite direction. Almost before she realised it, she was looking through an open door, into a long, narrow room as white as the living room. A woman sitting at a table jumped up, throwing a grey cloth over what Alex thought were a collection of guns arranged in front of her.

Her shoulder banged heavily against the doorframe in her rush to get out. 'Excuse me!' Alex whispered, her mouth instantly dry. The woman came running after her, sandals flapping.

'No, no, excuse me!' the woman said. The white shirt that billowed out of the waistband of her black skirt emphasised how thin she was. 'Please, Madame, what you like? Coffee? Tea?' Alex couldn't place her accent. Could she be a maid? Alex shook her head and almost ran to the living room, but the woman followed. 'A croissant? A tartine?'

'No, no, really.'

The woman stood by the door for a moment as Alex sat

down, hugging a white cushion. She looked at Alex closely and then laughed, showing a gold front tooth. 'Don't have to worry about guns, no bullets!' she said. 'Cleaning only! Very safe. Look!' She pointed towards the cocktail cabinet, and above it Alex saw a framed photograph of an elderly man with a gold trophy in what might have been a shooting range. 'Only sport, see?'

The woman glanced quickly down the hall, then took a step into the room.

'You nice lady from England Chez Maxie,'

Alex examined her tired face. 'I am *maman* Sammy!' She patted her breast.

'Of course,' said Alex, releasing her grip on the cushion. 'You work at the Eichenbaums' villa.'

'Sammy is a good boy,' his mother said in English. 'But Madame Julie in Eze finish soon. You tell Sammy if you need maid, ok? I have many experience. I work for Monsieur Barron long time.'

Alex was confused. 'Michael Barron?'

Sammy's mother made a disgusted, guttural noise while flicking her fingers, as if throwing something away. 'Not him! Uncle Barron, in photograph. Good Uncle Barron. But he only comes here one month, too busy. This boy Michael is not a good Barron. Bad, bad.' She sucked her teeth as if she'd found a worm in a lemon. 'Girls, girls, already! And not married one year. Bad.'

A door banged down the hall. 'Glad they don't like Madame Julie house. Too good for a bad man.' Sammy's mother's eyes shone as she backed out into the hall. 'Don't forget job!'

Alex heard Natascha call to Sammy's mother, in perfect French, asking her to bring her green bag. Then she appeared in the doorway, adjusting a tight green dress around her narrow hips. When she sat on one of the big white sofas, she was like an emerald dropped in the snow. She looked at Alex calmly, as if she were used to being admired. 'Sara's the cleaning woman,' she said. 'Michael's great uncle asked us to keep her on while we're here.' She rubbed at a mark on the green bag.

'Keeping all this whiteness clean must be a full-time job,' said Alex.

'Oh, she's not full-time, thank goodness. She comes in to keep everything ready for Michael's uncle, but she doesn't seem happy about doing anything we ask. We'll have to get all fixed up with that kind of thing.' Natascha looked at Alex hopefully, her smooth cheeks just starting to turn pink. 'You know, the help. I'm sure you'll be able to advise me.'

'I…' Alex thought immediately of Chantelle. 'I'd be delighted to help you.'

There was no mention of Michael until they were in Chantelle's Citroen, climbing above the port with the open sea glittering on their right.

'My husband had to see some people about a boat,' she volunteered suddenly, as if the excuse had just come to her. 'He sails.' She looked out at the sea. 'Do you sail?'

The tiny sailboat Rod had at one time kept at a public sailing club along the Thames probably didn't count in Natascha's world. In any case, Alex had no time to reply before Natascha said, 'I don't sail myself. All that being sideways nauseates me. Something to do with my inner ear. Michael doesn't understand.'

'I only like motor yachts – preferably moored,' Alex said, to be sympathetic.

'Oh, you do? Me too. Our boat was called *Natascha's Smile*. My father's boat, I mean. I loved it so much.' Natascha sighed. 'They've already sold it, though. We have, I mean. You can't change a boat's name, did you know that?'

Alex tried to remember the sailboat's name. How could she have forgotten? She could see it now, its faded blue sail rolled up as Rod pushed it along in the water one long-ago summer, Meghan and Beth trailing sunburned legs over the bow.

'Michael's probably in Antibes,' Natascha said. 'I don't like it there. I'd much rather be near Nice. Have you been here long, Mrs Coates? You seem to know your way around.'

They stopped at a traffic light near a small row of shops, including a butcher's. A delivery truck was parked outside, half mounted on the pavement. The Citroen was almost level with it. A man in a bloody white coat came out of the butcher's and pulled the back door of the truck closed, bringing a whiff of raw meat with it.

'Oh!' Natascha cried. 'I can't bear it!' She covered her nose and mouth with her hand. 'I'm not being precious, Mrs Coates. Michael always says I'm making a fuss, but honestly, I can't bear the thought of those poor animals in a slaughterhouse. The cruelty makes me ache.'

The light changed and Alex pulled away quickly.

'I guess you've realised I'm a vegetarian,' Natascha said. 'I've never eaten meat in my life, not once.' She giggled, and although Natascha was taller than her, Alex had the impression she was sitting beside a child. 'But don't worry, Mrs Coates. I don't nag people who eat meat.' She unclasped her green bag and took out a pair of sunglasses. 'At least, not any more.'

CHAPTER TWENTY-THREE

Liliane Valentin was on the driveway as the Citroen arrived. She grasped both of Alex's hands in hers, tilting her head and smiling as if greeting a dear friend. She led her around the car to be introduced to Natascha. Natascha seemed to grow an inch as she shook Liliane's hand briefly, dropped it, and walked back up the drive to look at the house from a distance. Liliane trotted after her.

Alex hadn't seen the entire villa before. She loved it even more when Liliane opened the shutters in one dust-sheeted bedroom to reveal a golden wall of bamboo in the overgrown garden, rustling hypnotically around a balcony. In the master bedroom beneath, the dressing room was lined from floor to ceiling with cedar drawers that still released a clean, woody odour when, at Liliane's urging, Natascha pulled them open. Each one had a worn ivory label on the front: *chaussettes de coton* – cotton socks; *chaussettes de soie* – silk socks; *mouchoirs* – handkerchiefs, petticoats, collars, summer pyjamas… Alex looked in as eagerly as Natascha, but everything had gone.

'It's adorable,' Natascha said. Liliane puffed up. 'But the house needs a lot of work. I don't know if my husband would have the patience. I don't know if I'm ready to take on something like this until I – we – are more established on the Riviera.'

Liliane was prepared. 'You won't have to lift a finger,' she assured Natascha, leading them back downstairs. 'I've got someone who can help.'

Standing in one of the archways to the airy living room was the odious Paulette Bitoun.

'Madame Barron!' Paulette's deep purple lips opened wide as she spoke. They were an exact colour match for the enormous stones on her necklace. The skirt of her mauve suit bound her tightly around the knees. She minced towards Natascha. 'We delight you are come to ze beautiful France,' she said in

English, grabbing the girl's hand. Her accent was strong.

'We're pleased to be here,' Natascha replied in French. She was unfazed. Perhaps, Alex thought, she meets people like this all the time.

'Paulette is my interior designer,' Liliane explained, as if everyone had one. 'I know that there is much to be done, but Paulette has such an eye. She has worked on some of the most beautiful properties in the area, haven't you?'

Paulette, who had placed herself squarely between Alex and Natascha without even a glimpse at Alex, touched her plump fingers to her cheek girlishly. Alex sighed.

'Yes, and many apartments in Paris, too. My work has even been in English magazines!'

'That's exciting,' Natascha said flatly. She continued the conversation in French. 'Perhaps you could give me your card, Mrs Bitoun, and I could call you another time.'

Whenever Alex moved, Paulette's bulk blocked her view of Natascha's face.

'But I have my portfolio with me. Please, let's sit down. Liliane, you won't mind?'

Alex realised that everything must have been pre-arranged between the two. Liliane had extended the oval dining-room table so that Paulette's work could be spread out. It was made of brilliantly polished oak, with room for 10, but there were only four chairs. Alex didn't sit down, but stood by the French doors that opened onto a now-weed-filled stone patio.

'The Valentin house has character, but it's time for modernisation,' Paulette was saying. Liliane, seated next to Natascha, nodded. 'For example, these windows – how can we enjoy the view? They are so narrow, so old-fashioned. Replacing them with folding glass panels would take years off the house.' She slid some of the pictures on the table around. 'Here, Madame Barron, is something I created for a house in Cannes – it belongs to an American banker.' Natascha looked at it briefly before turning to Alex.

'What do you think, Mrs Coates?'

Paulette squeaked.

'What would Madame Coates know? She is not a designer!' Paulette said. 'She's no more than a secretary!'

If Alex could have reached Paulette across the table, she would have hit her. She visualised herself doing it, happily. Natascha and Liliane were both silent, the air thick with their unease. Alex took the photograph.

'It's sweet for the provinces,' she said in English, enunciating so Paulette would be sure to understand, 'but it's not what we're doing in London and New York.'

'I agree,' Natascha said. That Paulette had insulted Alex could hardly have escaped her notice. 'I'd never replace these gorgeous windows with something so modern.'

Liliane looked alarmed. The great *amitié* she had clearly expected between her prospective tenant and the designer was not developing.

'In fact,' Natascha continued, 'I don't think I'd change much at all. I'd just want to refresh the look, tighten it up a bit. Sleek up the kitchen, too. My husband can't live without his wine cellar, his gym equipment...' She stood up and went over to the windows.

Liliane relaxed a bit, collecting up Paulette's photographs and piling them roughly on the end of the table. 'That might be best,' she said. 'I'm sure you'd bring fresh new ideas to the house. Everyone would be so thrilled with a change. *Alors*, I must tell you all about my secret suppliers in Monaco and Cannes!'

The colour of Paulette's jowls now matched her lips.

'You look a little warm, Madame Bitoun,' Alex said happily. 'Can I open the window for you?'

The designer was about to say something when Natascha yelped softly and placed both hands on the glass of the windows. 'Kittens!' she said. 'How adorable! Aren't they just so cute?' She pulled at the brass handle but it wouldn't turn.

Liliane jumped up from the table and peered out over the patio.

'*Ce n'est pas possible*,' she cried. 'It's not possible. I thought your gardener was getting rid of these creatures.'

Natascha laughed as three or four white kittens with black tails gambolled after their mother towards the hedge at the edge of the garden. It seemed to Alex that the child within her appeared quickly, and the emerald-green dress and expensive leather bag were nothing more than dressing-up clothes. Alex hoped Natascha had some kind aunts at home to watch out for her, friends to trust – someone in addition to Michael Barron.

'Why didn't your man finish the job?' Liliane turned to Alex. 'We simply cannot have these animals near the property.'

Paulette now moved to the window, too. 'Do you mean that Guillaume? Ha! My dear Liliane, let me tell you…'

'What are you talking about?' Natascha interrupted. 'The kittens are gorgeous. Look, there they go! Can you still see them?'

'They have to be got rid of,' Liliane explained. 'The noise! The smell!' She touched a corner of her Hermès scarf to her nose.

'I don't understand what you're talking about,' Natascha said. She jiggled the handle again. 'Do you mean putting them down! Nobody does that kind of thing now!'

Alex moved forward and turned the brass handle so the bar slid out of the sockets at the top and bottom of the frame, releasing the door.

Within a few moments, Natascha had run onto the lawn and found the hole in the rhododendron hedge. Liliane tutted.

'What are we to make of this, Mrs Coates? I didn't know *les Américains* were so devoted to animals. But isn't Madame Barron just *adorable*? Though I was expecting someone less capricious. Do you think she'll take the house? She seems to like it. The husband will have to see it, I suppose.' She sighed at the thought of the inconvenience.

The three women waited. The hedge trembled. Paulette said, 'Madame Charpentier would not have let this happen. Can you see it? Losing an important client through a hole in the hedge?'

Even the sound of the designer's voice was too much for Alex to bear and she went to find Natascha.

She was standing on the far side of the lawn of the villa on the Avenue Jean Cocteau, her back to the sea, facing the house. She waved at Alex.

'Have you found the kittens?' Alex called. The luminous sea sparkled behind Natascha.

'They ran under the door of that building.' She pointed to the garage where Alex and Guillaume had first seen the cats. 'Mrs Valentin doesn't really mean having them put down, does she? I can't bear to think about it.' Her eyes were moist. 'I couldn't live in her house if that's what she's capable of.'

'She spends all her time in Paris, you'd never see her. Don't let that influence you.'

'And that other woman! How rude!'

Alex laughed. 'She's not my favourite person either.'

They began walking back towards the house.

'Besides, I don't need a designer. I want to do all my own interiors. What I really want is to open a business, have a showroom or a boutique. But of course they're all dead set against it.' She folded her arms across her chest. 'Even my father, he said it wasn't our kind of thing. He wanted me to be an art dealer, but all those rich people and their money…' She laughed suddenly. 'Oh, I'm sorry. That sounds silly.'

'Not at all,' Alex replied. 'I know what you mean.' But she could barely believe her naiveté.

They had reached the smooth marble steps that led up to the villa's back *terrasse*. 'I like the look of this house much more than Madame Valentin's.' Natascha said. 'It's not big, but we don't want anywhere too big. Well, I don't, anyway.' Her eyes scanned the large garden. 'Is this house also available?'

What would Chantelle do? Alex knew from the files back at the office that Immobilier Charpentier oversaw the gardeners and cleaners here, and that Guillaume checked the building. He'd mentioned the owners rarely visited. Might they be interested in selling, if there were an irresistible offer?

'The owners don't use it often,' Alex said doubtfully.

Natascha beamed.

'Really? So maybe they'd consider selling!' She ran up the steps to the terrace and brushed her hand along the trimmed top of a lavender shrub. 'Please Mrs Coates? Can we give it a try?'

'Perhaps I could arrange for you to have a quick look inside before we think about getting in touch to ask the owners.'

Natascha clapped her hands together as Alex keyed in Guillaume's number on her mobile.

Guillaume tutted over the phone. Alex had the impression he thought she was committing an indiscretion, letting a stranger into the property, as if it were evidence of a particularly English lack of judgement. She wandered around the garage out of earshot of Natascha, cajoling him. The girl's hardly a stranger, she said. Wouldn't Chantelle have done the same? This might be the perfect solution. And anyway, the owners rarely appeared, hadn't he said so himself?

Guillaume relented. If Madame the American was prepared to wait, he could be there within 20 minutes.

Alex took a deep breath. She snapped a twig of rosemary from a bush along the drive, and crushed the leaves in the palm of her hand, inhaling the scent.

'We're in luck,' she said to Natascha, who was now sitting comfortably on the steps. 'The keys are on the way.'

Natascha stretched her long legs and said, 'We should go and tell Madame Valentin that we'll put her house on the longlist for now.'

She didn't get up.

'The thing is, now that she'd....' She wrinkled her nose in distaste and continued; '...that she'd put these kittens down, I don't think I even want to see her.'

She stood up and walked over to the garage where the kittens disappeared. She picked up a stick and pushed it underneath the door, as if trying to play with the kittens.

'They won't come out,' she said. 'They're scared. I hate it when animals are scared, don't you? All those poor cows to the slaughter. All those poor cats and monkeys, you know, for experiments. I just can't bear to imagine it.'

'You don't have to,' Alex laughed. 'Not with these spoiled little animals. Our handyman is taking the best possible care of them.'

Natascha appeared to cheer up.

'Come on, let's go and face the music.'

Paulette Bitoun tried her best to be included in the visit to the villa on the Avenue Jean Cocteau. She knew that house, she said, she had ideas that Natascha would find divine, she had a special relationship with a landscape architect who would replace the terrace with a deck… Natascha listened politely. They had gathered back in the dining room, and as Paulette droned on, she tottered closer and closer. Natascha stood her ground until the designer grabbed her hand. Natascha tore her hand away and moved closer to Alex.

'Madame Bitoun, I won't be needing an interior designer.'

Paulette's lips hung open in distaste.

'I prefer to do my own work. As a matter of fact, I've just been talking with Mrs Coates about setting something up here on the Riviera. Right, Mrs Coates? I'm sure we can exchange ideas though… in the future.'

Paulette at last looked at Alex. She would have smirked, but the designer's expression was so venomous that she felt momentarily rattled.

CHAPTER TWENTY-FOUR

Guillaume's pick-up was in the drive when Alex and Natascha pushed back through the hedge from the Valentin villa, but he was nowhere to be seen. He had already unlocked the front door, and Alex pushed it open hesitantly.

'Mmm, wood polish!' Natascha said, following behind. 'It reminds me of my boarding school. I love that smell!'

Her voice trailed off as Alex slid open the double doors to the living room.

'Well,' she said. 'Would you look at that.'

In the centre of the room was a huge black sculpture, polished until it shone. Alex and Natascha were reflected in the fat, round buttocks of a woman about nine feet tall.

'Now that's what I call a centrepiece,' Natascha said. She immediately put both hands on the buttocks. The voluptuous naked woman, standing flatly on both feet, with enormous arms crossed over her stomach, was smoking a cigarette. Each toe was like a little black ball, each forearm as big as a watermelon, each breast an ebony beach ball. Her eyes were closed and her mouth was formed into a sultry 'O' as if she were blowing smoke rings towards the garden.

'She makes me want to strip off and have a cigarette,' Alex said.

Natascha laughed. 'That's the sort of reaction an artist would be aiming at. She might be a Botero, a South American artist. My father had a couple of small ones. Isn't she amazing? Do you collect art, Mrs Coates?'

Alex thought the question was sweet. She and Rod had never had much money to spare – most of their pictures came from junk shops, or as gifts from friends.

'Michael wouldn't even recognise a Picasso!' Natascha smiled indulgently. 'But my father and I talked about art all the time. He was so passionate. He would be so distressed to know...'

Alex waited, hoping Natascha might say something about the family's art collection, but she simply bit the inside of her cheek, creating the suggestion of fines lines in her otherwise flawless white skin. 'Well, the estate, it's so convoluted. I wish I could... Oh, the lawyers will sort everything out, I guess.' She slapped the sculpture's buttocks lightly, and giggled.

They prowled the house together. Natascha was careful to close doors behind her and to open cupboards gently. Someone here loved cooking – the kitchen was stocked with well-used copper pots and pans, and a scarred butcher's block had been covered up with protective muslin. In the formal dining room, there were leather-bound photograph albums on a sideboard. Alex opened one tentatively. She glimpsed a young family in what was probably the 1970s – a swimming pool, a picnic, Christmas, pet dogs. Alex thought, how much money do you need to keep a whole house waiting for years?

She snapped the album shut as she heard Guillaume calling from the hall.

'Good, you're in,' he said. 'Will you lock up, or shall I wait?'

'We'll be done in a minute. Mrs Barron's in the living room. Guillaume, there are still some cats on the property. Mrs Valentin saw them.'

He shook his head, puffed his cheeks, scratched his wiry hair. 'I can't take care of every cat in the neighbourhood for the sake of that silly woman.'

Alex was just about to try convincing him when Natascha appeared in the hall. Alex would have introduced them, but the moment Guillaume saw the American girl, he seemed to freeze. He stared up at her face as if trying to place her, his eyes narrowing, then widening. He stepped back and the set of keys slipped from his hand onto the terracotta tiles. Natascha moved as if to pick them up for him.

'I think...' she began, but Guillaume cut her off.

'Raskilovich!' he whispered. Alex had never seen him look so concerned. He turned to Alex. 'Raskilovich!' This time there was reproach in his voice. 'Why didn't I think?'

He swiped up the keyring and walked back out the front door. Alex and Natascha looked at each other in silence as the pick-up's door slammed.

What the hell is the matter with him now, Alex thought. She began to apologise, but Natascha stopped her.

'Mrs Coates, don't worry. I'm used to it. Sometimes people have strange reactions to my name. I guess I can't hide behind being Mrs Barron after all.'

CHAPTER TWENTY-FIVE

The number of outdoor tables at Chez Maxie increased every day as the sun inched further along the *terrasse.* The blonde *serveuse* no longer had the time to smoke and chat on her phone. Now she ferried cups of coffee from the bar to the customers outdoors, sometimes an early glass of rosé or one of the odd drinks that Alex found peculiarly French – a *diabolo menthe*, the mint and lemonade mix that looked like washing-up liquid on ice, or the cold beer and grenadine syrup they called a *Monaco*. She ordered *un café*, resting one lump of sugar on her spoon and dipping it into the thick coffee until it had melted.

But there was no time for taking things slowly. Immobilier Charpentier had plenty to manage, not least the constant stream of people who dropped in every day to ask after Chantelle. Chantelle's accountant sent a shy young assistant to spend an afternoon with Alex, guiding her just enough to keep Chantelle's paperwork within the labyrinthine bounds of French law. Maxie and Françoise sent over customers they knew Alex would want to meet, including the concierge of Chantelle's apartment building, who promised to drop by with her post. Maxie said, 'Take advantage. Soon we'll get you all the right contacts.'

But there was one person Alex couldn't manage without. In the days that had passed since their meeting with Natascha at the Avenue Jean Cocteau, Guillaume had been less present than ever.

'Listen,' Françoise said to her, when yet again Alex asked if she'd seen him coming or going. 'He's been unpredictable for a long time, ever since…' her voice trailed off. Alex was standing at the bar waiting for her espresso. She was making her own coffee in the office less and less.

'But he seemed so shocked to see her. I can't figure it out. He couldn't possibly have met Natascha before.'

Françoise rapped the metal filter on the edge of the special drawer below the bar to empty the grouts. When she had filled the filter with ground coffee, she jammed it back into the Gaggia and secured it with a rough tug of the handle. As she waited for the cup to fill, she rested one hand on the handle and the other on her hip, reminding Alex fleetingly of an old engineer.

'Not face to face, at least,' Françoise said. The *serveuse* came in and out, calling the drinks orders at the bar. Alex waited for a moment of calm.

'Alright, I'll tell you a few things,' Françoise said eventually. She lowered her voice so that Alex could barely hear above the din. 'But never let Guillaume know. I'm telling you to make things easier for you.'

In between the interruptions, Alex learned about the death of Guillaume's daughter.

Cecile had been a beautiful girl, Françoise told her, a surprise to everyone, not least to Guillaume and his wife Therese, a tiny dumpling of a woman. When Cecile was born, Therese was an art teacher who gave private lessons in her own small studio. Guillaume – a cabinetmaker in those days, with his own business – made easels and frames for her students. The baby gurgled away in the corner of the classes.

They were a happy couple before the child was born, Françoise said. But when Cecile entered their lives, their joy was infectious. Unlike many Niçois men, Guillaume was proud to push his little daughter's pram around the streets, delighted when even strangers stopped him to comment on how remarkably pretty she was.

Getting everything she wanted didn't spoil Cecile. All the children, including Maxie, wanted to play at the Chapel house. But all Cecile wanted was to play with her animals, the cats, dogs, mice and birds her parents gave her.

'Too many, in my opinion,' Françoise said. 'Therese was like a zookeeper.'

Cecile was clever, too. But one day, when she was about 16,

there was an accident

An ironwork gate outside the school was rusty and loose, and it gave way as Cecile swung on it. Her face caught against it. A ragged metal point tore her cheek from below the eye to her chin.

'She looked like a ghoul,' Françoise said, running her index finger in a jagged line down her own cheek. 'No wonder she was so depressed.'

Therese and Guillaume were beside themselves. Their gorgeous girl, who had been so easy-going and loving, withdrew from them and everyone else, refusing to go back to school and rarely leaving the house. It would have been a tragedy for any child, but the angry red scar was such a contrast with her unusual beauty that if people didn't stare, they looked away. Therese gave up her studio to be with Cecile. Guillaume became moody and sour. He lost business, obsessed with trying to sue the school for negligence, building up debts in the process. 'It was about this time that he began to work for Chantelle,' Françoise said.

The scar began to fade. Cecile seemed quieter than she had been, but that happens sometimes as they get older, doesn't it, said Françoise.

Eventually, the girl's spirit returned. 'But Guillaume had changed. He was always waiting for something to happen after that,' Françoise said sadly. 'Some nasty surprise. He was never our Guillaume again after that.' Cecile had to redo a year at school, but went on to university, studying sciences.

'And then she went to work in Marseilles, for a big pharmaceutical company. I've got no idea what she was doing...too complicated for my little brain,' Françoise tapped the side of her head. Somehow even the scar itself turned into no more than a smooth, pale thread.

The pharmaceutical company was targeted by animal rights activists.

'It was ridiculous, really, they'd made a mistake. Cecile would never have worked anywhere that hurt animals. She and her mother were crazy about them.' She jutted her chin towards some photographs pinned behind bottles on the shelf above. 'Look, on the left.' Alex put on her glasses. In one photo, a thinner Maxie was kissing a puppy. Another woman, with her chin resting on top of Maxie's head, was facing the camera. Françoise moved a bottle aside so Alex could see. The dark-haired woman's smile was lop-sided, the skin of her cheek lightly pulled by a scar. 'She was always finding new homes for some poor beast she'd found. That's Honda. He was hit by a car. That's how he got that name.'

Françoise stood on her tiptoes to inch the bottle back into place. The activists weren't the sort to just march up and down with placards, she said. They were a sophisticated group with a lot of funding. One of them was even able to get a job as a driver for the director of the company. Cecile sometimes went to meetings with this director. He'd even drive himself, on occasion. But one day, the director was unwell, and couldn't attend an important meeting. He needed Cecile to go in his place. The driver had asked for the day off, so Cecile decided to drive herself. She went to pick up the car from the director's home.

'She insisted on taking the car,' said Françoise, hissing the 's'. 'Insisted. That's what the director said, we all read it in *Nice-Matin*.'

The animal rights activists used a home-made device which blew up when Cecile turned the key that morning.

'Oh my god!' Alex slapped her hand to her mouth. Her eyes shot to the photograph behind Françoise. She imagined her own Meghan climbing busily into her SUV one sunny morning, waving goodbye to the children, and her throat ached.

The *serveuse* called an order. Françoise stopped talking and lined up saucers on the counter. Alex pulled spoons and sugar from the box on the bar and placed them on the saucers for her.

Françoise continued. 'They were after the director, of course. It wasn't his fault. But Therese didn't see it like that.

At the funeral, the only time she moved was to scream at the director of the company. 'What a tirade,' Françoise said, with admiration. 'It wasn't as if the director forced Cecile to take the car and go in his place... Well, we could all tell Therese wasn't in her right mind.'

Four months later, she took a fatal overdose. Guillaume carried on. He did more and more work for Chantelle, finishing off jobs at night if he could, a solitary figure who began to avoid even his oldest friends. The following summer, no one was truly shocked when a Range Rover was set alight one night near the Beau Rivage hotel on the Promenade des Anglais. It belonged to the director of Cecile's company, who was on holiday in Nice – the one who'd asked Cecile to go to the meeting instead of him. No one was hurt then, but Guillaume, eventually, was convicted for the crime.

Revenge, thought Alex. Sal Eichenbaum was right.

'We stuck by him, of course,' said Françoise. 'He'd had such a difficult time. Chantelle couldn't have been more loyal. You might have done it yourself, under the circumstances. But the law is the law.'

Orders for wine and beer arrived with the lunchtime customers now. Alex tapped her watch to see it was still working.

'And the driver?'

Françoise puffed out her cheeks – a familiar gesture that said, who knows? 'Those animal rights people got everything wrong. Their conscience will give them what they deserve.'

CHAPTER TWENTY-SIX

Alex walked out into the blinding sunlight of the terrasse, feeling shaky with sadness.

Someone shouted, 'Mum! Mum, over here!'

At first Alex didn't look around as she headed for the office, but the call from one of the tables nearby was insistent.

'Were you ignoring me?' It was Beth. They hadn't spoken since their tiff on the beach at Villefranche, and now Alex examined her daughter's face warily. She was sitting at a table set for two, a glass of rosé in her hand. In front of her a paper bag bulging with lemons from the market lay beside a leafy head of celery. She smiled and clinked her glass with the one waiting on the table. Alex felt optimistic. She pulled out the chair beside her.

'Don't be silly,' she said, kissing Beth's forehead. 'If I'd turned around every time someone had shouted Mum I'd have broken my neck. Who are you waiting for?'

'You, of course. Maxie told me you were inside nattering with her mother. She said you'd probably want the roast monkfish.' Beth raised her eyebrows. 'It comes with some kind of tempura vegetables, *que les primeurs, bien sûr!*' Her imitation of Maxie's 'only the freshest young veg!' was perfect. 'I was afraid to argue.'

Alex sat down. She could see Beth was relaxed: her hair shone in the sunlight, and her eyes were bright. Alex wouldn't mention either Beth's work, or Raymond.

'You won't believe what I've just heard,' Alex said.

Beth was rapt as Alex repeated Françoise's story. She stopped while their lunch arrived, delivered by Maxie herself. She continued as soon as Maxie was chatting with the next table. When Alex had finished, Beth's plate was clean, but Alex had only just begun. Beth started to pick at the fried courgette flowers on Alex's plate.

'Poor guy, no wonder Guillaume is so weird,' Beth said. 'That would send anyone over the edge.' She ordered coffee from the *serveuse*. 'How's it going with the little princess? Has she decided on anywhere yet?'

Alex counted out the properties on her fingers as she summed up for Beth the visits she and Natascha had recently made together. Nothing was right. The Eichenbaums' magnificent cliff-top villa was too out-of-the way, the Valentin villa needed too much work, in addition to Liliane's intentions for the cats, the villa on the Avenue Jean Cocteau, despite its location and the stunning, buxom statue, was badly laid out, and Natascha didn't want to live in an apartment, no matter how grand. Unless Patrice LeBlanc decided to show the Menier villa, Alex's next hope was Ed Bronz's house.

She had already made a tentative appointment with Ed's housekeeper, Suzanne, to see the villa on the Avenue du Phare. ('Of course,' Suzanne had said when Alex rang. 'Monsieur Bronz instructed me to welcome you at any time.')

'Huh,' Beth said. 'Natascha's choosy.'

'She has a right to be, don't you think?' Alex bit her tongue the moment she'd said it.

'Did you know that husband of hers comes from a seriously unpleasant family? Father, grandfather, uncles – they're all lawyers and every one of them has something to be ashamed of, from frauds to shady investments.' Beth looked delighted with her information.

'That's how people get rich. How did you find out?'

'The internet, of course. As far as Michael Barron goes, it seems he's too dim to make any money – spending it is his speciality. I'd guess his family isn't too upset he's over here and out of their way. Miss Dithery seems to be just as clueless. She's always trying to give the money away, but when she does, it's to the wrong people. About eight years ago she backed an... Oh, Mum!'

Beth sat up straight so suddenly the table rocked.

'Mum, Natascha gave loads of money to an animal rights group in Europe nine or 10 years ago.' Beth stared intently at

Alex. 'Activists of some kind. They blew somebody up!'

Now Alex sat up straight. 'It can't be,' she said.

Beth continued. 'What if it was the group that killed Guillaume's daughter? Nothing happened to the woman who gave them the money, as far as I remember. She wouldn't have known they were going to actually kill anyone.'

Alex frowned. Surely it was an awful coincidence, and Beth had misread the information. But when Maxie came over with the bill, Alex asked her exactly when Guillaume's daughter Cecile had died. Maxie didn't need to think.

'I always remember,' she said, 'because it was a year after she turned up with Honda. He's getting on now, so it was...let's see... it'll be 11 years next month.'

Beth was like a dog with a stick, wanting to play but unwilling to drop it. Her delicate face was animated by a greedy interest.

'I'm going back to Menton right now, I need to check all of this,' she said. 'I'm going to find out if this really is the way it looks.'

'Don't go, darling, please. You can work at the flat.'

But within minutes Beth was gone, leaving the unpaid bill on the table.

At least we haven't argued, Alex thought.

As she counted out the euros, Alain Hubert's BMW pulled up across the street alongside a police car. She sighed at the thought of him seeing her hiding in that doorway. He made his way towards her, shaking hands and kissing cheeks. When he got to her table and stood above her, the sun shone directly in his eyes so that they looked like topaz.

'Now that we're alone, shall we explain ourselves to each other?' he asked.

Alex groaned. 'You mean the day when you saw me in the restaurant doorway? You first.'

He sat down. 'There's nothing for me to tell. Sometimes I lie awake at night remembering pieces I couldn't put together. I was reminded of something, that's all. People are quick to remind me I'm no longer a policeman, but I hate to leave things unfinished. What about you, Madame Coates? Why were you following Monsieur Bronz and his Russian friend?'

Alex sank down in her chair.

'I'm just nosy.'

'That makes two of us.'

She gathered her things. She had left the office expecting to have one quick coffee over three hours ago, and she was anxious to get back, but Alain seemed to be settling in.

'Have you been to the Russian Church here in Nice, Madame Coates?'

The green and gold onion domes of the Russian Orthodox Church were an unexpected sight to see sparkling in the Mediterranean sun, but so far Alex hadn't been inside.

'Once upon a time the Côte d'Azur was a playground for Russians. They loved the Riviera even more than the English did. That was before the Revolution, of course. The aristocracy left the snow of Moscow and St Petersburg behind every winter for the warm sunshine of the Riviera. Even years of communism didn't dull that light. Now, they're back, but they're more likely to be office girls than countesses.' Alain frowned in what Alex took to be disapproval. 'When I was a young man, things were different. If we encountered Russians, they had come out from behind the Iron Curtain, and there was likely to be trouble.'

Alex relaxed into her chair. Perhaps she wasn't going to get back to the office after all.

'Over the years, there were some memorable characters,' Alain continued. 'You know, Françoise and I have been friends for some time. Maxie's father, was a boyhood friend of mine. We used to go to all the same parties. Françoise was a wonderful dancer, can you imagine? I can see the two of them now, dancing in the garden at some house in Cap Ferrat.'

'Which house?' Alex asked.

'It might have been Monsieur Bronz's; it might have been somewhere else.'

'Ed owned that house back then?'

Alain shrugged. 'You're the estate agent. Why don't you find out? In those days I was just a young cop, *un flic*. Who would invite me anywhere? If I hadn't known Françoise and her husband, and my wife hadn't been a beauty, I'd never have set foot in such a house.'

Alain wasn't the sort of man to sit in the sun repeating the stories of his youth to anyone who would listen. He must have a point, Alex thought.

'You'd see the same people again and again,' Alain continued. 'I have a good memory for faces, it was a skill you needed in my job. One of the faces that kept coming round was another guy like me. You could tell he didn't really belong, but he always had a pretty girl on his arm and he drove good cars, so no one asked questions. I was jealous, I admit it. Everyone said he was Russian, which was a lot more interesting than being a local cop. We thought they were all either spies or defectors.'

Alex laughed. She too remembered a time when the Soviet Union was a mysterious place that occasionally spat out a treacherous tennis player or chess master.

If he hadn't been so envious of the foreigner's allure, Alain explained, he wouldn't have been so attentive. 'He had a way of coming and going like a cat. You'd notice him drinking or offering around his cigarettes, but when you looked for him, he'd be gone. So I decided to keep an eye on him.'

He shook his head as if remembering a youthful folly.

'He always seemed to be looking things over. You'd find him leaning against a wall or looking out a window, and you'd think he was just having a cigarette or enjoying his champagne. But he was taking in every detail.'

'Planning something?'

'I don't know. In any case, he didn't appreciate being followed. He must have known I was there when he did this to me.'

Alain held up his left hand, on which he wore a gold

wedding band. His waggled his little finger. A quarter of an inch was missing at the top, the nail was short and misshapen.

'He walked into the library of one of those big houses and I followed him. The room was empty and he simply stood in the middle, clinking the ice in his glass.' Alain whistled gently. 'Was he up to no good? I believed it in my bones, but savouring a glass of Jack Daniels is not against the law. But a few weeks after that, that house was burgled. Just a few paintings were taken, that's all. I wasn't on the case, but I heard about it. A coincidence? I was standing in the shadows beside a bookcase, I was sure he hadn't seen me. I waited a minute or two after he'd gone, then I left. He had closed the door. I didn't think about it at the time – it had been left open when we'd entered. I went to open it, when suddenly he was there on the other side, he banged it against my face, and when I grabbed the side to try to stop it, he slammed it shut.' Alain held up his finger again. 'That's where this went, somewhere on the floor of that library.'

'Ouch,' said Alex.

'Yes. But my pride suffered the bigger injury. He said he had forgotten his cigarettes, and he was right, there they were on the desk.'

'So he wasn't doing anything wrong after all.' Alex was disappointed.

'But before he mentioned his Gauloises, he whispered something. His accent was strong, and I was hopping with pain, but I'm quite sure he said, "Monsieur Hubert, next time it could be your entire hand."'

Alex shivered.

'And what happened next time you saw him?'

'So far he hasn't seen me.' Alain took out the familiar piece of gilt and played with it absently.

The *terrasse* was in full shade now. A small group of police officers, off-duty, were gathering nearby. Alain was already standing up, kissing cheeks, slapping backs. The police nodded politely at her, one or two shook her hand, but she didn't belong. It was time to go.

CHAPTER TWENTY-SEVEN

Chantelle had been difficult to contradict when she first told Alex about the apartment in Les Jolies Roses. '*Fabuleux!*' she'd said. 'I'd have it for myself if it weren't so perfect for you.' Chantelle had swung open every cupboard, demanding that Alex imagine her clothes hanging inside. She'd run the taps ('the water pressure!') and flushed the toilet ('often overlooked, *cherie*'), but she'd neglected to mention the noise. The gently increasing buzz of the market in the mornings, with its occasional laughter and shouts, was a welcome replacement for the ring of Alex's alarm clock. The noise that continued outside into the night, however, was less endearing. The drone of motorbikes and the clang of the tram, barely noticeable by day, could be irritating with the windows wide open, as they now often were. She'd give anything to be distracted by sounds she had always taken for granted: Rod's voice, his absent humming, the creak of his chair, his keys in the door, his footsteps.

She looked at the photographs on the end table beside her. Meghan and her children on a skiing holiday; Beth and Meghan at 10 and 12, sitting on the steps outside their house in London; Rod staring intently at her from under a Panama hat. She loved that one; she had taken it in Fayence just weeks before he died – he was laughing and frowning at the same time, an expression she knew better than her own reflection.

'What would you make of all this?' she said out loud. She imagined Rod and Guillaume deep in conversation about the merits of one type of drill over another. Rod would never find himself silenced, as Alex did, by Guillaume's shifty discomfort. He'd laugh off Alain's fanciful ideas, too, and easily manoeuvre the conversation round to something simpler, like the mileage on a new car. He'd charm Paulette Bitoun instead of antagonising her. He'd probably treat Natascha like a friend of the girls as teenagers.

Alex herself was unsure. Sometimes the girl seemed to need a mother; moments later Alex would feel like the secretary. Natascha bounced from childish excitement to cool authority within minutes. Perhaps that's what you were like when you were that rich, Alex thought. Was she herself intimidated by that wealth, or awed, as Chantelle appeared to have been? She could easily imagine Natascha giving her money away to an animal rights group, moved by generosity but misguided by sentimentality. When people saw her, they calculated the possible benefits of her wealth for themselves, like Liliane Valentin. Why would a girl like that put her trust in anyone?

When Alex tried to imagine Rod speaking to Ed, she simply couldn't.

She had opened a bottle of a Corsican red wine recommended by Maxie, and she now put her second glass down, untouched, among the photographs. 'No wonder I'm tired,' she said to Rod's photograph. His motionless face stared back at her until she fell asleep on the sofa.

The phone woke her an hour or so later. It was Natascha. Alex checked her watch – 10.30pm.

'I hope I'm not disturbing you, Mrs Coates, it's just that I wanted to ask you a big favour.'

Alex rubbed her eyes. 'It is a little late for me.'

'I'm sorry, I'm a night person myself.' Alex could tell she was in Mrs Barron mode, expecting attention. 'I've been thinking more and more about the possibility of opening a boutique here. I think it would suit me. I'd like to look at some stores. I don't mind exactly where at first. I know you'll be able to take me to the right places.'

Alex sat up slowly. 'You mean, clothes stores?' She hadn't been shopping for months.

'No, for me. I've decided I'd really like to try an interiors store, as I mentioned. Michael hates the idea of course, but I want to give it a go. What do you think? A good mix of things: fabrics, furniture, some antiques, some art. The kind of place

I'd like to find myself.'

Alex wondered if she were dreaming. Couldn't Natascha have called during office hours?

'We don't usually handle commercial premises, to be honest. And don't forget, we have an appointment in the Avenue du Phare tomorrow.' Alex felt proud of herself. She was actually saying no.

She was looking forward to the viewing at the Avenue du Phare.

'We don't have to find the store tomorrow.' Natascha laughed. 'We can start by checking some places out. How about Bellet? I keep hearing about it.'

Alex thought of the quiet café, the toothless waiter.

'It's not the first place I'd think of opening a boutique,' she said. 'It's not really that sort of area.'

'OK, let's leave that for later. Let's start with what you know in Nice, and we can move on from there.'

When Alex put the phone down, having confirmed her meeting with Natascha the following afternoon at the Avenue du Phare, Rod's photograph seemed to be scolding her, not laughing. The heiress, however sweet and lost she sometimes seemed, was used to having people at her beck and call.

'It's your own fault, Mum,' Meghan scolded in turn the next morning. 'You're in too deep. That girl sounds a bit unbalanced, if you ask me, a bit bi-polar.' Alex could hear dishes clattering and water running. She imagined Meghan marching around the kitchen in London, the phone squeezed between her ear and shoulder, loading the dishwasher. The children would be at school. Her daughter was always occupied, her hands were never still – like Rod, who'd felt lost without a project or a chore. When the clattering stopped, Alex could hear ferocious tapping on a keyboard. She knew Meghan was in the hall, checking her emails, sitting in a pool of light at the computer table that fit under the stairs. For the first time in a while, Alex missed her like mad.

'Oh, here's something from Beth!' Meghan mumbled to herself as she read the email through. 'Ha! She's still going on about that Ed character, she doesn't think he's for you at all. I agree…blah blah blah… Seems to think they're all a bunch of criminals…the heiress is… Hmm. That's pretty nasty, even for Beth.'

'What?'

'She says Natascha's leading you around by the nose like a dancing bear and she'd like to put a stop to it.' Meghan laughed. 'Can't imagine anyone leading you around by the nose, Mum.'

'Except you,' Alex said.

CHAPTER TWENTY-EIGHT

Someone had phoned while Alex was talking to Meghan, and she listened to the message as she was preparing to leave the apartment. At first Natascha's voice was unrecognisable. She was almost whispering, as if the effort of forming the words was exhausting. She couldn't have sounded more different from the night before.

'Michael wants us to spend the day with friends, sailing,' she said weakly. Hadn't Natascha said sailing made her sick? 'Can we rearrange our appointment for later in the week?' Alex listened again, to be sure. She thought she could hear Michael's voice in the background. She turned up the volume. There was a pause, as if Natascha was listening to him, then she said in a monotone, 'I'm looking forward to doing some sailing again.'

Alex didn't believe a word.

She rang Ed's house immediately to rearrange the viewing, expecting Suzanne's voice.

But Ed's voice on the other end of the line made her stand up quickly from the end of the bed as she was slipping on her shoes. She cleared her throat twice before speaking.

'But this is excellent news,' Ed said. 'That gives us both a free afternoon. Why don't I show you one of my favourite places in Nice?'

She accepted with an alacrity that surprised her. She even ironed the cream raw silk T-shirt Meghan had given her for Christmas, paying special attention to its flattering, square neck.

Alex had heard of the Villa Arson in the northern part of Nice. The name had intrigued her at first, but when she found it was an art gallery that held avant garde exhibitions, she'd been in no hurry to visit. Ed parked the Audi and they walked the last 10 minutes together. On their left was a line of villas, painted ochre and dusty pink, mustard and faded green. Ed and Alex amused themselves describing the colours they passed.

'As brown as burnt biscuits,' Ed said about one villa.

'Wasted white,' he said of a peeling front door that had been carelessly splashed with a coat of cream paint.

Alex laughed. Whatever language Ed had grown up with, his use of English was playful and imaginative.

On their right was an imposing wall made of boulders, terraced at its height by lush green grass and pines. The street climbed gently upwards. At the top, they walked through a gate into a courtyard. The wall, Alex could see, was part of a building enclosing a shady square. On the opposite side, 30 feet away, glass doors opened into a large, peaceful space.

'But where's the exhibition?' Alex asked. The walls were bare; she and Ed were the only visitors. He was wearing the shiny chestnut loafers that would make Meghan snort, and he tapped one of them on the floor. Alex wondered if he polished them himself.

'Look.'

The floor of the gallery was covered in a sheet of black plastic. Hundreds of small flaps were cut into it. When Ed bent down to open one, he read out the words he found there. 'Two roads diverged in a wood and I...'

'...took the one less travelled by,' Alex finished the line of the poem. She'd heard it a hundred times from the back seat of the car and at the kitchen table, as Beth had memorised it for a school pageant. She'd forgotten the last few lines anyway. Alex told Ed the story, still both mortified and amused at the memory of Beth's pained, pale face searching for her help in the audience.

'But this isn't art,' Ed said dismissively. He turned her towards the door with his hand on the small of her back.

The modern gallery building was built around a simple 18th-century villa, enveloping the villa's tomato-red walls as if a giant seed were germinating within a granite pod. The villa appeared to be used as offices; there was no way in through the glass walls that surrounded it. They walked past, down a long hall and out at the far end of the gallery.

'Goodness,' said Alex, confused. Scores of glass triangles rose from the ground around them. When she looked down through the nearest, she realised they were skylights for the gallery below. She and Ed walked among them, negotiating steps as the levels beneath them changed. The view around them was stupendous. Alex turned in a circle, scanning the blue horizon in front of her, dotted by the pink dome of the Negresco hotel by the sea, and the green hills behind. The weather was perfect: there was no haze to discolour the flawless sky or distort the clarity through which she could see in detail a minuscule sailboat crossing the Mediterranean. Alex drank it all in.

There was still no one to be seen. They leaned on the retaining wall, looking out over Nice.

'It's not a bad city, for a small one,' Ed said. 'I don't mind spending a few months here every year.'

It hadn't occurred to Alex that he didn't live in Nice year-round.

'Do you have other homes, then?' she asked.

'Paris would be ideal for another apartment,' he replied. 'Near one of my favourite restaurants. Or perhaps Budapest, because of the coffee.'

He also thought spring in London was refreshing, and the women in Istanbul pleasantly argumentative.

Alex realised he hadn't answered. Right, she thought. No more questions. She tried another tack. 'I couldn't manage another house. It's a relief to have so few responsibilities now. I could run off to South America tomorrow if I wanted.'

He continued looking out across the view.

'You're not a woman who would leave her job just like that.'

'Not until we've found someone to take your villa off your hands. It will be quite something to leave a house you've been in for more than 20 years.'

'Perhaps 30 now,' he said.

Alex calculated rapidly. So Ed had been in the Avenue du

Phare in 1980, at the time of *Nice-Matin*'s article about the policeman's broken jaw.

'Thirty years' worth of stuff to clear,' she said. 'Hard to decide what.'

'You are a widow, Alex. You've learned that "stuff" isn't important. What would you sell to have your husband back in your bed tonight?'

He stopped looking at the view and turned to face her, his clear eyes fixed on hers.

My soul, thought Alex, but she didn't reply.

'I could be gone in minutes,' Ed continued. 'Or I could stay for years. But the house could earn me a lot of money.'

Alex had relaxed, leaning against the warm wall, but she snapped back into Immobilier Charpentier mode at the mention of money. Chantelle would never have been lured off duty like that, forgetting that Ed was a client. She chattered about the benefits of sale versus rental as Ed listened, looking out over the roofs. Finally, he laughed and leaned into her so that their shoulders barely touched. 'You don't need to convince me. If I like your client, she can have it. But the thought of staying here has recently become more appealing.'

Alex didn't move away.

Suddenly there was a shout. They both leaned out over the wall. The street below them was a narrow dead end, shaded by the terrace wall and an apartment building. Alex couldn't see anyone at first, but then the blonde woman she had seen following Ed appeared in the verdant gloom. She was wearing shoes this time, low heels.

'*Salop!*' she shouted up, pointing at them. 'Bastard! Don't think I can't see what you're doing!' She looked around her rapidly, as if assessing how to scale the wall. There was no way she could do it. She ran off down the street.

'Ah no,' Ed said softly. He sprang away from Alex, reaching for his phone. He spoke to someone urgently – it might have been any one of those Slavic languages Alex couldn't recognise. When he finished, he touched her elbow again, and she turned back with him towards the building. He seemed pre-occupied, even alarmed.

'What is it, Ed? Who is she?'

'I'm sorry, Alex. Let's get out of the sun.' He was walking quickly. If the woman was trying to get up to the terrace, she'd have to go up the side, the way she and Ed had come. It would take a few minutes, but Nice was full of narrow steps that crisscrossed gardens and alleys. There was sure to be a shortcut.

By the time they had reached the glass doors, Alex was feeling warm. She was moving faster than she would have liked, guided by Ed's increasingly firm grip. Instead of heading back to the main entrance, Ed led her towards the villa at the centre of the gallery. He punched a code into the keypad, and the glass slid open. They walked to the front door, where Ed entered another code. The door clicked open. Alex hesitated, but followed. She was feeling even more anxious now that they were entering an area that was off-limits to the public. She could hear a photocopier swishing. As they neared the stairs, someone came up behind them, and called loudly. Alex inhaled sharply. When Ed turned around, the man relaxed.

'Ah, Monsieur Bronz. It's you. More research in the library?' It was a security guard, and Ed shook his hand as if there were no hurry at all.

'This is Madame Coates, a friend,' he said. The guard smiled.

They went down the stairs into some kind of archive. It was dimly lit, with row after row of storage stacks. Ed spun the wheel on one of the stacks until there was just enough room for them to fit between the last two cabinets. They squeezed in. Alex could see boxes tied with string and rolled documents. It had been a long time since she'd been in an archive; the odour of desiccated paper and ink was reassuringly familiar.

'Ed, I'm not sure…'

'We're nearly there.'

There was a fire door at the end of the row. Ed pushed it, steering Alex through. She quickly shielded her eyes against the bright sunlight.

'Are you alright, Alex?'

'What on earth is going on?'

'We'll soon be on our way.'

This time he put his hand on her waist; she wished she wasn't beginning to perspire through the pale silk.

They crossed a scrubby area at the side of the gallery, which seemed to be well below the terrace they had been on. She couldn't stop to think how it all connected; Ed's hand propelled her forward. They ran down some uneven steps and into a small archway in the wall. Alex could smell cats.

'Ed, I'm really…'

'Shh!'

She remembered the anger in his face on the night drive back from Monaco, but this time there was no fine wine in her system to dull the impression that she'd made a mistake to trust him. He was looking at her intently. He smiled but his impatience was clear.

'I don't think…'

'Be quiet now,' Ed said firmly. He put his hand over her mouth, and Alex was so shocked she didn't move.

They could hear footsteps on the other side of a door in the stone wall, running. When they'd faded, Ed took a couple of steps back. 'She won't come back this way,' he said. He lifted the latches on the door and they stepped out onto a deserted street. Alex realised it was directly below the terrace.

'What on earth was all that about?' She brushed strands of damp hair back into place. She suddenly didn't want to be with Ed any more. She wanted to get back to her apartment and slam the door. How dare he manhandle her like that?

'She's unpredictable,' Ed said. 'I'm sorry you had to see that. We ought to get back to the car.' He reached to guide her along the street, but she shook him off and walked ahead.

'Please, Alex. Don't think any more about this unfortunate incident.'

Beth was right – perhaps there was something sordid about

Ed. How could she have let him push her along like that? She felt silly and vulnerable, and now she was fed up with his shiny shoes and his vague answers. She flushed at the memory of her shoulder resting against his. She wiped her mouth. She wanted to speak to Meghan, not to tell her about this, but to feel the closeness of her, to imagine her in the busy, safe, familiar house in London. She kept walking.

'Let me take you home,' Ed called.

When she turned around, Alex said, 'No, Ed. Don't insist.' He stopped suddenly, as if immobilised. She continued on to the corner and out of his sight.

She slowed down, breathing heavily, by a shop with a tired display of fruit and vegetables. Something cold and sharp suddenly dug into her shoulder. She jumped, squirming away. It was the woman they had tried to avoid.

Did she really think that with those dark eyes and eyebrows, anyone would believe she was really blonde? Alex took in her puffy face and cheap dress, and momentarily felt sorry for her. Her gaze was unfocused. Had she been drinking, or taking drugs? She'd probably been pretty once. The woman said something Alex didn't understand, and when Alex didn't react, a tremor of fear passed over her face. Then she said, in French, 'He won't get away with it unless I let him. He knows that. He can't keep avoiding me.'

Alex pulled away from the blonde's cold fingers. The woman looked her up and down.

'You're not his usual sort.'

It sounded so coarse that Alex felt dirty. She turned away and hurried down the road, not looking back.

CHAPTER TWENTY-NINE

The folder beside the key cabinet in the office in which Chantelle, Guillaume and now Alex dropped their receipts had been empty when she'd left the day before, but there were a few dockets now. She leafed through them: petrol for the pick-up; door hinges, an electric socket. Recently, looking through the receipts was the only way she knew what Guillaume had been up to.

She pencilled the expenses into Chantelle's hardbound ledger. Then she erased them angrily. She'd entered them in the wrong column.

It wasn't the first mistake she'd made over the days since her visit with Ed to the Villa Arson. The memory of his hand over her mouth still hurt. She practised out loud the excuses she would offer Natascha for not accompanying her and Michael on the visit that would inevitably have to be rearranged to view Ed's villa. But her voice was strained as she heard the words echo around the empty office. She knew she would have to go, for Chantelle's sake.

One of the receipts was from a shop in Bellet, one Alex hadn't noticed before. Guillaume usually used the same suppliers – Alex could see it: receipt after receipt with the same few names. But in this new one, he'd bought a few pine two-by-fours, a roll of plastic cord, and some rat poison – all things he could easily need in the course of his work. But something was crossed out in pen and deducted from the total he wanted to claim: a dozen candles. Typical of him to be so precise, Alex thought, but wouldn't he be more likely to have his dinner alone under the bright fluorescent light of a small kitchen? She amended the total she'd entered in the ledger.

As she did so, Harry Bormann's number in New York flashed up on the phone. She looked at the office clock – he was up late to be calling her at this time of the morning.

'You are so not going to believe this, Alex,' he said,

breathlessly. She pulled another receipt from the folder and looked it over. She was used to Harry's enthusiasms now. He probably just had more hospital gossip to share. But he said, 'Chantelle said something. Alex, she *said* something! I couldn't wait to tell you.'

Alex put down her pencil.

'Harry! At last!'

Her heart soared. Chantelle would come back and take control again. She would make everything clear.

'What did she say?'

'Well, we don't know. It was French.'

Unfortunately, after Chantelle had spoken loudly and confidently, she had returned to her usual condition. The doctors nonetheless regarded it as a positive sign.

'I was reading to her from the *New York Post*, just some gossip about a congressman and a call girl. Maybe she knows him and had a few words to add. It wouldn't surprise me!' His giggle dissolved into a happy squeak.

Buoyed, Alex called Monsieur Quelin, the solicitor. 'In case you find someone,' she explained. 'Family. They'll want to know.' Next she phoned Guillaume, leaving a message.

Then she ran to Chez Maxie. Maxie was at a back table, irritably tapping and re-tapping figures into her calculator. Françoise was hidden behind the morning's *Nice-Matin*. When Alex told them the news, Maxie's tired eyes filled with tears. She pushed the calculator away.

'It's good news, but oh, our poor Chantelle, all alone with no one to understand her. *Maman*, who can we send?'

'*Les Américains* should set up a tape recorder,' Françoise suggested. 'Chantelle might be trying to say something important.'

'A good idea, *Maman*! like Great Uncle Fabrice, who had a stroke.' Maxie turned to Alex. 'For months he mumbled about the bathroom floor, but no one paid attention. After he died, the house was sold and guess what? The new owner refitted the bathroom, and what do you think he found under the floorboards?'

'Oh no,' said Alex.

'*Oh oui*! Ten thousand francs, and nothing to prove who owned them!

As Alex was leaving, Françoise called her back, waving the newspaper. There was a picture of Paulette Bitoun, in colour, resplendent in a neon orange evening gown. 'She's announced that she's opening her own interiors shop in the rue Alphonse Karr,' Françoise said. She put the newspaper on the bar, flipping it round so Alex could read, but she flipped it away just as quickly. 'Just what we all need,' Françoise sighed. 'Another shop for people with too much money.'

Alex tugged the newspaper back, and made a note of the street. Perhaps she should take a look.

Alex peered into the shops along the rue Alphonse Karr as she wandered along its wide, shady pavements. If you wanted soft suede shoes or pale linen trousers, scented soaps or embroidered guest towels, this was the place to look. The windows were full of upholstery fabrics draped artfully over antique chairs, and the fragrance of expensive candles puffed from every door. Alex lingered in front of a display that contained two tan-leather pouffes on which piles of tiny cushions teetered. As she bent down to check the price, a reflection glinted in the plate glass.

She didn't turn around. A blue Mini had slipped into a parking space behind her, and the driver and her passenger had begun to embrace passionately. Alex smiled, but after a few seconds, she could see the girl had begun to struggle. She was trying to push the man away. The man grabbed the girl by her long hair and kissed her violently, jamming his hand between her legs. Alex watched in the reflection, then walked on to the next window, full of pastel leather handbags arranged in circles. But with a sly second look, it dawned on her that the man was Michael Barron, and the girl was definitely not Natascha. Alex crossed her arms, hunching her shoulders. If she moved, she might attract Michael's attention. She put her face as close as she could to the shop window, her eyes focused on the reflection in the glass. She could hear the girl – an American – shouting, before being cut off by Michael's blundering kisses.

'I'm not playing…this game…Mike…. stop… I told you…not to marry her…we can't…stop!'

Michael more or less fell out of the car as she pushed him. The girl was still shouting, but he laughed at her through the window. He adjusted the crotch of his jeans with an aggressive tug. Alex heard him say, 'You don't have to worry about her, babe.' Alex started moving in the opposite direction just as her phone pinged. A text from Natasha: 'Come quick!'

Alex almost ran. It wasn't far to Natascha's building near the Negresco Hotel. As she waited for someone to answer the door, she looked around furtively, tensing and relaxing her shoulders. Michael could be on his way back right now, and she didn't want to see him. From a family of shysters, as Beth had put it. She wouldn't be surprised to hear about this at all.

Sammy's mother buzzed Alex in and opened the door. She gave her a conspiratorial smile as they headed down the hall.

Instead of the whiteness Alex expected, there was a rush of colour at the living room door. She was dazzled, hesitating. Sammy's mother pushed her in from behind.

Fabrics were flung all over the boxy sofas and trailed along the floor like wedding trains. A white pod chair that hung from the ceiling was spinning gently. Alex had the impression that it contained a mound of sea-blue tissue paper, but then she realised it contained Paulette Bitoun. Natascha rose out of a pile of huge geranium prints on the sofa the moment she saw Alex. She hugged her, put her lips close to Alex's ear, and whispered, 'Help!'

Paulette struggled, rustling, out of the pod. She patted the stiff silk layers of her dress back into position.

'Mrs Bitoun dropped in unexpectedly to show me more of her work,' Natascha said. 'She assures me that only the

Valentin house will do for Michael and me, and has come up with new ideas.' Natascha pointed to the boards propped up against the mirrored cocktail cabinet. They were covered with samples of fabric and pictures snipped from catalogues and magazines. 'Mrs Bitoun thinks a safari-meets-Blade Runner look might suit us.'

Natascha was trying not to laugh.

'Natural yet *sophistiqué*,' Paulette said. Her bright blue eye shadow was speckled with glitter. She selected fabric samples from the table and held up one after the other to Natascha's cheek. Whenever Natascha backed away, Paulette held another even closer. 'So essential for the décor to complement the owner's complexion,' she said. She started pinning samples to Natascha's cashmere cardigan. At last Natascha said, 'Mrs. Bitoun, I wish you had made an appointment instead of dropping in. I really must tell you that I don't think we're going to get along.'

'But what do you mean, Madame Barron?' Paulette simpered through a mouthful of pins. 'And please, call me Paulette. We will know one and the other so well during zis wonderful project together.'

'No, I insist. I'll be doing my own interiors. In fact, that's why Mrs Coates is here, to help me look for premises.'

'Of course she's not,' Paulette said. She removed the pins and glared at Alex. 'Madame Coates knows nothing about the Côte d'Azur. You can't trust her. She's an imposter!'

Natascha flushed. 'You can't say things like that about my friends in my own house, Mrs Bitoun. I must ask you to leave.'

Paulette's skin was even thicker than Alex had imagined. She held a zebra-stripe sample of fabric close to Natascha's face.

'Madame Barron, you're making a mistake. Why don't you let me help you? You need an entrée here in Nice. Why, I am opening my own showroom shortly. It's just a matter of signing the papers. We could work together.' Then she clapped her hands and bit her lip girlishly. Alex couldn't bear to look.

'*Mais oui*, a partnership! Bitoun-Barron Associates!'

'Absolutely not, Mrs Bitoun!' Backing away, Natascha unpinned the fabric samples and dropped them on the table. She swiped up the mood boards and held them out to the designer. Paulette finally seemed to understand. She started stuffing her things into a series of bright green alligator-skin portfolios, talking to herself as she did.

'I should have known. Rich Americans, English widows, my eye! They know nothing about anything. I shouldn't have wasted my time.'

Natascha drummed her immaculate nails on the table as she watched Paulette. As much as Alex disliked the designer, she didn't like to witness her indignity. She went to wait in the hall. A few minutes later, Paulette lumbered out, her portfolios dragging on the floor. Alex opened the door for her. A sample of metallic faux-leather fell onto the floor. Both women leaned down at the same time to pick it up.

'*Elle le regretera.* She'll be sorry,' Paulette hissed, so close that Alex could smell her make-up. 'She'll come crawling to me for help. No one will be interested in her when the authorities prove that her *papa* was a crook. And everyone will be laughing at *you*, Madame Coates.'

Alex recoiled as if she'd been slapped. She knew that of everything she'd been through, being insulted by this silly, rude woman was the least significant. But she shut the door firmly after the designer, leaned against it, and allowed herself to cry.

She straightened up quickly when she felt someone's arms slip around her. Natascha hugged her tightly. It had been a long time since anyone had enveloped Alex with such spontaneous warmth, and she cried even more.

An hour later, Alex held out a glass cup as Natascha poured mint tea from a turquoise teapot. She'd let her shoes slip onto the floor, and curled her legs up onto the roomy white sofa. Natascha took the box of tissues that had been resting between them and pushed it to the far side of the coffee table.

'I think we're done with these now,' she said. She smiled over the rim of her teacup, and Alex wondered again why she had been trying to fool this sweet young girl for the sake of a woman far away in a New York hospital.

'It's such a relief to have told you the truth about Chantelle,' Alex said. Natascha's fingers were warm from her teacup as they squeezed her hand. 'You deserve a real professional like her, not an imposter like me!' Admitting the truth had been like taking off an uncomfortable dress. Alex helped herself to another of the sticky cakes Sara had brought in with the tea tray.

'I understand,' Natascha said. 'Trying to be something you're not in front of other people is exhausting. I like you even more now that you've been honest with me. Not a lot of people are.' She played with a string of freshwater pearls around her neck. 'If Chantelle were to recover and come home tomorrow, no one could tell her that you haven't given things a damn good try.'

Alex sighed in relief. Why didn't Beth or Meghan say the same thing, instead of relentlessly nagging her to give up and go home?

'Now can I be honest with you?'

Alex tensed, but Natascha suddenly gave her another hug.

'Your daughters are so lucky! I like to think my mother would have been like you, someone I could be happy to be with.'

She jumped up to root through her handbag and came back with what Alex had thought was a slim diary. Alex could feel the bones in Natascha's shoulder as she snuggled against her. 'My mom and me,' she said, opening the diary and running her finger around the edge of a photograph inside: a woman with Natascha's eyes, exactly, holding a tiny baby. 'She died of cancer when I was about six months old.'

Alex put her hand to her heart.

'But look.' Natascha flicked to the next snap. 'My mom's

sister, May. She had a farm in Vermont. Whenever I wasn't at boarding school in Switzerland, or with my dad, I was there. That was the only place I ever really felt like me.'

In the photo, a round-faced, teenage Natascha was bottle-feeding a calf, watched by a heavy woman with windblown hair.

'But Aunt May and my dad had a huge argument, and I think it was over me. I guess my dad won, because I hardly saw her after that. Aunt May never even got to meet Michael. And then she passed away too, not long before we got married.' She shut the album and slid it onto the coffee table next to the tissues.

Natascha's beautiful, expressive face was easy to watch, and as Alex listened to her, Sammy's mother returned repeatedly with pots of sweet mint tea. The girl's eyes filled easily with tears, but she was also in the habit of twisting her mouth to one side when she thought something was funny. It wasn't flattering, highlighting the beginning of jowls, which somehow made it endearing. And she was an astute observer of others.

'I adored my father, and he taught me to love art the way he did. But I knew he was a very controlling man,' Natascha said. 'And of course he had the thing that made people do what he wanted. People will do anything for money. But not my aunt – she wouldn't let my father control her. All she wanted was to take care of her farm, and me. Dad thought she was crazy.' Alex watched the pearls slip in and out of Natascha's hands. 'The thing I regret most is that when my father and Aunt May drifted apart, I had to follow him. And his world never felt like my world.'

Now Alex put her arms around Natascha's shoulders. The girl leaned into her comfortably before pulling away and looking squarely at Alex. Her face was alight with excitement.

'That's why I want to live here, instead of in the US!' Natascha said. 'Sure, people here know who I am, but not everyone. There aren't so many people to make judgements about me and my family, and about our history, and about our money.'

Would Natascha touch on her father's art collection? Or on her involvement in animal rights? Alex didn't ask; it would be an admission that she, too, had been rooting out information, ready to make her judgement like everyone else. She felt a mix of guilt and disappointment when Natascha simply said, 'I don't want to do what people expect of me, I just want to be me, to live quietly with my husband.'

Alex didn't want to imagine what her husband and the girl who was driving that Mini could be doing right this minute.

'I've been in love with Michael since we were teenagers,' Natascha continued. She smiled indulgently. 'His father was a business associate of my father's. And besides, his family is so wealthy he's the only guy I could be sure wasn't after me for my money.' She laughed, then blew her nose, and even that was graceful. 'He's so into sailing, it was easy to convince him to come give the Riviera a try.'

'He's a good-looking man.' Alex said it as brightly as she possibly could.

'He sure is!' Natascha giggled, but then sighed. 'I just wish he wasn't *totally* into sailing. It's become kind of an issue between us, the fact that he spends so much time...' She bit her lip, and seemed to think better of continuing. She stood up suddenly, almost bouncing off the white sofa.

'So, there. I don't care if you're not Chantelle Charpentier! I like Madame Alex Coates just fine, and we're going to take on the Riviera together, right?'

CHAPTER THIRTY

Alex had arrived home to find Beth sitting at the round table, nearly hidden by a vase of lilac branches.

'You look worn out,' Beth examined her mother's face suspiciously. 'What's the matter with you?'

'I'm tired. I've just been listening to Natascha's life story.'

'Aha! Tell me!' Beth fidgeted excitedly. 'Did she say anything about the trial?'

'What trial? She didn't mention any trial.'

Beth's laptop was set up on the table. She tapped on the keyboard, then pointed at the screen. 'See? Just as I'd thought.'

Alex scanned some of the newspaper articles Beth had found. Following the death of Guillaume's daughter, there had been a lengthy investigation. It had taken the police several months to connect the company's driver to the animal rights group that had been protesting outside the research facility. Journalists from the local paper took several more months to unravel the group itself. They discovered that the son of a French politician had been involved, along with the ex-wife of a renowned local butcher. The activists were part of a wider group that operated in Britain and Canada, too. Once the British press had taken up the story, it was just a few weeks until they could name people who financially supported the group – including the 18-year-old daughter of multi-millionaire Uri Raskilovich.

'But she was just a girl,' Alex said.

'Are you making excuses for her? She was old enough to do what she liked with her money.'

During the trial, the driver's defence suggested that these well-to-do, well-connected supporters had threatened him. He had acted under duress. But the lawyers who represented Natascha Raskilovich ('And you'll never guess who they were – Barron, Barron and Barron, if you please,' Beth crowed) were ready for everything. The girl came away looking a complete innocent, someone who had thought her money was buying no more than milk for rescued kittens. The lawyers even successfully sued one of the British tabloids for libel, because they had unearthed a distant cousin who swore that Natascha Raskilovich had known exactly what was going on all the time.

Alex shook her head sadly. 'Poor Guillaume. How dreadful. To come face to face with someone you believe was involved in your daughter's murder...'

'Someone who was definitely involved, Mum. It's clear.' Alex pressed her lips together tightly. Beth's smugness was beginning to grate. Her daughter even had a few print-outs – she'd obviously spent a lot of time on the internet – and waved them in front of Alex's face.

'Alright, alright, I'll look at them later. I've got things to do at the office. Whatever you do, keep all that stuff well out of Guillaume's sight.'

Beth followed her down, wondering out loud about Natascha. Alex kept a look-out for Guillaume, hoping Beth would have the good sense to shut up if they saw him.

The first voice she heard on the answering machine was Odile Perrin's. The old woman from Bellet, whom she had first heard berating Chantelle, seemed in a more conciliatory mood, but her accent was still virtually impossible to understand. Alex and Beth listened several times together.

'I guess she doesn't know about Chantelle,' Beth said. 'She seems to be asking her for help. Too bad you can't slow this thing down, I could get what she wants then.'

Alex looked at her emails while Beth listened again. She had stopped paying attention when Beth snapped off the machine. 'She's calling all her neighbours names, but she doesn't want to be left in the mud they kick up. She wants to sell the piece of land Chantelle knows all about – the one that never produces any good wine. She says the Americans are so stupid they'll buy anything, so they deserve it, and she knows Chantelle can get her more than it's worth.' Beth laughed. 'Shall we save that to blackmail her with?'

This one would be delicate, Alex thought. Perhaps she should send Guillaume.

But Beth was intrigued. Alex described the small vineyards and the pretty countryside, but she avoided mentioning her dreamlike experience in the derelict château.

'Come on, we can go in the morning,' Beth said. 'There's strength in numbers. I can protect you from this old woman's potions and spells.'

Alex couldn't imagine her wisp of a daughter protecting her from anything, but for the moment being with Beth felt unusually effortless, and she didn't want it to end. She found Odile Perrin's address in the phone book.

CHAPTER THIRTY-ONE

Two large dogs with black scars on their shoulders barked excitedly at Chantelle's Citroen as soon as Alex pulled into Odile Perrin's yard the next day.

Beth closed her window. 'We could always reverse back out,' she said, dubiously.

The farmhouse was shuttered. Half of it looked like it was still a barn; a rotting wooden door yawned open into darkness. People bought these houses and painted them pink and planted lavender by the drive, but there were no frivolities here. The stone was bare, the earth in the yard trampled and rutted.

Alex turned off the engine. The dogs stopped barking but circled the car, letting out low growls.

'I'm not getting out first, that's for sure,' Beth said.

On one side of the house, green sheets pegged to a line billowed in the breeze. After a moment or two, a woman appeared from among them. She was tiny and bent, but she walked briskly towards the car. When she got to the driver's side, she stopped suddenly.

'*Hélas, tu n'es pas Chantelle!*'

'No, I'm not Chantelle, Madame Perrin. My name is Alex Coates. Please let me explain.'

The woman called the dogs to her side with a snap of her fingers.

'I work with Chantelle and Guillaume at the office in Nice,' Alex continued. 'Is it OK if we get out of the car?'

Odile peered through the window at Beth, who said *bonjour* with exaggerated cheeriness.

'You're English,' Odile said bitterly.

'We should've phoned first,' Beth whispered.

Alex got out. Odile grabbed the dogs by their collars. 'Yes, I am. This is my daughter, Beth. I've been working with Chantelle for a few months, but she's in New York at the moment.'

Odile wasn't impressed. She muttered unintelligibly and walked towards the house, snapping her fingers again for the dogs. Alex followed. When the old woman pushed the door open, there was a not-unpleasant whiff of fried onions and wine. She didn't go in, however. She turned to Alex.

'Tell me,' she said.

Alex explained everything, except the facelift. Odile didn't seem the kind of woman to be sympathetic to cosmetic procedures. Alex said simply that Chantelle had been taken ill in New York, and was unable to get home for now. Odile didn't seem alarmed or upset. 'Guillaume should have told me,' she said bluntly. By now, Beth had stepped out of the car. The dogs growled.

'Guillaume's been busy recently. I should have asked him to come when we got your message. I thought I'd look at that piece of land, and then I can tell Chantelle about it.'

'Chantelle will know exactly which piece of land I'm talking about,' the woman said sharply. Alex tensed with the effort of listening to her almost incomprehensible accent.

Odile looked hard into Alex's face. If she was trying to decide whether to trust her, she didn't seem to reach any conclusion. She made to go into the house.

'Guillaume's over there now. Tell him to come and see me.' She waved into the distance.

Alex had to ask her to repeat it several times before she was sure she'd understood. Odile was exasperated. 'For god's sake, I'll call him myself. He's over there. There!' She pointed in the direction of the ruined château. 'Where he usually is.'

She went inside and shut the door. The two dogs lay down in the dust, watching Alex and Beth get back in the car.

'That's curious,' Alex said.

'There's probably a few of these old peasant women about, she's not that curious,' said Beth, emboldened back in the safety of the passenger seat.

'No, I mean about Guillaume. Did I understand Odile

correctly?'

Why would Guillaume be hanging around the ruined château?

The sun was bright and warm. There would be plenty of light in the château to take a good look. Alex would never have done it alone, but as Beth had remained in good spirits, she'd be open to an adventure.

Beth walked towards the château from the road excitedly, imagining the people who might once have lived there, and why it had fallen into ruin. In this quiet place, Alex imagined briefly that the petite woman in front of her was still a child. She half expected Meghan to run out of the greenery and put her small, warm hand in hers. When they reached the ruined veranda at the back, it seemed even more overgrown than Alex remembered.

There was a sudden scurrying noise on the other side of the veranda. Alex grabbed Beth's arm. Two slim white cats ran off, panicked, hugging what was left of the wall. Alex had one quick glimpse of their black tails.

She'd seen them before.

'More scared than us,' Beth laughed.

She tested each step cautiously as she climbed towards the veranda.

'Can you imagine if we'd had something like this near our house at home?' Beth said. 'I'd have been playing here every day.'

Alex smiled. Her daughter had reacted exactly as expected, but she said, 'Rusty nails, broken glass, rotten floorboards... Do you think I'd have let you in here? Besides, in England it would have been boarded up.'

Through Beth's eyes, the building must be no more than a quaint ruin, stripped of its menace and transformed into a playground. Alex had surely misunderstood Odile – even a multi-skilled handyman like Guillaume would be overwhelmed by a job as big as this.

Beth shouted. She'd pulled open what was left of a small door, probably a cupboard, at the far end of the room. Alex hurried to her.

'Give me your key ring, Mum, that one with the little torch.' Alex handed it to her, and Beth shone it into the space. It was shallow, with just one shelf. Mildewed wallpaper lined the back wall. Mixed in with the earthy smell of vines and rotting wood there was the distinct odour of fresh candle wax. Beth flickered the torch from left to right. The shelf was clean, free of the dust and grit and mouse droppings that covered all the other surfaces; someone had been keeping it clear. In the centre of a mismatched group of candlesticks, there was a framed photograph. Alex recognised one of the faces easily: it was Guillaume's daughter Cecile. She was standing beside an older, heavier woman. Both were smiling. Beth reached for it.

'No! Don't touch it!' Alex pulled her hand away. 'We can't let him know we've been here.'

'Oh god, do you think this is something to do with Guillaume?'

Could it have been Guillaume, that day she had fainted in that endless hall? Is this why he hadn't shown his face? She felt profoundly sorry for him. To set up a shrine to your lost family in an abandoned ruin seemed close to madness. What did Odile mean, where he 'usually is'? Alex and Beth had intruded on something intimate, and she wanted to get out as fast as possible. She took Beth's arm and pulled her back towards the door.

Beth said, 'You're giving me the creeps,' but followed willingly.

At the café in the village, Beth ordered a *pichet* of rosé from the waiter who'd first told Alex about the château.

'Guillaume's totally weird,' Beth said. She had become more and more glum since they left the château. 'Everyone's totally weird here, Mum. You should get out now. Go stay with Meghan. Buy one of those flats she's always looking at.'

Alex watched the waiter. He didn't seem to recognise her.

She couldn't ask Odile about the château, that was certain. If she asked anyone at Maxie's, it might seem like she was prying. And she definitely couldn't ask Guillaume. What else could the waiter know?

'The whole situation is absurd,' Beth continued. 'Chantelle might never come back, that Ed guy gets worse every time I hear about him, and now we find out that Guillaume is...'

Alex interrupted her to catch the waiter's attention. She reminded him that she'd been there some time before, but he looked blank. He didn't seem to be in a chatty mood this time, and couldn't tell her, when she asked, when he last saw anyone near the château.

'You need some friends here, Mum.' Beth had barely stopped to listen to what the waiter had said. She launched back in. 'Who'd look out for you if something went wrong? I've got to get back to Paris soon. Why don't you talk about it with Meghan?'

Her voice was whining now. Alex felt her patience sapping. She left the money for the rosé on the table.

It was true, she didn't have real friends here, but until Beth had pointed it out, she hadn't thought about it. Her life was full of people – almost too full.

'Actually, I think Natascha and I might become good friends.'

The look of hurt in Beth's eyes took Alex by surprise, but before she had a chance to say anything more the waiter was by her side again. He'd been thinking, he said. 'No, no estate agents or Americans there recently,' he said, spinning his tray. 'Just the local kids, of course. And the man who feeds the cats.'

'The cats?'

'His daughter used to do it. I can't remember the story, I think she died. But I often see him on his motorbike. *Un fou*, I think.'

A madman, the waiter had said.

'Oh god,' said Beth. 'You've got to get out of Nice.' She marched back to the car without looking at her mother. Alex could tell from the angle of her shoulders that the day's pleasant complicity had come to an abrupt end.

CHAPTER THIRTY-TWO

Alex had procrastinated long enough about rearranging the viewing of Ed's house, until she received a telephone call from Suzanne. Alex had, unusually, been eating a ham and camembert baguette for lunch at her desk, and she munched hurriedly through a mouthful before she picked up the office phone.

'Monsieur Bronz asked me to telephone,' Suzanne said, as if surprised to be tasked with the call. 'He would like you to confirm when Monsieur and Madame Barron will be viewing the house.'

Alex reached for the diary, and asked when would be convenient. Suzanne said, 'Oh no, Madame Coates. Monsieur Bronz asked me to be sure to arrange a date to suit you.' She emphasised the word 'you' – *vous* – and Alex sensed a lively curiosity in her tone. They agreed some possibilities to suggest to the Barrons, and Alex went back to her sandwich.

'*Chérie*, you must stop being so *brittanique*,' Chantelle had said one day when Alex was first working for her. Alex had been eating a sandwich at her desk that day, too, and she'd bravely continued chewing under Chantelle's scrutiny. 'Watching you will give me a *crise*.' Her boss certainly wouldn't have dithered and procrastinated about calling Ed's house on the Avenue du Phare to reschedule an appointment for important clients.

Now Alex looked down at Maxie's *plat du jour* on the table in front of her and thought about how she had slowly begun to change her ways. A sandwich would no longer be enough to fortify her for the appointment. She had even asked Maxie to add some crispy *frites* to the veal kidneys cooked in port, and now she'd finished every last one. She'd have to leave shortly to meet Natascha and Michael.

When Alex looked up again, the professor was making his way among the tables towards her.

'Madame,' he said, pumping her hand. 'The Menier villa?'

'Not yet, I'm afraid.'

The professor perched his books on the edge of Alex's table and sat down.

'Madame Coates, I met a friend of yours the other day, Mr Bronz. A most unusual man.'

Alex gripped her hands tightly together under the table. So much seemed to have happened between now and the day that Maxie told her she'd seen Ed talking to the professor.

'Did you discuss your book?'

'That's an understatement.' The professor's eyebrows shot upwards. 'It seems Mr Bronz knows rather a lot about the architectural details of the Menier villa.'

Alex leaned forward.

'He seemed to be familiar with the shutters,' the professor continued. 'He had a surprising grasp of the details, the size of the elephants, for instance, the colours. A formidable man. But...'

Alex resisted looking at her watch. She'd need to leave very soon.

'But he was no help to me. Quite the opposite. He has made me doubt my own work. Is he a good friend, Madame Coates?'

Alex shook her head. Her cheeks flushed as she recalled yet again the pressure of Ed's hand over her mouth. 'An acquaintance, no more.'

'Then I'll tell you, what he said was strange. He told me there was no point in pursuing my research. He said that if there were any history of note in that house, it would bring sadness, not fame and fortune.'

'Oh! I wonder what he knows.'

'He described the house in detail. He even described the housekeeper.'

'I expect he knows her. What's odd about that?'

'I'm surprised I haven't come across his name before.' The professor took off his jacket, revealing arms as skinny as pencils. 'Do you think Mr Bronz might be writing his own book?'

Alex admitted anything was possible.

'When I told him that I had come across some documents, he laughed, Madame Coates. Laughed! And not in a nice way.'

Alex felt sorry for the professor. He was no match for Ed.

'Don't let him put you off,' she said.

'He seemed to suggest if I continued, harm would come to me.'

Alex could imagine Ed's cold expression. She'd seen it herself. But why would Ed bother to threaten someone as harmless as the professor? Why had the mention of some shutters on the villa riled him?

She patted the professor's ivory-white hand. She said, 'I'm sure Mr Bronz was joking. Perhaps you should talk to him again.'

The professor chewed at a nail on the other hand.

'I don't think so.'

Alex reached for her bag under the table and stood up. The restaurant was busy – the lunchtime rush. Maxie and the *serveuse* sailed among the tables; Françoise's head bobbed up and down behind the bar. When Maxie came to take the professor's order, she threw her hands up in mock despair. 'No more fritto misto, Professor. You'll have the veal, and I'll add some frites, you'll enjoy that.' She winked at Alex.

'A good choice,' the professor said, as if it had been his own. He pushed up shirtsleeves. Maxie swooped off, with Alex's empty plate in her hand, but was blocked suddenly by Alain Hubert. She kissed him on both cheeks.

'Maman is too busy to flirt today,' she said. 'Here, say hello to our friend the professor. He's worried about something.'

The professor frowned, but Alex said, 'Tell him about Monsieur Bronz. He's the police, after all.'

'I *was* the police,' Alain corrected her.

When the professor had repeated his story, Alain sat down. He took hold of Alex's arm, as if to keep her from leaving. He wanted to know what Ed had said, word for word, but the professor's memory was inexact.

'It was more of an impression,' the professor said, biting his nails. 'A suggestion of harm.'

Why was Alain taking the professor's story so seriously? Alex was cutting the time she had left to get to the Avenue du Phare fine now. She gently shook off Alain's grip and jiggled Chantelle's car keys.

'Have you come across many forgeries in your line of work, Professor?' Alain asked.

'In architectural details? I'm not sure what you mean. Fake cornices? False mosaics?'

'I mean, among the histories of these fine villas you're so interested in.'

Alex really had to run now.

The professor laughed nervously. 'If only I had, Monsieur Hubert. That would be just the sort of thing my publisher would love!'

CHAPTER THIRTY-THREE

There was no Audi in the drive at Ed's house, and Alex stopped holding her breath as she parked Chantelle's car – only a few minutes late. Monsieur Bronz was away, Suzanne said at the door, but he had asked that Madame Coates and her clients be made welcome.

'Usually he doesn't like anyone in here at all,' she said, as they waited for the Barrons to arrive.

A black convertible Porsche with a local '06' number plate rolled to a stop under the eucalyptus trees. When the gates closed automatically behind it, Natascha rose up out of the car wearing a white headscarf, black Jackie O sunglasses, and a tight black skirt. Michael wore chinos, and a navy double-breasted jacket with gold buttons. It was a look Alex disliked, and she disliked it all the more on him.

Suzanne, watching them arrive from the kitchen window with Alex, cupped her hands to her cheeks in delight. After offering them lemonade, she left the three of them alone.

Natascha picked up on Paulette Bitoun's style in the decoration as soon as she saw the flouncy chintz curtains in the first-floor hall. She rubbed them between her fingers disdainfully, smirking at Alex. At least the owner had kept Paulette on a tight rein, she said. Any damage could easily be put right.

Michael strolled around the house looking bored. It wasn't until he saw the large corner bedroom at the back of the house that he took his hands out of his pockets, and looked around as if he were calculating.

'Nat,' he announced. 'This could be a kind of playroom. There's plenty of space for my treadmill, and I could get my screens put up here.' He waved to the space above the bed.

'But honey, you can see the sea from here. Wouldn't it be better as our bedroom?' Natascha sized it up, biting the inside of her cheek, as Alex waited in the doorway. The ensuite bathroom, with its huge round window, contained a roll-top bath and a chaise longue.

Michael didn't reply.

In the dining room, the couple talked about replacing the Paulette-inspired wallpaper, an oversized jungle pattern, with something more subtle. 'We could bring over the Picassos,' Natascha said. 'I love those prints, they'd be just right here, they'd emphasise how graceful this room really is.' She leaned against the table, imagining the transformation.

'No way, Nat,' Michael said. 'Stick them in your study. We'll put my sailing shots in here. That's what you need on the Riviera!'

Natascha glanced apologetically at Alex.

Besides Ed's reading room, the only other room with any genuine personality was an L-shaped bedroom overlooking the drive. It was connected to the adjoining room – the sort married couples shared in another era. Alex barely remembered it from her first visit with Ed, when she'd been so nervous she'd hardly looked. The shorter part of the 'L' contained a king-size bed; the longer part looked like it was used as a dressing room, with a mirrored wall of cupboards and a contemporary blonde wood tallboy. It was spacious and calm, but the Barrons had only a quick look and continued on.

Alex stayed behind. This must be Ed's bedroom. She could hear Natascha's voice fading down the hall and waited a moment before partially sliding open the cupboard door. The smell of cedar floated out. She touched the soft sleeve of a jacket. There were tens of them, on cushioned hangers, along with pressed shirts in plastic film, folded pastel sweaters on the shelves, shoes with shoe trees in regimented pairs. What did she expect? She shut the door, and rubbed her finger marks off the glass with her scarf.

Next she inspected the top of the tallboy. There were no photographs, just a silver tray filled with loose change and two mobile phones. There were some cufflinks and a comb, a small silver Cartier carriage clock that was two hours fast, and a burnished leather document wallet, its zipper open.

It was quiet, except for Natascha's muffled voice somewhere in the house. Alex could hear her own heart. She noted where one edge of the wallet poked out over the tallboy – she could put it back exactly, no one would ever know. She touched it, then drew her hand away.

Was this the same document wallet she'd seen in Ed's hand, the day she followed him down Boulevard Gambetta?

Alex usually resisted the urge to peep in other people's papers if they were left in view. She'd want the same respect herself. But the familiar leather was tempting. She glanced over her shoulder, picked it up and half-pulled out the contents.

She recognised the grey-blue colour and grainy texture of the paper used for architectural drawings. She eased them out a little more, until she could see the name of the architects: Benkemoun, Nice. Just below that was printed 'Villa in Villefranche'. She wiggled the papers to get them neatly back into place, and as she did so, she noticed that the name of the client was Patrice Leblanc – that was the owner of the Menier villa! She could hear Michael's raised voice, perhaps on the floor above. She pulled the plans back out and unfolded them halfway. There was something handwritten in pencil across the top: she could barely make it out, the handwriting was messy. She realised the letters were Cyrillic. She turned the drawings over to see the other side: one room, from the looks of it, with three or four areas circled in the same pencil.

Alex was disappointed. No lurid photographs, no compromising letters. All she had discovered was that Ed, like the professor, had an interest in what might be the Menier villa – but why?

She eased the drawings back into the wallet, positioned them exactly on the tallboy, and turned to go.

It was then that she heard Ed's voice.

What was he doing at home? Alex's stomach somersaulted. Why had he come back? She dashed back into the adjoining room and closed the door behind her. She stopped to breathe in deeply, but her heart was pumping and she could feel heat in her cheeks. She fanned her face with her hands. Ed was getting closer, calling her name. If she went out into the hall now, she would bump into him. She went quickly to the window and stood there as if she were interested in something on the drive. She noticed the Audi parked between the Citroen and Michael's Porsche.

When Ed found her, her mouth was almost too dry to speak. The little crinkles of amusement that played around his eyes made it worse. Surely she looked as guilty as she felt.

'I think your clients are having a disagreement,' he said. He kissed her on both cheeks, surrounding her momentarily in his leathery scent, then stepped back and looked at her intently. 'I was hoping you'd still be here,' he said, almost whispering. 'I'm so sorry about the unpleasantness at the Villa Arson. Can you forgive me?'

Now, standing in front of him, just the two of them in this elegant room, Alex couldn't imagine why she had been so irritated with him at the Villa Arson. He waited for her reply.

'But that woman,' she said. 'You seemed to be afraid of her.'

'No. Only that you would let her come between us.' He moved closer.

Suddenly, Michael's voice became loud. It sounded as if it were travelling through the ceiling, and Ed turned towards the hall.

'Let's hope the argument's not about the house,' he said. 'Why don't you go and save them while I wait for you downstairs?'

Alex hurried, flustered, to the floor above.

'You're never happy,' Alex heard Michael say bitterly. 'Why do you always have some crazy plan? Just relax for once. You drive me up the wall.'

When Alex called to them, he sauntered out of one of the small attic rooms as if nothing were wrong, blocking the hall with his bulk.

'She's loving it, Mrs Coates. But me, I don't think I've made up my mind.'

Alex introduced Natascha and Michael to Ed downstairs in the reading room, where Suzanne had set out a plate of petit-fours on the coffee table. Ed and Michael talked politely about the view, the architecture of the house, the maintenance of the garden. They were both fluent in easy chatter. Natascha was quiet. She sat on the sofa and picked at a petit-four. Alex had the impression she was holding back tears, but Alex herself was still going over and over the moment in the bedroom at which she had heard Ed call her name. She flipped through one of the art books on the coffee table, trying to appear nonchalant, hoping her heart would slow down. Could Ed have seen that she was looking around his bedroom?

When Ed and Michael began talking about yachts, Natascha got up, sighed loudly, and wandered around the room. When suddenly she said, 'Oh, wow!' everyone looked at her. She was standing at the spot where Alain Hubert, too, had been taken by something on the wall.

'What now?' Michael said sharply. Alex found him more irksome with each passing minute.

'It's just like...no, maybe it's not. This photograph, Mr Bronz, is it you?'

Alex moved closer to take a look, too. It looked like Ed, younger and possibly happier. He had his arm around the shoulder of a child, a girl of eight or 10, in a summer dress. They were smiling, the same broad smile, the same deep dimples.

Ed hadn't moved. 'Yes,' he said. 'And my niece.'

'She's pretty,' Natascha said. 'Where was it taken?'

Ed frowned, confused. He walked towards Natascha and Alex, saying, 'I don't remember.' The three of them looked closely at the photograph. Alex wanted to put on her glasses, but it would have appeared too curious.

'It's an old photograph, as you can see. When I look at it, I can only see my niece.' He moved away, but Natascha lingered.

She was mumbling when she said, 'For a second I thought I knew that picture leaning against the wall in the background. There's not really enough of it to be sure.'

As far as Alex could see, only the corner of a picture was visible, full of shapes that reminded her of seashells. In fact it might not be seashells at all; it could be anything. She was surprised Natascha thought she could recognise it.

'Right,' Michael said briskly, 'There she goes again. Always on a flight of fancy.' He laughed, with neither kindness nor indulgence.

Natascha put both hands over her face. When she removed them, she laughed, too, without, Alex thought, any spirit at all.

'Gosh, I'm sorry. I just don't know what I'm thinking any more,' she said.

Michael took his car keys out of his pocket.

'It's time we hit the road, honey,' he said. 'So Mr Bronz, we're heading for a boat party tomorrow night in Antibes. You might be interested. Why don't you and your wife join us?'

'I don't have a wife to bring,' Ed replied. He looked directly at Alex. 'Which means I can ask Madame Coates if she would accompany me instead.'

Natascha clapped her hands, suddenly childlike. 'Oh, yes, please come, Alex. It will be so much easier if you're there!'

CHAPTER THIRTY-FOUR

There were several dresses laid out on Alex's bed at Les Jolies Roses, and she was looking through the scarves in her wardrobe. She had no idea what to wear on a yacht.

'No, a scarf won't do, Mum; too daywear,' Meghan said. Alex had called her as soon as she got home. 'It's got to be jewellery. What about the amber necklace?' Alex took it out of the box on the dresser. She laid it on each of the dresses, standing back to look.

'No, not right,' she said. 'It looks too formal with the shoes I have to wear.' Natascha had warned her that only bare feet or soft soles were permitted aboard the *Vanessa B.* She'd even offered to lend her some, but her feet were a size and a half bigger than Alex's. With no time to buy any more, the only shoes Alex could find were a pair of flat blue sandals. She rarely wore them – they'd seemed dowdy once she'd taken them out of the box and put them on at home. Now she saw them in a different light.

'That long necklace with the silver beads, the glittery one? Have you still got it?' Meghan was excited. She was having her hair cut and Alex could hear the Argentinean hairdresser offering his advice in the background.

Alex found the one Meghan meant and held it up against each of the dresses in turn.

'Tell me what he said again, Mum. I can't believe you're going to a party on a yacht.'

When Natascha and Michael Barron had driven away from the house on the Avenue du Phare, Alex was left alone with Ed. He had apologised again for what he referred to as 'the unpleasantness' at the Villa Arson, and hoped they could forget about it. Alex resolved to stick by her decision. She wouldn't ask him about the blonde woman, nor any more questions at all. Even when he began to tell her about the girl in the photograph, she bit her tongue. Where was this little girl now? Why didn't Ed seem to have any other photographs of her, or of his son? What happened to the room in which the photograph was taken so many years ago?

The no-questions policy seemed to work. Ed became talkative, but still divulged little.

Alex breathed in. 'He said he hadn't felt genuinely interested in a woman for years, until he met me.'

Meghan whooped. 'God, Mum, how corny can you get? And listen to you, you're falling for it! I wish Beth hadn't gone back to Menton, she could go as your chaperone. Now what about that blue jersey dress with the folds at the neck? Is it the same blue as the shoes?'

Alex flicked through the hangers and found the dress her daughter meant.

'Under any other circumstances, I'd be worried sick,' Meghan said, 'but since the Barrons are going to be there, it will probably be fine. I'm not telling Beth though. I don't know why she's been getting so agitated about Natascha. From what you've told me, she's just a poor little rich girl, lucky to have found you. Why don't you try the silver beads with the blue dress? No belt, OK? Does it look great?'

It did. Alex put the phone on loudspeaker while she changed. She described the effect to Meghan, admiring herself in a long mirror propped against the wall. The jersey dress had a silky shimmer. It draped loosely from the shoulder, hugged her around the waist and skimmed her hips. With the knot of beads reflecting the light, the look was chic without being formal. Even the shoes seemed stylish now. She was satisfied.

'Hair?' asked Meghan. The Argentinean burbled excitedly. 'Benicio says it has to be up.'

What Alex didn't mention to her daughter was that earlier, after dropping Beth off at the train station, she had parked next to Alain Hubert's BMW. As she got out of the Citroen, his sudden nearness made her jump.

'Suzanne told me about the Barrons' visit to the house on the Avenue du Phare,' he said. 'She thinks they won't be taking it. I'm sorry I wasted your time.'

Alex laughed. 'News travels fast; so much for discretion. And she may be right. But you never did tell me what it was about that picture on Ed Bronz's reading-room wall. Why did it surprise you so?'

Alain took the piece of worn gilt out of his pocket. He held it up.

'What do you see?' he asked. His hand had the kind of tan that never fades, but the taut scar tissue on the tip of his finger was white.

'A bit of old wood?'

'You could say that. My nephew Felix's brother-in-law found it lodged in the wall of the boot of a car he bought recently. A vintage Mercedes. Perhaps it was stuck in there, overlooked, for years.'

Alex remembered Alain's nephew Felix talking about that car the first day she met Alain at Maxie's. It seemed so long ago.

'How did it end up in your pocket?'

Alain nodded over his shoulder towards the police commissariat next to Maxie's.

'My old friends know what interests me. Have you been to the Monday antiques market in the old part of town?'

She nodded. She and Rod had been there on several furniture-hunts.

'You can find good things there, valuable antiques with a provenance,' Alain continued. 'You can also find things you shouldn't ask questions about. One day, when I was a young inspector, a cache of goods came to us from the market. One of the items was a painting – a bad painting, nothing valuable. But the frame! What a piece of work! It sat in my office for a time. What interested me was that it looked very much like the frame of a painting that had been stolen from Auguste Valentin. Of course Valentin had a photograph of the work, for the insurance – it was a Matisse given by the artist himself. I think you know the Valentin villa, on Cap Ferrat?'

Liliane Valentin was on Alex's to-do list – she really must

call her to confirm that after the performance with Paulette Bitoun, Natascha was not interested in the house.

'I was young then, I had dreams of solving every crime from Monaco to St Tropez,' Alain shook his head, smiling at his younger self. 'The stolen Matisse was eventually returned to the Valentins. They decided to pay the ransom for it.'

'I know,' Alex said. 'Liliane Valentin told me.'

'Usually a frame isn't important. It's the painting that counts. The painting is removed and the frame disappears.'

Alex nodded.

'So the Matisse went back to Valentin without its frame. Of course, when this one showed up in the antiques market, we had to let Valentin see it. If it had been stolen, we needed to prove it.'

'And Auguste Valentin knew it was his?'

'Of course! You don't forget a frame like that. I didn't anyway. I had seen it before.'

'In the Valentin villa?'

'No. I wasn't paying attention to the paintings on the walls at those parties, Alex. No, I had seen it in the hands of a thief.'

'Where?'

Alain shrugged. 'At a house on the Avenue du Phare. The one that got away, as you say in English.'

Alex remembered the article from *Nice-Matin*, the one that described a policeman shooting at a car.

'Ed's house?' she asked. 'But it didn't get away. Both the painting and the frame were eventually returned to Auguste Valentin – you just said so.'

Alain was opening his car door again. 'Haven't you been keeping up with the news?'

She'd been so busy, there hadn't been time. She shook her head.

'Françoise has just told me; she saw in *Nice-Matin*. Drouot the auction house in Paris won't officially authenticate the Valentin Matisse.'

Alex thought back to her conversation with Liliane. A

forgery for sure! The painting would be worth nothing now. The family would have to sell their beautiful house at any price.

'So the Matisse wasn't worth stealing in the first place,' she said. 'But I still don't understand how all this relates to the photograph at Ed's house. You know, Natascha had a similar reaction to yours when she saw that photograph, too.'

Alain hesitated, as if mulling that over. He looked at the piece of wood in his palm, and closed his fingers over it. 'What I saw in the photograph at Bronz's house looked like the frame of the stolen Matisse.'

He dropped the piece of wood back into his pocket.

'What are you saying? The frame is now at the auction house, with the Matisse inside it. Couldn't you get your friend to check if the piece you have is missing?'

'A fine gilt frame can be repaired easily.'

'Then you'll never know if the bit of gilt you have is from the stolen Matisse.'

What had Guillaume said, when they were talking about Alain? That he likes to keep himself entertained between the school gates and the nursery?

'An old cop sees a crime where most people see a coincidence,' he said. 'Am I rambling?'

But of course it was too late for Alex to ignore Alain's ramblings now. What did she know about Ed, after all? Was Alain really suggesting that years ago he'd had something to do with the theft of the Valentin Matisse?

There was one thing she was sure of when it came to Ed Bronz, however: she was looking forward to seeing him on that yacht tonight.

'Earth to Mum? Earth to Mum?' Alex grabbed the phone. How long had Meghan been waiting for her to say something? 'What were you doing? You don't have much time! I said, now, what about the bag? Oh, and Mum? It's OK, you know, about men. I think Dad would understand.'

CHAPTER THIRTY-FIVE

Alex felt underinvested rather than underdressed. The style aboard the *Vanessa B* was artfully relaxed, a look she knew required time and money to achieve. There was plenty of linen – comfortably crushed shirts for men; loosely tailored shifts or short, tight dresses for women. There was also plenty of silk – little designer cardigans to protect against the evening breeze, and jersey dresses that slid off brown shoulders, and clung to hips and thighs. Everything seemed sophisticated, tasteful, expensive. Alex's eyes were constantly drawn to knobs of gold and silver on men's wrists. Most of the women glittered at the throat or wrist or ear. The only diamond she could show off was the tiny chip in her engagement ring. Alex felt like an imposter – she *was* an imposter. But she knew she looked good. Ed's reaction when he'd met her at the door of Les Jolies Roses confirmed it.

It hardly felt like they were aboard a yacht at all. She and Ed had walked up the gang from the jetty, where the *Vanessa B* was moored stern in, gleaming in the moonlight. A small crowd watched the guests arrive, and Alex had her first inkling of what fame must be like. A ragtag gathering of passersby had stopped on the dock to enjoy the spectacle. Alex could have been among them.

They were shepherded across the deck to the main salon by one of the crew, a pretty, athletic-looking girl in a tight T-shirt and short skirt. Tanned, muscular boys in the same T-shirt circulated among the crowd of guests with glasses of champagne on silver trays. Ed handed one to Alex. He stood close to her, almost proprietorial. She didn't mind. He looked handsome in his grey and white seersucker jacket. Meghan would laugh at the style, but she couldn't see, as Alex could, how other women watched him.

The room was larger than she'd expected. It crossed the width of the yacht, some 30 feet. Alex couldn't figure out where it ended – there seemed to be a screen across the middle about 30 feet away. The guests were standing in groups, or sitting on long black leather sofas. There were several in the salon, arranged around coffee tables the size of beds. The pale grey walls were mostly bare but as Alex passed, she saw shapes emerging from the colour. They were life-size women's bodies, relief sculptures that emerged from the walls themselves, the wall covering drawn across them like silk sheets. They reminded Alex of corpses in a morgue.

As they wandered closer to the screen at the back, Alex saw it was full of hundreds of individual leafy plants tucked into the structure. Alex leaned on the rail of a circular staircase beside the living wall and saw that it continued down to the floor below. She could see the tops of other guests' heads.

'I hear they have a full-time gardener in the crew,' Ed said.

Alex munched happily on the rounds of canapés offered by the good-looking boys. Ed pointed out other pieces of art she hadn't noticed at first. The coffee tables were also display cases, each lit from within to highlight a collection of miniature paintings. She scanned the crowd – no Natascha. Ed introduced her to someone he knew, who brought over someone he knew. Each time, Ed put his arm lightly round her shoulders, but soon they had mingled into the crowd and were separated. Once, when she caught sight of him talking to a group near one of the sculptures, he smiled conspiratorially.

Alex jumped when she heard a familiar booming voice.

'That is some amazing fucking art!'

She seemed to be the only person in the crowd who cringed at Sal Eichenbaum's crudeness.

He was standing behind her talking to girl in a gold dress. When he put his hand on her perfect bottom, Alex gasped. He turned around. The girl smiled languidly at her.

'You're that estate agent,' he said. He was wearing a billowing black shirt, and looked like a Mafiosi. 'Too bad it didn't work out with those kids. Anyone else?'

'Not right now,' Alex said. She didn't want to think about

Immobilier Charpentier for the moment, not here. She didn't want to think about Sal Eichenbaum, either, but Julie appeared out of the crowd. She lifted her husband's hand off the girl's rear as absently as she would swat a fly. He stomped off towards the living wall, followed by the girl.

'Thank God you're here,' she said, kissing Alex. 'I was about to head home, but I'll have another drink now. This kind of thing isn't usually my scene.' Her long black dress scooped low to show off a beautiful necklace made of cords of entwined silver. 'Seen these?' She pointed towards a wall-light. There were eight or 10 in the salon, identical sheets of metal directing the light upwards, each one delicately filigreed with palm trees. 'Took me months! Dario's commissioned a bunch of stuff from me, so I feel I should show my face once in a while. He throws a good bash, anyway. You know Dario, right?'

No, she didn't know the *Vanessa B*'s owner, but now that she wasn't on duty for Immobilier Charpentier, she didn't mind admitting her imposter status. 'You're not really missing anything,' Julie said, without malice. 'Italian entrepreneur. If it doesn't float, he's not interested.' Her smoky laugh ended in a cough.

The Barrons had just arrived, and there was a ripple of interest as the couple made their way through the room. They stopped here and there to exchange air kisses. Natascha's black hair was drawn up, but a few ringlets had escaped. She looked fresh and confident, as if she were in familiar territory. She didn't scan the crowd the way everyone else did. She knew all eyes were on her. It was several minutes before she noticed Alex and Julie.

The good-looking boys had been refilling her glass so attentively that Alex had no idea how much she'd consumed. She felt lightheaded and happy. Natascha and Julie began talking about dogs, the kind of conversation only dog-lovers could have. They were making each other laugh, Julie raucously, Natascha more delicately, a giggle she couldn't contain. When Ed returned, he could barely find a pause in the conversation in which to say hello. Julie, Alex could see, found him charming.

The group of people around them expanded and contracted, but after an hour or so they were on their own. They sat on one of the sofas, which were so comfortable Alex took off her sandals, leaned back and put her feet up on the edge of the coffee table. She thought of asking Ed about his conversation with the professor, but the sudden, pleasant weight of his hand on her shin quieted her. He was telling her which of the miniatures he thought the most interesting, but the warmth of his hand on her skin, the gentle pressure, took up all her attention. She liked it. She liked the way his eyes met hers. No one, besides Rod, had touched her for years. But his eyes were suddenly drawn to something behind her. He lifted his hand and said, 'Isn't that Beth? Your daughter?'

Alex sat up and looked around vainly. Beth had gone straight back to Menton after their visit to the ruined château.

'It couldn't have been. Are you sure?'

It seemed so unlikely, but wasn't Alex here herself? How unlikely that was, too. Beth would have been just as surprised to see her – more than surprised, too, if she'd seen Ed with his hand on her mother's leg. She'd better go and find out for herself.

Plenty of people were now draped over the sofas. Sal Eichenbaum was splayed on one, his hairy belly exposed. She could see Michael Barron whispering in the ear of the girl in the gold dress. The man Julie had pointed out as Dario was surrounded by women who were busy comparing themselves to one of the shrouded wall sculptures. A dapper elderly man was picking stems from the living wall. He had one behind his ear, another in his lapel, and he offered one to Alex as she passed. But there was no sign of Beth.

Alex steadied herself to go down the circular stairs to the floor below. The steps seemed to be made of crystal; each one glowed a different colour as she moved. Was she making them do that? The effect was disorienting. On the last step, she stopped to look over the heads of the guests. This was another salon, smaller and darker. People were dancing to music that Alex now realised had been in the background all evening. She noticed Natascha's head bobbing among the group, and behind her, the moonlit harbour. The dance floor was in fact hanging over the water; part of the boat's side wall had been lowered like a drawbridge to create a balcony. It was a perfect stage.

Alex strained to see the faces in the crowd. A neon light made their teeth glow. Any of them might have been Beth. She went to the edge of the dance floor. Her first impression was that the dancers could fall right over the sides, though then she saw they were protected by a transparent, chest-high wall, the top embedded with a line of twinkling lights. When Natascha saw her, she put her arms up and waved, beckoning Alex to join in. Alex shook her head.

There were small bars on either side of the dance floor, each with a barman in the *Vanessa B* T-shirt. The top of each bar was made of the same pulsating coloured crystal as the staircase, and as Alex put the flat of her hand on the bar, it turned blue. When she removed it, it faded. She asked the barman for water. The crowd here was younger. It was as if Alex had deserted the parents in their penthouse upstairs and arrived downstairs at a nightclub for their beautiful children. Beth wasn't among them.

As Alex headed back towards the stairs, she saw people coming and going through a door just beyond it. She darted under the staircase and through the door, and immediately felt the night air on her face. She also inhaled a waft of sweet smoke. She was on a side passageway of the *Vanessa B*, where five or six people were leaning over the rail. One of them was Julie Eichenbaum.

'Smoking section,' she said when she saw Alex. She inhaled the joint she was holding deeply, and offered it to Alex.

'Haven't done for years, remember?' Alex said. 'No exceptions.' She didn't need to feel paranoid tonight. It was the last thing she wanted while chasing guiltily after Beth.

Julie shrugged, exhaled, and passed the joint to the girl next to her. 'She's adorable, that Natascha. I'm going to design some dog collars she can sell in that new shop of hers, what do you think?' Julie was amused with the idea. 'Maybe extend the range to silver dog bowls. For the pooch that has everything.' She laughed until there were tears in the corners of golden eyes.

Beth was definitely not aboard, and Alex was beginning to feel woozy. She needed to be somewhere quiet on her own for a few minutes before going back upstairs to Ed. She asked one of the good-looking boys for another glass of water, and gulped it down. What the hell were you thinking, she said to herself. How would this look to Beth? Rod had barely been gone for a year, and there Alex was succumbing to the advances of an outrageous flirt with a dubious history. She thought of the masculine, L-shaped bedroom in the house on the Avenue du Phare and tutted.

It was easy to get back onto the dock without going through the salon on the upper deck. A staircase led from the door on the dance deck to a gangplank where a few smokers were gathered, admiring the *Vanessa B's* towering hull. One of the crewmembers even offered to accompany Alex on her stroll to the end of the dock.

The yacht was quite a sight. It burbled with voices and music, its lights reflected magically in the water. Laughter burst from groups who looked even more glamorous from afar. Alex walked up and down beside it until her head cleared. Julie's hoarse laugh erupted above her as she passed beneath. There were no boats on the other side under the suspended dance floor. From this angle, she realised that the floor itself was transparent. The dancers could look down and see the water changing colour beneath their feet, lit by floodlights under the *Vanessa B's* waterline. Alex was impressed. If this was what Dario had thought up for his boat, what could his house be like?

As she watched the colours playing on the hull, there was

a scream from the direction of the dance floor, followed by a splash. Something had hit the water. More screams, then shouting. Faces appeared at the railings on each deck, amid more shouts. Alex saw something thrown from the lower deck – a lifebuoy. In the water, a person was flailing, splashing. Within seconds, two people had dived off the boat. They reached whoever had fallen in two or three strokes.

The floodlights that had been changing the water from yellow to green to red suddenly exploded into white: an emergency system. Alex could see the outline of legs pedalling frantically beneath the surface. Another two lifebuoys splashed onto the water from the boat as people continued to shout, but the person was safe now, hands grasping the lifebuoy. The two crewmembers who had dived in were beside the person, nudging the lifebuoy as if they were pushing a child in an inflatable toy. At the waterline, a door opened, a set of steps appeared. Hands reached out. They lifted the person up swiftly in one smooth movement, working together. It was a woman. Her hair hung in flat, wet cords across her shoulders, and she stumbled, reaching out to the arms beside her to avoid falling. As she disappeared into the blackness of the boat's interior, Alex realised with a dreadful start that the woman was Natascha.

CHAPTER THIRTY-SIX

Alex ran back up the gangplank, but if there was a door that would lead her down to the deck where Natascha had been pulled aboard, it was hidden behind the excited throng. She pushed her way through. A velvet rope cordoned the dance floor like a VIP area, and the dancers had by now shrunk away from the harsh illumination of the searchlight and decamped to the bars. Excited chatter had replaced the pounding music. Crew members were examining the transparent wall, but it appeared to be intact.

'Is she alright, the girl who fell?' Alex asked, several times. No one knew. After a few minutes, the searchlight clicked off, and there was a short, surprised silence in the darkness before the colours returned.

She pushed her way back to the salon, where a woman said, 'Typical Dario – something always happens at his parties.'

Ed had disappeared from the sofa. Julie was now stretched out in his place. She sat up the moment she saw Alex.

'Did you hear? That poor kid Natascha took a dive!'

'She jumped?'

'Who knows? Everyone's got a different story. Someone said she was pushed.'

'That couldn't be true,' Alex said. 'She must have slipped. Something must have given way.'

'You never know with a girl like that. Young, beautiful, stinking rich – it's a combination people love to hate.' Julie shifted on the sofa, lying on her side as if she were in her own bed. 'Your friend Ed, for example, he doesn't like her too much.'

'What?' Alex looked doubtfully at Julie. Her eyes were half-closed. 'What are you talking about? Ed barely knows her. Julie, you're not suggesting…'

'Of course not,' Julie said. 'But when I mentioned the Raskilovich fortune, he looked like he'd turned to stone.'

'What did you say?'

'I can't even remember. It was only a joke, for god's sake. I thought everyone in the world knew who that kid's father was – I guess I was wrong. Know what he said?'

Julie sat up, pushed out her jaw, knit her brows and in a deep voice, imitating Ed, she said, '"Raskilovich? That little bitch." Well, you could've knocked me over with a feather.'

'You misheard him, Julie. He wouldn't have said anything like that.'

Or would he?

'Nope, I'm sure that was it. He looked so mad. Kind of Jekyll and Hyde, you know? Sexy but dangerous.' She punched Alex weakly on the thigh and winked.

'When was this?'

'Just after I saw you in the smoking section. He came looking for you.' Julie was getting sleepy now, succumbing to the alcohol and dope. 'He needs to calm down. Men with tempers are no good to anyone.' She nestled her cheek on Alex's shoulder and within seconds had started to snore.

Had Ed really been so surprised to discover Natascha's background, or was Julie imagining it? And why would it make him so angry?

Alex scanned the crowd. The idea of Beth being in among them now seemed absurd. The little groups that had formed in gossipy excitement had reformed, smaller and more relaxed, pierced by laughter and drunken shouts. Julie at last coughed and turned to face the other way. As Alex stood up, she heard a crew member asking for her. He handed her a stiff, ivory envelope. The card inside was embossed with *Vanessa B* in gold, just as it appeared on the stern of the yacht. By the time Alex made out Ed's name at the bottom of the scrawled paragraph, the crew member's broad back was several feet away. Alex squinted at the words 'sudden terrible headache'. It happened from time to time, Ed wrote. He had to lie down; he couldn't risk driving her back to Les Jolies Roses. A crew member would make sure she got home safely. Could she forgive him?

Alex stared at the notecard for several seconds, as if studying Ed's handwriting would make it easier to understand why he hadn't come to tell her himself.

Part Three

CHAPTER THIRTY-SEVEN

Alex called Natascha's number four times from the taxi on the way back to Nice, but her phone went straight to voicemail. She imagined it lying on the seabed beneath the *Vanessa B*. At home, she called Michael twice, leaving messages.

Alex made herself some tea, and turned on the television to help dull the swirl of images in her head. By the time she'd left the yacht, news had circulated that the girl who'd fallen was unhurt. Dario's guests had talked about it excitedly. Even so, Alex couldn't banish the image of those legs trailing helplessly in the floodlit water. She gnawed at the idea of Beth having been at the party. Anyone could have invited her, of course. She'd find out all about it in the morning. But what if Beth had actually seen her there with Ed? The memory of the weight of his hand on her leg brought a flush to Alex's throat. When Julie's face, creased with laughter, came to mind, Alex laughed out loud herself. The American's openness was refreshing, almost disarming, but how could Alex believe what she'd said about Ed? He was unpredictable, yes, and moody, but Jekyll and Hyde was going a bit far. The sudden headaches could explain a lot.

She settled into the sofa and watched the news on an English-language channel, then flicked for a while before tuning in to a French news station. Along the bottom of the screen she could see the words *Le Butin Raskilovich* – the Raskilovich haul. She scrabbled for the remote and turned up the volume.

Auguste Valentin's Matisse was not the only painting whose authenticity was now in question. The journalists who put together *Le Butin Raskilovich* had unearthed clips of Raskilovich as a young man – Alex could see where Natascha's broad forehead and high, Slavic cheekbones came from. Uri Raskilovich, a Russian immigrant to the United States in the 1940s, had made his fortune buying land to develop shopping malls. By the time he was 30 – and an American citizen – the rental income from prime sites all over North America placed him on international rich lists. He was a notable patron of the arts. The Raskilovich Foundation, which he started in the 1950s, was devoted to bringing contemporary Russian artists out of the Soviet Union to the safety of United States and Europe at the height of the Cold War. Later, the foundation continued to support and publicise their work. Raskilovich himself was a respected collector of 19th- and 20th-century art.

Among the interviewees was one of the executors of the Raskilovich estate – Michael Barron, Senior. Alex curled her lip at the sight of the familiar disingenuous smile. Barron emphasised that the artworks discovered in a vault on one of Raskilovich's properties in New York state would not be – and would never be – put up for sale.

'And does the whole family agree?' the interviewer asked. Barron Senior was tapping his papers into a neat pile, ready to go. 'What about the daughter?' The conversation was voiced over in French. Alex strained to hear what Barron said in English.

'My partners and I represent Mr Raskilovich's daughter – my lovely daughter-in-law Natascha.' His perfect teeth flashed.

Alex frowned.

'But didn't Mrs Barron want the collection to be sold on behalf of the Raskilovich Foundation? Isn't that how the discovery of the Matisse forgery – possibly others – has come about?' asked the journalist. 'Why has the sale of the collection been put on hold? Why won't you let anyone examine it, Mr Barron? Why the mystery?'

Barron continued smiling steadily, ignoring the questions.

The report showed some of the paintings that had been discovered, which were in the process of being catalogued for sale before the estate had suddenly asked for their return. Alex even recognised some of them. It truly was a haul. Raskilovich had had a private collection worthy of a national museum. It had been so private that it had come to light only after his death. There was a clip of Natascha hurrying from an apartment building into a limousine, dressed in black, perhaps not long after her father's death. A reporter pressed a microphone into her face. 'What did you know about this hidden collection, Mrs Barron?' he shouted. Her face was hidden by dark glasses, but Alex could see she was chewing her lip.

The report ended showing Natascha and her father arriving at a ball held by the Raskilovich Foundation in Los Angeles. She was holding her father's arm, smiling at him, glowing with pride. He could have been her grandfather.

'How much does she now have to lose?' the journalist's voice asked.

She really is a poor little rich girl, Alex thought, closing her eyes. She was asleep within minutes.

CHAPTER THIRTY-EIGHT

Alex called Beth the next morning before checking the time.

'What do you want, Mum? It's so early.' Beth's voice was woolly.

Alex had been rehearsing this conversation since the first voices from the market below had floated up. Would – could – Beth admit anything about being aboard the *Vanessa B*? Alex cleared her throat. She began by suggesting Beth bring Raymond to lunch.

'Couldn't you have waited till later to ask that?'

'I wanted to give you plenty of time to get here,' Alex said. It sounded less convincing now than it had in the grey dawn light.

She could hear Beth yawn. 'I'm sure he'll say he's too busy with his work. He was up nearly all night. I don't think I'll make it either. But thanks for asking, Mum.' Alex exhaled. Beth sounded almost normal. But just as she seemed about to hang up, Alex quickly said, 'I went to an amazing party, Beth, you won't believe it.'

The silence seemed endless. Alex continued: 'Natascha and her husband asked me to a yacht party.'

Beth seemed about to say something, but there was more silence, Alex's shoulders tensed. 'It was quite something. And I bumped into Julie…'

'Why did you go with them?' Beth interrupted, angrily. She sounded fully awake now.

'They asked, darling. I didn't have a chance to tell you because…'

'Because you were too busy flirting with that crook and toadying up to that mindless girl!'

The venom in her tone threw Alex off balance. 'Beth, don't be horrible. You'd like Natascha if you gave…'

'I'll never like her! Does she think she owns people because she's got money? Guillaume's daughter died because Natascha thinks she can do whatever she wants.'

'That's not fair. It had nothing to do with her, you found that out yourself.'

'Fair!' Beth's voice was cracking. Alex bit her lip so hard it hurt. What would Rod do now?

'Sweetie, don't be like this. I'm sorry I woke you up. Let's talk later, when we've both had some coffee.' Beth's tirade continued: 'Unbelievable,' she was saying; 'I can't believe what's happened to you...'

A man's voice began to murmur gently in the background, and then the phone clicked off. Raymond. Yes, perhaps Raymond, like Rod, could calm Beth down.

In the days that followed the party, Chantelle's presence seemed stronger than ever. Alex could hardly open a file or a drawer without turning up yet another old note in Chantelle's elegant handwriting. People dropped in every day to ask after her – stallholders from the market, the pharmacist, the mechanic from the Citroen garage. Even one of the street cleaners put his head round the door one morning to ask when she was coming home. Everyone missed Chantelle. The scent of L'Eau d'Issey stubbornly pervaded the Citroen, despite the fact that Alex now always opened the windows before she started the car.

Alex was tired of being unable to tell anyone anything new. After the promising, if mysterious, comment to Harry Bormann, Chantelle had remained silent.

'I think she liked hearing all about the *Vanessa B*,' Harry told her. 'But of course I didn't say anything about Natascha's fall. Oh my, she would so not like to hear about that, not one little bit!'

Somehow Harry had been talked into volunteering for something called the Loved Ones Panel at the health centre in New York.

'It feels so meaningful, Alex,' he said with a long sigh. 'I guess I was looking for a caring role like this all my life, and I just didn't know it.'

Their almost daily conversations began to include gossip about other patients, and updates on their families, with whom Harry had now begun to socialise. One day, after Alex had hung up and was locking the office, she realised that she and Harry hadn't discussed Chantelle at all. She phoned him back quickly for news, feeling guilty.

Chantelle wouldn't recognise her collection of cuttings now. Alex had started to type out her notes for the dossier, and there was a sheet or two tucked into each alphabetised pocket of the folder. Whenever she found something new, Alex added the information. She photocopied the cutting she had found about the 1980 robbery of the house on the Avenue du Phare and filed it under 'C' for Cap Ferrat, cross-referenced to 'B' for Bronz. It seemed calculating, but why not? She hadn't heard anything from Ed since the party. Why shouldn't she treat him as just another detail?

The dossier's 'Z' pocket bulged with unplaced cuttings. She had been reading them as carefully as she could, but it was time-consuming. She was no longer hopeful they would turn up properties that might interest Natascha and Michael Barron, but she wanted Chantelle to come home to find that she had produced a useful resource. In any case, since the incident on the *Vanessa B*, the Barrons had virtually faded away. Michael had called to say Natascha was on the mend, but that was it. At the end of each day, Alex gave the dossier a contented pat before putting it back into its drawer. She had done her best.

At last there was a message from Ed.

'Alex,' he said, sounding tired and distant. 'Things keep going wrong between us. I've never had to apologise more often, nor to mean it so much.'

She listened to the message four times. For god's sake, she thought. How long will I put up with this ridiculous to-ing and fro-ing? It was just a silly crush, she told herself, what was I thinking? Forget him.

She deleted the message.

That evening she bought herself an expensive bottle of Bordeaux, one that Rod had always liked, and drank just a little more than she would normally have done.

A few days later, Natascha's number lit up momentarily on Alex's phone, but the ring didn't even have a chance to sound before it disappeared again. For Alex, it was the perfect excuse. She arrived at the Barrons' apartment near the Negresco with a huge bouquet of peonies. Sammy's mother opened the door.

'Aha!' she said, eyes narrowing. 'Come, come quickly.' She took Alex's hand firmly and led her to the living room.

Natascha was sitting on the white sofa, surrounded by paperwork in leather folders. The moment she lifted her eyes, she said, 'Alex! Thank goodness you've come!' She started shifting papers so she could get up. But she sank back into the cushions suddenly as Michael appeared at Alex's side.

'Great of you to come, Mrs Coates,' he said. 'We should have called you sooner. Natascha's much better now, just feeling a little embarrassed about that night. She's laying low for a while.'

Natascha smiled weakly and handed the bouquet of flowers to Sara. Her eyes were teary with irritation or fatigue.

'There's nothing to be embarrassed about. Everyone knows it was an accident, part of a balcony panel wasn't properly aligned. It gave way,' Alex said. That's how it had been reported in *Nice-Matin*. The article covered two pages, with photographs of the guests, in one of which Françoise had insisted she could see the back of Alex's head. Natascha pushed more papers aside and patted the sofa beside her. Alex sat. Michael hovered nearby, restlessly fiddling with his phones and throwing peanuts into the air before catching them in his mouth. He left the ones he missed on the floor.

'There was someone behind me,' Natascha said. 'I'm sure of it. But Michael says people will just think I had too much to drink.'

'You think someone pushed you? By mistake, of course,' said Alex.

'It didn't feel like a mistake, Alex. It was more like a deliberate shove.'

'But who on earth would do that?'

Michael stopped popping his peanuts. 'Nat, give it a rest. No one touched you, OK? It was an accident, it's over. Leave it alone.'

Natascha's face brightened when her husband wandered out of the room. She reached behind her back and held up a folder with a silver clasp. 'Look, Alex, I've been sourcing accessories for the store! It's the only thing that cheers me up right now. I can't wait to get going on it again, if only he...' She stopped talking as Michael walked past in the hall.

There were print-outs, pages torn from brochures, emails. Natascha had chosen designer candlesticks and fruit bowls, etched glass lampshades, painted occasional tables, and a selection of the kind of *objets* Alex had never understood: ostrich eggs arranged in baskets and sculptural willow-wood shapes to fill a corner. She could almost smell the room fragrance sprays. It would be a wonderful shop, she was sure, but Natascha could afford to launch an entire luxury brand if she wanted. How could this little business possibly keep her occupied?

When Michael reappeared, Natascha quickly pushed the folder under another one with 'For Signature' embossed on the front. He stood with his hand on the doorknob, and said, 'Thank you for coming, Mrs Coates. We appreciate it. My wife will be resting for a while. We'll let you know as soon as we need your help again.' Natascha gripped Alex's arm, but Michael walked out into the hall and turned to wait for Alex. Sammy's mother held the front door open for her, shaking her head sadly as she passed.

One afternoon shortly after the incident on the *Vanessa B*,

Julie Eichenbaum had turned up at Immobilier Charpentier, hauling Lolly in behind her. The dog had taken up almost all of the office. They had moved on to the *terrasse* at Maxie's, and Maxie had then moved them inside as the evening temperature dipped. The giant dog squeezed under the table, watching Honda warily.

Sal Eichenbaum, who had arrived in LA, called Julie several times in succession. The one-sided conversations lasted either less than a minute ('Yeah. Nah. OK. Ciao.'), or longer, as Sal sought Julie's opinion on everything, from what to eat, to how much the cinematographer earned. At last Julie turned off her phone. 'The idiot really thinks these little foxes are interested in him,' she volunteered about her husband. 'But take away his Oscar and his houses and he's just another fat jerk.' She shrugged helplessly, as if Sal's womanising was an endearing foible.

Meanwhile, the house in Eze was still for rent. Other estate agents had been to see it, but Julie seemed in no hurry. 'You know, most of these estate agent guys are no more professional than you, Alex,' she said, surprised.

A couple of days later, they met again. 'You look too English,' Julie blurted out. 'Like you're going to pick roses.' Alex smoothed her white cotton shirt. Her arms were beginning to get quite tanned now. 'Show a bit more shoulder or something.' Julie herself looked like she should be carrying a painter's ladder.

'You should talk,' Alex said.

'I don't have your looks. You're as sexy as hell underneath and you don't even know it, do you? No wonder that guy is crazy about you.'

Guillaume was like a cat, always around, but rarely for long. He came and went, leaving receipts and notes that Alex answered with messages on voicemail. The arrangement seemed to work: things ticked over, a sort of status quo was maintained, any real movement on hold until...until what?

Alex didn't know.

Until the solicitors, Quelin & Company, advised otherwise? Until Beth calmed herself down and came back to Nice? Until Natascha reappeared from her luxurious white cocoon near the Negresco? Until Alex decided to give Ed another chance?

When Patrice LeBlanc phoned one afternoon, Alex had to think hard before she remembered why the name had such resonance. The owner of the Menier villa! A contract had not been signed, LeBlanc explained, an agreement had fallen through; there was some misunderstanding with the letting agent in Paris. Did Madame Charpentier still have an interested party?

Alex felt as if her ears had popped. At last, something seemed about to happen. She made an appointment with LeBlanc for the following day.

CHAPTER THIRTY-NINE

When Alex opened her eyes to the spring light filtering into the bedroom at Les Jolies Roses, it took a moment to realise why she felt so completely awake: the Menier villa. Today, she would see Chantelle's favourite at last.

She dressed quickly and hurried through the market towards the Citroen. Bulbous globes of artichokes were stacked in piles on nearly every stall now, and Alex scanned the prices as she passed.

'We have the best and cheapest, Madame Alex,' someone called to her, holding out a bouquet of artichokes tied by their long stems. She slowed down to look, just long enough to catch sight of Guillaume in the crowd. A bunch of red carnations peeped from his canvas shopping bag. She edged closer to him while she examined the vegetables, pretending not to have noticed him. If he wanted to avoid her, he could, she thought. But he had seen her. He extended his hand.

'Such beautiful flowers,' Alex said. 'Where did you find them?' She didn't care, but she couldn't let him walk away. She would have grabbed his collar if she could. They were jostled by other shoppers with their bags and baskets. Alex watched his face as he told her about fixing a problem with some gutters, but as he spoke, his eyes never left the red onions he was choosing. He'd got rid of that blockage he'd mentioned, too – god knows what the tenant had been throwing down the drains. Oh, and there were definitely no more cats to irritate Madame Valentin. Alex knew. She'd seen the white cats with black tails in Bellet. He moved aside to let another customer near the piles of produce, and Alex grabbed his arm.

'By the way, did Odile Perrin get in touch? She's a character, isn't she? She wanted Chantelle to find a buyer for some land up there.'

Guillaume shrugged. 'She asks Chantelle to look at that field every few months – it's her way of keeping in touch.

Otherwise, she doesn't see anyone.'

'But you see her, don't you?'

He slung his canvas bag from one hand to the other. 'Odile is my wife's aunt,' he said. 'She brought my wife up. So I visit sometimes.'

Perhaps Guillaume and his wife Therese had played in the old château along with other local children, Alex thought. Perhaps they had fumbled and kissed as teenagers in its shadowy, tumbledown rooms. She looked at the bunch of carnations, and wished she and Beth hadn't uncovered his intimate shrine.

'Well, she sent my daughter and me packing,' Alex laughed. She didn't mention the Menier villa. Anything that raised the subject of Natascha Barron now would ruin the moment's precarious entente, but she could think of nothing more to say. She released his arm as he turned away.

As Alex got out of the car in front of the Menier villa, she was struck by the fresh smell of recently cut grass. It was blissfully quiet. Any passing noise was muffled by the clipped hedges and overhanging mimosa that hid the property from the road.

She looked up at the villa. It had none of the usual ornamentation, no bunches of plaster grapes, no floral friezes under the eaves. Its façade, two storeys high, was as flat as milk. The glazed black roof tiles shone in the sun. Low laurel hedges hugged the front of the house, making it look as if it were growing out of a neat green ruff. It might have been austere had it not been for the peacock-blue shutters, carved rather than louvred in the usual Mediterranean style. She noticed as she got closer that the latch between each pair was actually the metal trunk on a wooden elephant.

Patrice LeBlanc's grey eyes were humourless. '*Non*, Madame, there's nothing romantic about them,' he said, referring to the shutters. 'When I bought the property after the fire, I rebuilt it according to the existing footprint. My architects had no trouble finding a supplier for machine-cut shutters. It was a competitive price – cheap, in fact. The latches had to be made, of course, but they're so simple, any metalwork apprentice could do it. And besides, not all of them were destroyed by the fire.'

The same charming detail appeared on the inside of the shutters, which locked when the trunk curled round the tail of the animal in front. In the cool, dark dining room, Alex helped LeBlanc unhook the trunks and swing open the shutters to let in light. The room, like all the others, was empty. Faint scratches on the hexagonal terracotta floor tiles showed that the previous tenants had had a table for eight.

LeBlanc would never consider selling, he said. The rental income was too lucrative. He talked rapidly as Alex followed him around the house about the ratio of income to square metreage and rattled off the management fees he'd been quoted. He tapped his fingers on his thigh impatiently when Alex stopped to look at each room, as if he'd already decided that she'd be unable to bring him any clients. He fired questions at her with a cold smirk, as if he didn't expect the *Anglaise* to come up with the answers. Fortunately, Alex had done her homework. By studying Chantelle's other contracts, she was able to snap out answers on sliding-scale fees, on discounted insurance premiums, on renegotiating contracts... Alex felt smug. If the Barrons weren't interested, she might even be able to find other tenants. How pleased Chantelle would be with that!

She looked around the villa a second time while LeBlanc took a call in the reception hall. From the upstairs rooms, there was no sight of the alley between the villa and its neighbour, where she had first seen Ed and the Russian arguing beside the dark-green Mercedes. She could only imagine where it was, some 50 feet away.

LeBlanc had already had the house redecorated in preparation for the tenancy that had fallen through. The kitchen was fully equipped with a huge range cooker and marble countertops. The four bathrooms each had walk-in showers the size of Alex's bathroom at Les Jolies Roses. There were even two monitors for the security cameras discreetly placed beneath a shelf by the front door. Natascha and Michael could move right in. But something was lacking. Alex tried to imagine what Chantelle admired so much about the rebuilt house, but the only thing that was really appealing were the shadows that the shutters created. Alex snapped a couple of photos with her phone. She would show these to the professor: lines of sunny little elephants that plodded over the floors and walls in the darkened rooms. Nothing else in the house, unfortunately, lived up to their quirky promise. She sighed and put her phone in her bag.

Alex found LeBlanc again in one of the downstairs rooms, one she'd thought Natascha could use as a study. He was kneeling on the marbled floor tiles, running his finger along the grouting. 'Yes, Monsieur LeBlanc, you're right, it's ideal for rental,' Alex said as brightly as she could. 'I'll get my clients in to see it.'

'*Très bien*,' LeBlanc said. 'And I'll have this looked at. I don't know what's happening – it's the second or third time I've found grouting that hasn't set properly. I should never have replaced the old terracotta tiles. They weren't even badly damaged by the fire. Still, a minor problem. My housekeeper's husband has been trying to take care of it.'

A door slammed at the back of the house. LeBlanc winced. 'That'll be the housekeeper now,' he said. 'She's new. The woman I'd had for years died a few weeks ago.' He made it sound no more than an inconvenience.

They went into the hall. 'Maria!' LeBlanc called.

'I'm coming!' The accent wasn't French. Footsteps echoed around the empty spaces as the housekeeper made her way from the kitchen on the opposite side of the villa. LeBlanc's phone rang again and he moved into the study to answer it.

The footsteps stopped. 'Madame?'

Before Alex had turned completely around, she stepped

back in shock. So did the housekeeper. It was the blonde woman that Ed had worked so hard to avoid.

'What are you doing here?' the woman whispered. She came uncomfortably close to Alex and stared angrily. 'You're in on it, too?'

'I don't know what you're talking about.'

They pulled away from each other as LeBlanc returned.

'Ah, there you are, Maria. This is Madame Coates. She may be showing some tenants around shortly.'

Maria's broad smile transformed her into someone benign and biddable. She virtually curtseyed to LeBlanc.

'Of course, Monsieur. *Enchanté*, Madame.' Alex's scalp prickled. She stuck close behind LeBlanc as he led her outside.

'Let me show you the grounds. The gardeners have been in, but the pool still needs...' He stopped abruptly. 'Is everything alright?' Alex's heart was thumping beneath her breastbone, but she nodded.

'Well,' LeBlanc continued. 'You don't need to know all this yet. To be honest my former housekeeper and the agency in Paris arranged everything between them like clockwork. All I did was bank the cheques.' He talked as he walked ahead so that Alex hurried to keep up, but she was no longer listening. What could the blonde have meant? In on what? What could she and Ed be involved in together?

'None of this was damaged by the fire,' LeBlanc was saying. He waved towards the summer kitchen. Like many old villas, the house had an open stove in a portico for use when it was too hot to cook indoors. Alex had seen summer kitchens equipped with cutting-edge gas ranges, wine coolers and ice makers, but this one retained the simplicity of an earlier era. It was attached to the house with a tiled roof that protected an old stove and a ceramic sink. Olive-wood logs were piled up against the wall. The spot behind the open grill was blackened from years of use. The scene overlooked a grassy slope down to the empty pool.

'That's sad about your former housekeeper,' Alex said

weakly. 'What with the other deaths attached to the house, I mean.'

'And inconvenient,' LeBlanc said. 'But let's not mention that. Come, I'll show you the pool house.'

The main building's proportions were echoed in a miniature version a few feet from the pool. The pool house had been added just a few years ago, LeBlanc said. It had two spacious showers, two mirrored dressing areas with heated towel rails, and a lounge. One wall was entirely open to the pool.

Alex glanced back up the slope of lawn to the house. One of the elephant shutters remained open, and she imagined Maria there, watching. 'It's hard to find good help, isn't it? How did you find Maria?' Alex's voice was shaking.

'A stroke of luck. I met a local man through a mutual acquaintance in Paris, just after my housekeeper died. Conversation came round to it, and he offered me his housekeeper. She'd been with him for years. Thank god it's worked out.'

Alex said, 'Do I know him?'

LeBlanc shrugged. 'Listen, Madame Coates, I must be going. Give me a call. Let's get this deal done.'

As they were shaking hands by the Citroen, LeBlanc remembered. 'Of course, Bronz. That was his name. Somewhere near St Jean Cap Ferrat.'

Alex was momentarily relieved – she could see it all clearly. The woman just an embittered ex-employee, she thought. Ed probably had to get rid of her for some reason. But as she reversed the car on the gravel drive, she remembered that the housekeeper who had been with Ed for years was Alain's old friend Suzanne.

CHAPTER FORTY

Alain Hubert's BMW was parked outside Maxie's, but there was no sign of him at the restaurant. It was quiet on the *terrasse*, as it often was when late afternoon was becoming early evening. Three young women were drinking tea in the last strip of sun, and Françoise was standing in the doorway. She tapped the table beside her as Alex was walking past.

'You look like you need a glass of *rosé*, Madame,' Françoise called. Alex smiled. She had been thinking too hard on the drive back from the Menier villa. She told Françoise about the house with its beautiful shutters, about Patrice LeBlanc and the summer kitchen and the pool house. But she didn't mention the housekeeper.

Three times now. First, tearful and barefoot, calling after Ed in the street. The second time, shouting at him by the Villa Arson. And now appearing in the Menier villa, the new replacement housekeeper recommended by Ed himself.

Alex sipped the wine Françoise set on the table. 'You're in on it, too?' What could the woman have meant? Did she think Alex was sleeping with Ed? Well, that was understandable. Was *she* sleeping with him?

Her train of thought was interrupted by a little cry beside her. She looked up to see Beatrice, the teller from the bank, more orange than ever.

'You look so worried, Madame! Has something happened? Our dear Chantelle?' She sat down and stretched across the table towards Alex.

'No, no. There's nothing I can tell you.'

'What a dreadful situation. And you're doing so much to keep the business on its feet. Everyone in the *quartier* has noticed. I hope it's not too much for you?'

'Oh, no. Everything's fine.'

Alex sensed a shadow of disappointment on Beatrice's face. There was no one within earshot, but the bank teller stretched even closer and lowered her voice.

'I shouldn't tell you, but my manager is concerned. He's been speaking with the *administrateur judiciaire*. The overdraft.' Beatrice's fingers wiggled in front of her as if she were typing.

Alex shifted in her chair, angling her body away.

'It would be helpful if a new lease were signed quickly, or a sale agreed,' Beatrice continued. 'Perhaps the American millionaires?'

'They haven't made any decisions yet.'

'A shame. Perhaps you should give them a nudge? The sooner the better, Madame, for Chantelle's accounts.'

Having dropped her little piece of information into Alex's lap, Beatrice sat back happily. 'I can't stay,' she said, as if Alex had urged her to. 'I must prepare my husband's dinner.'

Alex ordered another *rosé* as soon as Beatrice was gone. Surely this was a more pressing thing to worry about than who Ed was sleeping with? She was going to have to take a careful, critical look at Chantelle's hardbound ledger.

She jumped when she realised that the hand putting her glass of wine on the table was Alain's.

'Françoise thinks you were disappointed with the Menier villa,' he said.

'She's right. I had such hopes for it, but there's no reason to assume the Barrons won't like it. Or the professor. But there's a housekeeper there, the owner said she'd worked for Ed Bronz.'

Alain stopped playing absently with the little piece of gilt frame.

'Could that be right, Alain? I thought Suzanne had always been Ed's housekeeper.'

'I don't keep up to date with everything Suzanne does,' Alain said. 'But I'm sure she's been working for him for many years. Why?'

'And she wasn't sharing the job with anyone? An eastern European woman?'

Alain's eyes glittered. 'Alex, tell me what you want to know.'

Should she tell him? She wasn't even sure what there was to

say. But Ed's house interested him, and Alain would make more sense of these connections than she could. He stood beside her, waiting. Perhaps this was one of his police interview techniques, unnerving people until they talked.

'It's just that the owner of the Menier villa told me his new housekeeper used to work for Ed Bronz. I thought it was odd. I remembered Suzanne; she was so worried Ed would be angry about calling the police.'

Alain thought about it for what seemed a long time.

'She may have worked for him somewhere else,' he said at last.

Yes, of course! How stupid of her. A simple explanation. Alex threw her hands up. Why hadn't she considered that possibility? But all the same, this was beginning to make her skin crawl.

CHAPTER FORTY-ONE

When she got back to Les Jolies Roses, seeing a plate and one of her crystal tumblers in the kitchen sink quickly emptied Alex's mind of any thought of the blonde. An empty bottle of water on the countertop was surrounded by breadcrumbs.

Alex stopped to listen for a moment, holding her breath. She stood outside the guestroom door, then tapped lightly. There was no reply. Alex cracked open the door. Inside, a pile of papers was balanced on the folding table that served as a desk. Beth's laptop was open beside it, connected to Alex's printer. The teenage Beth would never have left this sheaf of papers out for anyone to see, Alex thought

When the girls were young, Alex had tried never to pry. Meghan, in any case, was an open book. She trailed around the house after Alex telling her every detail of her life. It wasn't unusual for Alex, exhausted by the minutiae of Meghan's passing crushes and girlish feuds, to shout at her in irritation. Meghan was unfazed. She'd simply take up where she'd left off later. Alex was rarely interested in the prattle itself, but she loved Meghan's self-absorbed confidence, her absolute faith in the fact that she was the centre of everyone's attention.

Beth was the opposite. It was only through Meghan's chatter that Alex and Rod discovered details they would have preferred not to know: that Beth was smoking, that she'd been to a party at a notorious squat, that she lied. Alex and Rod refused to threaten or punish her. There was no point in slanging matches. But they reached the conclusion that the more attention they paid, the more secretive Beth became.

Prying, as Alex knew, could backfire. Beth had tried several times to keep a journal like Meghan's, which was usually left open on the kitchen table, but she didn't stick with it. Nonetheless, one day when Alex was doing the laundry, the key to Beth's lockable teenage diary had fallen out of a shirt pocket. Alex showed it to Rod, but he laughed and told her she was asking for trouble. The key sat in the laundry room, tempting her, until eventually she had given in.

Alex had been shocked by the venom she encountered in Beth's diary. 'She's a bitch' was written several times. It didn't take long for Alex to realise who Beth meant as she flicked, horrified, between pages, but whatever she had done wasn't clear. It didn't matter. She tucked the key back into the seam of Beth's shirt pocket, fighting off a sick, tearful feeling for weeks.

The feeling flooded back now as she noticed the light on Beth's laptop was illuminated. She nudged the screen gently, and it lit up: Beth's inbox. 'Don't,' Alex whispered. 'Don't.'

But she leaned towards the screen. She saw the name of Beth's tutor in London. Alex scanned the text. 'Excellent progress,' she read. 'The photos you've sent show a wonderful development in your style…keep going!' Alex didn't need to see any more. It was good news. She should have known Beth would get on with it; that was her way. Why had she ever doubted her? Beth must have been so stressed, quietly working away in Menton to meet her deadlines. Of course she'd been a bit snappy.

It was a reflex to straighten up the papers on the desk, and Alex slid them into a pile before she realised what she was doing. The word 'Raskilovich' jumped out at her. She read on.

'That's some grudge you have about Natascha Raskilovich! What's she ever done to you? My advice is to be friends – even if her father's collection does turn out to include stolen work, she's not a criminal herself. Calm down! Tame that malicious energy for your own work.'

It was signed affectionately by someone called Carrie – yet another friend Alex had never heard of. What had Beth been saying? She fanned out the rest of the papers with the tip of her finger, but nothing caught her attention. She touched the screen, but there seemed nothing else from anyone called Carrie. Malicious energy; Alex said the words out loud. She shut the computer. Yes, it was a good description for Beth. She had rolled in and out of the apartment like a sudden storm.

Alex was brushing her teeth when her phone buzzed in the living room. She automatically checked the time. Beth wasn't likely to call so late, but Alex ran for the phone, expecting her anyway. Natascha's voice took her by surprise. The girl was whispering, despite the talking and laughter Alex could hear in the background.

'Can you meet me tomorrow in the Old Town?' She sounded anxious. Alex strained to listen as she noted the time and place Natascha had chosen. 'But please, if you happen to bump into Michael, don't mention it, OK?'

The next morning, Alex arrived at the restaurant Natascha had chosen in plenty of time. There was no room for tables outside the little bistro; there was just a window and a door, lace curtains drawn so that it appeared closed. The rue Droite, like most of the Old Town's medieval streets, was narrow – Alex could stand outside the restaurant and with a bit of effort, reach across to the ochre plaster on the wall opposite. Even at midday in high summer, these ancient buildings would be cool and dark. They towered above her.

Now, as she waited, she noticed another carved medieval lintel above a doorway. In this maze of alleys, ordinary people had been cooking, eating, doing their washing, fighting and probably waiting for each other just like this without interruption since the 15th century.

Natascha arrived looking tired. She kissed Alex on both cheeks and hugged a red paisley wrap around her shoulders as if she were cold.

'I chose this place because Michael would never come here,' she said, linking her arm in Alex's. 'He hates the Old Town. He's claustrophobic.'

The restaurant was minuscule, with close rows of wooden tables and traditional chairs with rush seating. Michael would look like a giant in a doll's house here.

When they had settled, Natascha sighed loudly. 'Oh, Alex,

it's so good to see you. Everything's been horrible since Dario's party.'

Even pale with exhaustion and on the verge of tears, she was beautiful.

'I was so sure someone tried to hurt me on that boat,' Natascha said. 'Michael absolutely refuses to listen. He won't even let me talk about it. He keeps telling me I'm crazy and that he's worried about me. He asked the maid to lock up his uncle's pistol collection, for goodness sake.' She seemed to think this was funny, and smiled briefly. Her face was so easy to watch, but could Beth be right, that Natascha was spoiled and manipulative? Or was she really the lonely girl who could trust no one, the girl Alex had pitied during their first meeting?

'Michael says I need to rest, that I'm not strong enough to see anyone yet. He even checks who I've phoned. He shouts at me if I want to go out. Where can I go? The only people I know here are friends of his. And you, of course.' Her hand popped out from under the paisley shawl to squeeze Alex's arm. 'The maid lent me her phone to call you.' She shook her head in disbelief. 'He wants me to go home, back to New York.'

Alex poured water from the carafe. Perhaps she should give Michael some credit. After all, setting yourself up in a foreign country without the support of your husband verged on petulance, and going back to the US would make sense for everyone. If Natascha were to return now, perhaps Beth would calm down. And Guillaume would definitely feel more comfortable. Even Paulette Bitoun would be happy to see the elegantly retreating back of Natascha Barron. Natascha's eyebrows arched higher than usual as she waited for Alex to say something.

'Maybe that would be for the best.'

Chantelle would have considered this a form of treachery, sending away potential clients, and Alex briefly imagined her shocked face.

'You don't really believe that, do you?' Natascha said. 'People have been telling me what to do all my life, Alex. They always say they have my best interests at heart, but it never looks that way to me. Michael used to understand that. We both wanted to get away from everyone who told us what to be and how to act. But now even he is trying to tell me what I think. Someone wanted to hurt me on that boat. I'm not crazy!' She rapped the table.

'But who would want to hurt you?' As Alex whispered the question, Guillaume and his bizarre, sad family shrine came to mind. It was a ridiculous idea, of course. Guillaume was nowhere near the boat.

'You'd be surprised. A lot of people hate the name Raskilovich.'

Alex remembered Julie's imitation of a furious Ed on the *Vanessa B.*

'When I meet people for the first time, I can see it in their eyes,' Natascha continued. 'They hate me for being something they aren't. Richer than them; younger, luckier, maybe prettier. My father had enemies, and they hate me for being his daughter.' She chewed the inside of her cheek furiously.

'Michael's only trying to protect you,' Alex said. 'I'm sure he doesn't want you to feel this way.' But she didn't believe a word of what she was saying. She wouldn't put anything past Michael Barron.

Natascha's eyes filled with tears. 'I really love him, Alex. But now that we're married, I'm beginning to think maybe he's just like the rest of them.'

Alex waited for Natascha to say more. She had ordered *porchetta*, the restaurant's local speciality, and the waiter now slapped the enormous slice of stuffed suckling pig onto the table. The pork crackling looked irresistibly crisp, and the various meats it contained looked perfectly tender. It smelled delicious. Natascha winced. She'd ordered spinach ravioli.

'His family, I mean,' she said. 'The Barrons. They're awful, Alex. They've got money and influence coming out their ears, but they just want more. I'm tired of people like them. I fell in love with Michael because he was different. He didn't care about all that, but he's changed. He wants to control things now too, starting with me. Someone tried to hurt me on that boat and he refuses to let me think it's true.'

Natascha picked at her ravioli as Alex tried consoling her. It was crowded on the yacht's dance floor, she told her. That railing, well, often things that look marvellous aren't quite up to the job. There's sure to be an explanation.

But Natascha's mind was made up. 'This whole business with my father's private collection isn't helping,' she said sadly. 'Maybe I've been letting all the estate matters get to me.'

Alex put down her knife. Perhaps she was about to hear Natascha's side of the story.

'I've read one or two things about that,' she said.

'See? I feel so exposed. Everyone feels entitled to an opinion.'

'Oh, no, Natascha... I didn't mean...'

Natascha patted Alex's arm again. 'Not you, of course. You're my friend. I mean people who'd be pleased if my father's pictures turned out to be forgeries. People who want to make him look an old fool. He loved those pictures. We had so many beautiful works of art when I was a child, but my father never displayed his favourites. They were for the two of us alone to share, that's what he used to say. He told me they were the ones my mother would have loved. When he was dying, he told me he'd sold them. He said there would be no pleasure in them for me alone. Why would he say he'd sold them if he hadn't? Why would he lie to me?' She searched Alex's face. 'Do you know where they were found?'

Alex sighed. Yes, she did know, but she wished she didn't. It had been reported in the newspapers, and it had been covered in the documentary she'd watched on TV the night of the party. Everyone knew it, and no one was likely to forget. She took a sip of water and waited to let Natascha say it herself:

'Those pictures were found inside the family mausoleum, with my mother, when my father was buried. Can you imagine what he must have gone through to get them there?' Natascha covered her face with her hands. 'She was the only other thing in the world that he loved, besides those paintings.'

'And you,' Alex said.

Natascha shrugged, and wiped tears from her cheeks She'd barely touched any of her lunch and covered it with her napkin. Suddenly she smiled. 'But at least the situation has got the wind up the Barron family!'

'Why?'

'I wanted those few pictures to stay with my parents, where my father wanted them to be forever.' Natascha said. 'But the Barrons won't accept that. Even Michael is on their side. Now that everyone's going crazy about their authenticity, everything's on hold. As well as my father's secret pictures from the mausoleum, there are all the pictures in the main collection. Which ones are fakes?'

She seemed to have cheered herself up, and ate a mouthful of bread with relish. When she finished chewing, she said, 'No one will touch any of them until they're authenticated. And if they're forgeries, those pictures won't be worth a dime!' The thought was making her glow. 'As executors, the Barrons won't get much reward for their labours, will they? They'll be the fools.'

'But what about you?'

'I don't care. Even if my father was duped on his favourite pictures, so what? He won't know now. They gave him, and me, so much pleasure. And I don't care about the money. With my beautiful new shop, I'll earn my own money for once.' A tan kidskin wallet appeared from underneath her shawl, and she took out several 20-euro notes. 'Don't you have any more properties for me to see? I really need to get out of the apartment.'

As they left the restaurant, they hesitated just outside the door, deciding on which direction to take. That was just long enough for Alex to notice a red polka-dot ribbon tied in a huge bow bobbing above the crowd, coming their way.

'Damn!' She grabbed Natascha's arm. 'Get moving! Paulette

Bitoun!'

Natascha giggled, and put her hand in Alex's. All eyes were on Natascha as they walked quickly down Rue Droite. When they reached the angle with Rue Rossetti, Alex looked back.

'I don't think she's seen us. Keep moving!' But it was too late. The designer's voice rang out behind them.

'Yikes! Don't look back!' Natascha laughed. When the open door of a church appeared on their left, she ran up the steps, pulling Alex after her into the gloom. Alex breathed in the peculiar combination of incense, wood polish and candle wax. They huddled towards one of the baroque chapels, backs to the door, and Alex lit a candle. She handed the taper to Natascha, who whispered in a shrill voice, 'Oh no!' and pulled her on. 'She's here! We'll have to make a run for it. This way!' Alex glimpsed Paulette standing near the doorway, blinking as her eyes readjusted to the shadowy interior. As Paulette moved deeper into the church, Alex and Natascha hid their faces by turning inwards towards the exuberant cherubs and golden plasterwork, as if they were tourists, and walked back out the door on the other side.

They ran up some steep steps and stopped, sweating, about half way along. On the shady side of the street, they leaned against crumbling walls to catch their breath. Before they had a chance to speak, Paulette's absurd bow appeared in the crowd below them. She turned in the opposite direction. Alex and Natascha ran round the nearest corner and kept moving. Natascha grabbed Alex's hand and squeezed it. She was radiant.

'She'll never catch up now,' Alex said, after a few minutes. After the noontime lull, the streets of the Old Town had filled up again. Businesses that had closed for lunch reopened their doors onto the streets. Aromas drifted out from the dark interiors: lavender, garlic, fresh bread, coffee, pastis. A queue had formed outside a butcher's shop, where rabbits and chickens hung upside down from the doorframe. As Natascha pushed past, she yipped like a dog in distaste.

After several turns, they slowed down.

'Now where?' Natascha asked.

Alex was lost. As she was looking up, vainly, for the street signs, Natascha cried out, 'There she is again. Run!' Alex didn't look back. She pushed through the crowd, repeatedly murmuring '*Excusez-moi. Pardon.* Sorry.'

'This is ridiculous,' she said, breathlessly, after they'd turned another two or three corners. 'Let's stop.'

They brushed past the customers sitting outside a café and headed inside straight for the *toilettes* at the back. Natascha pushed the door eagerly; she banged into someone and the door bounced back. An angry face appeared from the other side: it was Julie Eichenbaum. When she saw them, she started to laugh.

'Jesus' Julie said. 'What have you two been up to?' They squeezed into the small space. Julie, too, looked flushed. 'I've got an excuse,' she said. They talked to each other's reflections in the mirror above the sink. 'I've been trying to get away from a crappy designer who's been hounding me all day.'

Alex and Natascha cried out in unison. 'Paulette Bitoun?'

They told each other their stories over coffee in a secluded corner of the café. Unfortunately, Julie said, Sal and Paulette had hit it off. He'd let Paulette think that she could work on his next building project. But of course there was no imminent building project, and Sal had left his wife to explain.

'She just won't listen,' Julie said. She held an unlit cigarette in one hand and her silver lighter in the other. 'How many ways can you say no way José?'

Natascha's laugh floated above the café's afternoon hum. Their unexpected chase has altered her mood like a drug.

'She spotted me buying olive oil and that was it. I had to leg it. She wants to get her hands on our place in Bellet but it's just not going to happen.'

Alex stopped laughing.

'You have a place in Bellet?'

'It's a dump,' Julie said. 'I don't know why we bought it, it was a crazy idea. We have to get rid of it. We thought we could rebuild, but you know. Time. Money.'

'There we go again,' Natascha said. 'I keep hearing about this Bellet place. I should take a look.'

'You keep hearing the name because my son's a journalist and I asked him to write about it for the *New York Times*,' Julie said. 'I figured it would help sell the old château we bought up there.' She looked sheepish. 'You have to use what you can, right?'

Alex sat back with a gasp. Julie kept on talking, almost lighting her cigarette several times before remembering smoking wasn't permitted. Alex understood. The crazy foreigner that the waiter in Bellet had mentioned; Julie fit the description perfectly.

As Julie described the derelict château and their plans to renovate it, Natascha's eyes gleamed. She stuffed her paisley shawl into her bag. The more she talked to Julie, the brighter she seemed to grow. By the time they parted, she planned to turn the château into the most exciting interiors and crafts boutique in all of southern France.

CHAPTER FORTY-TWO

The next morning, watching Alain Hubert and Françoise banter at the bar, Alex suddenly thought, of course, Alain has been in love with her for years. His presence here was nothing to do with the Police HQ next door, nor the old friends to see, the gossip to share. How could she not have seen it before? As Françoise chattered to Alain, she barely raised her eyes from drying glasses and restacking cups and saucers on the shelves behind her. He followed every move. When she laughed, he smiled and leaned back from the bar, as if pushing himself away from a table, replete.

Alex stirred sugar into her second *café* of the morning. What did Rod and I talk about during all those years, she thought. She tried to remember. Whether Meghan should have a bigger bike? Should they sell the car? Who would call the plumber? Wasn't Beth like her grandmother? What films are on at the cinema? Alex's throat tightened. She remembered Rod's fingers curled around a cup of tea across the table from her as they talked. How many times had she seen that? How gradually those fleeting moments amounted to something so precious.

When the professor stepped between Alex and the bar, she jumped. There was a shoulder strap attached to his briefcase now, and it pulled at his collar, exposing the blue-grey skin of his neck.

'I hear you have been to the Menier villa!' He sat down. Alex didn't bother to ask how he knew. Information flowed around Maxie's like seawater around tide pools. She nodded.

'And?'

'It was lovely,' Alex said. 'You were right.'

The professor squirmed happily.

'The shutters, Madame? What do you think?'

'Well, they're pretty. The way the trunks and tails form the latches, very clever. And the shadows they throw on the floor,

I...'

He was almost purring, but he thumped his skinny hand on the table.

'I've decided that I won't let that Ed Bronz put me off,' he said. 'I can use whatever I like in my book!'

'Of course, it's your book,' Alex said. She thought of the architects' drawings of the Menier villa in Ed's bedroom. Perhaps Ed had realised she'd been in there after all. She was sure the professor wouldn't notice her blush.

'But Madame Coates, do you think this is definitely the house referred to in my documents?'

He hauled his briefcase onto the table. Alex stopped her cup from toppling off just in time. Both Françoise and Alain glanced over. The professor unsnapped the buckle and Alex forced a smile at the reappearance of the plastic folder.

'Look,' the professor said. 'I've found this letter in the family papers.' He licked his lips and started to read. 'It describes a house with a distinctive black roof and elephantine shutters,' he read. 'That would prove the shutters are original to the Menier villa, wouldn't it?'

'Elephantine can just mean big,' Alex pointed out.

The professor shook the letter in frustration. 'It's my bad translation. In elephantine style,' he said, waving his arm in front of his face like a trunk. He scanned quickly. 'Yes, here, look: it's describing a party with lots of artists.'

'Oh my!' said Alex. 'That's a good start for your publishers.'

'Unfortunately I can't make out any names.

Alex sipped the dregs of her coffee and sighed. She pushed the folder back towards the professor.

'You could include the villa in your book anyway, you know. The shutters are worth it on their own. Not everything needs a secret.'

He looked at her doubtfully.

'If I don't fatten up my book with intrigue and romance, I'll never find a publisher. Oh, why must it all be so difficult, Madame Coates!'

Alex could see that at the bar, Alain's attention was now divided between Françoise and the professor. He wandered over. Before he had a chance to say anything, the professor was thrusting his documents into Alain's hands. Alain looked at a few of them, stopping at a photocopy of a crumpled, childish sketch.

'What's all this?'

Alex felt crumpled herself as the professor launched back into his familiar story.

'As I've told Madame Coates, it's a batch of documents I came across. They would be of no interest to anyone but architectural historians.'

The professor rooted self-importantly in his briefcase and showed Alain another folder. 'I'm writing a book, you know, about architectural details in the area.

'Yes,' Alain said. He took the folder and leafed through it eagerly, surprising both Alex and the professor.

'Is this all you have?'

'So far, but...'

'They're all copies?' Alain interrupted.

'Of course, but what...'

'Good. I'll borrow them for a few hours if you don't mind.' Alain put the folder under his arm and then he grabbed Alex's hand. 'And you. I might need someone who can speak English. Let's go.'

CHAPTER FORTY-THREE

'Mum, you mean, Alain took you right *into* the police station? They let *you* inside?' Meghan's voice squeaked through the receiver.

The sweet odour of melon filled Alex's little kitchen at Les Jolies Roses as she listened to her daughter. She tucked the phone between her shoulder and ear as she continued slicing the orange flesh.

'We were only there for a few minutes. It was like any old office, really,' Alex said. 'Nothing exciting.'

Alex herself had been surprised the evening before when Alain had ushered her straight into the commissariat next door to Maxie's. He introduced her as '*une amie*' as they made their way to a second-floor office, where the window looked out over Maxie's *terrasse*. The offices were quiet; work seemed to involve staring at computer screens. Alex was disappointed. Alain led her to a small cubicle and offered her a chair next to a paper-strewn desk. For a few minutes he chatted with the very young man in the next cubicle about Nice's recent footballing debacle against Marseilles.

'My former *adjoint* is on sick leave,' Alain explained to Alex, finally sitting down behind the desk. 'This is his office.' He looked around disdainfully. 'How can you concentrate in a place like this? There's no room to put your feet up and think. No wonder he's sick.'

Now Meghan, on the phone, listened to her mother tell the story. She said, 'I don't know why I expected any better from the French police. What did Alain do then?'

Alex gave Meghan an edited version of the professor's research.

'Alain went through something on the computer,' Alex said. It had taken a while. Alain didn't appear to be technologically adept, but whoever happened to be passing the little cubicle seemed happy to help. He paused for each person, even a tearful receptionist who spent too long complaining about her feckless brother. Alex fidgeted as Alain listened, watching him pick over what the girl said as if gauging what to store and what to discard.

At last he'd found what he was looking for. He turned the screen to Alex, but it seemed nothing more than a badly photocopied handwritten letter in French. She peered closer to the monitor. It would take hours to work out the handwriting. Alain enlarged the screen, then smoothed out the professor's photocopy of the sketch on the desk. He opened a drawer and scrabbled among the papers until he found a magnifying glass.

'I asked a friend of mine in Paris, an old *commissaire* like me, to send me some information. Something's been keeping me awake at night. I hate that, don't you, Alex? When you can't sleep?' He examined the photocopied drawing through the magnifying glass. 'It's so easy to send information around now – nothing but attachments to an email. I prefer having real things, like this.' He shook the professor's file lightly. 'Sometimes you can see the details more easily when you can touch them. Here, for instance.' He pointed to some spidery lines on the childish drawing, and gave Alex the glass.

She shook her head and handed it back.

Alain said, 'Here it is again.' He zapped the image on the computer screen up in size again, and Alex saw the same spidery knot of lines.

'It looks like the same thing, on both documents. What is it?' she asked.

'Just some initials. On the screen is the record of a police interview, signed by the interviewee. The other is a drawing, maybe a sketch. Could that be signed by the same person?'

He held the photocopy against the bright office light. 'Look carefully. You can just about see the letterhead on the back of this drawing showing through. Perhaps the person, a child even, I don't know about art, drew on whatever could be found. On the back of a sheet of paper that had been thrown in the wastepaper basket, maybe.'

Alex narrowed her eyes, but she still couldn't make anything out.

'This is the record of an interview with someone called Oleg Zhurkov.' Alain tapped the screen. 'Those are his initials. My friend the commissaire sent me this copy.'

'A criminal?'

'That's never been proved. This interview took place more than 30 years ago, when Zhurkov was under surveillance. But he disappeared shortly after, so the commissaire informs me. Would you like to see a photograph of him?'

Alex nodded. Perhaps the professor would have his intrigue and romance after all.

Alain clicked slowly on the keyboard until he pulled up a couple of faded photographs. Alex looked closely at the dark-haired man, who, in both pictures, was sitting in a café, reading a French newspaper.

'Imagine him older,' Alain said.

Alex tried. She added weight, some grey, and tiredness to the round face. Suddenly she could see the man she'd seen several times with Ed.

'Oh my,' she said. 'The man with the Mercedes.'

'That's who I see too, Alex.'

'But what does this mean? Why was he under surveillance all those years ago?'

Alain took the piece of gilt frame out of his pocket and rolled it round gently in the palm of his scarred hand.

'We thought he might have been connected to some art thefts. But it was a long time ago, as I said. Nothing was ever proven.'

'Then why are you interested in him now? What's in the professor's letters?'

'Nothing incriminating. But it's not really the letters I'm interested in. It's this.'

He held up the initialled drawing and angled the secretary's mirror so that they could both see its reflection.

'What does it say?"

Alex looked carefully. The mirror image made the faint letterhead on the back of the drawing show through more legibly.

'It's your name!' Alex said.

'An odd coincidence,' Alain said. 'By the way, where is our friend Ed at the moment?'

'I haven't seen him for a while, Alain.' The memory of them sitting on the sofa on the *Vanessa B* flitted through her mind. 'What's he got to do with your name on this piece of paper anyway?'

At that point, Alain's phone had rung, and as he answered it, he strolled out of the commissariat as if he still did it every day. Alex had no choice but to follow.

He was subtle, this old cop, she thought with irritation. The idea that Ed had been involved in something was now well and truly planted in her brain.

Meghan, on the other end of the phone, groaned. 'Mum, I give up. I warned you, but you wouldn't listen. Look at you! Wandering around police stations! You're coming home and that's that. I'm calling Beth right this second!'

Alex laughed. 'Calm down. Don't worry. And definitely don't tell your sister about this.'

The melon Alex had been slicing at the table by the window was just as she'd hoped it would be: exactly the right amount of sweetness and juiciness. She calculated that there were probably just a few hours when all three factors combined perfectly. She started to eat it, looking out over the lights coming on in the buildings across the street. Why had Alain wanted her to see that interview from decades ago? He might as well have led the professor into the commissariat. Why did he ask her about Ed Bronz? Ed definitely knew the Russian, both she and Alain knew that, but so what? If Alain thought she could provide any information, he was mistaken. In any case, it had been a couple of weeks now since she'd even heard from Ed.

She sank her teeth through a chunk of melon. A brief rush of heat travelled up her neck as she remembered Ed's hand on her shin. Should she feel a fool? Or should she admit that in fact she would be happy to see him again?

Night had fallen outside. She snapped on the table lamp, and a reflection in the black windowpane stared back at her: a woman, sitting quietly on her own, the simple lamp, the pretty plate, the ironed tablecloth. Is that me, she thought? Her phone was on the table, too. She picked it up and scrolled through the numbers until she reached Ed's.

The front door slammed loudly before she pressed Call.

Beth.

She put the phone down. She smiled as she waited for Beth to appear through the door, fixing the expression almost instinctively. The woman reflected in the black window would look pleased to see her daughter; no recrimination; no irritation; no exasperation.

'Sweetheart, there you are! Just in time for the last bite of the most perfect melon ever.' Alex held the bowl out.

'Why is it so dark in here? What's the matter with you?' Beth turned on the overhead light, then sat down and ate the melon, shoving her greasy hair behind her ears with juice-covered hands. The circles under her eyes made her look grubby. When she'd finished, she drummed her fingers on the table without looking at her mother. Nothing Alex thought of saying felt safe. She waited: Alain's little trick.

'Raymond's gone,' Beth said eventually. 'I don't care. I didn't like him that much.'

Her downturned lips showed that she didn't mean it. Had Beth cared that much for this man? Alex felt a pang of guilt. Rod would have noticed in an instant, but she apparently hadn't seen what was right under her nose. She'd been so involved with Immobilier Charpentier she hadn't noticed the most important thing.

'I'm going to stay in his flat for a while. The rent is paid for another month.'

Alex leaned towards Beth, but she sat back in her chair, out of reach.

'Menton's quieter than Nice,' Alex said. 'But come back whenever you like,' she added quickly. 'You know I want you to be here.'

'You don't care one way or another, do you?' Beth looked at Alex for the first time since she'd sat down. Her skin was papery and pale again. There was an eyelash on her cheek that, once, Alex would have blown away.

'Beth darling, of course I care. I just want…'

Beth put her elbows on the table and buried her face in the crook of her arm. Her narrow shoulders shuddered as she sobbed. Alex reached across and held her awkwardly just above both elbows. When Beth looked up, she said, 'Mum, I can't think straight any more.'

Tears stung Alex's eyes. 'Then I'll think for both of us, sweetheart. And the first thing I think you need is a good night's sleep.'

Beth nodded and wiped away tears with the back of her hand, and let Alex lead her to the guestroom. She pulled away abruptly as Alex pushed open the door.

'You've been going through my stuff!'

'No, of course not. I'd only come into this room if I thought you were here.'

But it was too late. Beth stuffed her laptop into its case. She ignored everything Alex said, stumbling around the room as she gathered up the few things she had left. She crammed what she could into the laptop case. Alex reached for her several times, but Beth shrugged her off. She was out the door within seconds. Alex called down to her from the balcony, though Beth couldn't, or wouldn't, hear. By the time Alex had run down the stairs after her, her daughter had disappeared. She could barely see through her tears as she ran back up to the flat.

She phoned Meghan back.

'It's her work, Mum. She's been really unhappy with everything she's been painting. It's making her touchier than ever, if that's possible. She'll be alright. She'll get on with it eventually. Give her some space.'

Alex slammed the guestroom door shut. She paced the flat, absently picking books off the shelves in the living room, then replacing them. Beth was more than touchy; she seemed angrier and more fragile than ever. Alex ironed a shirt, paying extraordinary attention to the cuffs and collar, but all she could see was the image of Beth's inconsolable eyes.

What would Rod do?

What would a *good* mother do?

Alex knew she couldn't keep her distance any more.

Chantelle's car was parked a five-minute walk from Les Jolies Roses. There was a map in the glove compartment, and Alex was sure she'd be able to find her way to Menton. She didn't have the address, but she'd call Beth when she got there. Perhaps she'd have calmed down by then. Traffic was light, it wouldn't take more than half an hour. She might even get there before Beth arrived by train. She would wait for her in the station car park.

But as she pulled onto the autoroute towards Menton, Alex knew it was pointless. Beth probably wouldn't answer the phone if she saw her mother's number. She might not even be heading back to Menton at all. She might sit at a café somewhere in Nice, and change her mind. Perhaps she had even let herself back into the flat and was waiting for Alex, feeling sorry for herself.

'You can't think straight either, can you?' Alex whispered aloud, gripping the wheel.

The car in front of her as she got off the autoroute to go home looked familiar. A silvery-blue Audi. Ed's car.

The Citroen's headlights momentarily illuminated the interior, and Alex could see there was someone in the passenger seat. The car slowed for a red light. Alex was close behind. Should she beep? Of course not. She didn't really want to know who was sitting next to Ed. She stayed behind the car because she had to – it was the way back home. But at the next red light, where she should have turned, she saw the person in the passenger seat pull the driver towards her. She assumed it was a her – she couldn't make out the figures in the dim interior of the car, but it was a sensuous move, one the driver didn't resist.

'Bastard,' said Alex, out loud. But she couldn't mean it – they were hardly lovers. They were barely even friends. She had no claim to Ed Bronz. But when the light changed to green, Alex stayed with them. She would try to get one quick look at that woman, just so she knew. 'Not his usual type,' the blonde woman, Maria, had said. Well, she'd get a good look at Ed's 'usual type' now, wouldn't she?

CHAPTER FORTY-FOUR

It was impossible to go fast in Nice, even late at night. There were too many traffic lights and too many haphazardly parked cars, and it was easy for Alex to stay a couple of cars behind the Audi. She followed it past the squat, solid villas of northern Nice, and then west. When it stopped suddenly at the top of Boulevard Gambetta, Alex jerked the Citroen to a halt, too. Everyone in Nice double- and even triple parked – no one would notice her. But the Audi took off again. Several cars passed before Alex could get moving, and now she wasn't exactly sure which tail-lights ahead of her to keep an eye on. She sped up, overtaking a van, before she noticed one of the cars ahead turn off to the right. She slowed as she reached the turning, trying to see. A car behind her beeped angrily, and she swung the Citroen round the corner.

She'd been on this street before. The memory came flooding back, making her cringe. The restaurant where she been caught by Alain, waiting in his car opposite, was brightly lit and crowded. She crept past. If anyone noticed her here, they'd assume she was looking for a parking spot. Further along, there was an intersection. No sign of any moving cars, let alone Ed's. People were probably tucked up in their beds in the buildings along these back streets, the way she should be. The car must have crossed the intersection. She'd move on just a bit to see...

She was dazzled at first by the gleaming onion domes of the Russian church. They were lit up from below, the five round roofs tiled like green fish scales. Even during the day it looked completely out of place amid the palms, but here, at night, glowing between the apartment buildings, it was magical. She knew it was here of course – there were still Russian businesses gathered around it, catering to the community that moved close to its orthodox church. She slowed down and glanced at it, mesmerised by its fairy-tale appearance.

She was forced to slam on the brakes suddenly. In front of her, the door of a parked car had opened wide. Alex's first reaction was to press the horn or to shout in irritation, but then she saw Maria. Alex's heart was beating wildly now. The blonde didn't even bother to look at who she'd brought to a sudden halt. She slowly put one foot then the other out onto the road, as if she were stepping out of a sportscar. With Alex's headlights in her eyes, she wouldn't be able to see who was in the Citroen.

Alex looked around rapidly for Ed. She couldn't see him anywhere – he must still be in the car. Could she get past without being seen? She waited for Maria to close the door. At last Maria nudged the door shut and as she was squeezing between the Audi and the car behind to get to the pavement, Alex accelerated past. She didn't think she'd been noticed – just another car passing; it was a good thing Chantelle's Citroen was common enough. She drove on another few metres, and pulled into the space in front of a garage. She adjusted her wing mirror so that she could see back down the street towards the Audi. Her hands were damp and her shoulders tense. When the driver's door opened, she felt like a cat watching for a mouse to pop out of its hole. But it wasn't Ed who climbed out.

It was Zhurkov.

Alex scrunched down. Zhurkov opened the rear door of Ed's car and leaned in to pull something from the back seat. Alex craned her neck for a clear view, but now he and Maria had returned to the street side of the car. She stretched across the car and put her hand out of the window to adjust the rear-view mirror, but Zhurkov and Maria were crossing the road. They turned down the next corner, out of sight.

Alex looked at her watch. Half past eleven. It was too late to phone Alain but she felt anxious. He'd want to know what she'd seen. She couldn't keep this to herself until morning. She was sure she had his number.

He sounded sleepy, and there was a television on in the background.

'No, it's not too late, Alex. Tell me.'

She didn't mention the fact that she thought she'd been following Ed Bronz, nor that the Russian, Zhurkov, had been driving Ed's car. She told Alain what she thought he'd want to know: that Zhurkov had a burnished leather document wallet, and that she had seen it in Ed's bedroom.

It wasn't until Alex got back to Les Jolie Roses that she allowed herself to think of Beth. There was no sign of her. The shutters on Maxie's and Les Soldats across the street were firmly closed. She gave Beth one last call – unanswered – before she went to bed.

CHAPTER FORTY-FIVE

Alex had become so used to the sounds of the *marché* that they rarely woke her now, but she lay in bed the next morning listening to thuds and rattles muffled by her closed window. She reckoned they'd started about 5.30am, when she had already been fighting for hours to stop her mind from prowling among the things she couldn't understand. There was probably an explanation for everything; there usually was. Why shouldn't the Russian be driving Ed's Audi? And the leather folder – well, surely she was just tired and emotional after Beth's tears. What had made her call Alain with the hare-brained idea that he should know about it? He was infecting her with his absurd possibilities.

Walking would help. It would pass the time until she could ring Beth. She'd be asleep now, and sleep was what her daughter needed most.

Alex headed northwest in the misty early morning air, climbing the steep concrete steps that sliced between properties lining the hillside. Seen from below, these houses sat on top of each other. As she walked, Alex saw they were each set in their own dewy, deserted gardens. Observing was like a form of meditation: a cat carrying a kitten behind an overflowing rubbish bin; swathes of pink blossoms arcing through metal railings; a pile of dusty flour sacks outside a boulangerie.

But she couldn't stop her mind flitting anxiously from image to image, memory to memory, and going nowhere. She stopped in front of two villas, struck by masses of crimson bougainvillea against their cupcake-pink façades. Between them, Magdalene blue sky. The rooftops of the city below spread out towards the glowing aquamarine sea. She could be standing inside a child's colouring book.

'And that's where you belong, the way you're behaving,' she said out loud. 'It's time to go back to being a grown-up.'

Back at the office, she patted her pockets the minute she saw the red light flashing on the office answering machine. She didn't have her mobile. Had she left it in Chantelle's car? The blinking display told her there were seven messages waiting – they must have all been left while she was tossing and turning this morning in bed. Beth? Meghan? Had they been trying to get hold of her? Alex tripped on the wastepaper basket in her rush to get to the phone.

All but one of the messages were from Harry.

'She's awake! Call me!'

'Alex, where are you? Call me!'

'Call me, it's urgent. Anytime!'

'Where the hell *are* you?'

Alex threw her keys on the desk, next to the dossier. Chantelle was awake! She would be home soon. Suddenly the scent of L'Eau d'Issey seemed to be all around. She realised it had been there in the office all along; a feminine note beneath the aroma of coffee and paper.

How much time did she have? There was plenty to do. The most important thing was to make sure that by the time Chantelle got home, Mr and Mrs Michael Barron were Immobilier Charpentier's most satisfied customers. She knew that Natascha would give her a glowing reference, but that didn't matter. Chantelle was a businesswoman, and her prize was the society couple's signature on her dotted line – and their money in the bank. This was all she had asked Alex to set in motion, and that was what Alex intended to achieve.

Harry was wide awake in New York; he answered the phone after one ring.

'Can you believe it, Alex? I'm so happy! Just one look from her is all the reward I need.' He broke off regularly to blow his nose. 'I feel like, me and Chantelle, we're on a voyage together, you know? Like adventurers? And we've reached the top of the mountain range, and we can see the other side?'

Alex waited through his sobs. She could have cried herself. It was as if the merry-go-round she'd been on was slowing down, and the dizzy feeling was lifting.

But Chantelle was not sitting up in bed and reading gossip magazines. Despite being unusually responsive, Chantelle had not yet spoken. By now, Harry knew everyone on the medical team. 'Frank's optimistic,' he said. 'He's the best neurologist in New York, and he thinks it's just a matter of time. And Irene, she's seen this before. She's powering up the physical therapy from tomorrow morning. She says Chantelle will be up and at 'em before we can say *ooh la la.*'

As she listened to Harry, she scanned the wall of photos. At last, at last, she thought. It will all be so much simpler when Chantelle takes charge.

She wanted to listen to all the messages again, and her hand was still on the answering machine when Guillaume opened the door, trailing the odour of woodsmoke. He frowned the moment he saw her.

'No, no, Guillaume, it's good news!'

He looked her directly in the eyes, and Alex noticed for the first time that his were pale green. He must have been good-looking when he was young, before things had gone so wrong.

Alex translated Harry's messages for Guillaume as they listened together.

'You're right, it is good news,' he said. His hands rasped as he rubbed them. 'We can hold on now. Can't we?'

'We haven't been doing too badly. I think Chantelle will be pleased.'

'It hasn't been easy for you, Madame Alex'

'It hasn't been easy for either of us, Guillaume. If it hadn't been for you, I would have had to shut up shop and give the keys to Monsieur Quelin or the *administrateur judiciaire.*' Alex was about to say thank you, but Guillaume was shifting impatiently from foot to foot. Alex wondered fleetingly what he and Harry Bormann would make of each other.

Guillaume went to the filing cabinet, and Alex knew from the rustle of papers that he was fastidiously filling in the times of his comings and goings.

The silence shattered as Natascha and Julie Eichenbaum exploded through the door. Natascha's pale green tunic, embroidered with tiny flying birds, made her look fresh and cool. Julie, in her overalls, was as tousled as a bedsheet. She gripped Lolly's collar with both hands.

They had bumped into each other in the market, Natascha explained. Alex was aware of Guillaume moving into the kitchen behind her, well out of sight of the two women.

'She's full of fire, this kid. I love her. She's trying to convince me to sell her that old château in Bellet,' Julie said.

'But I said I have to consult my realtor first,' Natascha laughed.

'And I said I'll have to consult mine.' Their amusement was infectious. Julie punched Alex on the arm. 'Come on, we want to go up to Bellet for a look. What do you say? Come with us.' The dog's massive nails pattered excitedly on the floor.

Alex strained to hear what Guillaume was doing in the kitchen. Even with his weak grasp of English, he would have understood that they were talking about Bellet.

'Yes, please come, Alex. Think of it as work!' Natascha flashed a smile. The woman reduced so low by the incident on the *Vanessa B* was on a high now. She grabbed Julie's arm. 'You introduced me to Julie after all. If there's a sale, she owes you. Business is business, right?'

Natascha yelped as Guillaume stepped out of the kitchen. She put her hand to her embroidered heart.

'Oh my God, you scared me,' she said, in French. But her manners, as ever, were impeccable. She sat down again and smiled sweetly. Guillaume glowered. Alex flushed with embarrassment for him.

'We've had good news,' Alex said. 'Chantelle…'

'Jeez, of course, you guys are working,' Julie interrupted. She smiled at Guillaume and switched to French. 'We should've thought about it first. Excuse us for barging in. I can't imagine why anyone would want to buy that dump in Bellet, but let the kid take a look. Alex, think about it. We'll be next door having coffee.'

They bustled through the door, energy sucking out along with them.

'I know who she is,' Guillaume said. 'She owns the château in Bellet.' He looked confused, almost hurt. Alex noticed his long eyelashes, so unexpected against his leathery cheeks. She felt sorry for him. 'What does she mean, buy it? Who's buying it?'

'No one, Guillaume. Natascha just wants to look, that's all. She won't be interested. Not even Chantelle could engineer that!' She laughed, but Guillaume was stony-faced.

'Why does she want to look at it? There's nothing there for a girl like her. Chantelle would know that.' He shut the door behind him without saying goodbye.

Alex agreed with him, but there was nothing she could do. As silence settled over the office once more, she noticed that the light on the answering machine was still flashing – there was one last message.

What now, she thought. How much more can I take?

It was Ed.

'Alex, you deserve to know a few things about me.' She thought she could hear the tail end of a Tannoy announcement in the background, as if he were at an airport. 'Things I want you to know. We need to see each other again. Please return my call.'

CHAPTER FORTY-SIX

Alex deleted Ed's message. She was convinced she was shaking. She held her hands out above the phone expecting to see them tremble, but they were perfectly still. She placed her hand on her stomach, and felt her heart beating calmly. She rubbed her eyes, knowing it would smudge her mascara, and hoped desperately that when she opened them, Rod would be walking through the door of Immobilier Charpentier. But all she could see was the morning sunlight beginning to creep through the panels of the property ads in the window. For not much more than a second, her face creased. Then she sent Beth a text asking her to call as soon as she could, and pulled Chantelle's make-up mirror out of the drawer to fix her eyes before going next door to Maxie's.

It wasn't too difficult to convince Natascha and Julie, sitting on Maxie's *terrasse* with Lolly, to head for Bellet without her. As soon as they left, Alex rushed inside the restaurant. Before she had opened her mouth, Françoise smiled broadly.

'We've heard the news!'

From Guillaume, of course. Why had she bothered to think she could share the good news about Chantelle herself? For once, she'd imagined being the person who knew something first.

'At last something to give us hope. We've been waiting long enough, eh?' Françoise put an espresso in front of Alex and said, 'You've done a good job. Chantelle will be satisfied.' She opened the morning's *Nice-Matin* and placed it on the bar for Alex to see. 'But let's hope your pretty client doesn't have a chance to look at the newspaper today.'

Alex recognised Michael Barron instantly. He looked surprised in the photographer's flash, but the woman who was kissing his neck was oblivious. She was clearly not Natascha, as it claimed in the caption beneath the picture, which described the opening of a new nightclub in Cannes. Alex couldn't be sure if it was the American girl he'd been kissing in the Mini, but it didn't matter.

'Naughty, naughty boy,' Françoise said. She put the newspaper under the bar.

Alex could have hit him. She gritted her teeth at the thought of Michael's smug face as she walked up Avenue Borriglione towards the car. She found her phone under the driver's seat. Only one missed call, from Ed – no message. He must have called the office just afterwards. She breathed in deeply as she sat in the car, and then dialled Alain's number.

'Good, it's you,' he said as soon as he picked up. He didn't give her a chance to explain that she'd changed her mind about what she'd seen in Zhurkov's hands; it was probably nothing. She wanted to apologise for bothering him with her silly idea. 'Meet me in front of Maxie's.'

'Alain, I...'

He rang off before she could say no.

Alex, resigned, sat on the edge of the *terrasse* to wait for him. She pulled up Beth's number on her phone, and was just about to press Call when the stallholder whose asparagus she liked so much planted himself in front of her.

'Such good news!' he said, pumping her hand. He smelled of earth and pastis. Soon there was a little crowd around her, everyone talking about Chantelle – everyone expected her back any day. Alex put her phone away. She gently put everyone right, but she was sure the facts would soon mutate back into gossip. What surprised her most was how many people knew exactly who she was: the *Anglaise* who was taking care of everything for Chantelle.

She jumped up when she saw Alain walking towards her.

'Alain, it was a silly idea, I couldn't see clearly...'

He stopped dead. 'Excellent news about Chantelle!' Alex wondered where he'd found out – he couldn't have been to Maxie's this morning. His face was even livelier than usual, full of restrained excitement. 'You know, we could go into the commissariat again and you could look through lots and lots of photos in big binders. That's how it used to be. But I'm learning a lot about how things are now.'

He looked very smug as he swiped his scarred finger over the screen of his phone. He offered her his reading glasses as he held it out to Alex. A photograph. She examined the image he was offering her carefully. A mug shot of a good-looking man with large eyes and full lips. His hair was brushed across his forehead; long sideburns – he would have been trendy years ago. The name "Oleg Zhurkov" was written beneath the photograph.

'From your friends in Paris, I assume,' Alex said.

'I'm getting to like this technology after all. Except sometimes.' He took a stiff envelope from his back pocket and extracted a photograph. 'I spent all night looking for this at home. I had to go through a lifetime.' The photograph had obviously faded over the years, but Alex was still struck by the colours. A group of people dressed for a party, cigarettes and cocktail glasses in hand. First, she recognised Françoise. Her dark hair was piled up on top of her head and she was wearing a long, yellow, sleeveless dress. She was the only person not smiling at the camera. Instead, she was looking up at the man next to her: Alain.

'You!'

'I don't matter,' Alain said. 'The next man.' He was heavier now, more tired looking, but he hadn't lost that watchful look. Even posing for the photograph, his attention seemed to be on something else.

'The Russian.' Alex said. 'Oleg Zhurkov. That's how he looked in the photo taken in the café.'

'It took me a while to believe it when I first saw him again looking at Maxie's menu. Sometimes when I see a pretty girl or a good-looking kid in the street, I think, *ouf*, that looks like my old friend so and so, where have they been? It's a shock to realise it can't be; those old friends are as grey as me now.'

Alex nodded. She knew exactly what Alain meant.

'So when I saw Zhurkov again, I had to be sure it was the

same man.'

'The man who made you lose part of your finger?'

'The very same.'

'Revenge won't get it back, Alain.'

'You've misunderstood me, Alex. A bit of skin is hardly worth an act of revenge. All I want to know is whether I've been right about something all these years. And our Russian friend might help me find out at last.'

'Right about what?'

Alain returned the photograph to the envelope.

'Have you heard from our Mr Bronz yet?'

She shook her head.

'There's something else you could help me with too, Alex.' She took a step back, wary. 'I want to talk to Natascha Barron.'

CHAPTER FORTY-SEVEN

Back at Immobilier Charpentier, Alex put the *fermé* – closed – sign on the door. She checked to see if she could find the message Ed had left earlier, but it was definitely gone; she felt guilty, almost treacherous. It had been nearly two weeks since she'd seen him on the *Vanessa B.* When she returned the call, she was going to make sure it sounded as if she hadn't noticed those days go by.

She used Chantelle's mirror to put on some lipstick – Chantelle herself did that, Alex had noticed, preparing herself for a difficult call. She tried not to remember the pang of jealousy she'd felt believing Ed was in that car with the blonde. She breathed deeply before dialling.

She put the phone down again moments later very gently. She needn't have bothered with the lipstick, and she dropped it back in her bag. Had she misunderstood the tone of Ed's message, the one she'd deleted? He'd just now sounded polite but brusque, as if she were no more than a business call, arranging a lunch date. Perhaps he hadn't intended his call to be personal at all. She wrote down the name of the restaurant Ed had suggested in Monaco so fiercely the tip of her pen broke through the paper in her notebook. Had she been misreading absolutely everything?

She looked at the wall of photographs of Chantelle, the butterfly amid soberly dressed men at estate agents' dinners and civic reunions. She certainly didn't look like a woman who could ever feel embarrassed or unsure of herself. Well, if Ed just wanted to do business, that's what Alex was there for.

She went over their brief call again. Perhaps he'd answered when he was busy. Was he in the middle of a meeting? After all, he had business in Monaco – he'd said so during their cool, impersonal conversation. Had she seemed too eager? Should she have said no to lunch? But how silly of her to think he was calling her personally. If he still wanted to rent out his house, she'd take care of it on Chantelle's behalf. In any case, after lunch she could pass through Menton on her way back to Nice. It would give her another chance to try to see Beth.

The next day, the noon sun was burning the glamour out of Monaco. Alex shut the Citroen's windows against the noise that reverberated off the close-packed apartment blocks as she sat in a traffic jam by the port. Her back was damp beneath her crisp cotton shirt, becoming damper with every motionless minute.

When at last she could park and had started walking towards the restaurant, she noticed Greenwood's gallery. It was – or in fact wasn't, as it turned out – Raymond's gallery; she couldn't forget the old Yorkshire name, so unexpected here among the chic French jewellers and Italian designers. Two windows each displayed one large, unframed painting: a pair of monochromatic grey seascapes. She slowed down to look. She wouldn't mind one of those – simply seeing them through the window cooled her down. As she searched for the signature, she became aware of someone looking out at her from behind the painting. Her eyes readjusted rapidly to see Alain. He motioned her to come in. She looked at her watch, and calculated she had a few minutes to spare.

'What on earth are you doing here?' she said.

The gallery was airy and spacious, each wall filled with one stormy seascape. Alex could almost feel the wind coming off the canvas and whipping her hair. She and Alain were the only visitors, but there were voices from behind a felt screen at the back of the room.

'I'm just looking at the art, but it's not "my cup of tea",' Alain said, in heavily accented English. Perhaps he spoke more English than he let on.

'I'd take one,' Alex replied in French. But when she saw the prices, she changed her mind. Alain beckoned her to a corner out of sight of the felt screen.

'I'm following up on something your daughter Beth told me

this morning,' he said.

'Beth? This morning?'

Alain gripped her shoulder, as if to steady her.

'Back in Nice, at Maxie's,' he said kindly. 'I thought she was waiting for you.

Beth back in Nice? Had she been looking for her? Why hadn't she called? How could they have missed each other?

'Don't look so alarmed, Alex. Your daughter was fine. She was talking quite happily to Françoise. She told me that Ed Bronz used to buy and sell a lot of paintings.'

'You didn't need to learn that from her, did you?' Alex said. She knew she sounded defensive. 'Besides, there's nothing wrong with that.'

'Especially not for Greenwood's. Beth says they organised an auction of Ed's pictures back in the Seventies – a good sale, lots of international interest.' They moved from one stormy seascape to the next. 'I wanted to see if Greenwood's could find an old catalogue for me. See?'

He flicked through a slim brochure. The photographs of paintings were black and white, giving it a dated look. The names were a litany of 20th-century European art: Picasso, Léger, Cocteau, a smattering of Russians.

'These are minor works, apparently. They're probably in private collections now. But Beth was also able to tell me an interesting fact.'

Alex sighed. She should have known better. Beth, the sly child, working hard on her own agenda when she had seemed so heartbroken about Raymond.

'Beth's been able to locate six or seven of Bronz's paintings.'

She was obviously spending much more of her time online than on her own canvases.

'Where?'

'Here and there,' Alain said. 'Provincial museums, minor collectors. People often treat paintings as property. They invest hoping that a work will increase in value as it hangs on the wall. And when it does, they sell it. Sometimes before they can sell, they have their property examined more closely. That's happened with some of Ed's artwork. And do you know what? It seems that two of these were forgeries.'

Alain's self-satisfied smile irked her. 'I guess it doesn't reflect well on Greenwood's. Are you saying Ed was duped?'

'What if Ed did the duping?'

Alex laughed. The owners of the voices behind the screen came out to see what was going on – two young men in stylish, thick-rimmed glasses. Alain waved them away and lowered his voice.

'In the late 1970s, the house on the Avenue du Phare is purchased by a nondescript company. People come and go, a family spends time there, there are some parties,' he said. 'But no phones, no utilities, nothing is registered directly to that address. Probably an investment, maybe a holiday home, even a tax dodge. The house does, however, appear to have regular business with a transport company based in Switzerland.'

'How do you know all this?' Alex had stopped looking at the paintings and was facing Alain squarely.

'The longer my former *adjoint* is *en maladie*, the more easily I can work his computer,' Alain replied. 'You know, Hubert isn't an unusual name. I have more cousins than I can count. But my family is here, on the Côte d'Azur. When I was younger, the thought of cousins in snowy Switzerland was appealing. So when I noticed my family name on the side of that transport company van, I wanted to know about them.'

'And?'

'No cousins. No Huberts. Not even a genuine transport company in Switzerland,' Alain said. He didn't look at all disappointed. 'But I kept that to myself, and I kept my eye on that house in the Avenue du Phare.'

'And when you noticed the young Zhurkov going in and out, you fixed it so that the police would take a look.'

Alain cocked his head. 'Bravo, Madame! How do *you* know all this?'

She told him of the cutting about Ed's house in Chantelle's

dossier. She remembered that a policeman's jaw had been broken, and that shots had been fired at a car.

'I was a good shot,' Alain said proudly. 'But not good enough. I hit the car twice at the bottom of the driver's side door. If I'd pulled the trigger a fraction of a second earlier, I would've had him. You can't get away with breaking a policeman's jaw.'

They had walked around all of the seascapes and were back where they started.

'Do you remember the professor's papers?'Alain asked. 'I wasn't interested at first, but I couldn't get them out of my head. It was seeing the name Hubert showing through that paper with the sketch. And seeing that strange little initial on it, like a spider. I'd seen it before, and I remembered it. And that's when I had my friends in Paris send me all of Oleg Zhurkov's records.'

'But if I recall the newspaper cutting correctly, nothing was found,' Alex said.

Alain took the piece of gilt frame out of his pocket and held it in the open palm of his hand.

'The piece of frame your nephew Felix's brother-in-law found in the car,' Alex said.

'No,' Alain replied. He took out another piece of frame, about the same size and shape. He held them together for Alex to see. They fitted into each other, a perfect match; two pieces broken off the same frame. He held up the one in his left hand. 'Felix's brother-in-law found this one lodged tight behind the door panelling of that car a couple of months ago. It could have been stuck in there for years.' Then he held up his right. 'And I found this one that night years ago in the grounds of the house on the Avenue du Phare. A piece that fit perfectly into the frame I believe was in the hands of Oleg Zhurkov, which I believe is the one that turned up at the antiques market in the Old Town.'

'From the painting that was stolen.' Alex looked at them carefully. The gilt on the piece in Alain's right hand was worn and dull.

'The frame of what I think is the original Valentin Matisse.'

279

'You've kept this little piece of gilt all these years?'

'I told you, a case that played on my mind.' He put both pieces back in his pocket.

'So you think the Valentin Matisse was in Ed's house, and that Zhurkov was handling it when you showed up.'

Alain nodded. 'I think he got it out of the house that night when I and my colleagues arrived, and he was challenged. Maybe other paintings were moved around before that – no one questions a delivery van parked in a driveway, unless your name happens to be the same as the one on the side. But after that night, nothing. The Valentins chose to pay the ransom for their painting, and everything came to an end. Not even a report of any art thefts around here for years.'

One of the young men in glasses came out to say they were closing for lunch. Alain lowered his voice further.

'And why was the Valentin Matisse in the house on the Avenue du Phare? Ed Bronz's house?'

Alex turned towards the door.

'I'm meeting Ed for lunch, Alain. That's why I'm here in Monaco.'

Alain slapped the catalogue against his thigh. 'Then you might find out.'

CHAPTER FORTY-EIGHT

As soon as Alex left Greenwood's, the midday sun hit her. She moved to a shady doorway for a moment and breathed in deeply, considering what Alain had just told her.

It wasn't surprising that Ed Bronz and Oleg Zhurkov knew each other, she thought. The Russian community couldn't have been large on the Riviera at that time, during the Cold War. It was natural that people from the Eastern bloc would seek each other out. If Zhurkov had committed any crime, it didn't necessarily follow that Ed knew anything about it. And if some of Ed's paintings had been forgeries, it was a shame, but it was none of Alain's business. It was certainly none of Beth's. Alex exhaled loudly and stepped out of the doorway.

She had kept Ed waiting for 20 minutes, but he was reading *Le Monde* as if he were sitting in his own study. He stood up when she arrived, kissed her cheeks lightly and pulled out her chair. They could have been business colleagues, like most of the other diners in the elegant Japanese restaurant.

Perhaps that is all they were.

Alex's shirt began to feel clammy in the air conditioning.

Ed chose for both of them from a menu printed on what seemed to be pale blue rice paper. The restaurant had been his suggestion; the black-clad waitresses referred to him as Bronz-san. He told her about a visit to Japan many years ago, and made her laugh. He seemed tired, giving her the opportunity to lead the conversation, but she didn't know where. Now, with all that Beth and Alain had planted in her mind, everything she thought to say would sound curious, so she said little. Ed didn't try to fill the gaps. The hum of the electricity that had connected them on the *Vanessa B* had gone quiet. Alex shivered.

She avoided Ed's eyes. He simply paid closer attention to the expertly prepared sushi. At last, he placed his chopsticks on their porcelain rest. When he clasped his hands together, Alex noticed for the first time that there were Cyrillic letters around the edge of his gold ring.

'I've behaved unforgivably,' he said. There was a fraction of an instant too much stress on the last syllable. Alex had almost stopped hearing his accent, but this reminded her to listen. 'Please excuse me.'

'Nothing to excuse. You're a busy man. It's a shame that the Barrons don't feel your house is right for them, but Immobilier Charpentier would be happy to continue searching for a suitable client. We…'

Ed reached across the table and covered her hand with his. 'Please, Alex. I'm not here to talk about my house.'

Alex waited.

'I should have spoken to you soon after the night on the yacht. I should have told you how much I was enjoying your company.'

She sipped her green tea.

'But things get in the way,' he continued. 'Just when you think you're on top of the situation, along comes something – or someone – new.'

He smiled.

She was wary, of his changing moods, of the unexpectedness of her reactions.

'Yes,' she said, 'My life is so different here.' She immediately realised Ed might think she was referring to him. She tried to backtrack. 'I mean, I'm meeting so many people. Natascha Barron and Julie Eichenbaum, for instance, are such lovely people,' she said. 'Even though Natascha is so young, she's so refreshing. She's had a difficult time getting over that fall from the boat, but …'

Alex heard her own voice chattering, and wished she hadn't started. How could she have forgotten what Julie had said? Hadn't it been the mention of Natascha that had made Ed so angry on the *Vanessa B*? And here she was jabbering about her. How stupid could she be?

It was too late. Ed pulled back from the table. 'I don't

want to talk about that woman! I don't want that to ruin everything now.' His raised voice sounded ugly in the serene surroundings. Alex stopped talking. There were goosebumps on her skin.

Other diners turned in their direction. What had Julie said? Dr Jekyll and Mr Hyde. He had frightened her. Alex had been frightened, too, at the Villa Arson, evading Maria. She was frightened now. Ed put his hand over his eyes, and sighed. Why hadn't she seen him as the person Beth saw: a ladies' man, not to be taken seriously? Or as the person Guillaume had warned her about: a man not worth knowing. Alain, too; what was he trying to suggest, with his fanciful suggestions of long-ago art thefts?

Alex stood up as the waitress delivered an arrangement of fresh mango, fanned out on the plate to look like a wave, flecked with tiny pieces of red chilli cut into the shape of jumping fish. She stared at it momentarily, but left the restaurant.

As soon as the blast of heat hit her outside, she slowed down and looked back. Would he follow? What did he see in her anyway? Perhaps a conventional English widow was just as exotic to a man like Ed as he was to her. If she walked away now, there wouldn't be another chance. She stood with her back to a sun-warmed wall, and waited. She would give him five minutes, and then she would walk away.

After seven minutes, he appeared. She began walking and he broke into a jog catch up.

'Who do you think you are that you can speak to me like that?' she said.

They were walking uphill now, in the direction of the Citroen. He stayed close beside her.

'I do nothing but make mistakes,' he said 'I'm so sorry.'

'Why do you hate Natascha Barron?'

'Because she reminds me of everything I've lost. Or I should say, of everything I allowed myself to lose.'

'Like your art collection?'

For a moment Ed said nothing. They were both breathing deeply with the effort of the incline. Alex waited for him to ask how she knew, but he said:

'Olya sold it. My wife. My ex-wife. She hated it, in the end. I didn't really care, just a few pictures I regretted.' His forehead had begun to glisten in the heat as they continued on towards the Place du Casino. It made him seem vulnerable. 'I had a small picture by Monet, one that no had known existed. It wasn't included in the catalogue raisonée – the definitive list of all works by the artist. It took me a long time to prove it was a Monet. I miss that one.'

'You're lucky to have had something like that, even for a short time.'

'Lucky? I don't know. Olya sold it to spite me because she thought I was greedy and proud, and she was right. She thought she had married someone else. She didn't want her children to have a father like me.' He took a handkerchief out of his breast pocket and wiped his forehead. 'I kept the house on the Avenue du Phare because I thought Olya would come back. She loved that house. We were happy there until...'

Alex thought of what Alain had told her. An offshore company owned the house, people came and went. But she could see Olya now – she imagined a tall, slim woman in a long dress, laughing in the shade under the eucalyptus trees. She remembered how Ed had looked as he drove her home through the dark after their dinner with Beth in Monaco. It was how he looked now – lonely.

They had reached the Citroen.

'Why did she leave?'

'I started out as a painter, like Olya. I was idealistic, in that way young people are. And then I became a sort of art dealer. But Olya thought she had married an artist. My clients weren't the kind of people she wanted to know. She couldn't accept it, even though it had given her a life she could never have imagined.' Alex noted how the bright sun picked out the lines around his eyes. 'I trusted people I shouldn't have trusted, and

I lost others. And now all that might come back to me, to get in the way again.'

'What's it got to do with Natascha?'

He shook his head. 'I can't tell you here.'

'Is it connected with Maria?'

The look on Ed's face made Alex regret it immediately. Ed seemed shocked. 'I don't remember telling you her name,' he said coldly.

She stepped into the shade of a shop awning opposite the car. She wasn't about to tell Ed that Alain Hubert was rooting about in the past, trying to make sense of fragmented memories. Nor would she tell him what Maria had whispered to her: 'You're in on it, too.' But she said, 'I saw her at the Menier villa, that's all. I thought the owner Patrice LeBlanc said you'd recommended her as a housekeeper, Ed, but I might be wrong. It's my French. Sometimes I get the wrong end of the stick. It was just work; that villa could be perfect for Natascha and Michael Barron.'

'The Raskilovich girl living in the Menier villa?' He shook his head, as if in disbelief.

'Why not? It has everything they'd need.'

'Yes, I used to know the Menier villa well.' He stared at the ground, frowning, as if he'd forgotten Alex was there.

'It's hot, I should get back to Nice,' she said.

As she opened her bag to find the car keys, Ed took her arm. It was a gentle move, not at all threatening.

'Alex, if I have to go away again, think well of me. Ultimately, I am a stupid man. I used the only talent I had to hang myself with.'

She nodded.

'But if I'm still here, I don't want to be lonely.'

He kissed her on one cheek, then on the other, pressing his warm skin against hers. She didn't want to move, but she drew away when she noticed a passing teenage girl giving them a wide berth, and unlocked the car.

When she got back to the office, she found a note had been slipped under the door. It was from Alain. 'How was your lunch? And when can I meet Madame Barron?'

She dropped it in the bin. She wouldn't be playing his game of snaring Ed Bronz, and certainly wouldn't be helping him question Natascha. Instead she left a message on Natascha's phone, asking if she and Michael still wanted to view the Menier villa.

CHAPTER FORTY-NINE

When Julie Eichenbaum called to ask Alex up to the villa in Eze the next day, Alex had almost forgotten that she and Natascha had been to see the old château in Bellet. Alex sat watching Julie's cigarette smoke curl out of the window of her studio. The ashtray on her worktable was filled with white snakes of ash as Julie bent over her pieces of silver.

The visit to Bellet had been a mixed success. Alex sat on the edge of the Bank of Hollywood safe as Julie explained. 'I'm a nutcase for having ever bought that pile of stones, but Natascha must have seen what I saw once,' she said.

As she and Natascha had roamed the château together, they had imagined completely redesigning it, demolishing everything except the façade. They had reconstructed the forged-iron veranda, saved what they could of the parquet floor, and added semi-circular picture windows to the main upstairs rooms, so Natascha could always see over the surrounding vineyards.

'She's got great ideas, but she's all over the place,' Julie said. 'With her money she could buy all the Galeries Lafayette department stores in France, so why does she want to run one little design business?'

'She just wants something of her own, I think. Something she can control.'

'So she should get a dog.'

The monstrous Lolly was lying under Julie's silver-scattered worktable, and she rubbed her toes in his side. 'Right, Lol? Go live with her. Jeez, Natascha couldn't keep her hands off him. Got a new girlfriend, huh, Lol?' The dog grunted. 'Anyway, it was a good thing Lol was there, because without him we would never have known that someone was hanging around.'

Alex held her breath.

Julie and Natascha had arrived at the old château near midday. The gates were chained shut, which had surprised

Julie. She couldn't remember ever having had a key. They had climbed over the crumbling wall nearby, leaving Lolly, too massive to carry or push over the wall, tied to the gate. 'I knew he'd be fine,' Julie said. 'You'd need elephant tranquilliser to steal him, and he'd never go with anyone except me.' But after they'd heard him bark, Natascha insisted on going back to check. She scrambled over the wall and discovered that someone had tried to unleash him. His collar was half undone, and the leash around the gate had been picked at. Natascha was sure she'd caught a glimpse of someone disappearing on foot round the bend in the lane a few metres ahead.

'I guess he's a valuable dog,' Alex said.

Natascha and Julie had then found a break in the wall just low enough to tempt Lolly over. They returned with him to the château.

'I'd forgotten how creepy it can be in there,' Julie said. 'When I bought the place it wasn't so overgrown. I better sell it before there's nothing left. You can't see a thing once you're away from the windows.'

Alex knew the dark, dense feeling inside the château. What had at first seemed like a child's paradise now made her unspeakably sad.

'Natascha couldn't have been happier, though. She was making drawings and taking notes like no tomorrow.' Julie stopped filing long enough to inhale on a cigarette. She looked directly at Alex. 'But that dumb jock husband of hers will never let her take on a project like that.'

'It could work. You could add a little restaurant and a café. Turn it into a destination. It's a pretty area. There's room for parking.' Alex could see it now: one elegant showroom after another, filled with exquisite upholstery fabrics and furniture, a thoughtfully positioned antique; chandeliers.

'Call the mayor of Bellet,' Julie mocked. 'Ask him for a tax break.'

She and Natascha had been just about to leave when Lolly started barking again. Thinking he wanted to frighten the turtledoves nesting in the beams, Julie let him off the leash. He ran to a small door in the far wall of the main room and started scratching at it.

Oh god, Alex thought. She knew that door.

'They could probably hear us scream in New Jersey when the guy jumped out and ran off,' Julie said. 'Bet he was as scared as us. He must have been hiding the whole time we were there.'

'Did Lolly go after him?'

'Of course not, he hid behind me! He's a gentle giant. It looked to me like the guy was spying on us. That's strange, don't you think? Hiding in a closet?'

'All the local kids know the place, apparently.'

'I know what they get up to in there. I did stuff like that myself when I was a kid. But that's no excuse. It's dangerous, and it's trespassing.'

'You didn't get a good look at him?' Oh, how she hoped not. Who else would be behind that door?

'Too dark. We ran in the other direction as fast as we could.' Her hoarse laugh made Lolly jerk awake.

'And neither did Natascha?'

'She said he wasn't a kid, that's all.'

Alex's throat tightened as she imagined Guillaume's distress. He must have followed them from Immobilier Charpentier that morning, once he heard that's where they were headed. How he must have hated knowing Natascha would be there, a trespasser in his private grief. How innocently the girl provided reasons to be hated.

Julie pushed aside her metal files and polished the piece of silver she'd been working on with a rag. She held it up under a magnifying glass, and Alex saw that it was a perfect wine bottle, complete with label and cork.

'In any case, that escapade might have put Natascha off the château,' Julie said. 'I'm glad you're taking her to see that Menier place tomorrow. That's more up her alley. She's getting back to where she ought to be after that dip she took off Dario's boat.'

'Do you really think someone could have tried to hurt her on that boat?'

'Not for a minute. But you get rich, people hate you. Believe me, I know. They try to get at you in other ways.'

Alex waited for her to say something else, but she had chosen another small file, and hunched over her work. The only noise was the faint scrape of metal on metal, and Lolly's satisfied groans.

'You going to stop mooning around about that Ed?' Julie said after a few minutes, startling Alex. 'You're staring out that window like a lovesick teenager.'

'I wasn't even thinking about him,' Alex said.

'Yeah, right. Those dangerous types are under your skin before you know it.'

'Actually I was thinking about Beth.'

It was true. Despite all Alex's calls, she had missed the one time Beth had rung back because she was in the shower. She'd listened to it again and again: 'I'm glad about Chantelle, Mum,' Beth had said, 'because soon you can get out of here and go home where you belong. Call me as soon as you know when she's coming back.' It was meant to hurt Alex, and it worked.

Julie gave a helpless shrug. She rooted in one of the drawers until she found a thin silver chain, which she slipped through the eye at the top of the cork.

'Gorgeous,' Alex said.

'Here. Give it to your daughter.'

When Alex tried to refuse, Julie slipped it in the breast pocket of Alex's T-shirt.

'OK, so keep it for Chantelle, give it to her when she gets home.'

Alex touched it through the fabric. Everyone was eager for Chantelle Charpentier's return.

'She still has a long way to go,' Alex warned. 'Opening your eyes is only the first part of a long process.'

Julie said, 'Ain't that the truth.'

CHAPTER FIFTY

The garlicky aroma of Maxie's fresh pesto sauce curled into Alex's nose, and she realised it had been too long since she'd sat down at the restaurant for a proper meal. The plate of gnocchi was huge, but Alex would finish it easily. She loved the pudgy texture of the potato dumplings.

'Made right here in our kitchen,' Maxie said. She looked proudly at the three bowls on the table. Natascha leaned over hers and wafted the rising steam towards her nose. She had returned Alex's call about visiting the Menier villa almost immediately, eager to see it quickly. She had suggested meeting at Maxie's beforehand.

'Isn't this just the cutest restaurant, Michael? I've been dying to eat here.'

Neither Natascha nor Michael could have known that they were attracting more attention than any other table. The sous-chef Sammy, who rarely ventured beyond the kitchen door, came out to stock the bar with lemons, taking furtive glances at the rich Americans who employed his mother. Françoise climbed on her ladder more often than usual to rattle among her stock of bottles. Even the chef appeared mid-service, to shake hands with customers. Three tables away, Beatrice from the bank stared at the glossy couple, transfixed.

Michael nudged the gnocchi around his plate before trying a mouthful. When he nodded contentedly at Natascha, she beamed.

But when Alain came in, Alex put down her fork. Of course he would have heard the Barrons were coming – Maxie had told almost everyone when Alex reserved the table. Natascha laughed happily at something Michael had said; he tucked a strand of her hair behind her ear. Alex felt a twinge of guilt as Alain approached them, but he smiled widely at her as if this meeting was entirely coincidental.

Alex introduced them reluctantly. 'Wow, that is so interesting,' Michael said, once she'd explained that Alain was a retired police chief. Michael turned his full, sparkling attention to him, and Alain inspected Michael with his amused twinkle.

'I dreamed of being a cop when I was growing up,' Michael said through a mouthful of gnocchi.

Alain pulled up a chair.

'Many boys 'ave 'zis dream.'

Michael and Natascha frowned as they strained to understand Alain's thick accent, but Alex was as impressed as she was surprised. Alain's English was hesitant, but serviceable.

'I am sorry to know zat your family is 'aving a zeft,' Alain said. Natascha smiled politely, confused.

'I think he's talking about the collection,' Michael said. He looked at Alain as if examining a caged animal, and said loudly: 'Are you talking about the theft in New York?'

'I have always had an interest in this kind of thing,' Alain said. 'If it's no trouble, can you tell me about this?' He slipped a folded photocopy out of the breast pocket of his shirt.

Oh no, Alex thought. Couldn't he have been more subtle?

As soon as Natascha caught sight of the paper, she looked at Alex in alarm.

'I don't think we should be discussing this. There are so many uncertainties... The legal issues. Michael?'

But Michael had already taken the print-out. He looked at it briefly, proprietorially, and passed it to his wife as if dismissing it. Alex strained to see.

'Why are you interested?' Michael asked.

'This painting is not well known. But it's one I've always wanted to see myself. Do you know it?' Alain asked

'Of course,' Natascha said. 'It belonged to my father. But the private collection will never be displayed. I'm sorry, you won't be able to see it.'

'But the painting in this photograph was taken in Paris. At

Drouot, the auction house. It belongs to the estate of an artist called Auguste Valentin.'

Natascha was flustered. She looked at the picture again. 'Perhaps I'm not recalling this correctly. If you have specific questions, you should consult my lawyers. I'm sorry, Mr Hubert.'

She raised her chin stubbornly, and handed the photograph back to Michael, before continuing with her gnocchi. The imperious millionairess, Alex thought, is nowhere near as pretty as the poor little rich girl. She was glad, however, that she hadn't actually invited Alain to join them. He reminded her of a terrier straining at the edge of a rat hole.

'Of course,' Alain said. 'But did you see this painting in a photograph at Ed Bronz's house, on the Avenue du Phare?'

Alex quickly took a gulp of her wine. Natascha bit the inside of her cheek. She squinted, or perhaps frowned, towards the picture.

'Mrs Barron said she didn't want to say anything else, Mr Hubert,' Michael said. He handed the print-out back to Alain, but Alain didn't move. He waited, his eyes fixed on Natascha, until Michael dropped the print-out on the table.

After an uncomfortably silent moment, Alex asked, 'Is it, Natascha?'

Natascha nodded. 'I thought so, Alex, but I must have been mistaken. It's no business of Mr Hubert's, in any case. I'd prefer not to discuss anything to do with the estate. Now, I just want to think about the Menier villa.'

CHAPTER FIFTY-ONE

They never reached the Menier villa.

Michael had insisted on driving. This time, he'd borrowed a friend's Ferrari and Alex, despite the absurd squeeze in its rear seats, had climbed willingly into the low-slung car. Natascha put on her sunglasses. If she didn't want to attract attention, this was clearly the wrong car to be in. Alex had waved at Maxie and Françoise regally from the back as the car roared away from its parking spot in front of the *terrasse*.

It was like a fairground ride. As Michael darted in and out of traffic, the roar of the engine made conversation difficult. Alex gripped the armrest each time he swerved, but the car responded powerfully. She shouted, 'Chantelle's car will feel like a rowing boat after this!'

Not long after they had passed the turn-off for Villefranche, Michael's phone rang. He answered it, slowing down slightly. Natascha put her hand on his arm, but he shook it off.

'Later,' he said. 'Uh-huh. Call me. I'm in the car. I'll...' A motorcycle roared past, and Alex didn't know exactly what happened. Michael threw the phone into Natascha's lap and gripped the steering wheel with both hands. The Ferrari began to sway. Natascha screamed. Alex dug her nails into the edge of the leather seats and pushed her knees into the back of the driver's seat. The car fishtailed, throwing her around. The seatbelt burned into her neck. She had a fleeting memory of the girls, their profiles, in the pew beside her at Rod's funeral. The girls. Oh, don't let them have to go through this grief again.

The wall that divided the road from the villas on the hill below was suddenly right beside the window. She noticed how lovely the top of the palm trees looked, so green against the sky, just as the Ferrari scraped the wall. The noise was ferocious, the metal itself screeching in pain. The car bounced. The window on Natascha's side exploded into her seat. Alex imagined her face being peppered with hailstones. Natascha was screaming, 'Don't hit him, don't hit him!'

It was over within seconds. The Ferrari swung to a stop, its engine still purring like a leopard after a kill. A shocked cyclist in full Lycra stood looking at the car, uninjured, holding onto his bike. There were specks of blood on Alex's hands. No one said anything. The tinny voice coming from the phone pierced the quiet. 'Michael?' A woman's voice, an American accent. 'Michael? What's going on, babe? Oh, my god baby, are you OK? Mikey?'

Natascha picked up the phone and threw it with all her force at Michael. It bounced off his shoulder. They both scrabbled for it; Natascha got hold of it under Michael's legs and threw it through the window with a frustrated scream. He tried to brush pieces of glass from Natascha's lap, and to pick them out of her hair, but each time she shoved his hand away.

When he looked over his shoulder into the back seat, he said, 'Jesus Christ.'

CHAPTER FIFTY-TWO

The windscreen had shattered into gravelly pieces, small shards scratching Alex's hands and face. Natascha, with her large sunglasses, had barely been touched. The emergency team who arrived, sirens bleating, within minutes had insisted they go to the local hospital. Alex's hands were orange with antiseptic now; she had insisted they didn't put it on her face. Her eyes still ached from the light they had shone on her as they slowly picked over her face for slivers of glass. She examined herself in Chantelle's desk mirror, thinking she looked as if she had chicken pox.

In the emergency room, she had walked to and from the water cooler several times just to get away from Natascha's incandescent pain. She hadn't said a word to Michael from the second she shimmied over the gear shift and out of the undamaged driver's door. She wouldn't look at him. He had begged her to talk to him, oblivious to Alex and the emergency team. The more she ignored him, the angrier he became. Finally, he left them at the hospital. The last thing he said, addressing Alex, was, 'I could kill her. I could honestly kill her.' Natascha sobbed into her hands, and all Alex could do was stroke her hair as they waited for a taxi to take them home.

Alex had wandered restlessly around her apartment in Les Jolies Roses before calling Meghan.

'Where the hell is Beth?' Meghan had asked unhelpfully. 'She should be there to make sure you're alright. I'm calling her now.'

'Don't, darling. They're just scratches. They'll heal.' The thought of Beth slinking and sulking around the apartment had made Alex sigh, so that even Meghan, generally immune to any distress other than her own, stopped insisting.

Alex was returning Chantelle's mirror to the desk drawer when the front door of Immobilier Charpentier opened. A chubby, middle-aged man with a genial smile strode towards her, his hand outstretched. He looked familiar.

'*Bonjour*, Madame. My name is...' He stopped instantly as he saw her face, his mouth open, his eyes widening in surprise. It only lasted a second, but Alex instinctively raised her hand to her mouth and nose. She'd have to get used to this reaction. She'd find herself a big hat, she thought, even if it looked more ridiculous than her scratched face. She'd seen a floppy blue sunhat in the boot of Chantelle's Citroen; it would be perfect.

The man quickly recomposed his pleasant smile and continued: 'My name is Boubil. Dominic Boubil.'

Of course! Alex glanced up at the wall of photographs behind him. There was Boubil, the estate agent, thinner in some of the snapshots, chunkier in others. Alex had barely noticed him before, but now she saw he was looking at Chantelle affectionately in every one.

'There's hope,' he said, when she told him the gist of Harry's daily reports: Chantelle was responding to her treatment, weak but improving, still far from her old self. Alex's throat tensed as she told him. With the smell of the emergency room still in her nostrils, she suddenly imagined the white sheets, the tubes and bags, that Harry always avoided mentioning in detail.

'But business is business,' Boubil said. 'I'm here because I want to ask your advice about a shop on the rue Alphonse Karr.'

Boubil asking for her advice! She wished Chantelle was here to witness it.

'A mutual acquaintance of Chantelle's and mine tells me that Chantelle has promised it to her, but nothing has been signed. This client is particularly interested in the site.' Boubil's eyes darted over the tiny scratches and bruises on Alex's face as he spoke. 'I'd like to take it on, on my client's behalf.'

She must have looked confused, because Boubil said, 'We've done this sort of thing many times, Chantelle and I.'

'But I don't know which shop you mean.'

'It's Chantelle's shop, her own property. It's large, for the position. Quite an investment, one she made years ago. She's so clever about spotting potential.'

Of course there was no reason for Alex to know anything about it. She was beginning to forget that she had been here only a short time, that in fact she barely knew Chantelle – or her business – at all.

'Can you tell me who the mutual acquaintance is?'

'You may know her; a designer. Paulette Bitoun.'

Boubil offered to find Alex a glass of water as she spluttered. Had the perfect site for Natascha been right under her nose all along?

What would Chantelle do if she were in Alex's position? Alex waved Boubil towards the kitchenette to give herself time to think. When he returned, she drained the glass of water while he rubbed his hands anxiously.

'I'd prefer not to anticipate Chantelle's decision,' she said, pleased with how professional she sounded.

Boubil nodded.

Alex made up her mind. Chantelle couldn't possibly want anyone but Natascha to have her shop, and particularly not the awful Technicolor Paulette Bitoun.

'Perhaps it's best for Madame Bitoun to wait a little longer,' she said. 'I'll have to consult Chantelle's representatives, Quelin & Company, before we can even begin to think about it.'

Boubil's smile faded along with the prospect of a quick deal.

As soon as she had closed the door behind him, Alex went through every file in the office, every drawer and cardboard folder, every box and binder. Nothing. She took out the fat dossier, and dumped the still-unorganised contents of the 'Z' section onto the desk. She scanned each piece of paper ravenously before stuffing it back in.

And then she noticed a white plastic bag hanging from a hook inside one of the small kitchen cupboards. Boubil must have opened it when he was looking for a glass. The bag – ordinary, nondescript – had been there since before Chantelle left, but if Alex had noticed it at all, she must have thought it was empty.

Now she took it off the hook and set it on the desk. It was full of papers Chantelle might have been taking home, or perhaps had forgotten to file. She emptied them out. Here was the lease for a shop on rue Alphonse Karr, a receipt for the final rental payment and return of a *caution*, the deposit, the final survey of its condition. The lease had run out just days before Chantelle's departure. There was also a brochure for a business that had occupied the premises. Alex breathed in the inky smell of the pages, and flipped through the pictures. It had been a showroom for beds and exclusive bed linen. She ignored the four-posters and carved wooden sleigh beds, and looked at the backgrounds: beautiful plasterwork in a series of bright, spacious sets. If this was in fact the shop on the rue Alphonse Karr, it would cheer Natascha up no end.

She checked the key cabinet, jangling her way through every tag until she found the right one.

CHAPTER FIFTY-THREE

Natascha had taken to calling Alex every day since the accident on the way to the Menier villa, sometimes two or three times. She even dropped into Maxie's, sitting on the *terrasse* with a *citron pressé* and waiting for Alex to join her when she had the chance. Each time Alex spotted her there among Maxie's tables, she had the impression that Natascha was an elegant bird of some kind, a flamingo, which had landed mistakenly on the pond of a public park.

'Things are good now with Michael,' she insisted, the one time Alex had asked. 'I've convinced him my store is a great idea.' But then Natascha whipped her sunglasses off the top of her head and put them back on her nose, resolutely silent. Alex didn't ask again.

Now, as they were nearing the shop on the rue Alphonse Karr for the first time, Natascha said, 'Your mind is really somewhere else.' She put her hand on Alex's shoulder.

'Sorry?'

'I've been talking to myself for 10 minutes! You haven't heard a word, have you?'

It was true, Alex hadn't been listening to Natascha, not since she'd spotted a blue Mini parked on the corner as they had turned into the street. There was sure to be more than one in Nice, Alex reasoned, but she was watchful all the same. Last time she'd noticed that car, Michael had been kissing another woman inside it.

'I was saying, maybe we could work on the store together, when Chantelle's back, of course. It would be a great partnership, the three of us, don't you think?'

Natascha was excited about the shop on rue Alphonse Karr, almost childishly over-excited. There had been no sign of Michael at the apartment. Alex steered Natascha across the road to avoid passing close to the Mini.

The shops around them were selling parasols and blow-up mattresses, tourists were wandering towards the sea with straw beach mats rolled under their arms, but after a few minutes of walking, the streets had become quieter and cooler, the people more elegantly dressed.

'This must be it,' Natascha said. 'Oh, Alex, it's just like you said!' She looked up to take in the full double-fronted shop, with its wide doorway set back from the tree-lined street. Alex tried all the keys before finding the one that unlocked the heavy metal grille as Natascha counted the pedestrians walking past.

'Lots of people passing by,' she said. 'Think what I can do with this window to tempt them in!' Alex was aware of someone standing on the other side of the street, looking at them, but when she turned to see, the person stepped into a doorway. She turned back to the shutter. Just as she heaved it up, Natascha jumped in towards her.

'Paulette!'

Alex groaned. She glanced across the street.

'No, look, she's coming down this way.' Natascha pointed in the other direction. 'Quick, Alex!'

As soon as they were inside, Natascha slammed the door behind them, making the glass rattle. They ran from the windows to the back of the room, stumbling over what seemed to be packing materials.

'Did she see us?' Natascha flattened herself again the wall. Alex dropped down on her knees behind a counter.

'No one would recognise me in this get-up,' Alex laughed, taking off Chantelle's blue sunhat. But Paulette had pressed herself against the shopfront, peering in with her hands cupped around her eyes. Her body was outlined against the backdrop of intense sunlight, her ample hips bubbling underneath the edge of her belt.

'Perhaps she didn't realise it was us. She'll go in a minute. Let's see the back first,' Alex said. She pulled Natascha beyond the view of the window, deeper into the dark.

The three large showrooms were empty. Years' worth of

customers' footsteps had worn trails in the parquet floor, but the odour of wax polish mingled with the smell of fresh paint and new sheets. Either Chantelle had taken care of this herself, or her tenants had been unusually conscientious. The premises were spotless.

'Now this is an option,' Natascha said happily. 'Definitely!' Then she added quietly, 'I could move right in, I don't care what Michael says.' She pointed out where she could put three antique armoires from Normandy, which she planned to use as display shelves. They paced out the spot that Natascha thought she could divide into showrooms using vintage striped canvas from old beach tents. She had already asked Julie to find another bank safe in which she could display the jewellery Natascha would commission. 'I could put it here, next to one of those antique cash registers.' She stood at the back of the largest room, playing with an invisible till. She held out her hand for Alex's imaginary money.

'It's more realistic than Bellet,' Alex said.

'For now. I could cut my teeth here before I expand. I'll learn fast. I'll have this store going in no time.' Her long legs folded under her as easily as a foal's as she squatted on the floor, taking papers from her file. She'd already ordered a few things, she said, vintage stuff she might not be able to find again. Michael didn't know, of course, but she didn't want to miss out on anything. She held up a leaflet showing a Chihuahua wearing a collar made of what looked like mosaic tiles. 'Hand-painted,' she said. 'Cute, huh? I couldn't resist.' She held up one picture after another, asking for Alex's opinion. It would be the sort of store where Alex might look, but never buy. Still, there'd be plenty who would.

Alex had almost forgotten about Paulette Bitoun when she saw a shadow at the window. She shrunk back against the wall. There was a sudden rap on the glass. Natascha grimaced. They'd been spotted.

Paulette was inside the moment Alex opened the door, bombing the shop with her powdery scent. Lacy black bra straps drooped from the armholes of black sleeveless top. A copy of *Paris Match* was pinched under one flabby arm. The wide belt that squeezed her flesh out like dough was made of yellow patent leather, with an enormous heart-shaped gold buckle. When she saw Natascha, she bared her little teeth.

'You've heard about my new shop,' she said in English. She pushed herself up towards Natascha's face to give her a kiss on both cheeks, causing Natascha to grimace even more. She ignored Alex.

'How exciting,' Natascha said flatly, in French. 'Where is it?'

Alex shifted from one foot to another. Perhaps she ought to have mentioned some of the background to Natascha, about Dominic Boubil, but it had seemed unnecessary until now.

'But Madame Barron, it is exactly here in your nose. Zees are my shop. I will call it after my nickname. Pu-Pu.'

Alex coughed.

'You mean, this store? But Mrs Bitoun, I'm considering taking the lease on these premises.' Natascha looked helplessly at Alex. 'As soon as possible.'

Alex said, 'But Madame Bitoun, your agreement hasn't been formalised.'

Paulette fixed her tiny eyes on Alex. She drew in a breath to speak, pausing momentarily to examine Alex's spotted face. She launched in again rapidly, in French. 'There is no question that this shop will be mine,' she said. 'Chantelle knows I want it. She knows it is perfect for me.'

'But the lease hasn't been signed.'

'Madame Coates, the lease is a formality. This is how we do things here, but how would you know that? Chantelle knows I will move in soon.'

'I'm sorry, Madame Bitoun, I can't confirm that until we have news from Chantelle herself.'

With each indignant breath, Paulette's stomach ballooned out over the edge of her belt. 'This is impossible!' she shouted.

'I'm sorry, Mrs Bitoun.' Natascha seemed touched by the designer's distress. She stepped towards her.

'No!' Paulette threw up her hands, batting Natascha's arm brusquely away. It may have been an accident, Alex couldn't tell. Natascha lifted both arms up as if to protect her face, just as Paulette pushed her backwards. She seemed to poke Natascha in the ribcage.

'Who do you think you are, coming here as if it's your playground? I've read about you, you and your cheating husband. Don't think you can ruin my plans for the sake of your little holiday. You won't have this place!' Drops of spittle landed on Natascha's cheek. 'Give me the keys!'

Natascha had flattened herself in horror against the wall where her beach tent showrooms would fit. She inched closer to Alex.

'Madame Barron doesn't have them,' Alex said. 'I have them. Why don't we try to calm down and think this through?'

But Paulette wouldn't calm down. She stamped her feet on the parquet. 'If Chantelle were here, I would already be open for business! I would be dealing with people who understand the Côte d'Azur! Look, look!' She flicked through the pages of her copy of *Paris Match*, her hands shaking with rage. She held a full-page photograph under first Natascha's nose, then Alex's. A denim-clad older man was posing astride a motorcycle in the middle of a living room. She couldn't see clearly, but even a quick flash of the mix of lurid, neon-coloured patterns on the walls and chairs made her feel giddy.

'My design! In *Paris Match*!' Paulette said.

'*Très jolie*,' Natascha said weakly. 'Very pretty.'

'*Jolie*? Pah, what do you know?'

'There's no call for rudeness, Mrs Bitoun.'

Natascha's reprimand was the last straw. Paulette's blotchy jowls quivered. 'You'll have to go,' she shouted. 'You'll have to go and I'll make sure you do.'

She didn't bother closing the shop door as she left.

Alex and Natascha were as still as statues as they watched Paulette waddle angrily across the street. Eventually, Alex breathed out.

'She's gone.'

'She's unhinged,' Natascha said. 'Does she really have a right to this property?'

'Nothing is signed, and as far as I understand it, Chantelle would rather stay in a coma than do Paulette Bitoun a good turn.'

'Then let's make this work, Alex. I'll take it! Can I get started straightaway?'

Alex hugged her. She was sure Chantelle would want this, but nothing could be finalised before she'd spoken to Monsieur Amedeo Quelin about it.

'Could I have a set of keys, though? Just to get some people in for quotes? An architect?'

'We ought to wait a bit,' Alex said, but Natascha was already pushing her lower lip out girlishly. 'Shouldn't you discuss it with Michael?' She sucked her lip back in instantly and shook her head.

'Alex, I'm surprised you of all people would think I can't make decisions without my husband.' She acted out her little pout again and said, 'Now, those keys, pretty please?'

CHAPTER FIFTY-FOUR

'Money talks,' Françoise announced matter of factly from behind her copy of *Nice-Matin*.

'Not to me,' Maxie said. She put a plate of grilled sardines in front of Alex. The skin was crisp and golden, pulling away like wrapping paper from the translucent bones.

'I waited a month for a decorator to give me a quote when I had the hall painted,' Françoise said. 'But see, after only a few days this rich American's shop is crawling with architects who can't wait to tell her how much money she can give them. *Bon appetit*, Madame.'

Alex nodded, her mouth already full. She'd seen the photograph of Chantelle's shop herself in that morning's paper. *Nice-Matin* was hardly renowned for investigative reporting: the only way they could have discovered that Natascha Barron was interested in the premises was if someone had told them. 'American millionairess to set up shop locally,' the headline informed its readers. Alex tutted. Considering that the article also stated that the American millionairess had unfairly trumped 'a beloved and world-famous French interior designer' to get her hands on the property, Alex knew that that someone had to be Paulette Bitoun.

Alex mopped her plate with a slice of baguette. Today, at last, she was going to see Beth, and planned to leave for Menton as soon as she'd finished lunch. She couldn't do it on an empty stomach.

The previous evening, Meghan had said, 'Beth's really not sounding good, Mum. Honestly, what a bore. Why can't she just pull her socks up?'

Alex had run her fingers over the tiny, scratchy scabs on her cheek and could think of nothing to say. If Rod were here, what would he do? But Rod wasn't here. He wouldn't be here in future. She'd said it herself to Beth on the beach. She'd looked at the photograph of Rod staring at her from under a panama hat, the one she knew as well as her own reflection in the mirror. She'd stared angrily back.

Meghan continued, 'There's only so much time I can spend on the phone cajoling my sister, Mum. I mean, Tim's in Singapore again, and the children run me ragged. She's got to get on with things herself. She ought to just give up on her bloody painting, she'd feel better. I even offered to lend her some money, but she says that's not it.'

'She doesn't need money, surely? I'd give her whatever she needed.'

'I don't know what she needs.' The note of genuine worry in Meghan's voice had been an unfamiliar one. 'But she's fixating on Natascha, too. It's not healthy, Mum. I don't know what's gotten into her about that girl. What's Natascha done to her?'

'Nothing. She's missing Raymond, that's what it is,' Alex had suggested. 'She's taking out her anger on Natascha instead.'

'Well, you'll just have to sort her out. It's getting ridiculous. I'd do it myself if I could get away.'

How could Alex possibly sort Beth out? It had always been Rod's job. He'd been there to talk to her teachers, to ignore the detritus of drunken teenage parties, to listen without a shadow of disbelief on his face as Beth reeled off little white lie after little white lie. He'd been there to knock softly on locked bedroom doors, and to sweep up smashed plates without recrimination, while she, Alex, had hung back, watching him do it. What help could she possibly offer Beth now?

'Oh, keep up, Mum. Beth couldn't have cared less about Raymond,' Meghan had said. 'She misses Dad.'

Alex had idled over a second coffee after her lunch of grilled sardines. Whatever consoling, conciliatory phrases she practised for Beth as she watched the market stallholders pack away their unsold produce, they seemed to come out wrong.

She'd left the Citroen behind the old train station. Now, as she walked in its direction, she could see someone sitting on the hood of the car, feet up on the front bumper. She stopped. Neighbourhood kids, she thought; perhaps one of the stallholders, whose trucks and vans packed the car park every morning. As she got closer, she recognised the slight shoulders. Alex was too surprised to fix her usual neutral smile. She hurried towards Beth, both fear and relief churning her stomach.

'I was just on the way to see you, darling. What are you doing here?'

Beth didn't take off her sunglasses as Alex hugged her tightly. Her shoulders felt limp through the worn fabric of her shirt, neither resisting nor returning her mother's affection. She was thinner than ever.

Alex said, 'You saved me the drive to Menton.'

But Beth, having let herself in to Les Jolies Roses to collect some things, now wanted to go back.

'Darling, is that all you came for? I could've brought your stuff to you.'

Beth threw her scruffy yellow knapsack into the back seat of the Citroen as soon as Alex had unlocked the doors. She retuned the radio to an English-language station and sat with her hands in her lap, looking straight ahead.

Alex put the key in the ignition, and despite the heat inside the car, she took Beth's hand. She said, 'Stay here in Nice. We need to take care of each other.'

Beth said, 'Ha.'

Alex put the Citroen into reverse. It spluttered and cut out. Beth clasped and unclasped her hands impatiently. Alex tried again. The car coughed a few times, then stopped. Eventually there was only the click of the ignition.

'Battery,' Beth said. 'The weirdo guy probably has cables to jump-start it.'

Why was she here if all she wanted was to provoke another fight? Alex tried the engine again. It caught twice, but faltered each time.

'You'll flood it.'

'I could walk you to the train station,' Alex offered, but as she heard herself say the words, she gripped the steering wheel angrily. It sounded as if she couldn't wait to see Beth go. She reached for her, but Beth was already arching over the seat, trying to grab hold of her knapsack in the back, her hand pulling awkwardly on the door handle at the same time. Her sunglasses fell off into the back of the car, and Alex could see her daughter's eyes at last. It felt like the first time they'd looked at each other in years.

Beth stopped in mid-stretch. 'What the hell happened to your face?'

'Some scratches from broken window glass. It'll go.'

The skin around Beth's eyes was dark grey. As she examined her mother's complexion, she was so close, their cheeks could have rested against each other. Alex wanted to put her arms around her, pull her in close. She was longing for it to be easy.

'I've got some vitamin E cream. It's good for scars. I'll bring it next time,' Beth said.

'Thank you, darling. I'd appreciate that.'

Beth turned to face forward now, without grabbing her knapsack. Alex held her breath hopefully as Beth fumbled underneath the seat for her sunglasses. She pulled out Chantelle's battered blue sunhat instead.

'Is this yours?'

Alex laughed. 'I know, it's not my usual style. I wore it for a few days to protect my face. Actually, I think I was trying to hide. I...'

'Yes, I've seen you in it.' The bitterness in her voice cut Alex short. 'You were with Natascha. You came out of a shop on Alphonse Karr. I saw you both. All lovey-dovey with the little princess. I didn't believe it was you, I couldn't believe you'd wear something so ugly. That's how much you've changed since Dad died. But how stupid of me; who else would have been playing happy families with that silly girl?'

She was out of the car door within seconds.

The thongs on Alex's leather sandals cut into the space between her toes as she walked after Beth. They weren't made for speed. The yellow knapsack was easy to follow, but before long it had disappeared into the crowd. She stopped and turned back, hopelessly, just as she reached the railway bridge before the train station. She used her mobile to call Meghan. No answer. She was probably collecting the children now. Alex left a message. 'Can you call me, sweetheart? I've just seen Beth. Do you think there's any chance at all that you could make it to Nice?'

CHAPTER FIFTY-FIVE

Rod had known that words like *bougie* could mean spark plug as well as candle, but for most things technical, Alex was dependent on the pocket French-English dictionary she kept in her bag. Even after she looked up *démarreur*, Guillaume's explanation made no sense. He tried again, more slowly, but she wouldn't have known what a starter motor was in English.

He took an oily rag from his toolbox and wiped his hands before explaining the problem to her for the third time. She wanted to say, it doesn't matter, I don't care, just fix it, but his patience prevented her. He pointed to parts of the engine, making sure she could see, and drew diagrams on a greasy paper bag. He looked her straight in the eye, and she tried hard not to look as if she were about to cry. The lump she'd had in her throat since seeing Beth had begun to ache now. There was no shade in the car park behind the old train station. The hot metal of 60 cars radiated around them, and Alex's light gauze shirt felt like a blanket. When Guillaume finally dropped the hood back down, she unclenched her fists.

'The parts will take a day or so, and it'll be fine for a while, but Chantelle will have to buy a new car.'

Guillaume had followed her back to the office, where Alex drank an entire glass of water in one go, standing at the sink in the kitchenette. Guillaume didn't even look warm. He made notes at the back of the office, pulling papers in and out of binders as he copied details into his ragged diary.

Meghan wouldn't possibly be able to get to Nice for a week or so she said, when Alex got hold of her. Tim was in Berlin and the nanny had gone home to Poland for a wedding. 'Don't worry, Mum. I'll call Beth every day. She'll be OK.'

Alex rang Beth repeatedly. Tears welled again in her eyes to hear Beth's cheerful voicemail message, one she'd recorded months ago. Her daughter's lips as they formed the words seemed so close. She longed for the chance to make things better. But what was the point in leaving message after message?

'*Ça va*, Madame? OK?' Guillaume had filed the binders back into place and was standing beside her.

'My daughter. She has some...some...' A tear had spilled onto one cheek. How could she put it to a man whose daughter was gone forever? She inhaled the odour of engine oil on Guillaume's overalls as he waited for her to finish. She put her hand to her eyes, and as she did so, he reached out tenderly for her wrist.

Oh my god, Alex thought. She pulled her arm away in surprise, rubbing it. The memory was suddenly clear: Guillaume had been there that day in the old château. He had tried to help her when she fell. He'd been afraid all this time that she would realise it was him, with his strange, sad shrine. How could she say to him, my daughter doesn't want to speak to me? How could she admit that everything she did made her daughter unhappy?

But she said tersely, 'My daughter hasn't been well, it's nothing to worry about.' It sounded rude, as if she were rejecting his compassion. She regretted it immediately.

Before he had turned away, Alex's phone lit up. The display showed 'Natascha Barron'. Guillaume must have seen it, and Alex let it switch to voicemail.

'Has she made her decision yet?' That furtive glance again; not quite looking at anything.

'She's already getting people in to give her quotes,' Alex said. 'Haven't you read about it in *Nice-Matin*?'

'I don't bother with *Nice-Matin*,' he said. 'It's nothing but lies.'

CHAPTER FIFTY-SIX

As Alex passed Maxie's *terrasse*, she could see a half-finished beer on the table in front of Alain Hubert. He drained it the moment Alex, without slowing down, waved. She'd been in no hurry to see him after the lunch with Natascha and Michael, but as she turned the corner by the commissariat, she saw his reflection in the building's plate-glass window catching up with hers. He caught her by the elbow, and gently lifted the brim of the floppy blue sunhat.

'That won't scar,' he said. 'I've seen worse.'

'It's been more than 10 days now. It's much better.'

'I've got an idea,' he said, taking a step towards the commissariat.

'I'm meeting the Barrons,' she said, looking at her watch pointedly. 'At the Menier villa.' Natascha's feverish enthusiasm hadn't stopped at the shop. She had badgered Alex to arrange another viewing of the Menier villa as soon as she could.

'Ten minutes,' Alain said. 'No more.' He was already holding open the door of the commissariat. 'I promise.'

Why couldn't she resist?

At lunchtime, the offices were virtually deserted and they reached the *adjoint*'s cubicle without any of the usual interruptions. Alain tapped the computer awake. He turned the screen towards Alex so she could see clearly. She was expecting more of the professor's letters, or more photographs of Oleg Zhurkov, but Alain pointed to a folder marked 'Raskilovich'.

'You've obviously done your colleague in Paris a lot of favours,' Alex said, but Alain didn't seem to hear. He opened the file and suddenly scores of images lined up, one in front of each other. Alain clicked through them rapidly. Alex had glimpses of painting after painting, blazes of colour and shape, portraits and landscapes, blocks and lines. Alain tapped on the keyboard until he came to a painting that seemed familiar:

bright colour, a window opening onto a sunlit blue sky, the fronds of a palm tree. Around the edges was a radiant pattern of what could be seashells.

'Matisse?' Alex asked

'Good. The Valentin Matisse.'

'The one being valued in Paris by the auction house. The one they say is a forgery.'

'Well, no. There is one at the auction house, it's true. But in fact these particular shots were sent from New York, by an old friend of my colleague in Paris.'

'You lot are awful,' Alex said. 'Go on.'

'They're photographs of the secret collection, the one found in the Raskilovich mausoleum.'

Alex could almost feel Alain's breath on her cheek as she looked at the screen. She backed away.

'You know that this painting was stolen once, from the Valentin house on Cap Ferrat.'

'Alain, we've already been through this. The Valentin family paid the ransom, and it was returned.'

Alain took a photocopy out of his pocket just as he had done at the lunch with Natascha. 'Was it? It's the painting in the background of the photograph at Ed Bronz's house. Natascha Barron recognised the painting itself. And I recognised the frame. The frame that was eventually returned, separately, to Auguste Valentin.'

He took the pieces of gilt from his pocket and fitted them neatly together, holding them up in front of Alex's eyes. She recoiled instinctively.

'It's just a frame.' Alex stood up. 'What's Ed got to do with it, Alain? I thought you were after Zhurkov.'

She didn't really need to ask. Ed had been an art dealer. Beth had already suggested that some of the work he'd sold had been forged. She didn't want to believe that he had been knowingly involved.

Alain waited, examining the painting as if he were enjoying it in a museum, until Alex said, 'Why don't you leave this in the past? What's the point? What could you do about it anyway? There must be a statute of limitations.'

Alain touched his scarred finger to his temple. 'Not here.'

Alex snatched up her bag. 'I'm late for the Barrons,' she said, and made her way back to the front door.

CHAPTER FIFTY-SEVEN

Natascha and Michael were waiting for her at the train station in Villefranche. There was a new car now, a shiny black Monaco-registered Jaguar, which nobody mentioned. Michael snapped his chewing gum all the way to the gate of the Menier villa.

'I really hope this one is right,' Natascha said brightly, but her voice was strained. 'Now that I'm getting the store underway, we need to get settled. Don't we, Michael? I'm getting lots of quotes for the work. I've seen an architect with great ideas. Now we just need to get things signed, don't we?'

'Sure thing. Soon as we can.' Even though the air conditioning was on full, his window was wide open and his arm hung out, tapping on the outside of the door. Alex pulled her seatbelt tight.

'I understand you're from a family of lawyers, Michael,' she said.

'Oh yeah. Long line,' he said. 'Three generations. Grandpa, Dad, Uncle Jim and my brother Will, but it started out with my great grandpa.'

'And your cousins,' Natascha added. 'Don't forget them.'

'Yep, cousins too.'

'Can't get away from Barrons in New York,' Natascha said. Michael slapped her playfully on her thigh, but Natascha wasn't smiling.

'And the law doesn't tempt you, Michael?'

'Me? No.' Tap tap. Snap snap. Alex caught his eyes briefly in the rear-view mirror. It was as if he was checking to see if he was irritating her. 'There are enough Barrons practising law as it is.'

'Michael loves sailing, right? He can do a lot of sailing here on the Riviera.'

'Can do a lot of sailing around New York,' he muttered, but Natascha appeared not to hear. They were turning into the drive, and she craned her head out of the window.

The silence that had struck Alex last time she'd driven up to the house was now filled with birdsong so loud it muffled Patrice LeBlanc's voice as he greeted them at the door. Alex strained to hear anything from the rest of the house – footsteps, a radio – but there was nothing. She tugged the blue sunhat down over her head, as if it would hide her from Maria.

'My goodness, these are just adorable.' Natascha lifted the elephant trunk on one of the window latches as they went into the study. 'Alex I could sell something like this in the store!' She pushed them open and leaned on the sill, looking down into the garden. 'Michael, come look!'

The pool shimmered in the sun; two blue and white parasols were open above white-painted iron tables. 'Now that's more like it,' Michael said. LeBlanc winked at Alex. 'Always get the pool ready,' he whispered. 'Works with the foreigners every time.'

In the kitchen Michael opened and closed the door to the walk-in cold store several times, then said to Alex, 'You could open a bar in here.' For the first time, she could understand why his white smile might be appealing.

She left them to wander around the garden with LeBlanc, her ears ringing with the sudden quiet they left behind. That's when she realised Maria was standing behind her.

'He told me to leave you alone,' she whispered.

Alex whipped round, pulling her bag closer.

'Who?'

Her teeth showed nicotine-yellow through a sneer. 'Who do you think? He said you don't know anything, but why have you been following us?'

'I haven't been following anybody, don't be ridiculous.' But then she looked at it from Maria's angle, and it was true. She had been following Ed the first time she laid eyes on Maria, barefoot in the street; she'd been creeping along the road near the Russian church after seeing her in the car; it was now the second time she'd shown up at the Menier villa. If you were unstable, it might not look good.

Natascha's laugh, relaxed for once and floating up from the garden, seemed to come from an impossibly long way away. Alex's chin trembled.

'What do you want?'

Maria jerked her head towards the study behind them. 'How much is this worth to you?' A toolbox sat on the marble floor, near a pile of protective white sheeting. Someone must have been fixing the grouting LeBlanc had complained about.

'I honestly don't know what you're talking about.'

The flicker of the CCTV monitors under the shelf by the door caught Alex's eye. One of them switched to the alley, now empty, where she had first seen Ed arguing with Zhurkov. Her stomach lurched when she realised Maria must have been watching her even then.

How much was what worth?

Alex pursed her lips so they would stop quivering, and then guessed, 'Paintings?' Perhaps Alain was right after all. What else could it be?

'I don't care who gets this stuff, as long as I get paid. Your fancy friend with his fancy house thinks I don't know what he's looking for. I'm tired of his lies. How much?'

Of course a woman like Maria would only want money. Her skin must have been glowing once, but now it was pasty from cigarettes and worry.

Alex guessed again. 'I won't pay more than Ed,' she said. Her knees were shaking so hard that her skirt trembled.

Maria took one of Alex's snowy, pressed cotton shirt-tails and rubbed it between her fingers, and dropped it. She said, 'Then go to hell.'

Maria padded silently back down the hall towards the kitchen. As soon as she heard the door shut, Alex ran into the study. From the window, she could see over most of the grounds at the back of the house. LeBlanc was on his phone by the side of the pool; Michael appeared by the pool house but disappeared again, walking and talking.

The toolbox was unlocked. She lifted up the top tray. It was virtually empty – a couple of pristine hammers, a set of unused pliers. Underneath there were more tools, all new, and a folded plan.

Natascha called from not far away. 'Cooee! Where are you?'

She'd seen that blue-grey paper before. The architectural drawing by Benkemoun. In Ed's bedroom; the one she tugged out of the leather document wallet. The same Cyrillic notes; the same circles.

'Alex? Come out, come out, wherever you are!' Natascha sounded happy. Alex pushed the drawings back into the box and shut it. She reached the front door just as Natascha did. Michael and LeBlanc followed behind. Natascha took both her hands. 'He loves it,' she whispered to Alex. 'At least he says he does. This can make everything go back to how it was!'

LeBlanc came with them back to Nice in the car, keen to sort things out and get back to Paris. He sat at the front with Michael, talking horsepower. When a dark-green Mercedes passed them on the other side of the road, Michael whistled.

'Yes, it's a handsome car, that. It belongs to my housekeeper's husband,' LeBlanc said. Alex stopped talking to Natascha in mid-sentence.

'Her husband?'

'Yes, he'll be going to the house, I expect. He's offered to give those marble tiles another go.'

'He needn't bother,' Natascha said. 'We're going to pull it all up and replace it with parquet, aren't we, Michael?'

CHAPTER FIFTY-EIGHT

The florist at the corner opposite the commissariat had tried to deliver flowers several times, judging from the number of notes stuck to Immobilier Charpentier's door. At first Alex thought they might be from Natascha, a thank you. But that would have been impossibly quick work – they'd only dropped her off a couple of hours ago. Natascha and Michael wanted to drive her all the way home, but Alex had needed to walk. She'd meandered from where they left her in the lively back streets of the port along the edge of the Old Town, through the gaudy Place Massena and then uphill towards home. She stopped halfway up to scroll through the numbers on her phone.

Alain.

Ed.

The park next to her had exploded with excited screeches as children from a nearby school flowed into the playground, throwing bags and bikes onto the grass.

Alain *or* Ed.

Why would the architectural plan she'd seen in Ed's house be in the Menier villa? Maria knew Ed wanted something in there. And Alex had seen that architectural plan change hands between Zhurkov and Ed, the day when she'd followed them. The day Ed had come out of Maria's building. Whatever it was, it was something Alain Hubert would be happy to know about.

She clicked on Alain's number, but the staccato siren of an ambulance that had been droning in the distance roared up behind her. She hung up. Someone will be relieved to hear that, she thought, watching the ambulance pass, as relieved as she had been that day in Fayence.

Alex had called the emergency services the moment she'd seen Rod stumble towards her through the back door in Fayence, looking equally alarmed and surprised. She dropped the cast-iron casserole she'd been washing at the sink, cracking the terracotta floor tiles, and ran to him. His skin was already grey. What was she supposed to do? All those newspaper articles she'd read over the years, the posters she'd barely noticed in doctors' waiting rooms, what had they said? She led him to the sofa. He wasn't wearing a shirt she could loosen – it was already hot, and he'd been working in the garden. There was no aspirin in the house to give him, either. She remembered that – that was one of the things she should do. He kept his eyes on her face, trusting her. She wouldn't panic, for him. Even now, whenever she tasted bile in her mouth, she remembered that moment. When she'd finally heard the siren, his eyes were watery with fear. She'd been saying something, nothing, just comforting words, but he stopped her, and whispered, 'Don't be lonely.'

How could she have gone back to London after he died? The girls didn't understand that staying in Nice made the years ahead of her seem less empty. How could they? They both looked to the past for comfort, but Alex had to look forward, to find another life; her next life. What had Chantelle said? *Comme un chat.* Like a cat.

She started walking again. She'd made her decision. She scrolled to Ed's number, and dialled. She listened through his voicemail message in French and English, and then said, 'Ed, it's Alex. What do you have to tell me?'

Before she closed the office, she realised she should collect the delivery from the florist. She re-applied her lipstick in Chantelle's desk mirror as she listened to Immobilier Charpentier's message. Three unidentified callers, who left no message. She could hear an impatient intake of breath on each one. She listened again, thinking it could be Beth, but of course how could she tell from a breath?

The florist beamed from behind her stem-strewn worktable when Alex walked in. She ran into the back room, wiping her hands on her canvas apron, and reappeared with an arrangement of huge chive flowers and lavender wrapped with a purple ribbon.

'Oh, Madame,' she said. 'I took the order! I wrote the message! I can speak English, you know, I understand everything.' She looked as proud as a schoolgirl, and held out a little envelope. Alex balanced the flowers on the table to take it, the lavender tips tickling her skin. The florist's handwriting crossed over it boldly.

'O appy day Alics,' it said. 'I send flours to mark the special occasion. Chantelle speek. Call me rite way. Kiss and ugg from Ari.'

The florist giggled when Alex had finished reading. 'Chantelle speaking again! I've already told tout le monde. Everyone!'

She'd worked quickly. As Alex walked back to the office, her face hidden behind the chives, the pharmacist called to her from the entrance to his shop: 'Good news, Madame!'

Back in the office, the clean scent of the lavender rose from her hands as she spoke to Harry. He was overexcited, his voice breaking like a teenage boy's.

'I knew something was going on last night,' he explained. 'She was different. I can't really explain. I just knew. So yesterday evening I go down to the canteen for coffee with Miguel – he's the head nurse, remember? Chantelle was peaceful. And when I get back – I mean, vwa-lah! She's looking at me like, where's my coffee? I couldn't believe it!'

Harry was busying himself alongside the medical team, who had leapt into action to sustain Chantelle's recovery.

'She has a long way to go,' he explained gravely. 'She's only speaking French, but she makes sense, that's what the nurse Alphonsine tells me – she's from Port au Prince, remember? And Chantelle understands everyone. I told her if there was anything at all she needed, I'd get it for her. And do you know what she said? Paris Match!' Harry giggled ecstatically.

Chantelle's physical response was promising, but the fact that she was speaking only French concerned her team. Alex understood. It was exhausting to speak a foreign language. It would be the last thing Chantelle would want to do. Alex decided she'd wait before getting as excited as Harry.

The rest of the *quartier* wouldn't. Maxie's blonde *serveuse* tapped Alex on the shoulder as she was locking Immobilier Charpentier's door. Alex dropped the keys in her bag, but she could hear her phone ringing and pulled it out as the *serveuse* started to speak. She was as excited as the florist. '*Madame* says to tell you that you must be sure to come to the restaurant the day after tomorrow,' she said, giggling. Alex could see it was Ed calling. She pressed answer, but poised to speak, let the happily impatient *serveuse* deliver her message. 'We're planning a celebration for Chantelle! *Madame* says to tell everyone you know that we're having champagne at Chez Maxie. We'll be serving a special cocktail aperitif. *Madame*'s invented it herself – it's called Champagne Chantelle!'

Ed was laughing on the other end of the line. He must have heard every word. 'I'll try to make it,' he said. 'But meanwhile, nothing would make me happier than seeing you again.'

CHAPTER FIFTY-NINE

When Alex's taxi stopped outside Ed's house on the Avenue du Phare, the morning sun glinted off the windows. At the door, Ed touched her chin and turned her face to one side. 'What the hell have you done?'

'Does it still look awful?' She'd thought the scratches across her nose and cheeks were less angry now, but of course he hadn't seen her since the accident. 'I was in the wrong place when a window broke.'

He looked at her doubtfully and stood aside to let her in.

'You still look beautiful.'

He sat in the desk chair in his reading room, facing her on the sofa. Suzanne brought them glasses of water on a lacquer tray. She brushed her index finger across her lips as she put one in front of Alex.

Ed said, 'Thank you Suzanne. That will be all.'

When her bustling in the kitchen had stopped, Ed came and sat beside Alex. He crossed his legs, exposing a thin maroon sock. She wondered, did he choose them himself?

'I can't tell you how happy I am that you called.'

She smiled. 'So many things feel uncertain.'

'I'm not sure where to begin.'

They sat in silence for a moment, he more comfortably, it appeared, than Alex. She stood up and went to look at the photograph that had interested Alain, and then Natascha. 'Your niece?'

Ed nodded. He said, 'Tatiana, my brother's child.' He didn't move from the sofa. 'We called her Tati.'

'Why would Natascha Barron think she recognised the painting in this photograph, Ed?'

Ed shifted uneasily, but the flash of irritation Alex saw in his eyes disappeared in an instant.

'I don't know. Why would she?'

'She thinks she recognised a painting from her father's

private collection. Alain Hubert thinks so, too.'

Ed's eyes narrowed. 'This is a surprise, Alex. I can't imagine why you would be discussing such things with either of them.'

'They've both been in this room before, remember?'

'Yes, I remember.' He joined her beside the photograph, squinting down his nose at it. 'Isn't it strange how you can look at something for years, and then suddenly see a detail you hadn't noticed before?' He reached up to touch the photograph. 'This was a green dress, a new one. She came to show it off. But you're right, the painting. How stupid of us.'

He seemed confused, and Alex suddenly felt guilty. Whatever he had done, whatever he had been, it was no business of hers. It was nothing but curiosity that had brought her to him.

'Why do you want to know about this, Alex?'

'Your photo came up in conversation, that's all. Natascha's father was an art collector. You know that, surely.'

He moved back to the sofa, leaving a sudden cool emptiness beside Alex.

'I didn't know who she was at first, not until your American jeweller friend told me. It doesn't matter. She doesn't matter.'

'Hubert thinks it looks like a painting that's been found in New York,' Alex continued. Ed glanced at the spot on her throat where she knew her heart was pulsing hard under her skin. 'And like one that used to belong to Auguste Valentin, which is in Paris.'

'How would he know about that? And why would he care?'

'I wasn't trying to find any of this out, Ed. It's been in the newspapers.'

He sighed.

'Tell me about Alain Hubert. I'm sure he was happy to have found his way back into this house at last. With your help.'

It seemed cruel.

'Oh no, Ed, it's not like that. I didn't help him. I didn't know anything until he started digging around. That's what I wanted to tell you. He's got this idea that...' When she said it out loud, it began to sound even more absurd. Perhaps Guillaume was right: Alain was just keeping himself entertained. She sipped some water and continued. '...that Oleg Zhurkov was a thief. That he stole paintings. That you used to...to be involved.'

Ed's cheeks twitched. 'How?'

'By copying them.' She got the words out quickly, and they lay between her and Ed like stones flung through a window.

'And you believe this, Alex?'

'I don't know. I've got no idea, Ed. Is it true?'

Now he went to the French window. The tangy fragrance of eucalyptus floated in as he opened it. He turned to face her, and for a moment she felt she was being appraised.

Then he said, 'Come with me.'

She took off her low heels to follow him across the lawn.

She hadn't realised there was another building down a small incline at the end of the garden, hidden among masses of oleander. Ed took his time going through the keys to find the one that opened its wooden door. The building was low and square, with a tiled roof that rose into two dormer windows; no more than a solid shed. The stucco was grey and chipped now; there were spiderwebs in the peeling shutters. Alex put her shoes back on to walk across the dried twigs on the flagstone patio.

When they entered, motes of dust swirled in the sunlight.

'This is where my brother first worked,' Ed said. He stood in the centre of the empty room with his hands behind his back. 'I've haven't been in here for years.'

'Your brother?'

'When we were children, we lived in an apartment the same size as this room. Four of us.'

As her eyes adjusted, Alex noticed paint speckling the floor.

'My parents were artists,' Ed continued. 'In the Ukraine in the Fifties and Sixties, life wasn't easy for artists, especially if you were considered dissidents, as my parents were. My brother was an artist, too. From when he was three or four years old, Alex, you should've seen what he could do. You could put anything in front of him, and he could copy it almost perfectly. It was his party trick.' The odour of stale linseed oil appeared when Ed started pacing from one end of the studio to the other; Alex thought of Beth. 'Thanks to my parents, we were surrounded by art, and artists. I had little talent myself. But I could recognise it.

'For every birthday, my brother and I received exceptional gifts, paintings and sculptures that were sometimes made just for us. Imagine!' He sighed. 'No one outside the Soviet bloc valued this work at the time, of course. Who knew about the talent among us?'

Alex brushed dust and pigeon droppings from a windowsill, and leaned against it. Ed paced again as he talked.

'One man understood this cultural wealth, though. The girl's father. Raskilovich. I met him when I was studying art history in Kiev. He found ways to get artists out of the country, did you know that?'

'The Raskilovich Foundation,' Alex said. 'He brought artists out of the Soviet Union during the Cold War. I saw a documentary about it.'

'He wanted to give artists the chance to develop their talent in Europe and the United States. A noble aspiration, don't you think?'

Alex nodded.

'Yes, I thought so too, at the time. I couldn't wait to introduce him to my brother. I followed him around like a beggar trying to get him interested. Finally, it worked. My brother left.'

'And came here?'

'Raskilovich arranged it. At first he studied in Paris. But when he came to work here in the South of France, he asked me to join him. How could I have turned him down? My parents urged me to go, even though they would be on their own. So, we made it work.'

Alex knew it wasn't as simple as it sounded.

'My brother was living here, on the Avenue du Phare. It was hard to believe. The last time I'd seen him in Kiev he was sharing a shabby room, and then...' Ed waved around the space. 'And then this. He was doing well. Commissions from collectors. Small museums even bought his work. It was like a dream, Alex. I was so proud. Of course he could never have afforded a place like this, but I didn't understand that until much later. We didn't discuss practical things.' Ed laughed. 'He wasn't a practical man, my brother.'

Alex remembered what Alain Hubert had said: the house was bought by some kind of offshore company. The *Nice-Matin* article in the dossier reported it belonged to Russians.

'I started to do well myself,' Ed continued. 'At first I helped to sell the art of our friends to other friends. We used to have small exhibitions here. Parties to introduce new work.'

'In this building?'

'And in the house. People spilled out all over the garden.'

Alex thought of the young Alain Hubert and Françoise, with her hair piled on top of her head. She said, 'Like a dream.'

'We had parties at the Menier villa, too. I think you know it. Rodolphe Menier was a collector himself. He was a good friend to us. His villa was a beautiful wreck. The parties were wild.'

Alex smiled at the thought.

'Soon enough I established a small gallery in Monaco. I bought some important pieces. Uri Raskilovich asked me to buy and sell some work for him. He had an amazing eye, Alex. He was a rare connoisseur.'

Alex recalled the work she had recognised in the documentary.

'By then I had married Olya. She's an artist, an even better one than my brother was.'

Ed was pacing again.

'She hated Raskilovich. She saw through him the first time she met him, with me, when we were young. And she was right. He wasn't what he appeared to be at all. His secret collection...' He stopped and turned to Alex. 'I want to trust you.'

Alex started at the sudden change of tone. She cleared her throat.

'You can,' she said.

A breeze had blown up outside, and leaves from the patio skittered in through the door.

Ed said, 'Why do you think the work in that collection was hidden for all these years?' He stopped by the windowsill and looked intently at her before starting to move again. 'Most of them were stolen.'

'Stolen!' Alex whispered. 'Why would Raskilovich steal paintings? He had the money to buy anything he wanted.'

'Why? Ask your little friend Natascha.' He put a strong accent on the name, like a threat. 'The only ones he wanted were those he couldn't have – the ones that weren't for sale, like the Valentin Matisse. He was bored by what he could buy. A very rich man's affliction.'

Alex walked to the far end of the studio. The stuffy heat was making her uncomfortable. She pulled the hair up off the back of her neck and said, 'Did Raskilovich get hold of the original Valentin Matisse? It's in the private collection, isn't it? The Valentin family's painting hasn't been authenticated. Theirs was a forgery. It's been in the news.'

Ed was by the door now, and Alex followed him out. The breeze felt almost cold.

'I know it's a forgery. It was painted right here in this room. By my brother. Jonas's party trick became a profession.'

Alex gasped. Alain was so close to the truth.

'It was the last one he worked on.' Paint flakes dropped from the door as Ed slammed it behind them. 'I was an idiot, Alex. I didn't see what was happening for years, right before my eyes. I rarely came into this studio. It was my brother's space. One of the few times I entered was when that photograph of Tati was taken. Jonas was working on that last painting, the Valentin Matisse. She followed me down to the studio in her green dress.' Ed brushed the leaves off a bench on the patio. 'Jonas had been copying stolen paintings for Raskilovich ever since he left Ukraine.'

'And you really didn't know?' Alex desperately wanted to believe it.

'I didn't Alex, honestly.' He opened his hands to her, then let them fall on his thighs. 'But I found out. Jonas said I was deliberately blind, but that's not true. I couldn't believe it at first, perhaps. Of course there were signs I should have understood. It's easy to say once you know what you were looking at, though.'

'You told Olya?'

'She loved it here. There was my son. He and Tati used to play right here, in this garden. I was happy. I didn't want it to change.'

It wasn't hard to imagine: children's voices on a summer night, the excited warmth of small bodies resting against hers for seconds before running off again across the garden.

'Did Olya know what was going on?'

'I made sure she didn't. I lied to her.' Ed sat down on the bench. He slumped, elbows on knees, as if he could no longer hold himself up. 'You know, Jonas had always been afraid that Raskilovich could hurt our parents. He had a lot of influence in the Soviet Union. I think that's why my brother did this. He had his own career, Alex. He was a successful artist. He didn't need to do it. Why else would he have done it?' He looked at Alex as if begging her to answer.

'He was afraid. Fear makes people do unnatural things,' she said.

'Our father died just after I left, but when our mother died, years later, Jonas tried to stop working for Raskilovich. He told him it was finished. But Raskilovich liked his set-up, having the paintings he wanted stolen to order, sending them back to their owners as copies. Jonas's copies.'

It was the story Liliane Valentin had told Alex: the family had paid the ransom for the stolen painting. For nothing, Alex thought. All they'd got in return was a forgery.

Ed continued: 'Raskilovich forced my brother to keep working for him. He threatened his family.'

'But Jonas could have exposed Raskilovich! All those stolen paintings?'

Ed smiled at Alex indulgently. 'Forgery is a crime. My brother would have hung himself by exposing Raskilovich. But you're right. He tried to protect us. He put together names and dates, photographs, documents; the things that could link Raskilovich to the thefts and the forgeries. Raskilovich's money bought this house, you know, but it was linked to Jonas's name. That's why it's mine now.' Ed laughed, as if at the absurdity of it. 'He gathered everything, the fake bills of sale, the knocked-up transport documents that were used to move things around, all of it. It would have been a catastrophe for Raskilovich if anything had got out.'

Transport documents, Alex thought, with a start. Hubert of Switzerland.

'Did you move things around yourself?'

'Not physically, of course. There are people who know how to do things like that. As I said, my brother wasn't a practical man. He couldn't believe that Raskilovich would ever let him go, and the documents were an insurance policy.'

Ed reached into his back pocket and pulled out his wallet. From inside he took out a small photograph, and held it up for Alex to see.

'This has always been my favourite,' he said, as she took it. Ed's niece, in a swimsuit, was sitting on what might be a pool lounger between two men, laughing hard as she looked up at the older one. He was quite old: his bald head sinking into his shoulders, but his smile was lively. On the other side, a man who looked like a young Ed. They were all squinting into the sun.

'Tati adored her father. She was an artist at heart, too, always drawing on anything she could find, just like he did at her age.'

'Where is Jonas now?'

'I told you about Rodolphe Menier, the art lover. That's him, there.' He pointed to the bald man. 'We spent a lot of time with him, talking about art. The children loved him. His villa then was like a museum. Floorboards would crumble under your feet. Some of the rooms had to be closed up. Menier didn't seem to care. So Jonas slipped into one of those rooms and buried his documents under the floor.'

Alex suddenly felt giddy. I know where it is, she thought. That's what Maria was talking about; there were no paintings. She was now aware of the sweat on her palms, and handed the photo back to Ed.

'Jonas thought it was safe. But Alex, you know how children are. We all came and went so easily between the Avenue du Phare and the Menier villa. Tati must have seen him do it.' He put the photograph away and returned the wallet to his pocket.

'Perhaps she thought that her father was playing hide-and-seek,' Alex said.

Ed shrugged. 'It was a terrible mistake. Raskilovich rarely came to our home, but he came to threaten Jonas face to face. And when they were shouting at each other, when Jonas told him about hiding the documents, Tati heard them fighting. She told Raskilovich she knew where they were, in Uncle Rodolphe's house. She must have thought she could make them stop fighting.'

'She was afraid,' said Alex.

'Raskilovich was an evil, vindictive man. He would do anything to protect himself. A few weeks later Menier's place went up in flames.'

'Oh god,' said Alex. 'The fire.' The Menier villa was destroyed by fire in 1980. She thought of the heaps of smoking timbers photographed by *Nice-Matin*. 'He had it burned down.'

'Yes. He set that fire, I'm sure of it. Not himself, of course. Raskilovich was a monster, and he knew people who were monsters. He had it burned down. And with it he killed Rodolphe Menier and my brother, who was asleep, in the house at the time.'

'I'm sorry, Ed.'

'And my niece, Tatiana.'

Alex patted Ed's back as if he were a child.

Eventually he said, 'Months later, I told Olya the truth. I admitted I had known for a long time what Jonas was doing. She left me without even packing a bag. I thought it was grief, and that she would come back, with my son. I waited here. But they're gone forever. She blames me for Tati's death, and she's right. It was my fault.'

'Oh, Ed. But she's wrong. It was Raskilovich's fault.'

The sun had travelled behind the eucalyptus trees, and light flickered in and out of the leaves over Ed's face.

'The discovery of the Raskilovich secret collection will expose a lot of ugliness. Things could eventually point in this direction. And if my brother's documents aren't found and destroyed soon, it could prove that I was part of it.'

'But it was years and years ago.'

'Would you believe it, Alex, if an art dealer sells his own brother's work, a forger's work, then claims innocence?'

They sat in silence, Alex's hand resting lightly on Ed's back. Mosquitoes were beginning to buzz. After some time, Alex said, 'Will you be able to get the documents out of the Menier villa?'

Ed shrugged. 'That's up to the man you saw me arguing with the day we met. That's the sort of thing he does. That's why I got in touch with him again after so many years. I need his help. I don't even know if the documents are still there. They may have been destroyed in the fire. I can't risk not knowing. I must destroy them if they still exist.'

'What if Alain could get hold of them?'

Ed turned to her quickly, twisting more gracefully than she would have thought possible. 'Why would he even imagine something like those documents exist?' He stared at her pointedly, and she felt alarm.

'I wouldn't tell him, Ed. Honestly. But he's interested in Zhurkov. If he can connect you both, and Maria... You said yourself she was unstable.'

'Maria?'

'In the Menier villa. She must need money, or she wouldn't have asked me how much I'd pay for whatever she thinks you're after. I didn't know what to say, how could I? I thought a painting might have been hidden somewhere... this isn't my usual field, you know.'

She crossed her legs and folded her arms.

'Maria! I should have known. She and Zhurkov are nothing but thieves. She has no idea what I want from that villa, the madwoman. She thinks we're stealing from the owner, and all she can imagine is that I'm cheating her of her cut. Fool. Only Zhurkov understands what this means to me. Alain Hubert can't learn that those documents exist!'

'But Alain isn't interested in exposing you, Ed. He just wants to know that he was right about what was going on here in this house. And he was, just about, wasn't he? He was the police officer who shot at Zhurkov when he was challenged, when he moved the painting out of the house.'

'That idiot,' Ed said, punching one fist into another. 'Zhurkov spent months dreaming about that damn car when he got back to France. I told him to forget it.'

'It's the last piece in an old puzzle as far as Alain's concerned. He doesn't know there are any documents.' She laughed uncomfortably. 'He doesn't know you set Maria up as the housekeeper. But he thinks something is going on.' She waved her hand as if to dismiss the idea, but she glanced nervously at Ed's face.

He shook the back of the bench angrily. 'Alex, this isn't a game! This is my life! What is it to him?'

Alex shifted on the bench, inching away from him, and stood up. She could leave right now, run back across the humid grass; she could run all the way to St Jean. Suddenly he looked exhausted and sat down again next to her with his head in his hands.

'My head,' he said. 'These outbursts, they cause unbearable

headaches. Sometimes it's so bad I can't think.'

'Natascha wants to put parquet over that floor, in any case. No one will ever know even if they are there. It's over.'

'What? Cover the floor? The girl will really be taking the house?'

'There would be time to find the documents if they really are still there. I'll be able to help.'

Ed was pale. He turned his head sideways, as if moving away from the pain. 'We have to get the documents. She can't stop this now.'

'You can't blame Natascha. I don't think she had any idea what her father was doing. She wants to get away from all that. She wants to be…ordinary.'

He pressed the heels of his palms into his eyes. He almost stumbled once or twice as they walked back in the direction of the house.

'Ordinary? You can never be ordinary with that much money. I won't let that name ruin everything for me again.'

Inside the house, he headed immediately for the stairs, stopping at the bottom to look sadly at Alex. 'This isn't how I wanted our meeting to end,' he said. 'I don't want you to go, but my head… I can't control what I'm doing. Let me call you a taxi.' He stumbled back towards her, but Alex put her hand on his chest.

'I can do that myself,' Alex said, 'Try to sleep.'

CHAPTER SIXTY

Alex felt like a bomb had gone off, and that she was standing among the debris. She wandered back and forth between the kitchen at Les Jolies Roses and the living room, flicking through the numbers on her phone as if she would suddenly find the strength to speak to someone, anyone.

The dossier sat on the coffee table. Its accordion folds were stretched flat now. Alex would find another one before Chantelle came home, a fatter one. She squeezed the brochure for the exclusive bed shop on Alphonse Karr deeper into the 'B' pocket, noting with satisfaction that it covered Boubil, beds, Barron and even Bitoun. She folded up the plastic bag in which she'd found the shop papers, squashing it into smaller and smaller squares, until it too fit into the pocket. If only everything worked out so easily.

The 'B' pocket also contained the photocopied article about Ed's house. She reread it, imagining a young Alain watching dejectedly as a sporty little Mercedes escaped into the dark. She leafed back to where she'd put the original, under 'C' for Cap Ferrat. Then she flicked to 'M', where she found the article about the fire at the Menier villa. It was a cutting from *Le Monde*, much more reputable than *Nice-Matin*. Even so, it got the facts wrong. It reported that the fire that killed artists Rodolphe Menier and Jonas Brazinskas, along with a nine-year-old child, had been caused by faulty wiring. A reasonable assumption, thought Alex, considering the neglected state of the villa. In her mind's eye, she saw the child running towards the old artist, proud of the drawing she'd done for him on the back of an old bill she'd found crumpled and thrown away in her father's studio. She shook her head to get rid of the dreamlike image. It was time to tell people the good news about Chantelle.

Meghan was first on the list.

'Well, thank god!' she said. 'I was beginning to worry. Now

you can come home and you can bring Beth back with you. Do I still need to come over? We'll need to get the moving company sorted. How much of the furniture did you bring from Fayence? You won't need it all at once, will you? Make Beth help. It'll stop her from moaning and whining, won't it?'

As Meghan made plans on the other end of the line, Alex made a note to call the storage company in Fayence. There were plenty of things in those boxes that would look perfect here in Les Jolies Roses.

Guillaume had said nothing for several seconds after she told him – Alex wondered if perhaps the line had cut out. But of course he's already heard, in the *quartier*, she thought, embarrassed. She repeated herself. 'I heard you, Madame.' Again, silence. When he spoke again, his voice was tearful. 'Of course I won't miss the party at Maxie's. How could I?'

Amedeo Quelin's obvious relief surprised her. 'They haven't been easy to deal with, these Americans,' he confided. 'They have a rather more informal approach. No one has ever called me Amy before.'

Alex covered the mouthpiece so he wouldn't hear her laugh.

Michael answered Natascha's phone. 'Who? The estate agent we met in New York? Oh, yeah, right. Thanks for letting us know.' Alex should have hung up when she heard his voice. Had she really thought they would have a free evening to spend at a little neighbourhood *fête*?

But Natascha had phoned back half an hour later. Alex could barely hear her. 'He's asleep,' she whispered. Alex told her about Chantelle, about the party. 'I'm ecstatic!' she said. 'Michael says he wants to look over the store in Alphonse Karr tomorrow evening, but yes, I'll talk him into it. We'll be there, for sure.'

She even left a message on Beatrice's extension at the bank. Chantelle's account would need some sympathetic attention when she returned and it was worth keeping Beatrice on side.

And she was going to have to tell Beth.

She opened a bottle of Château de Bellet *rosé* and leaned on the railing of her balcony. The leaves of the trees opposite hung listlessly, and the purr of a passing car was magnified in the hot, still air. As it manoeuvred into a parking spot outside the Café des Soldats, she realised it was the Audi. She watched the top of Ed's head as he passed beneath the balcony and rang the bell. She downed half the glass in one go before opening the door.

'I'm sorry, again,' he said. 'These sudden migraines have affected me all my life.' His forehead still seemed creased with pain, but he said the usual headache had never arrived. She could have moved aside to let him in, but she didn't. She waited, aware simply of how pleased she was to see him. He pressed against her body as he kissed her on both cheeks, and she could smell laundry powder and musky cologne. She had one hand on the doorknob and a cold glass of wine in the other, and it seemed that only the weight of his body against hers was holding her up. 'I don't mean to scare you,' he said. His lips brushed over her ear as he spoke.

'I need to put my glass down.' She felt like a teenager leading Ed to the sofa. He picked up one of the photographs on the end table, and Rod stared intently at him from under his panama hat.

'My husband,' Alex said.

Ed put it down gently, in exactly the same spot.

His skin was softer than she had expected, his body firmer. He kissed her tentatively at first, offering her the chance to refuse. When she didn't, he said, 'Let this be the next part of our lives.'

They were both woken as the front door slammed. The wind, Alex thought sleepily, but the muslin curtains were motionless by the open bedroom window. She reached for the bedside lamp. Ed sat up and looked around him in the unfocused way of someone roused from a deep sleep. The alarm clock showed 7:06am.

'What the hell was that?'

Alex's long white silk T-shirt was hanging over the back of a chair by the window. She got out of bed for it. There was a knock on the bedroom door. Beth's knock: a loud, angry rat-a-tat-tat, completed just as her pale face appeared around the half-open bedroom door.

'Oh god,' Alex said softly.

Beth's head disappeared after a fraction of a second, but that would have been all she needed.

Alex slipped the T-shirt over her head. She found Beth in the kitchen, holding a paper bag from the boulangerie downstairs.

'What have you brought?' Alex said. 'Shall I get us some plates?'

'How could you, Mum?'

'I know it's not easy, darling.'

'But he's nothing like Dad, he's so different.'

Alex took the bag from her hand.

'No one will ever be like Dad, Beth. I wouldn't want anyone to be.'

'But he's not our sort of person.' Beth had seen the silk T-shirt many times before, but the way she looked at it now made Alex pull the fabric further down her thighs. She moved around Beth as she made coffee and laid out the croissants and brioches on a plate.

'Have you heard any of my messages? I've been trying to get in touch with you for ages.'

'I've lost my phone charger,' Beth answered. Alex knew she was fibbing.

'I was going to call again this morning. Chantelle is better. She's talking! There's a party for her tonight at Maxie's.'

Beth looked up hopefully. The black sweatshirt she was wearing seemed far too heavy for the weather.

'So you'll be coming home?'

'Not yet, darling. Will you come to the party for Chantelle tonight? I'd love you to. They ask about you at the restaurant.'

'We can go home together, can't we?'

Alex had never lied to her children. 'I'll take you home, Beth.

But I'll come back. There are things for me here.' She put three mugs on the table.

'Like kowtow to the Russian princess? Is she going to be at this do tonight?'

Alex ignored the barb. 'She'll be at her new shop on rue Alphonse Karr. She's so excited about it.'

What was Ed doing? Hiding in the bedroom? Slipping out like a guilty lover? Alex hoped not. She strained to listen for any movement over the gurgle of the coffee maker.

'What about him?' Beth jerked her thumb towards the bedroom.

'I hope he'll be there, too.'

When the coffee was ready, Alex followed Beth to the spare room, mug in hand, and watched her while she sullenly gathered her few last things together. Alex's throat tightened to see Beth's fingers vainly pulling at the zip of her bag.

'Please, darling, please. I can't make Dad come back. I can't finish your paintings. I can't stop my life where it was.'

'You stop it for them.' She pushed Alex's hand away when she tried to help her with the zip. 'For Natascha and for Ed.'

The front door clicked quietly and Alex knew that Ed had left the apartment. Beth didn't appear to have heard. Alex gripped the handle of the mug with such force she was surprised it didn't break. She bit the end of her tongue till it hurt so that she didn't actually throw the mug at her daughter. The wave of disappointment that washed over her sucked the air from her lungs so that she couldn't speak. She put the mug down, trembling with anger, and went back to her bedroom. She was just about to give in and cry when she noticed, written on the mirror, the word 'Soon'. Ed must have used her lipstick.

She heard the door slam again as Beth left.

CHAPTER SIXTY-ONE

'For you, they're on the house,' Maxie said, handing Alex her second Champagne Chantelle cocktail. 'I've used a little orange liqueur made by my ex-sister-in-law in Menton and a *soupçon*, just a touch, of cranberry juice to control the sweetness. What do you think?' Françoise had already explained that the scent was to remind everyone of Chantelle's signature eau de toilette. 'I knew you'd like it,' Maxie said, before Alex replied. 'The cranberry juice gives it the colour of Chantelle's lips, *non*?'

Alex examined the frosty glass doubtfully, but Maxie was already shouting to Françoise for more bottles. People were milling around by the bar and outside under the awning, giving the gathering a cocktail party air. Harry's bouquet of chive blooms and lavender was arranged in a wine bucket by the till. Alex hadn't eaten anything all day, but she shook her head when the blonde *serveuse* came round with a plate laden with squares of oniony *pissaladière*. Every few minutes, she checked her phone to see if there'd been a call.

Alex scanned the crowd. There was Alain's nephew Felix talking to the Citroen mechanic. At his elbow Beatrice was deep in conversation with the pharmacist. She barely recognised a group of stallholders from the market, dressed now in freshly pressed shirts and laughing loudly on the *terrasse*. Alain was listening to the receptionist from the commissariat. Alex had to keep putting her glass on the bar to shake hands or kiss cheeks. She felt like family at a wedding.

When she saw Paulette Bitoun hovering at the edge of the crowd, she ducked for the *toilettes*, but it was too late.

'I thought Chantelle was already back,' Paulette said, behind her suddenly. 'But I see I'll have to wait a little longer.'

Alex rattled the handle of the locked toilet hopefully. Paulette's grey roots had begun to show, and Alex had a moment of pity before Paulette opened her mouth again.

'This misunderstanding with my shop will be taken care of

the moment Chantelle's home,' Paulette said. 'You'll see.' Alex rattled the door handle again. Paulette didn't move. 'I hope Madame Barron won't be making any interior changes. I don't want to have to undo things in my showroom.'

'She can do whatever she wants, Madame Bitoun. She's there now, in fact.'

Paulette's mouth opened into a speechless, wrinkled 'O'. Alex just about fell into the toilet when the door opened. She locked herself in and patted cold water on her cheeks.

There was no sign of Paulette when she came out. As she made her way back to the bar, the professor shambled into her path.

'Marvellous news!' He raised his glass to her, swaying slightly. His cheeks were bright red.

'Yes, we're all looking forward to seeing her back.'

He focused on her nose. 'Oh, yes, but I don't mean Madame Charpentier. Also marvellous news. I followed your advice.'

Alex froze. 'What advice?'

'To speak to Monsieur Bronz again. I was encouraged by some of Maxie's excellent Côtes de Provence. A bottle, in fact, at lunchtime.'

'You spoke to him this afternoon?'

'Just now. I think he was on his way here. I met him outside.'

Ed outside? She stood on her tiptoes to see above the crowd. 'And what is the marvellous news, Professor?'

'I told him point blank, I said...' He stood squarely on both feet and threw out his chest, making Alex think of a small boy. 'I said "You can't threaten me. I have friends in the police."'

She would have laughed if she hadn't been so horrified. What would Ed think she'd been saying to the red-nosed professor?

'And?'

The professor exhaled rapidly. 'He tried to pass me by, but I stood my ground. I told him that he wouldn't get away with it.'

She scanned the crowd again. Was Ed really here?

'You have to bluff a bit in life, Madame. I told him Alain

Hubert knew all about the documents.'

'Oh no, Professor! No!' Of course Ed would think first of the documents he was so eager to destroy. But would he pay any notice to the ineffectual professor?

'Oh dear,' slurred the professor. 'Shouldn't I have said anything? He was a bit frightening, to be honest. He said, "Damn, damn, damn Raskilovich!" Then he took off.' The professor hiccupped, and Alex reached out to steady him. 'Your Monsieur Bronz would benefit from some meditation techniques, don't you think?'

There was barely room to move inside the restaurant now. Maxie beamed as she cruised the crowd, but Alex had to get outside into the evening air. She pushed past Alain, who caught her elbow, but she shook him off. A few feet away, she walked into a puff of cigarette smoke.

'Sorry, Madame! It's my break, y'know?' Sammy, the sous-chef, guiltily threw his cigarette butt into the road. Next to him stood his mother, Sara. She slapped her forehead the moment she saw Alex.

'Aiee, lady, I tell you he is a bad boy.' She spoke in English.

'One cigarette won't hurt,' said Alex, absently.

'No, Sammy is a *good* boy. I mean Mr Michael Barron! Madame Natascha crying, crying, he shouting, shouting.' She shook her head dramatically. 'He say, you better gone, everyday same thing. You better off dead. He say that to his wife!'

Sammy pulled at his mother's hand.

'Maman's tired, y'know?' he said to Alex. He led his mother further up the street. She craned around to Alex to say, 'He dangerous. Why she marry a bad boy like that?' Sara turned to her son, slapping his back. Alex started towards the restaurant. The queasy feeling in her stomach was turning to distinct sickness. She really shouldn't drink on an empty stomach.

When she felt the buzz of her phone against her breast, she stopped in mid-step outside the commissariat. Julie's name on the display made her smile with relief.

'On my way, honey,' she said. 'Don't let 'em down it all

without me. Sal's back, too. We're looking for a parking space.'

'*Asshole, learn to drive!*'

Julie talked over her husband's voice, oblivious. 'We just met your guy, Guillaume. Looked in a hurry.'

'That's good. He, of all people, should be here.'

'Yeah, if he's coming. We met him in the supermarket. I was buying dog food, he was buying rope, for chrissake. Each to his own, huh?' That smoky laugh. 'He asked me if it was true I was selling the château. I said, sure, when Natascha's finished with her new store, she's moving right onto it. No sense of humour that guy, huh?'

'*Move it, dickbrain!*'

Alex's heart was pounding. Guillaume never read *Nice-Matin*, he'd said it was full of lies. He'd think what Julie said was true – that she was selling to the Barrons. Tonight everyone seemed to have the wrong idea about Natascha Raskilovich Barron.

Maxie handed her another Champagne Chantelle as she sat down at the only *terrasse* table left. Alex scanned the crowd again hopefully, but she couldn't find the faces she wanted to see. She put her hand over her mouth in horror as it dawned on her that everyone with a reason to hate Natascha Raskilovich Barron knew exactly where she was tonight. Guillaume, thinking his shrine would be destroyed by the very person who made it necessary; Ed, with his stinking tempers and his lost life; Paulette Bitoun, a future snatched away by her wealth; even Natascha's handsome, deceitful husband.

'*Mon dieu*, Alex, have you seen a ghost?' It was Alain. She scrambled past him. People were still trying to shake her hand but she pushed on. Damn the Citroen, what was the matter with it? She'd have to take the tram. Maxie called to her as she ran down towards the stop, but she ignored her. Someone grabbed her arm, and she tried to wriggle away. Whoever it was held on tighter, dragging her to a stop.

'Mum!'

She turned to see Meghan.

Alex drank her in: her neat, highlighted hair, her stylish trainers, her little suitcase on wheels. She looked momentarily frightened before taking charge. Alex held on to her now, beautiful, practical, bossy Meghan.

'We need to get to Natascha.' Alex took Meghan's suitcase and ran with it. Meghan followed.

People on Maxie's *terrasse* called after them.

'What is it, Mum?' Meghan was pulling at her hand. 'Where are we going?'

There was a tram further up the tracks, clanging towards them.

'Follow me!'

They ran towards the tram stop 50 metres away. Alex stumbled as she stepped onto the platform. Meghan pulled her up. There were only a few people waiting on the platform, and Alex pushed past them as the tram doors slid open, banging ankles with the suitcase.

'Give me that,' Meghan said. 'What the hell is going on?' They stood in the centre of the carriage, panting.

'What are you doing here?'

Meghan was breathless. 'It's Beth. She sounded so strange this morning, so I just thought, right, I'll go, I'll get a flight, and I did. Here I am. I didn't have time to explain it to you. Beth knows I'm here. What's wrong with you all?'

The trip was only three stops, but why was it taking so long? Alex swallowed hard.

'Mum, you look frazzled. Have you been drinking? Tell me what's going on!' Alex couldn't speak. She looked helplessly at Meghan, who put her arms around her and stroked her hair.

They got out in the centre of town, pushing past the tourists who crammed on behind them. Alex ran. Meghan kept up the pace beside her, her neat little suitcase in her hands now, bouncing, falling over, banging her shins.

'Where are we going, Mum?'

Alex could hear her running footsteps and her breath. They elbowed through the throng of people who were lingering in front of each restaurant, deciding if they liked the look of the place. Some of the shops were open, the ones that sold sequinned T-shirts, baseball caps with 'French Riviera' embroidered above the visor, fringed beach wraps. They turned onto rue Alphonse Karr, where suddenly it was calmer. There was a small clutch of tourists in front of Natascha's shop window. Alex stopped momentarily to take it in, shocked.

There was a mannequin dressed in a dark-blue dress, with a red silk headscarf knotted around her neck to match pouting, painted lips. Through white-framed sunglasses, she seemed to be watching the crowd. She was sitting akimbo on the floor, leaning against a pile of wooden packing crates; her face, partly hidden by a Panama hat, was resting in the crook of her raised arm.

Alex hammered on the window. 'Natascha! Natascha!'

More window-shoppers stopped to look.

Alex ran to the door, but it was locked. She grabbed Meghan's suitcase and heaved it against the glass. It shattered inwards. Meghan screamed.

Alex scrambled across the shards and over the samples of striped beach hut fabric on the floor. It was dark, but she remembered the layout. She ran down the short hall and round into the main room where she could get to the window display.

'Call an ambulance, Meg. Dial 112, they'll speak English.'

As she reached the folding doors that led into the window display, she stumbled on something soft. She jumped back.

Shafts of streetlight filtered through the seams in the folding doors. They lit up what seemed familiar to Alex, folds of grey-black denim.

'Jesus,' Meghan shouted from behind her. 'What the hell?' She pushed past her mother and knelt on the floor, hugging her sister. 'What's happened? What have you done?'

The light fell across Beth's grey eyes as she looked up at her mother over Meghan's head. They were filled with tears.

EPILOGUE

Every time Harry Bormann walked into Maxie's, the conversation lulled. People stopped chewing and forks halted mid-way between plate and mouth. He didn't understand, of course, when Alain said to Chantelle, 'How much more tanned can he possibly get?'

Chantelle lifted her cheek for Harry's kiss.

'He's more stupendous every day, Alain, you can't deny it,' she said.

Her hand shook as she put down her champagne glass, and Harry deftly moved it away from the edge of the table. His T-shirt could have been painted onto his perfect torso.

'I can't leave her alone for a minute, can I? I've only been at the beach an hour,' Harry said. 'Alain, are you being a bad influence again?' He wagged a finger at the old policeman, before turning towards the bar. 'Françoise, *plus de champagne, s'il te plait!*' No more champagne! Please! His accent was atrocious, and his girlish voice was completely at odds with his remarkable physique. 'Chantelle, are you ready for your nap? You know how important it is.' He put his hands on his hips and waited while she slowly uncurled herself from her chair. He and Alain hovered over her, but she waved them away.

'*Oui, mon chéri.* Yes, let's go.'

Customers scraped their chairs aside to clear the way for Chantelle's cane, with its ebony handle. She rested her free hand on Harry's muscled forearm.

When they had passed, customers made the usual comments. '*L'Américain* is devoted to her, swears he won't leave until she's strong enough…' 'Weeks in a coma in *l'Amérique*, at her side all the time…' Then they lowered their voices, because they knew Maxie and Françoise didn't like it discussed: 'The awful business with the death of that girl…'

Alain leaned on the bar as Françoise made his *café*. Outside, Harry tucked Chantelle into the passenger seat of the Citroën parked in front of the restaurant.

'She's better every day, eh?' Alain said.

Françoise nodded. 'She's lucky with that boy. Imagine how much she'd have to pay for a nurse. Between him and Guillaume, she has the most loving care in all of France.'

'And Alex. Don't forget Alex.'

'That's business, Alain. Alex is taking care of business. Oh, look, there she is now,' Françoise said.

Alex, arriving at the restaurant, waved at them through the window as she sat down in the shade of the awning.

'She's a good woman, the *Anglaise*,' Alain said. 'She stuck it out.'

'She certainly did. And she still puts on a brave face. Can you imagine how she felt that night?'

'She was fond of that poor little rich girl. She put on a fine performance at the inquest.'

Françoise leaned across the bar, lowering her voice. 'But she fought tooth and nail to protect her daughter. Can you believe the police even considered Beth a suspect at all?'

'They have to see it from every angle. It could have been anyone, as Alex pointed out. Paulette Bitoun – fear of losing your business is a powerful motive. Of course we knew it couldn't have been Guillaume, but if you look at it objectively, it's understandable. He's never gotten over his grief, and he held Natascha responsible for the death of his own daughter. That husband, well, I could see in a minute that he was a fool. He was making a mess of his life, but he couldn't possibly have carried out murdering his own wife.'

'Alex's daughter is much better now, that's what Harry says.' Françoise uncorked a bottle of rosé and handed it to the blonde *serveuse*. 'She was so jealous of Natascha, and she was going through her own grief. Did she go to the shop that night with the intention of harming her? We'll never know. But what she said at the inquest, oh, it broke my heart.'

Alain nodded. Everyone had heard how desperately Beth Coates tried to stop Natascha from aiming her uncle's gun at her own heart. 'The poor girl, it wasn't much of a life with all that money,' he said. 'That night in the shop on Alphonse Karr, Natascha told Beth that she recognised Guillaume the first time she saw him. She knew she'd been partly responsible for the death of his daughter. And she hated herself when she realised that she was using her money to damage Paulette Bitoun, however much she disliked her. That would make you depressed for a start, but then she knew she'd made a terrible mistake marrying that womaniser. She must have been in a terrible state that night. Not much of an advertisement for being rich and beautiful.'

Françoise set out her cups and saucers on the bar.

'Look, there's Beth coming now. Funny little thing, that one. They'll be waiting for Ed.'

They watched as Alex and Beth laughed with Maxie outside in the shade of the awning. Maxie took their orders and came back to call them out to her mother at the bar. She slapped a tray down on the countertop.

'I can tell you're gossiping, you two,' she said without looking at them. 'Stop it. We have a restaurant to run.' She headed for the kitchen.

Out on the *terrasse*, Alex and Beth were joined by Ed Bronz.

'I heard he's buying her an estate agency of her own,' Françoise said, stopping to watch them kiss. 'What I don't understand is, why did Ed turn up at the shop that night? Could he have had something against that poor girl, too?'

Alain rubbed the two broken bits of frame together inside his pocket, clicking them into place so they formed one piece. He could have had Zhurkov, easily. Zhurkov was a thief when they were all young, and he was a thief now. But to prove it, Alain would have had to take Ed Bronz away from Alex.

He put the pieces of frame on the bar and walked outside to say hello to Alex and Ed. Françoise wiped them up with her dishcloth, and threw them away.

ACKNOWLEDGEMENT

With gratitude to the many friends who had faith in me when I had little in myself, and who inspired me to continue my relationship with Alex Coates, in particular Christie Hickman and Katia Lief.

ABOUT THE AUTHOR

Suellen Grealy

SUELLEN GREALY was born in London, educated in Dublin and New York, and started her working life at an advertising agency on Madison Avenue. She returned to London in her twenties, where she worked in interior design and in magazine journalism. Neither of these was as challenging as running a small restaurant with her French husband in Nice, where they both still live.

Printed in Great Britain
by Amazon

82829778R00205